ARTEMIS 3

THE JOURNEY

DAVID MILLER

FIRMAMENT BOOKS

First published 2023 by David Miller in Australia

Published by Firmament Books.

ISBN 978-0-6457134-0-4 (E-book) 978-0-6457134-1-1 (Paperback) 978-0-6457134-2-8 (Hardback)

Cover Design: Book Cover Design by 100 Covers. Original cover created by Tim Young from public images, including the NASA images archive.

firmamentbooks.com

davidmiller.online

For Katrina, as we live together our story within the masterpiece of God's love story.

A brand new story of strength, fortitude and growth inspired by the astronauts of the 21st century.

Mike and Sue prepare to make history for NASA on the Moon ... but is it the history they expected?

A geologist with a passion for space, Mike Trellis enjoys carefree life.

As a US Navy test pilot and young mother, Sue Bright dreams of being the first woman on Mars.

Mike and Sue are new trainee astronauts for NASA as it prepares to return to the Moon after 50 years. Do they have the right stuff that their predecessors had? They have the desire, but do they have the knowledge, the ability, the fortitude and the worldview to succeed? Can they and their diverse team unite to overcome the dangers of space travel? Or will their actions derail their mission and their lives? And what place does faith have in the life of an astronaut in the 21st century?

Other nations are racing to access the resources of the Moon first. Will they disrupt the Artemis 3 mission?

And will the mission be remembered for reasons they expect? And how will they cope?

Artemis 3: The Journey is David Miller's first novel. An avid reader since childhood, growing up during the Apollo and Space Shuttle eras, he has a passion for space, science and faith.

Contents

1

— • —

Mike Trellis didn't know he was going to make history during his lunar mission, Artemis 3. That was his fellow astronaut Sue Bright's role as the first woman to walk on the moon just five days ago. He wasn't even supposed to be on the mission. He was originally the backup scientist for the mission until George Scorby was diagnosed with thyroid cancer.

Mike and Sue worked through the now very familiar process of preparing for their fourth EVA on the moon. They prepared their xEMUs (Exploration Extravehicular Mobility Unit), each cross-checking their work and assisting each other in donning the suits, all the time careful not to accidentally launch themselves into the ceiling of the lander in the low gravity environment.

Mike easily lifted himself up and through the hatch on the back of the suit. In zero-G, he had stretched from his normal six-foot frame to six-foot-one, so on the moon, he was somewhere in between. The xEMUs had been designed to accommodate a wide range of body types and accommodated his fit but average build.

Sue was likewise an average build, five-foot-four (on earth). She had had long black hair until astronaut training when she needed to shorten it to shoulder length for practical reasons.

As they depressurized the airlock, they each checked their xEMU systems to ensure there were no leaks and that the systems were operating correctly. Mike could feel his pulse and breathing rate rise slightly. This part of the mission was one of the riskier yet most exciting as they explored places no human had been. If something went wrong, there was only one other person here to help. A robotic device might be able to assist, but they were very much alone out here.

2

WEDNESDAY, MAY 17, 2017

Today was the day of 'The Call'. Mike was expecting it sometime this morning, which made focussing on his work as part of the JPL Mars Science Laboratory Curiosity Rover team difficult. As a member of the geoscience team, he was involved in planning the next activities of the rover during the morning and then reviewing the results of the science experiments in the afternoon. It took all of his concentration to follow the morning discussion regarding Curiosity's operations. It was currently driving towards Vera Rubin Ridge. At least he wasn't the lead today.

This was the second time he had applied to become an astronaut candidate with NASA. Each time more people applied, reportedly 18,000 this time. That he was even part of the shortlist was a miracle. He hadn't even finished his PhD for his first application, but he had interned with the JPL Mars team.

Mike had grown up watching Space Shuttle missions on NASA TV. He'd been captivated by the thought of exploring outer space. His father, John, a software developer, had been in elementary school during the Apollo program and had nurtured Mike's interest. They often watched TV launches together and even trekked from their home in Colorado Springs to Florida's Space Coast to watch the launch of USS Discovery in August 2001.

Throughout school he'd been fascinated by science, especially under-standing how the earth and other planets had formed. Mike had been single-minded in his desire to become an astronaut. He'd attended Space Academy during Junior High and later the Advanced Space Academy, building some long-term friendships.

He had decided to study for a Bachelor's degree in Geological and Envi-ronmental Sciences at Stanford University, California. After graduating, he studied for a Doctorate in Geology from the University of California, Los Angeles, taking as many opportunities as possible to undertake research on NASA projects, including internships at JPL.

It had been disappointing to receive a letter informing him that he had been unsuccessful as a candidate in 2013. But he had at least gotten past the first cut and had an interview with the Astronaut Selection Board. This time he'd made it much further, with a physical, more interviews and some team activities.

"So, Mike, are you happy with that plan?" asked Georgie, today's Mis-sion lead.

Startled from his thoughts, Mike nodded, "Ahh, that's fine." Fortunate-ly, he didn't have any serious interest in the activities planned for the day. The priority was driving at the moment, but visibility reduced the drive distances that could be planned to around 50 metres, so there were many additional opportunities for additional science.

"That's great. I'll pass the plan on to the engineering team. Data from Sol 1699 should be available this afternoon."

The team all stood and started filing out of the meeting room. As Mike got to the door, he felt his phone vibrate. His pulse began to race as he looked at the number, calming down as he saw his girlfriend's number.

"Hi, Emily, what's up?"

"Hi, I just wanted to check if you were right to go to Jane and Karl's tonight?"

"Ahh – sure, should be ok."

"Great. Have you heard anything?"

"Not yet, and I don't have any missed calls."

"Ok, talk to you later."

"Bye", he said as he hung up. Emily was the only person he had told that today was the day. His team members at JPL knew he had applied and had been to several meetings, but since the last meeting was more than a month ago, they had mostly forgotten about it.

Mike returned to his office, checked his emails, and returned to his analysis of some recent images.

He heard a knock on his door and looked up to see John, another scientist on the team.

"Are you coming out for lunch?"

"Sure. Sorry, I got lost in that analysis."

"Have you got anything happening this weekend?" asked John as they headed off to the nearest cafeteria.

"It's pretty loose. We might visit Emily's family on Sunday."

"You interested in going to the Dodger's game?"

"Who are they playing?"

"The Reds."

"I'll think about it. Got a bit going on," hedged Mike.

"Ok, but we'll have to get tickets soon."

They entered the cafeteria. Mike ordered a chicken enchilada and John a roast beef sandwich, and they found a table in a not too busy area.

As he took a bite of his enchilada, Mike's phone rang. Jumping up and almost choking, he looked at the number and seeing a 281 prefix definitely increased his adrenalin.

"You right?" asked John.

"I've gotta get this," answered Mike, regaining his breath. "Mike Trellis."

"Hello, Mike. This is Alan Pointer from the NASA Astronaut office in Houston. How's your day going?"

"Ummm, Hi Alan, err, just coughing up an enchilada."

"Great, ahh, glad you are enjoying that. So, it was good to meet you as part of the Astronaut candidate selection process."

"Yes, Alan, it was an interesting and challenging experience." Mike returned John's curious stare as he tried to control his breathing. Fine thing for a potential astronaut to cough their lunch across a room. He could see the cleaner hovering in the background.

"So, Mike. We are impressed by your qualifications, your experience in geoscience, especially at JPL, and the way you participated in the team activities. We would like to offer you a job as an astronaut candidate."

Still standing, he decided sitting was a more dignified option than fainting and managed to say, "Sure".

"I'm certain you'll make a fantastic contribution to our exploration of outer space."

"Thank you, sir. I've wanted this for so long."

"Well, Mike, we will be announcing this in June, so please only tell close family for now. We don't want it leaking before the announcement with the Vice President."

"I understand."

"Ok then, welcome to the team. Someone from our office will be in touch shortly to organise everything."

"Thank you, Alan, I'm honoured, and I look forward to it".

Mike ended the call and put the phone down. He'd just been accepted into one of the most elite groups of people on and off the planet!

"Everything ok?" asked John.

"All my dreams just came true!"

3

— • —

Thursday, June 8, 2017

The previous three weeks had been hectic. Mike had immediately rung Emily and told her the good news. Then he had rung his parents, who were thrilled by the news. The following day he'd received a call from a liaison at the astronaut office to organise a trip to Houston to prepare for the announcement, including measurements for his blue uniform. A NASA TV crew had interviewed him. He'd got basic training in handling media questions. He'd had to organise leave from JPL for visits to Houston and give his notice. He never got to that Red's game with John.

Yesterday he'd arrived in Houston with Emily and his folks. He'd meet the other 11 astronaut candidates—a very diverse group, with many women and many were military. Everyone was very excited. They had received their uniform, got more media training and gone through a rehearsal of the announcement.

So now here he was, about to meet the Vice President of the United States of America, and the NASA Administrator and face a press conference!

The other candidates were highly capable. He'd met a couple during the interview process as they gathered in groups of 20, and yesterday they had a chance to get to know each other better. There were only two other scientists, a couple of doctors and several pilots, including a woman, Sue

Bright. Given the current focus on returning to the moon, he wouldn't be surprised if she was part of the first moon mission.

As their names were announced, they entered the auditorium and stood in front of a mock-up of the Orion capsule, internally lit, with the hatch open so the audience could glimpse inside. No longer was this class going to fly in space shuttles and not even, hopefully, the Soyuz. They would train on the Orion, the SpaceX Dragon and the Boeing Starliner. While most of them would no doubt visit the International Space Station (ISS), their focus was on getting to the Moon and Mars.

Mike found Emily and his parents in the crowd and gave them a wave. Not one for large events, still, he took a deep breath and smiled. He figured there would be many more such events in his career, so he'd better get used to them, and he sat on his stool on stage.

The event was a celebration of the candidates and NASA and America's role in space. The NASA Administrator welcomed them to the family. The Vice President of the United States of America, a fan of NASA, commissioned them as future heroes of the country as they ventured back to the Moon and onto Mars, invoking the name of God to bless the class, NASA and the nation. And, of course, there were opportunities for questions from the press.

After the event, many came to shake his hand and congratulate him. Finally, Emily and Mike's parents were able to hug him.

"Mike, we are so proud of you seeing you up there with the rest of the class," said his dad, John.

"Yes, everyone is so skilled and experienced, and fancy 18,000 people applying," his mother Clare said.

"And you got to meet the Vice President!" bubbled Emily.

"I'm not sure a handshake qualifies as 'meeting'," said Mike. "It looks like we are moving on to lunch now, so let's get some food."

They followed the rest of the class into a nearby dining room, finding seats at a table with another astronaut candidate, Christina Pak, and her parents.

"Christina, these are my parents, John and Clare and my girlfriend, Emily," said Mike.

"Mike, thank you," said Christina. "Wonderful to meet you all. These are my parents, Ann and David."

They all greeted each other.

"So, Christina, whereabouts in the States are you from?" asked Clare.

"We live in Orange County, California. My parents moved from South Korea to the US before I was born."

"Oh – such a big city! I don't like big cities. We are from Colorado Springs, and it just keeps growing, but at least it isn't too big. We visited Mike once in LA, but it was just so big and crowded. But I'd guess you all would be used to that."

Mike glared at his mother, changing the subject. "Christina is another of the scientists in the class. You're a biologist, aren't you?"

"Yes, I studied at Berkeley and did my doctorate at Stanford. Currently, I'm working at NASA Ames. Emily, what do you do?"

"Wow, they are great colleges," said Emily. " I'm an intern in robotics on the Mars Rover, Opportunity."

"Ok – so you met Mike at JPL?"

"Yes, we've only been going out a couple of months. This whole astronaut thing has happened so quickly!"

"Doesn't feel like it for me," quipped Mike, "it took two years from when I applied. And that was my second attempt."

"I still can't believe I got through," replied Christina. "Even after all the interviews, I didn't think I had a chance."

The waiter appeared with their set salads, and they settled into a discussion about the application process and their experience of the event. The

NASA Administrator walked around the tables and thanked the families for attending.

At another table, astronaut candidate Sue Bright was eating lunch with her partner, Ron and all of their parents. Alan Pointer, from the Astronaut Office, had joined them.

"Ron, we are thrilled to have a pilot of Sue's calibre as a candidate. I'm afraid we will be taking a lot of her time during the next few years," stated Alan.

"I'm sure. That's not going to be anything new. The Navy has kept her pretty busy."

"That would be true, so I guess you are used to long-distance romance?"

"Well, most of the time I've known her, she has been studying or operating as a test pilot, so she has mostly been at home. Moving to Houston is going to be a big change. I need to try and find some work here."

"Have a chat with our recruitment office. There are few roles that we don't have. I'd be surprised if we couldn't find you something."

"That would be helpful. Thank you, sir."

Ron turned his attention to the turkey sandwich that had just been placed before him.

Sue pondered the discussion. Ron hadn't been overly supportive of the move involved. They'd only just gotten settled into their new place. And he'd only just started a new job as an electrical engineer at a defence contractor, so the idea of moving and a new job just wasn't appealing to him.

4

Sue's parents were surprised by her choice of the Navy for a career. They knew that she'd been interested in space and aviation. After all, she had gone to the Advanced Space Academy during high school. Studying aeronautics at MIT, she was recruited by the US Navy and trained as an F-16 pilot. NASA recruited many good military pilots, so it was a shot to become an astronaut.

Sally Ride's career as a NASA astronaut inspired 12-year-old Sue's imagination. Imagine being in space. Imagine being the first woman to do something. Maybe she could be the first woman on Mars, or perhaps the Moon? She'd figured that flying was the best way to achieve that, and who didn't like planes?

She'd always been more interested in building and doing things than in dolls. She loved hiking and camping, but she'd been obsessed with flying. She also loved watching birds, especially eagles flying. They were so majestic, gliding on the air currents, with barely a movement of a muscle.

Sue's father was an electrical engineer working in power distribution, and her mother was a paediatrician. Their family had always been very focused on science. Her brother worked in software development, and her sister was a paramedic.

Her family had moved fairly frequently when she was a child, as her father moved from project to project. However, they lived in St Louis,

Missouri, for most of her high school years. One of her science teachers was interested in space and often used NASA materials in class, encouraging her to attend the Advanced Space Academy.

Space Academy was fantastic. Sue got to make friends with so many others from around the country who, like her, were interested in science and space. And they got to do simulations of space missions. She even got to be the mission commander!

Sue had been so excited to be accepted to MIT for their aeronautics course. There weren't many women in the class, so she got a lot of interest from the guys. She'd focussed on space systems subjects in her undergrad degree as much as possible. During her final year, a US Navy recruiter had convinced her that she could become a jet pilot, so she signed up.

Training to be a pilot in the US Navy had been tough. While there were now more women in the armed forces, it was still a heavily male-dominated environment. But the guys had been fair and had helped her, and she had been able to help them in return. She was so glad that today it was more usual for a woman to be a fighter pilot. After two deployments, she had completed a Master of Science in Systems Engineering at the Naval Postgraduate School and became a test pilot.

While studying for her masters, Sue met Ron, and in 2015 they had a daughter, Jessica.

The Call had come just after she'd returned from a test flight and was changing out of her flight suit.

"Lieutenant Commander, this is Alan Pointer from the NASA Astronaut office in Houston."

"Good morning, sir."

"Good morning. I hope that you are in a position to talk."

"Yes, sir. All good, sir," she replied as she stood in the changing room in her underwear.

"We at NASA were very impressed by you at the interviews a few weeks ago."

"Thank you, sir."

"Would you still be interested in an astronaut role at NASA?"

"Absolutely, sir!"

"Well, Sue, we would very much like to offer you a position as an Astronaut candidate."

"That is an honour, sir, and I would be excited to accept."

"Great! Well, we will organise for orders to be prepared for you, and you should hear something shortly. Have a great day."

"Thank you, sir. I look forward to the journey. Goodbye."

Sue fist-pumped the sky and then figured she better finish changing before calling Ron.

Suitably attired in her uniform, she called Ron, "Hi Ron, I just heard."

"Did you get it?"

"Yes," she screamed, "I'm going to be an astronaut."

"Wow, ok, then, umm, when do you go?"

"I don't know yet. I'll get orders soon, I guess."

"OK, well, I'm happy for you. We'll talk later. I have to go."

"Right, bye."

Sue looked at the phone. Ron didn't seem all that excited by the prospect. It had been a very long shot, but he knew this was her dream. Ron worked for one of the defense contractors on fighter jets, and he wasn't quite as gung-ho as her fellow pilots. In fact, he was way nerdier, but they'd been able to relate about the engineering systems. And they both loved the outdoors and had several camping adventures under their belt. One of the advantages of not being deployed to a ship!

5

— · —

Monday, August 14, 2017

Today was it, the first day of astronaut training. It had been a crazy month for Mike. He'd finished working out his notice at JPL and taken two more trips to Houston while he found a single-bedroom apartment in Clear Lake.

The apartment was pretty nice but basic. One bedroom, walk-in robe, bathroom, small galley kitchen, lounge, dining and a small balcony. The complex had a pool, laundry and gym, and he could have a pet if he wanted. He doubted he would have time, and he'd need to look at buying a house anyway since he expected to be here for years.

Emily was staying in Pasadena as she would be going back to school. Mike suspected their relationship wasn't going to progress.

He'd packed up his apartment in Pasadena, sold a lot of stuff, shipped the rest to Houston, hopped in his RAV4, and began his road trip.

Last week he'd spent a lot of time replacing the stuff he'd sold, such as his couch, bed, dining table and fridge. He had actually camped in his apartment the first night, finding a Chick-fil-A a mile away for dinner. He was now fairly well set up, for a bachelor, and had spent a bit of time familiarising himself with Clear Lake and Houston. How crazy is it when one of the freeways is called 'NASA Bypass' and another main street is 'Space Center Boulevard'!

One thing for sure, it was hot, peaking just under 100 deg F (37 deg C) all week. And humid! Wow. Mike was very glad about the air-conditioning in his car and apartment. And then, there were the cockroaches, flying cockroaches!

So, waking early at 6 am, he jumped out of his new queen size bed, heading out to the pool for a morning swim to stretch out his muscles. He returned home for a shower, dressed in a shirt and tie, and grabbed some cereal.

Mike checked his Facebook. Some Aussie friends seemed to be laughing at their deputy Prime Minister turning out to be a New Zealander. What a laugh. Less of a laugh was the news of the landslides in Freetown, Sierra Leone, killing 500. That put things in a bit of perspective.

Taking a selfie and recalling the need to manage his public profile, he posted, "First day training as an astronaut!"

He grabbed his things and headed to his RAV4 to drive to the Johnson Space Center (JSC).

JSC was the home of the NASA Astronaut Corps, with most based here and much of the training located here or nearby.

After navigating through security, Mike found his way to the correct car park and into the NASA Astronaut Office, where he found several other candidates already gathered.

Alan Pointer walked over to Mike, extending his hand. "Mike, good to see you. Have you got settled in?"

"Yes, thanks, Alan. I've got an apartment in Clear Lake while I have a look around for somewhere to buy."

"Good idea. There are a lot of places available, and you'll be around here for several years, so a good time to buy. Did your move go ok?"

"Yes, got everything packed up. The drive was fun, and my stuff arrived last week."

"Great! We will get started in about 20 minutes, so grab yourself a coffee or juice. There're some donuts over there. Don't expect them every day, but we wanted you folks to feel welcome and help you settle in."

"Ok, thanks, Alan."

Mike looked around the room, heading straight to the coffee.

"Hi Mike, welcome to Houston."

Mike turned to see who it was. He said, "Christina, good to see you. How did your move go?"

"Pretty busy. While we were here in June, I looked at a few houses with realtors and purchased one, moving in just last week. I'm still living in boxes!"

"Wow, organised! I'm renting an apartment. I'm going to look around and see what I like. Real estate is much cheaper here than near JPL, so I guess buying makes sense.

"So, what do you think today holds?"

"I suspect a lot of briefings and hand-holding!"

"Hi, Christina, Mike. You going to let someone else get at the donuts?"

Mike turned to see Sue, smartly dressed in a pantsuit.

"Sure, Sue, I guess we better get something."

They poured themselves coffees, Christina got an orange juice, and Mike selected a doughnut. Another candidate, Andrew Glover, joined them.

"Damn hot and humid here," said Andrew.

"Yes", agreed Mike and Christina.

"Gets this bad in Maryland in summer," commented Sue.

"I prefer desert," said Andrew. "You guys got any idea who should be class leaders?"

"I reckon Sue here would be a good leader," offered Mike.

"I agree," said Christina.

Sue was blushing now. "I think it's a bit early to know who the top dogs are quite yet."

Just then, they heard Alan calling the group to attention.

"Folks. Welcome again to Johnson Space Centre. If you want to make your way into the briefing room, we will get underway shortly."

The group made their way into the room, finding seats. They didn't need to wait long.

"Good Morning. Welcome to Johnson Space Center. My name is Chris Forest, and I'm NASA's Chief Astronaut.

"Ladies and gentlemen, you have begun a journey of exploration. Yes, of space, the Moon and even Mars, but also of yourselves. You have been chosen from amongst the largest group of applicants in NASA history. You already excel in diverse careers, of which you can be rightly proud.

"From today, you are no longer leaders. You are rookies. You will discover that you have so much more to learn, and we will help you with that. You will have to learn to become a team, trust each other, work together and save each other's lives when there is no one else to help.

"You are going to need to learn how to cope when you are isolated in a tin can with three of your crew with only a comms channel to link you with home. You will have to learn systems, learn science, and learn to live without gravity.

"This class is 'doing the next thing'. We expect you will not just go into earth orbit but go and live on the Moon and Mars. You will fly in spacecraft that have not yet been designed! And, to do that, you are going to have to cope with situations that we have only yet dreamed about, and you will have to solve them.

"We will help you. We will train you. We will test you. We will invest in you. We will annoy you! And you will deal with it, and you will ask for help because failure is not possible. And you will fail if you don't ask for help. And then, once again, you'll be leaders.

"Mental health is one of the biggest factors we in the Astronaut Corps deal with. You will have problems, and it is ok to ask for help. You all have just moved, some with families, and you have just changed jobs. For anybody, that is a stressful situation. If you are struggling, start asking for help now. NASA needs you healthy in all aspects.

"Being in space is fantastic. It is like nothing else, and I hope and expect that all of you will one day experience that. I suspect some of you will experience things I haven't, such as walking on the Moon or Mars. Do take the time to experience those things. Remember them, record them. That is what will make the work and the discomfort, and the frustrations, worthwhile.

"Class of 2017, welcome to NASA."

Everyone applauded.

Alan took the floor as Chris Forest sat down.

"Thank you, Chris. Candidates, the next two years are going to be very busy. You are going to visit all of NASA. You need to know what we do because one of your roles is Public Relations, and another is staff morale. You will encourage and motivate the staff by turning up at a facility. That will take some getting used to. You will also need to learn Russian, the basics of the ISS systems and the spacecraft you will fly, including the Soyuz, Orion, and other vehicles, and train in EVA operations. All before you are approved as Astronauts and be available for selection for a mission. And then you'll do more learning. You will be learning for the rest of your career.

"So, today, you will meet the team and get an orientation to JSC.

"Also, as a group, you need to select your class leaders over the next week. Be ready next week to tell me who they are."

Then the briefing began.

6

—◇—

TUESDAY, APRIL 12 2018

Sue struggled into the extravehicular mobility unit (aka EVA suit) with the help of the suit technicians. It was not easy. On earth, the suit was actually very heavy. This was the first time that she was going into the Neutral Buoyancy Laboratory (NBL) for training. Mike was her training partner. It made sense to have a pilot train with a mission specialist.

The last nine months had been as busy as promised. Most weeks, the class visited one facility or another. There had been survival training., and they'd had a geology field trip. She'd even got to learn and perform maintenance on the T-38 jets. But this exercise was probably the closest to being in space that she'd come. The ISS trainer mock-up was close, but you weren't floating. In the NBL, she'd be floating as she would in space, in a space suit!

Her partner Ron had settled in ok. They'd bought a red brick 3,500 square foot, two-storey 4 bedroom house in Seabrook. Ron had managed to find some remote work so he could stay home and look after their now three-year-old daughter, Jessica. He still didn't seem to be overly happy, but he was supportive. Being a young mother and Astronaut Candidate was a tricky combination. However, NASA understood, with many candidates also having young families. Jessica was now old enough for them to let her be in childcare a few days a week, and Ron could focus more on work.

Sue was finally properly in the legs and bottom half of the suit, and it was time to climb into the torso. The assistants helped her get under the torso and climb up into it. There wasn't a lot of room to move, and the lower part of the suit weighed her down. After several minutes of struggle, she finally got her arms into the sleeves and her head out the neck and rested while the team secured the lower half of the suit to the torso. Then they fit her gloves and added the weights to make her neutrally buoyant in the tank.

Sue could just make out Mike going through the same process nearby. The process took over an hour, and most of it had to be performed with others' assistance. She imagined what this task would be like for just two people on the moon helping each other. The suits wouldn't have the same weight there, but it would still be awkward and even slower.

Mike seemed a sensible guy to her. He was driven in different ways from the military guys she had spent most of her Navy life with. In some ways, not unlike Ron. More thoughtful, and, well, somewhat geekish, and definitely fitter. They got on fairly well, but this was the first time they'd been on the same team. That was probably part of the training, she thought. She had noticed that teams were mixed up, and they were constantly being monitored by trainers, especially on the various training trips they had undertaken, such as the survival and geology training trips.

Finally, they were both ready and standing on the platform, back to back, prepared to be lifted into the pool. Given the all-clear, the pneumatic crane lifted them up, across and then down into the pool, where final leak checks were performed and tweaks made to the weights on the suits to ensure they were neutrally buoyant. The pressure in the suits was above atmospheric pressure to counter the water pressure. The suit air mix had less nitrogen and a greater oxygen concentration. The training was expected to last about 6 hours, so measures were required to avoid the bends.

As the water washed over her helmet, Sue controlled her breathing. She had done Scuba training, so she was familiar with being underwater, but this was different. The air blowing into the suit was somewhat noisy, and if something went wrong, it wasn't as simple as swimming to the surface and taking a face mask off. In fact, the briefings and training had been very clear on procedures to clear their ears. A former astronaut, Leland Melvin, had been injured during such training when the Valsalva device used for this purpose was missing.

"Control to EV1. Are you ready to proceed?" she heard through her headset.

"EV1 Roger," Sue replied.

"Control to EV2. Are you ready to proceed?"

"EV2, copy that. Ready to proceed," Mike sounded nervous.

"Control to divers take EV1 and 2 down to 10 feet."

Sue felt them move down. Wearing the suit, there was no way that she could propel herself, so divers moved her around. She felt the pressure build in her ears and used the Valsalva device to clear her ears. She tried forming fists with her hands. There was resistance, but she could do it. Looking around, she was amazed at how clear the water was.

"EV2 to Control, I'm having trouble clearing my ears."

"Ok, EV2. Divers, take EV2 up to 5 feet."

"Control, EV1. I'm fine here. Can we proceed deeper?"

"Roger EV1, divers descend EV1 to 20 feet."

"EV2, Control. Ok, I've cleared my ears, ready to descend."

"Copy EV2. Divers descend EV2 back to 10 feet."

Sue now felt more pressure and noticed the divers adjusting the weights on her suit. Her legs were trying to float up, so that wouldn't be helpful.

"EV2, are you ready to descend to 20 feet."

"Roger, Control."

They made their way down the ISS Truss mock-up and began the process of swapping batteries between a pallet and the battery rack as an exercise in using tools. Sue found it took some practice to find the tools on her work platform on her stomach. It was hard to see them, and then the gloves made it hard to grasp them. It took time to get used to their feel.

After about 1 hour, Mike and Sue started to work together to move the batteries. Until then, they had been familiarising themselves with the necessary techniques.

"Control to EV1 and EV2. Can you both please translate along the truss to pallet B34."

"EV1. Copy."

"EV2. Copy."

They both started to move along the truss from their current locations, making sure to remain tethered to two locations. Another habit that they needed to learn. They needed to stay connected to their spacecraft. They would have an emergency pack that could give them some thrust if they floated away, but it was minimal, so the tethers were very important, and they needed to learn how to manage them and not get tangled in them.

Arriving at their workstation first, Mike's initial task was to get his feet into the foot restraint. Not as simple as it sounds when you can't see your feet. The process was akin to kicking at a bike-toe clip without being able to see it until your foot got in. After 5 minutes, he finally had his right foot in, which made it a bit easier to get his left foot in. And then he needed a rest!

Sue entered his field of view, holding a large electric screwdriver, which she handed to him. It was weird. He expected it to be heavy, but because it wasn't actually real but a plastic mock-up to be neutrally buoyant, it just floated. He manoeuvred it onto the large nut they needed to remove. Then a diver switched it out with an actual device (which did have mass), and

Mike could remove the nut. Without the foot restraint, he would have just rotated around it.

He repeated the exercise for another 5 nuts. He and Sue could float the battery module away from the pallet.

"Ok, Mike, I'll move this to the battery array."

"Copy. I'll just free myself from these restraints."

Finally arriving at the worksite, Mike and Sue aligned the module over the mounting screws.

This time it was Sue's turn to use the foot restraint and the screwdriver. Nothing happened quickly, that was for sure. The tools floated, so if you didn't secure them, they drifted away. A couple of times, Mike needed to retrieve the screwdriver for Sue as it had moved out of her reach.

As they returned to the pallet, suddenly, Mike's progress stopped.

"Control from EV2, I seem to have snagged on something."

"Control, EV1. I can see Mike's tether has caught on one of the cooler structures we are passing."

"Control copies."

"Mike, can you backtrack a bit, and I'll try and free you?"

"Sure."

Even though they were surrounded by divers to move them around and swap out equipment, obviously, they let situations like this develop to help with training.

"How's that, Sue?"

"Yes, that's enough. I think I've freed it for you. Now I just need to get out of the way so you can move again... Ok, you are free to keep translating."

And so it progressed for the six hours of training. Finally, they were able to return to the surface and extract themselves, with help, from the suits.

"How are you feeling after that, Sue?" asked Mike.

"I'm exhausted. That was pretty intense, and nothing works quite the way you expect."

"Yeah, I know, and there is so much going on. Managing tethers, managing the tools, working out how to grip stuff."

"So, are you heading home now?"

"Yeah, I've got a contractor coming around to quote on some renovations."

"Really! So you are making some changes to your new place?"

"Yeah, the bathroom is a bit dated, as is the kitchen, and the whole place needs painting. I don't need a floral bedroom!"

"Ha, ha, I don't know. Brings out your feminine side, Mike!"

"Yeah, right. Anyway, hopefully, the place can be fixed up for summer. I better get going. See you tomorrow."

"Ok, have a great night."

7

— • —

TUESDAY, JULY 23 2019. CLASS 2017 GRADUATION

Mike walked out of the double shower bathroom and watched his girl-friend, Lisa sleeping on the bed. They'd only met three months ago, and she worked in the Office of STEM Engagement at JSC, and they'd met at an event for educators that the astronaut candidates attended.

He changed into a shirt, tie and trousers. Today he had a meeting with the Chief Astronaut, the first since he had finished and passed his candidate training. He was now available for assignment to missions. There had been a lot of political announcements about returning to the Moon in 2024, and he hoped he would be part of it, although he would be surprised if any of the inexperienced candidates were assigned to the first manned flight to land on the Moon, Artemis 3.

He pondered the likely assignments as he poured himself a bowl of Wheaties. Probably backing up someone on a mission or maybe a flight to the ISS. He wasn't super keen on that idea because it would probably dis-count him from any of the early Artemis launches. Unless NASA increased the number of launches, most ISS missions were relatively long stays.

"Hi, I didn't hear you get up," said Lisa as she entered the kitchen.

"You were out of it."

"You are all dressed up to see the big chief. I like it," she said as she wrapped her arms around him.

"Ok, I've gotta leave soon. I guess you are going in later?" asked Mike, extricating himself from her embrace.

"Yeah, I don't have anything booked till this afternoon. I'll cook an egg for you."

"Thanks," Mike answered as he ate his cereal.

Mike finished his breakfast, said goodbye to Lisa, hopped in his car and drove the ten minutes to the Space Centre down Middlebrook Drive.

Sue was already waiting outside Alan Pointer's office. He had recently been appointed the Chief Astronaut, having commanded one shuttle mission, flown on two others, and commanded the International Space Station (ISS) during a 4-month mission. Before joining NASA, he had been a test pilot in the USA Air Force. He was well-liked by the Astronaut Corp and seen as a tough but fair leader.

"You can go on in now", said the secretary.

Sue rose and walked into the large corner office of the most powerful astronaut in the corps.

"Good morning, Lieutenant Commander. Come on in and take a seat. I hope you weren't waiting long."

"Good morning, sir. I haven't been waiting that long."

"Great. And how's your family?"

"They are well, sir. Jessica will be starting pre-Kindergarten this year. Ron is quite excited to be starting his new job at JSC next month. I think he has had enough working from home."

"And I hear congratulations are in order. You are expecting another one?"

"Yes, sir, we are due in January. I figured this was the only window of time to have another child and not drastically affect my flight prospects."

"Yes, I think you will have a very busy year. I'm not sure Ron is going to have much time in the office, though!

"We would like you to play a pivotal role in the next lunar landing," Alan continued. "We want you to be the first woman to walk on the moon."

Sue just stared at him.

The Moon.

The first woman on the Moon.

She'd just finished the candidate's course!

She knew she had done well, but she did not expect this.

"Ahh, sir, I think you just said that you want me to be the first woman on the moon. Did I hear that correctly?"

Alan smiled and laughed, "Yes, Sue, I did just offer you a place in history. Would you like some water?"

Wow, she'd expected one of the other experienced women in the corps to have that role. "That would be an honour, sir, but aren't there more experienced women available?"

"Please call me Alan, Sue. No, there aren't, really. With the Soyuz problems and the lack of our own launch capability, we don't have anyone of your calibre for the role. By the way, did I mention that you would be the commander?"

This just got better. She'd be leading the mission!

"Sir, do I really have the confidence of NASA, or is this a political decision?"

"Good question and you don't hold back! No doubt politics is playing into this mission a lot, and we probably wouldn't have the funding without it. And yes, there is a lot of pressure to have a woman land on the moon. But you have truly impressed your classmates and us. We think you are the right person for the job. There will be another woman on the mission Christina Pak as Mission Specialist 2. However, she would only land in exceptional circumstances.

"So, as part of your preparation, we want to get you to the ISS as soon as possible. Assuming that you are fit, we want you to fly on the Starliner to the ISS in October 2020 as Deputy Commander and stay on the station for one month. That will give you both space and command experience. How does that sound?"

Yes, Sue thought, it was going to be a busy year.

Arriving at the JSC, Mike found a park near the Astronaut Corps building and arrived early for his meeting with the Chief Astronaut. The secretary asked him to take a seat and if he wanted anything to drink. Asking for some water, Mike took a seat.

Mike looked up to see Sue being escorted out of the office by Alan Pointer.

"Good morning, sir, Sue," he said.

"Good morning Mike, come on in," welcomed Alan. "Thanks again, Sue. We will talk again very soon."

"Thank you, sir. Good morning, Mike. I'll talk to you later."

"So, Mike, have you had a bit of a break since the candidate course finished?" asked Alan. As he turned and led them back into his office.

"Yes, sir. I went back to Colorado Springs to visit my family, and Lisa and I had a week in Hawaii."

"That's great, and call me Alan.

"So, now that you are on the available to fly list, I guess you are wondering what your first mission will be?"

"Yes, I would be excited to know how NASA would like to use me."

"Well, we have been working through our options. With the SpaceX Dragon and Boeing Starliner still not yet operational, we are still reliant on the Soyuz. We are not planning for any of your class to train on Soyuz. If we need to fly another mission using Soyuz, we will man that from existing corps members. We want to focus your class's training on Dragon, Starliner and Orion, with missions to ISS and the Moon."

Mike swallowed. That confirmed he had a good chance of a moon mission.

"As you know," continued the Chief Astronaut, "the target to put the first woman and the next man on the moon in 2024 is aggressive. And clearly, there is a political push for it to happen within the next presidential term. But that means that funds are available, so we need to work with that and succeed. And we are planning flights a bit differently.

"We want you on an Artemis mission as a mission specialist."

Mike's heart skipped. There was a real chance he would walk on the moon. Mind you, there was also a real chance he would just orbit it!

"Sir, that would be amazing."

"I'm sure it will, but we have to get you there first. You need space experience. We would like you to be a mission specialist on ISS Expedition 67 in May 2021, returning in June 2021 on a Dragon, a short stay."

Wow, thought Mike, that is a timeline speedup. Astronauts can often train for five years for a mission. "That's very soon."

"Yes, but you already have the basics, and given the short mission, you'll be trained in a subset of the ISS experiments. There will be other mission specialists focussing on the others. View that mission as a training exercise. You will be doing real work, but your focus will be on Artemis.

"One of the great things about the Artemis program is that we can dovetail the primary and backup crews between the missions with little re-training since the systems and missions will be similar.

"So, we want you to be a backup mission specialist on Artemis 3 in 2024. George Scorby will be the primary. The commander will be Sue Bright. The Deputy Commander is John Packers, and mission specialist 2 is Christina

Pak. They have all been informed. We are still talking to people for the backup roles."

This was now a momentous day. Mike was a backup role not just for a seat orbiting the moon but for the next moonwalk! If he understood correctly, the first woman on the moon would be Sue, and the next man would be George, while Christina would stay in the Gateway in lunar orbit.

"Would you like some water Mike?" asked Alan noting Mike's distraction.

"Sure, thanks."

Alan poured him a glass. "I know that's a bit to take in, but there is more. Are you ready for it?"

Mike sipped his water, took a few breaths, and then replied, "Yes, go on."

"So, your primary mission will be Artemis 5 as the mission specialist in 2026. That will be a 30-day mission with 1 week on the moon with four members landing in a reusable lander.

"Are you happy with these options?"

Mike thought about it. He couldn't fault their selection for Artemis 3. Sue was an obvious choice as commander and selection for the first woman on the moon. She was smart, a good leader and capable. He could see that George was in the team as an experienced astronaut. In fact, it was surprising there weren't more experienced astronauts on the mission.

"Alan, I'm a bit surprised there are so many from our class on Artemis 3. I expected there to be more experienced astronauts in the team."

"Yes, I understand, but so many had extended tours of the ISS that we are concerned about their exposure. We really need Dragon and Starliner operational, so we can cycle astronauts through ISS without that impact on their health. There will be two on Artemis 2, which will prove the Orion in Lunar orbit.

"So, what do you think?"

"Sir, it will be challenging, but I accept the missions."

"Fantastic. I know you will contribute significantly to all those missions. Great to have you on board. We will be in touch about your schedule shortly. And I'll let you know who the rest of the Artemis 5 crew will be soon.

"I'll be talking with the other members of your class over the next couple of days. Please keep this confidential until then. You can talk to those members of Artemis 3 that I listed."

"I will. Thank you, Alan."

After shaking hands, Mike left the office and headed to his assigned workspace.

8

— . —

TUESDAY, JULY 23 2019. CLASS 2017 GRADUATION

Mike sat at his desk in the space shared by all his astronaut class. Once they got their assignments, they would relocate to different areas, possibly one of the astronaut corps workspaces nearby.

To be listed on three crews as primary or backup at the same time was unheard of. Things were definitely changing in NASA. He had so many questions. He realised that he didn't even know who was on the crew to the ISS on Expedition 67, nor Artemis 5, but he did know who was on Artemis 3.

He nodded at Sue across the room, who smiled his way as he logged into his computer. He discovered an email about Expedition 67 had just arrived. It appeared that John Packers, who would be deputy commander of Artemis 3, would be in command of Expedition 67. That was a helpful crossover. Andrew Glover from his class would be a Flight Engineer remaining on the ISS together with David Hopkins, a Canadian Astrophysicist. Looking around the room, it appeared Andrew wasn't at his desk.

The email detailed a preliminary meeting scheduled for the next day and a room location for desk assignment the same day. That's efficient, thought Mike.

The following email contained information for Artemis 3, with an initial briefing for primary and backup crews on Friday. Some lucky NASA scheduler was going to have a fun time coordinating all these interlocking mission schedules!

Mike opened his calendar application only to discover that most of his days were now blocked out with events starting Wednesday for the next couple of weeks. Someone must have been working on this overnight!

Mike looked up to see Sue standing beside his desk.

"Christina and I were going to grab a coffee. You want to join us?" she asked.

"Sure."

The three of them headed out of the room and down the hallway.

"Can you believe it?" asked Christina as they walked to the elevators. "We are going to the moon!"

"Well, you two are. I'm just backup," replied Mike.

"You'll get your chance," said Sue as they entered the elevator and selected the floor, and they were joined by some other staff. They kept quiet on the ride down, studying their phones.

They ordered their coffees and found an isolated table.

"I'm still surprised our class is playing such a big role so early in Artemis," commented Mike. "The experienced astronauts will be fuming!"

"I must say I was shocked this morning when Alan told me," said Sue. "I thought they would have gone with a safer option since I'll be having a baby in January."

"It's so great you decided to have another one, Sue, "said Christina, glancing at Mike. "I still need to find the right guy, and now I'll have to wait five years before I could even try. My parents will be so pissed."

"Have either of you met John Packers?" asked Mike, keen to change the topic.

"I have," said Sue. "He's U.S. Air Force, Colonel. He was part of my survival training group, although not on my team, so I didn't spend that much time with him."

"He's going to be my commander on my trip to the ISS," said Mike. "I wonder how he'll go being deputy commander to you on Artemis 3?"

"I'm sure he'll be fine. He's a professional," stated Sue.

"Yeah, but isn't this all political? Not saying that you aren't capable, Sue, but hell, there have to be at least six experienced women in the Corps who could be in your role. They are clearly going for fresh young faces for the Moon. And whoever had three missions to prepare for?" asked Mike.

"You got 3?" asked Christina.

"Yeah, an ISS on Dragon, backup for Artemis 3, and Artemis 5 primary."

"There is definitely politics involved. I'm sure some of the corps will be put out, but damned if I'm going to miss a moonwalk if I have the option," said Sue.

"You're both lucky. All I'll get to do is look at the moon. When are you guys going to ISS?" asked Christina. "My flight is June next year on a Starliner."

"I'm scheduled for October next year on a Starliner as well if I'm fit," answered Sue.

"And I'm on a flight with Andrew and John Packers in April 2021 on a Dragon. I guess Andrew is on Artemis 4 or 5."

Christina stood up. "I've got a meeting to get to. Are you guys finished?" She took the cups and walked to the trash can; dropping one, she bent to pick it up, Mike admiring her fit physique.

"Ahem," coughed Sue, interrupting Mike's gaze. "Do you know George Scorby at all?"

"A little. He's Canadian, but he was on the Station for half of last year. He's a good guy and knows his stuff. He's a Geologist, so makes sense for him to be on the mission and for me to back him up, I guess."

"Are you sure you're cool with this?" Sue asked.

Mike felt her hand on his knee. "Not a lot I can do about it, is there? If Ron is happy, I can't complain."

"Ron doesn't know. Who knows, it might be his."

"I'm not into playing happy families."

"She likes you."

"Who?"

"Christina."

"I'm not one of the 'chosen'."

"You heard her. She wants a kid. She just needs to think you are one of the 'chosen'."

"She's not my type."

"Not what I just saw." As she leaned forward, "or what I feel." Mike inhaled and swallowed. He found strong women difficult.

Standing, he said, "I have to go", and fled the café.

9

It had happened after their last assessment in the Neutral Buoyancy Lab. It had been a hard 6 hours performing various tasks while being closely observed. They had passed, and Sue and Mike were elated. Ron had taken Jessica to visit with his parents since it was such a busy week. Sue had suggested they get dinner to celebrate, so they met at Chelsea Wine Bar overlooking Taylor Lake.

They'd started by sampling a few Belgian beers, and they'd both tackled the Shepherd's pie, together with a Californian Rosé Pinot Noir. As the night progressed, Mike found Sue becoming increasingly amorous, and it wasn't long until they found themselves back at his place.

They'd woken the next morning knowing they had crossed a line they had been warned not to cross and decided that while it had been fun, they shouldn't go there again.

Which had been ok until Sue announced she was pregnant. She and Ron had been trying for another child, not that Mike knew, that so there was no knowing who the father was. They'd decided just to wait and see, and Sue would deal with Ron if she had to, and then Mike started dating Lisa.

The rest of the day was pretty hectic for Sue and Mike, making arrangements and packing up their desks.

Sue arrived home to find Ron playing with Jessica in their backyard.

"Hi, I'm home."

"Mummy, mummy, look what I made," said Jessica, handing her an indecipherable crayon drawing.

"Aww, that's great. Have you had a good day?"

"Yes, I drew, had snacks, played in the balls, and Sally did a poo."

"Right, well, that's fun. Hi Ron, honey, how was your day?"

"Great, I got that project finished before I had to pick Jessica up, so a good day. What was your meeting about?"

"Well, they wanted to talk to me about future missions."

"Mummy, I'm going to play dolls."

"Ok. Jessica, just stay where we can see you."

"So, what missions?"

"Oh, Ron, it's amazing! They want me to be the first woman to walk on the moon!"

Ron stood there gaping.

"I know, it's crazy, I would have figured someone from an earlier class would do it, but there are 2 women from my class on the mission!"

"Wow. I guess that's good, but isn't it going to be dangerous?"

"Well, you know nothing I do isn't, but it will be as safe as possible."

"Umm, what about the baby?"

"Oh – that's fine, the moon walk won't be until 2024 at the earliest, and they want me to go to the ISS later next year first."

"Right, so you have 2 missions!"

"Yeah – isn't it great!"

"Ah, sure," Ron said hesitantly.

"But you can't tell anyone."

"Of course not. We'll tell family, but we have to keep quiet until they announce the crews, and that might be a while yet, especially for the moon walk."

"I guess you are pretty set on this."

"Oh Ron, this is my dream. The only thing better would be landing on Mars!

"Let's get Jessica fed and to bed. I've got plans for you," she said with a twinkle in her eye.

10

— • —

Mike arrived at JSC the next morning, picked up a box of his stuff and located his new desk. Andrew Glover, a tall, fair-skinned pilot from his cohort, arrived a minute later.

"Hi Andy, looks like we are on the same ISS mission."

"And lunar mission, Artemis 5."

"Really?! I didn't know that."

"I only heard late yesterday. I'll be deputy commander."

"And all of us actually land on the moon."

"Have you met John Packers or David Hopkins?"

"No. Sue was saying John seemed ok."

"Good morning, gentlemen. I gather you are Mike and Andrew?" asked John Packers, entering the room. "And this is David Hopkins."

"So, you are the newbies leapfrogging your elders!" said David as he shook each of their hands with a smile.

"We are as surprised as you," said Mike. "It's all moving quite fast."

"You don't know the half of it. You're lucky you don't have to squeeze your butts into a Soyuz. They don't have a Russian masseuse on the station to fix your back, either. So, Mike, you're a scientist?" asked John.

"Yes, sir, geologist."

"And you, Andrew, a pilot?"

"Yes, sir, aeronautical engineer, and I was an assistant professor at MIT," answered Andrew.

"Ok, Professor. I think we better go up in a T-38 tomorrow and you can show me your stuff," replied John. "David here has already enjoyed that experience yesterday, but he was already blooded."

"Thank you, sir. I'll look forward to it. David, how long were you on the station?" asked Andrew.

"Six months. Still can't stand straight. At least this time it will be shorter, and who would turn down a flight, right? You're both on Artemis 5, aren't you?"

"Err, well, if you know then, yes, we are," answered Mike.

"And you're a backup on my moon shot, Artemis 3, Mike," said John.

"You are?!" exclaimed Andrew.

"Umm, well, sorry, I couldn't tell you. And my chances of actually going are pretty slim."

"What role?"

"Mission specialist 1, backup."

"Shit – the moon walk."

"Only the backup. You'll be more surprised who the commander is."

"Not one of our group?"

"Can't say."

"She's gotta be damn good to get my job," said John. "Right. We've got our first familiarisation with the Dragon tomorrow. I know you boys have had initial training on it, but this is our first as a team. And I want us to know the damn thing inside out and be able to strip it down and rebuild it so that when it craps out on us, and they all do in some way, we can fix it. These SpaceX guys are always changing things, and I don't like change.

"Get your stuff stowed away, and let's see what else they've planned for us."

The team arrived at Ellington Field early the next morning and suited up to fly two T-38 jets to Los Alamitos in California and drove to SpaceX's facilities in Hawthorne for training.

Mike and the others settled into their seats in the SpaceX Dragon 2 mock-up trainer. The capsule design was very clean and futuristic. It felt very modern. Mike's seat was on the outside left, without a control screen which was reserved for the Commander and Deputy Commander. Of the three US spacecraft, the Dragon 2 was the smallest, however, there was still plenty of room for the 4 of them. He was glad he wasn't flying in a Soyuz, in which the astronauts are literally crammed, suffering excruciating leg pain.

Their exercise today was a basic familiarisation exercise, getting used to the vehicle layout, entry, and getting into seats in gravity. The command team received a very brief overview of the controls and layout. Their training would occur in a different simulator, although the entire flight was automated.

There was room for cargo pallets beneath the seats and a toilet they'd be able to use before rendezvousing with the ISS.

After that brief introduction, they went to be fitted for their Dragon suits which would protect them in case of cabin depressurization and keep them cool during the flight.

Earl, one of SpaceX's space suit engineers, introduced himself. "Greetings, gentlemen. Today we are going to fit you for your SpaceX Dragon suits, just like this one you can see here."

Earl pointed to a beautiful white, sleek suit displayed next to him. They had a few carefully placed black patches, a strip down the side and black boots. The face shield was clear, with a white helmet. Very stylish. It matched the interior styling of the Dragon.

"NASA has sent us your measurements, and the suits are adaptable, so we should have you all fitted out today.

"You'll notice that, unlike other suits, there is a zipper around the inner seam, so you enter from the bottom of the suit. The gloves do zip open, so you can use your hands to zip up. The gloves are very flexible and will work with our touch screens.

"How do we connect to the ship for air and comms?" asked Mike.

"There's a port on the upper right leg where you plug in the connector for air, communication and cooling," answered Earl.

"So these suits will protect us in a decompression?" asked John, with a hint of incredulity.

"Yes, sir, these suits conform to all of NASA's requirements. They keep you at the right temp, with atmosphere, and let you communicate.

"Each of you will find your suits over here with your name on them. Once you've got yourself familiar with them, you can go into that locker room and change into the undergarment and come back, and we will help you put the suit on.

Mike took a look at his new suit. It was pretty different to the other suits NASA astronauts had worn. For one thing, it was white, not blue or orange. Secondly, it was stylish! He examined the zipper around the inner seam of the legs. Weird place for a zipper, but it did seem to make for minimal openings. The action was smooth, so it didn't look like it would be too difficult to operate.

Mike also studied the gloves. They were small. Definitely not the over-sized gloves of the Apollo era.

Heading into the change room with the others, he found his allocated undergarment and got changed into it.

"They are pretty cool suits," said Andy.

"I don't care what they look like," said John, "as long as they don't kill me."

"Let's hope they are as comfortable as they look," chipped in Mike on his way out of the room to put his suit on.

"Ok, Mike, I'll be giving you a hand putting on your suit," said Steve, one of the suit engineers. "I suggest you unzip the gloves first, then open the helmet before unzipping the inseam."

Mike did as he was told, unzipping each glove opening. Steve showed him the buttons to press to release the helmet and allowed it to flop back. He then unzipped the inseam.

"Ok. Now comes the fun part. You basically need to dive into the suit from the bottom. Make sure you put your arms into the sleeves as you would with a sweater."

"Ok, I guess that doesn't seem too bad."

Steve held the suit as Mike entered it with his arms above his head. He found the sleeves and was fairly easily able to get his arms into the sleeves, and in the process, his head was out of the helmet opening.

"Great, now just be careful not to whack your head with the helmet. Have a seat here and put your feet into the suit's boots," instructed Steve.

Mike slipped his feet into the boots. They were comfortable and lightweight.

"Fantastic. Now you want to zip the inseam up. Make sure everything is tucked in as you go."

"Yep, I guess I don't want any nasty surprises," joked Mike.

"And you don't want any leaks!"

Mike was glad he had left the gloves off for this exercise. He could envision how a lack of sensation would make cleanly zipping up a suit an issue.

"Ok, then, let's zip up your gloves. Are you left or right-handed?"

"Right."

"Ok, then I suggest you zip up your right hand first as you'll find it easier to use your right hand in the glove to zip up the left."

Made sense to Mike, so he zipped up his right glove opening quite easily. It was a bit harder to zip up the left glove, but he did find that he could hold the zipper reasonably well with the right glove on.

"Fantastic, Mike. Let's just quickly close up the helmet, and you can have a go at releasing it with your gloves on. If anything goes wrong, I'm right here to let you out!"

Mike took a few deep breaths and then pulled the face shield down. It really cut down the external noise, which was part of its function during launch, and he could hear himself breathing. Using both hands, he felt around the chin area of the helmet for the buttons to release the face shield, which popped up.

"Well, that was easy, and it was very quiet inside," said Mike.

"Yep, that was well done. Have a few more goes to get used to it. You'll be wearing that for a few hours, and we want to make sure you can open it if it accidentally closes during the training."

After practising the helmet opening manoeuvre until he was comfortable, he was then prepared for a pressure test.

"So Mike, connect this umbilical above your right knee. You'll find a cover there that will open, and this can connect."

"Ok ... yep, I can open it, and let me just connect it."

"Turn it a quarter turn, and it will latch. To disconnect it, you need to push it in slightly."

"Ok. there, it is latched. Oh, a light came on in the helmet."

"Yep, that's so you know you have a good connection. Have a practice connecting and disconnecting."

After a few successful attempts, Steve instructed Mike to close his helmet. Mike could feel cool fresh air near his face. And he also noticed his body feeling a bit cooler.

Mike heard Steve's voice in his helmet, "Mike, can you hear me?"

"Yes, Steve, loud and clear." Obviously, there was a built-in microphone and speaker in the helmet.

"Fantastic. You don't need extra headsets with our suits. Less to fiddle with. I'll do a pressure test if that's ok with you."

"Sure, go ahead, Steve."

Mike felt the pressure increase in the suit, with the familiar pressure in his ears. But he didn't hear a lot of noise from the air movement, which was great. In fact, the suit was quite comfortable.

"Mike, could you please make some fists with your hands and tell me how they feel."

"Sure, Steve, they feel fine. Not that hard to do."

"Fantastic. Well, for the test, can you please stand up for a moment and take a brief walk for a few feet, don't forget the umbilical is attached. We just want to make sure that movement doesn't trigger a leak."

Mike stood up. Being a suit for flight, not space walking, it was light and comfortable, although it was a bit puffy under pressure. He took a few steps, not something he would be able to do in space!

"Thanks, Mike, that looks good. Please have a seat. You can recline if you want. We will run this test for 15 minutes to make sure everything checks out. I'll give you a pad that will Bluetooth connect to your suit so you can get used to the gloves, surf the web, and watch some video or play music. If you have any problems, ask for me or control, and we'll get you out."

"Ok, thanks, Steve. Any chance for a Mocha in here?"

"No, sorry, Mike, but there is a drinking straw on the left there."

Makes sense, thought Mike. If things went pear-shaped, he could be stuck in this suit for a few days, so he'd need to drink, which would mean, hmm, nappies, otherwise known as maximum absorbency garments (MAG). Ahh, the indignity of space flight. He'd missed that item in his dressing. The suit had enough room, but he'd have to wear them for future training.

"Steve, this is Mike."

"Yes, Steve, is there a problem?"

"No, just letting you know that I neglected to put on my MAG."

"Thanks for letting me know. There does appear to be enough room in the suit to accommodate it."

"Ahh, you newbies! MAGMAN you are, Mike," said John across the comms. Great, thought Mike, I don't want that as a call sign! He didn't know he was sharing communications with the others. He started looking for some music on the pad.

After passing the pressure test, he could open the helmet again.

"OK, gents, we are going back into the Dragon, this time in our suits," instructed John.

They walked over to the mock-up, entered and sat in their assigned seats—all a painless exercise.

"That was too easy," said Andy, "they'll let anyone do this soon."

"That they will," replied David.

Earl entered the Dragon after them. "You will find that you can cleat your heels into the chair by sliding them in from the outside while pressing your heals against the foot rest. Could you please all practice that action a few times."

Mike found that the action was easy to perform and required deliberate action to free his foot.

"And gentlemen, could you please attach your harnesses."

Mike found his four straps and harness lock and secured himself. He looked around and noticed that all had succeeded.

"A reminder, gents, that the evacuation order is Mission Specialist 2, Mission Specialist 1, Deputy Command and Commander. Evacuate, Evacuate, Evacuate. This is a drill."

Damn, thought Mike, a drill. First, undo the straps. He slammed his fist into the harness lock, releasing all straps, pushed and twisted his heels and headed for the hatch, as he was first to leave as Mission Specialist 2, glancing back to check on the others.

Then he realised his mistake.

All their helmets were closed.

They gathered outside for the debrief.

"Well, MAGMAN, what'd you do wrong?" asked the Commander.

"Left my helmet open," answered Mike.

"Correct, and why was that a problem?"

"There might have been noxious gas or a vacuum."

"Yep, although we'd all be dead if it was the later and we had to evacuate. Remember, we apply our basic procedures from our other craft, and the first thing in an emergency is close the helmet."

"Yes, sir."

"OK – thank you, Earl. Gents, back in we go."

They spent the next two hours practising various procedures, strapping in, evacuating, connecting up umbilicals, and assisting each other out of the Dragon as if unconscious. It was tiring.

11

—·—

Thursday, June 4 2020

Sue stood in front of the environmental control in Tranquility, Node 3 of the International Space Station (ISS) training mock-up at JSC. She was halfway through resetting the system as a part of her training for her flight to the ISS. Even though she would only be on the station for a month, she still needed to be familiar with system operations and able to perform necessary tasks in an emergency. Until now, most ISS crews had years in which to undertake training. She had less than one year and also three months of maternity leave for the birth of her son Jerome. And the COVID-19 pandemic definitely had not helped.

The birth had been smooth and uneventful. Jerome was healthy, and Ron had been fantastic looking after Jessica. There had been the late nights and lack of sleep, but NASA had been great and given Ron a lot of paternity leave. Within a week of getting home, she was at the gym every day to aid in the process of changing her body from that of a mother to that of an astronaut. There wasn't a lot of time to enjoy motherhood!

She looked around the mock-up. All the other team members from her mission were also here performing simulated tasks, wearing masks. Christina was in Columbus working on an experiment. Eric Hipps, the Commander and veteran of 2 space shuttle missions, was in the US Lab Destiny and also going through a procedure on its life support systems.

Flight Engineer Steve Davidson was in the Harmony Module checking electrical systems. He had spent 168 days on the ISS and would remain there and be replaced by a current ISS crew member on their mission in October.

Sue heard her name on the communications channel near her. "Tranquility, CAPCOM, Sue, can you please complete item 12 on your checklist."

"Copy that CAPCOM," she replied on the communicator.

Today they were simulating on-station operations, with communication procedures, moving around the station, and whatever else the trainers thought they would throw at the team.

Item 12 required Sue to toggle a switch and report a displayed value, so she toggled the switch and read the value.

"CAPCOM, Tranquillity. I have that figure for you."

"Sue, go ahead."

"132.7″

"Copy that 132.7."

Suddenly there was a high-pitched warble sound, the emergency alarm. Sue attached her checklist to the test unit, turned and walked into Node 1 and located the emergency checklist. Being first there, she made a call on the communications channel.

"Unity, CAPCOM, Emergency Alarm 1102."

"CAPCOM, copy."

Sue checked the fire panel and laptops to determine where the fire was detected. The alarm was in the Destiny Module

"Unity, CAPCOM, alarm in Destiny."

"CAPCOM copy."

Sue picked up a flashlight and breathing mask, walked to the Destiny Module, and saw the commander lying on the floor. She also smelt smoke and noticed some around a cabinet. Christina and Steve both appeared at the other end of the module.

"Christina, check Eric. Steve, assist me with this checklist. The alarm is in this module," instructed Sue. "Destiny, CAPCOM"

"CAPCOM, go ahead, Destiny."

"Commander incapacitated, MS rendering assistance, FE assisting me. Smoke in Destiny."

"CAPCOM copies."

"The panel shows an alarm in cabinet 41B. Ventilation isolated," reported Steve.

"DESTINY, CAPCOM, alarm 41B, ventilation isolated," reported Sue over communications. "Steve power isolate cabinet 41B."

"Isolating 41B, CONFIRMED." Reported Steve.

"Steve, check for smoke in 41B. Christina, how is Eric."

"Eric, for the drill, is unresponsive and not breathing," reported Christina.

Great, thought Sue, double emergency, and I'm now command. Keep cool.

"Steve, stand clear of everything. Which panel was Eric working on?" commanded Sue.

"41B," said Steve.

"Ok, isolate all cabinets in 41 before touching them; they might be live. Christina, get the medical kit from Node 3," instructed Sue. "DESTINY, CAPCOM medical emergency, command unresponsive and not breathing for drill. We are isolating all cabinets in 41."

Christina returned with medical equipment.

"Steve, are you ok checking the cabinets by yourself, and I'll assist Christina?" asked Sue.

"Yes, sure," replied Steve, opening cabinet 41B.

A trainer appeared with a mannequin, and Eric quickly left the module.

Christina started CPR on the mannequin. She would have to do this in space by 'standing' on the opposite wall.

"DESTINY, CAPCOM, initiating CPR."

"CAPCOM, COPY."

Sue located the defibrillator, opened the mannequin's shirt, and applied the pads as Christina continued to perform chest compressions. She heard a panel opening.

A trainer said, "On examining 41B, you find a smoking component but no active fire."

"There's a smoking component in 41B, but no fire," reported Steve to Sue.

"Thanks, Steve".

The defibrillator began giving instructions, "Do not touch the patient."

"Everyone clear of the patient, Christina. Stop CPR."

"DESTINY, CAPCOM, no active fire in 41B."

"CAPCOM COPY"

"Shocking patient in 3," reported the defibrillator

"Everyone clear", said Sue.

"2 ...1 Shocking, Monitor patient," announced the defibrillator.

"Patient is breathing and has good colour and is responding," stated a trainer.

"Great, Christina, can you please administer oxygen by mask."

"DESTINY, CAPCOM, patient is breathing and responsive after CPR and one shock. Administering oxygen."

"CAPCOM copies, PSYCHE would like to talk to you."

"COPY, DESTINY, PSYCHE, go ahead."

"PSYCHE, DESTINY, can you please move the commander to Node 3 and insert an Intraosseous device, give fluids and connect the BP, ECP and Blood oximeter, please."

"DESTINY copies, Christina and Steve will perform," said Sue via the communication system. "Christina and Steve, can you please take our patient to Node 3 and follow PSYCHE's instructions on GROUND to AIR 2. I'll sort out things here."

"PSYCHE Copies."

"Sure, let's go, Steve," replied Christina.

Christina took a deep breath.

"DESTINY CAPCOM"

"CAPCOM, go ahead, DESTINY."

"Can PSYCHE talk with Christina on GROUND to AIR 2 in NODE 3? And I need to work the fire issue with you."

"CAPCOM copies. Drill terminated."

"Well done, Sue," said Eric, returning to the module.

"Thanks, Eric, don't play with those electrics again!"

"Easy day for me!" he said, smiling.

"Ok, guys, let's gather out in the meeting room for a debrief in 5 minutes," said Robert, their lead trainer.

"Great, I need some water," said Sue. They left the module and headed to the training room to meet with the others.

That evening, Sue arrived home to her double-storey house in Seabrook, parked in the garage, and took a deep breath. After a busy day, she could think of better things than getting home, feeding and bathing children. Sometimes she missed coming home and just lounging with Ron, drinking wine and enjoying each other.

She tore herself away from her daydream, got out of the car, and entered the house through the internal door into the lounge room.

"We're in the kitchen," called Ron.

Sue dropped her bags and found her daughter Jessica helping set the table for dinner. When Jessica saw her, she ran to her, crying, "Mummy, you're home".

Sue caught her and gave her a kiss and hug, asking, "Hi, sweet pea. How was your day?"

"It was great. We read Cats and Hats."

"Ok, that's fun."

She kissed Ron and swept up Jerome from his bassinet. "And how's my little man?" she asked, blowing on his tummy.

"He's been great," answered Ron, "but he's probably ready for a feed. How was your training."

"Hectic," answered Sue, sitting down. "Hey, Jessica, why don't you finish setting the table while I feed Jerome." To Ron, she said, "We had a scenario in the ISS where Eric was incapacitated, so I had to command, deal with a fire and handle a medical emergency."

"Wow, how did that go."

"All went well. Everyone did their job well. But it would be different in space. Stuff will just be different. You can move someone more easily. Fire behaves differently. How was your day?"

"Same as usual. I managed to get some sleep with Jerome earlier, which was good since I didn't get much last night." Turning to Jessica, he said, "Hey Jessica, why don't you show mummy your drawing?"

"Ok. Here, mummy – this is for you!"

"Oh wow. Very pretty."

"It's a cat."

"Oh, of course it is. A very blue cat."

"With yellow eyes."

Sue nodded, wondering why the eyes were so close to the tail. "That's great. Why don't you give it to Daddy to put on the refrigerator."

"Ok."

Yep, handling a double emergency and communications with CAP-COM is a cinch.

12

— · —

Friday, November 20, 2020

They secured the hatch of the Boeing Starliner and floated down to their seats. Sue was sad to be leaving her new friends on the ISS after 25 days on board. Steve, from her team, was staying while Julie was returning with them. It was amazing how the isolation deepened the bonds of friendship while speeding around the planet in oversized cans.

They had all donned their flight suits prior to boarding, so apart from securing a few items, they only had to secure themselves and begin their checklists.

"CAPCOM, USCV-3″

Sue answered as Deputy Commander, "USCV3, go ahead, CAP-COM."

"Hatch locks all report secured."

Sue secured herself in her seat with the belts and connected her suit to the Starliner spacecraft. She and Eric began working through their checklists.

"Well, ladies, I'm pleased to be in command of the crew with the most women on it in NASA history," said Eric. "Welcome aboard, Julie, for our short flight back to Earth."

"Thank you, Commander. It's a pleasure to join Sue and Christina as well as yourself for this little trip home," replied Julie.

"Sue, can you please initiate a leak test in conjunction with the station."

"Yes, Sir," replied Sue and continued on the radio, "Station, this is USCV3."

"USCV3, this is Station; go ahead."

"We are ready to perform leak tests. Can you reduce pressure in the dock, please."

"Copy that, reducing dock pressure."

Sue changed her screen configuration to display environmental systems and monitored the cabin pressure to watch for changes that might indicate a faulty seal.

"What are you looking forward to when you get home, Julie?" asked Christina.

"A shower. Even better, a bath."

"I can agree with that. The pressure is holding. Good seal," replied Sue.

"Ok, let's go through the undocking checklist," replied Eric. He and Sue then proceeded through a number of system checks to ensure they had a working spacecraft before undocking from the ISS. "All looks green. Request clearance from Houston to undock, please."

"USCV3, CAPCOM," said Sue over the radio.

"CAPCOM, go ahead, USCV3."

"We have completed undocking checklists, all green. Requesting clearance for undocking."

"Standby USCV3."

"FLIGHT, Go, No Go for USCV3 undock. GUIDANCE"

"Go."

"OPS."

"Go."

"COMMS."

"Go."

"SURGEON."

"Go."

"ISO."

"Go."

"GROUND."

"Go."

"RECOVERY"

"Go".

"ISS."

"Go."

"FLIGHT, USCV3. Go for undocking."

"USCV3 FLIGHT Copy, go for undocking," replied Sue. She looked across at Eric, and he nodded and pressed the Undock button on the display. Sue then confirmed on her own screen, and the crew heard the latch motors as they disengaged the latches holding them to the ISS. The rest of the undocking procedure was automated, so the crew only needed to monitor the process in case they needed to take over.

Sue felt a slight movement as the spacecraft became free from the ISS. A display in front of her reported latches all open.

"USCV3, CAPCOM, latches open," reported Sue.

"Copy."

"Ladies, time to sit back and enjoy the ride," said Eric.

"USCV3 thrusters enabled," reported Sue on the communications channel.

Sue was not about to sit back and enjoy. This was one of the more dangerous parts of the trip. If something went wrong, it wouldn't just endanger them but also the crew on the ISS. She felt a slight push, and thrusters gently fired to move them away from the ISS.

"2 metres," Sue reported. "3 metres ... 4 metres ... 5 metres." She felt another push. "Burn 0," She reported on the Communications channel. To the crew, she said, "10 metres ... 15 metres ... 20 metres ... 30 metres."

"Burn 1," Sue reported on the radio. They could see out of their windows the earth rotating, and after a minute, they could see parts of the station out the windows.

"Wow, there goes my home for the last 6 months. Goodbye, ISS," said Julie.

It was a spectacular sight, thought Sue as she monitored the manoeuvre.

"USCV3 outside the Keep Out Sphere," reported CAPCOM on the communications channel. This meant that the Starliner was now outside a 200-metre safety zone around the station.

"Burn 2," reported Sue over the communications system. The crew felt another push, and they could see the station slowly move below them as they moved into a slightly higher orbit.

"Wow, that's amazing to see the station silhouetted by the Earth," said Christina. "Where are we?"

"Looks like we are over Brazil," replied Eric. "And we should have sunset in 5 minutes."

"I'd love to go to Brazil, especially to visit the Amazon," said Sue. "Not sure when I'll have time, maybe in a couple of years with my kids."

"I bet they'll be happy to see you," said Julie. "I know mine will be. I bet Bobby is refusing to go to bed."

"So, he's four, isn't he?" asked Sue.

"Yes, and 6 months is forever for him. He'll have changed so much," replied Julie.

"Oh wow, that must have been hard for you, being away from him at that age," said Christina.

"Yes, it's been tough at times. It's part of the price we pay, though," replied Julie.

"Just make sure you have lots of time with him over the next couple of months. Don't let NASA steal any more time. He'll need you," said Eric. "We are coming up on burn 3. Is everything secure?"

Everyone replied affirmative, and shortly later, a longer thruster burn occurred, and their separation rate from the ISS increased.

"Ok, ladies, you are free to leave your seats. We've got about an hour before we need to start fluid loading," said Eric. Fluid loading referred to the practice of drinking a substantial amount of fluids to ensure that the crew was able to maintain their blood pressure on landing.

Christina released her belts and floated to the hatch to look at the view. Sue joined her.

"Amazing to think that next time we are up here, we'll be on the way to the Moon, isn't it?" asked Christina.

"That will be something else," replied Sue. "In fact, there it is, beautiful!"

"Anyone for snacks?" asked Julie. "We have dried apple, macadamia nuts, some strawberries, and some cookies."

"I'll have the apple," replied Sue. She heard a metallic knock. "Did anyone hear that?"

"I heard something, don't know what," said Julie.

"Oh, look, I can see a meteor shower in the atmosphere."

There were a couple of more knocks.

"Everyone back in your seat, and connect life support," instructed Eric. "I think it's a meteoroid cloud."

Everyone swiftly flew back to their seats, connecting their life support hoses and buckling their straps. More knocks could be heard on the outside of the spacecraft.

"USCV3, for CAPCOM," said Eric over the communications."

"Go ahead, USCV3."

"We appear to be traversing a meteoroid cloud."

There was a particularly loud bang, followed by a whistling sound, an alarm, and Eric grunted.

"Close helmets," instructed Sue. She looked across at Eric, who was clutching his chest and saw red fluid floating from him. "Christina, Eric is injured; treat him. Get his helmet closed. I'm taking command." And then, on communications, she said, "USCV3, CAPCOM, Emergency, cabin depress, Eric's injured, I've assumed command." She acknowledged the depressurisation alarm.

"USCV3, copy, Emergency, depress and injury."

"Is everyone else ok?" asked Sue as she looked around the cabin for damage. She could just make out a hole on the opposite side of the cabin. The pings on the exterior had stopped as quickly as they had started.

"I'm ok," replied Julie.

"And me", Christina replied. "It's hard to stop the bleeding with his suit pressurized."

"Ok, Julie. I think we are through the cloud. Get a leak repair kit and try and seal that small hole over there," pointing across the spacecraft.

"I'm on it," Julie replied, releasing her belts but remaining connected to the ship's air supply.

"USCV3, CAPCOM, we think we are through the cloud, and we've identified what we think is the leak. We are working to seal it, and Christina is helping Eric, although the suit being pressurised is not helping stem blood loss."

"CAPCOM copies, note you still have 93 minutes until decel burn."

Sue took a deep breath, pulled out her pad and found the depressurisation checklist. She checked the rate of loss, and it wasn't too high; in fact, it appeared to be falling, so Julie's work must be having an effect. Other systems appeared to be operating normally, apart from a power system, which had failed over to a redundant system. They were travelling service module first, which gave them a lot of protection from such strikes ahead of them in their orbit, but somehow an object with enough energy had struck the top of the spacecraft.

"USCV3, CAPCOM, depress rate decreasing, systems nominal, other than PSM1, redundancy operating."

"CAPCOM copies."

"How's that fix going, Julie?" asked Sue.

"Almost done. Then we need to wait 3 minutes for it to set before pressurising."

"Great, I can see that it's already starting to help. Julie, how's Eric."

"He is breathing but not responding. At the moment, all I can do is apply pressure to the wounds," replied Christina.

"Ok, hang in there, we should be able to pressurise in a few minutes, and then we can take his suit off," said Sue, and then on communications, "USCV3, CAPCOM, we should be able to pressurise in 3 minutes. Eric is breathing but not responsive. We can only put pressure on wounds at the moment."

"CAPCOM copies. We are going to bring you in an orbit early, so the first alternate landing site is in Utah. The team there is prepping for you now, including an emergency medical trauma team. So decel burn in 32 minutes."

"USCV3 copies," said Sue, turning to Julie, "Julie, while you are waiting can you get the medical kit for Christina, please."

"Sure. 1 minute left," replied Julie, and she crossed the cabin to retrieve the medical equipment. She opened it out and strapped it to a grab handle. She went back to the repair site. "You should be able to re-pressurise now."

"OK, thanks. USCV3 CAPCOM, attempting pressurisation."

"CAPCOM Copies."

Sue elected the environmental screen and enabled the pressurisation. She watched as the pressure slowly returned to normal. "How is the seal holding, Julie?"

"It looks good. I've got another layer to glue on once pressure has stabilised to help protect it."

"Ok, Christina, how's Eric doing."

"The same, but I need someone to replace me. Holding this pressure is hard work."

"OK, I'll be with you shortly." Sue checked the system status, and the pressure was stable and normal. "Ok, Julie, pressure is stable; apply the patch." On the communications channel, "USCV3, CAPCOM, pressure stable, patch holding, we are working on Eric's wounds." To the team, she said, "Ok, we all leave our suits on and closed. We will need to open up Eric's to expose his wounds. Christina, we'll have to work quickly. You grab some combine dressings to put on them. Then I'll keep pressure on the wounds while you unstrap him."

They would have to get Eric out of his seat to unzip the suit from the back. It appeared that the entry wound was on his upper back right shoulder, and exited around his lower ribs on the left.

"This doesn't look good. He probably has bleeding in one or both lungs," said Sue. She opened his helmet and noticed blood around his lips. "Julie, can you get the oxygen resus kit. We need to give Eric oxygen and support his breathing. Eric, can you hear me? No response to voice. Eric, can you feel me?" said Sue, squeezing his trapezius muscles. "No response to pain."

Sue doubted they could get Eric back into his suit if they needed to. They'd have to try. She discovered what Christina had meant about applying pressure. They either had to push against Eric while bracing against the spacecraft or hold pressure with their arm muscles. Not something easily done for long.

Christina and Sue bent Eric over and unzipped his suit, pulling his head and upper body out of the suit. For the moment, they left his arms in the sleeves, and they could now reach the wounds and apply the combines and pressure.

"Ok, Christina, you wrap the bandages around these wounds while I hold them. Actually, that chest wound is sucking. Put a non-adherent dressing on it and tape it."

Julie now joined them with the oxygen resuscitation bag valve mask. And supported Eric's breathing.

"CAPCOM, USCV3."

"Go ahead, CAPCOM," replied Sue.

"Sue, just letting you know you now have 28 minutes till decal burn. How's Eric."

"Eric is unresponsive, breathing. The entry wound right scapula, exit wound left lower ribs, sucking. We are bandaging and supporting breathing."

"CAPCOM Copies. Do you want to continue with early re-entry?"

Sue thought about it. They would be pushed to get Eric bandaged, stabilised and back in his suit for the burn, but she doubted he would survive an additional 90 minutes during another orbit. "Eric needs to get on the ground ASAP. We will continue for the early descent."

"His colour looks a bit better," said Julie.

"Good. We need to try and get some observations done once we finish bandaging him. Damn, this is hard in zero-G!"

"I've got the sucker taped. I'll bandage around that shoulder wound now," said Christina.

"We need to get some fluids into him," said Sue.

"And us," said Julie, reminding them of the need to fluid load.

"Ok, once Christina finishes bandaging, she will grab our drink bags, and I'll set up intraosseous access for fluids. That means we will need to expose his legs, so we will have to take his suit mostly off. Shit, let me talk to the ground."

"USCV3, CAPCOM, I need to talk to SURGEON."

"SURGEON, go ahead."

"Thanks. I want to give Eric fluids which would require taking him out of his suit. We haven't done any Obs yet, but he has aspirated blood and lost at least 500 ml. Given time constraints, he would likely not be in his suit for decel and probably landing."

"SURGEON, I concur. Life support exceeds the benefit of the suit."

"USCV3 copies."

"Here's your water, Sue," said Christina. Sue took a long drink. She didn't remember this scenario in training!

"OK, Christina, help me get the rest of his suit off, then you put the oximeter on one of his hands and try a get his blood pressure. I'll run a line. We all need to be back in our chairs in a bit over 20 minutes."

Sue and Christina worked to get Eric's suit off while Julie kept supporting his breathing with the bag valve mask. Sue then inserted a line directly into his tibia while Christina got some observations.

"I've got some Obs," reported Christina while Sue gently squeezed the saline bag.

"Call the Obs down to Ground," instructed Sue.

"USCV3 for SURGEON," said Christine over the radio.

"Go for SURGEON."

"Obs for Eric, SPO2 92 Pulse 115. BP 90/60. We now have a line and providing saline."

"SURGEON Copies."

"CAPCOM 22 minutes to decel."

"USCV3 Copies."

"Drink up, ladies. I don't think we can do much more for Eric right now. How are those wounds?" asked Sue, drinking again from her water bag.

Julie had a closer look at the wounds and reported, "No significant bleeding."

"Good. Christina, why don't you take over bagging, and Julie, get some fluids into you."

Christina took over the bag valve mask helping Eric breathe.

"Right, so next, we need to get Eric back into my chair," said Sue. "Christina, let's float him down into it. Put his suit down at his feet. Julie, if you can strap him in for us, Thanks."

They sat Eric back in Sue's seat and strapped him in.

"Julie, why don't you get into your chair and then take over the saline. I'll take another set of observations."

After a few minutes, Sue reported on the communications, " USCV3, CAPCOM for SURGEON."

"SURGEON, go ahead."

"We've got about 400ml Saline into Eric. SPO2 93, Pulse 108, BP 95/70."

"SURGEON copies, go ahead with another pint of Saline. Make sure you all are doing your fluid load."

"USCV3 copies, we are attempting fluid load."

Christina located more drink bags and distributed them to Christina and Julie, giving Julie another saline bag. "Keep drinking," she reminded them.

"CAPCOM, USCV3 5 minutes to burn."

"USCV3 copies," said Sue. 'Christina, you'll have to get into your seat in a minute. I'll get an oxygen mask set up for you, then get strapped in myself."

Sue hooked up a therapy mask and handed it to Christina, then sank into the commander's chair and strapped in. She needed to adjust the straps a bit. She then brought up the navigational display; all systems still showed green.

"USCV3, CAPCOM, all systems green. 3 minutes to burn. We are putting Eric on a therapy mask."

"CAPCOM copies."

"Christina, get in your chair," Sue ordered.

Christina disconnected the resus mask from the oxygen supply, connected the therapy mask, put it on Eric and quickly slid into her chair on Sue's right and strapped in.

"All set?" Asked Sue. She could hear Eric's rasping breaths.

"USCV3, CAPCOM, ready for the burn."

"CAPCOM Copies, execute."

"Hold on, ladies," said Sue and counted down to the burn.

Suddenly they all felt weight for the first time in weeks, even months. The 15 minutes seemed to last forever.

"How is everyone going?" Sue asked after a couple of minutes.

"I'm fine," reported Christina.

"I'm ok. It's getting better," said Julie.

"Are you able to keep squeezing the fluids for Eric?" asked Sue.

"Yep, the acceleration helps."

Sue was surprised by how smooth the acceleration was. They weren't moving around too much, and she found it easier to move her arms around after a few minutes. She looked across at Eric, and could still see his chest rising and falling, which was good. They'd left the oximeter on, so she could see that his pulse rate had fallen a bit, and his oxygenation was still not too bad.

"USCV3, CAPCOM", said Sue on the radio.

"CAPCOM, go ahead, USCV3."

"The burn seems to be going well. All systems are nominal. Eric is still breathing, and we are continuing with fluids. His SPO2 is 92 and Pulse 100."

"CAPCOM copies. Telemetry looks good."

Eventually, the burn finished.

"CAPCOM, USCV3, 5 minutes until service module separation."

"USCV3 copies," said Sue. "Christina, can you please check Eric. He seems to be breathing ok, so I don't think we'll bother with the bag/valve mask."

"Sue," said Christina, unbuckling herself. She floated around behind Eric's chair, felt his pulse, took observations and checked his wounds.

"USCV3, CAPCOM for SURGEON", said Christina over the communications.

"SURGEON, go ahead."

"Eric is breathing with rasping, gurgling sounds, short, 15 per min. Pulse 102, BP 100/70. SPOs 93. No sign of additional bleeding. He's looking a bit pale and clammy."

"SURGEON copies. You can't do much more for him now. Keep him on O2. Finish that second bag of saline. And make sure the rest of you have consumed all your fluids, please."

"USCV3 copies," replied Christina.

"CAPCOM, USCV3, 1 minute to service module separation."

"Get back in your chair, Christina," instructed Sue.

"I'm on my way," replied Christina.

"Ahh, so much to drink," said Julie.

"Yes, I know," replied Sue, "we didn't quite get the timing right, so expect problems on the ground." They should have finished drinking their allocated fluids 1 hour before landing. They'd be on the ground in about another twenty.

"Separation in 3, 2, 1," reported Sue. "Now we are on the home run."

They kept monitoring Eric for the next 15 minutes.

"Ok, everyone, please tighten your belts. Things are going to get rocky," warned Sue.

"CAPCOM, USCV3, you should be about to start re-entry. See you on the ground. Medical team standing by in Utah."

"USCV3 copies. Thank you, guys, for your help," replied Sue. Damn, she thought, her family would be at the wrong site. Everyone's family would be at the wrong site! She hoped they knew what was going on. But what about Eric's family!

The spacecraft began to be buffeted as they started encountering the atmosphere at an incredible speed. This was only the fourth Starliner vehicle to visit the ISS. Sue hoped that everything worked as expected. It was still early days for the Starliner.

A glow slowly surrounded the vehicle as they got deeper into the atmosphere, and the shielding which protected them heated up. No longer was it black outside but a strange hue of yellow and white. Sue monitored the spacecraft systems. All normal. She didn't want to have to deal with another emergency. She checked the environmental systems. The temperature was ok, and the pressure was ok. The last thing they needed was for plasma to leak into the craft.

The intensity of the glow increased, and the buffeting became greater. Sue felt the movement as the craft banked to slow down further. Suddenly there was a small pop as the parachutes deployed, and Sue felt herself pushed deeper into her seat. There was another jerk as the main chutes deployed. The panel said all had deployed correctly, and she could see out of her window one of them against the blue sky. Blue sky, she hadn't seen that for a month.

"USCV3, CAPCOM. Chutes deployed," she reported over the communications.

"CAPCOM copies, looking good, Sue. Ground has you in sight."

Sue felt the movement of the spacecraft as they swung under the chutes. Nothing they could do now but wait. She looked across at Eric again. She could hear his rasping breath again now that it was quieter.

"Wow, how was that!" exclaimed Christina.

"Firey," said Julie.

"Yeah, all I saw was that strange glow out the window," said Sue. "About 30 seconds to cushion deployment."

They heard the pyrotechnics that filled the landing cushions with gas, and about 10 seconds later, they felt the jolt as they landed back in the USA.

"CAPCOM, USCV3, making safe systems."

"CAPCOM copies. Welcome home. The extraction team are about 5 minutes away."

"USCV3 copies."

Sue looked across at Eric. He wasn't breathing! She took a deep breath, unfastened her belts and tried to sit up slowly.

"Christina, are you able to get up and help me with Eric? He has stopped breathing. Remember to sit up slowly," said Sue.

"Sure," replied Christina.

"Can I help?" asked Julie.

"I doubt you will be able to," replied Sue, "I'm about to throw up as it is. Can someone stop the world from spinning?"

This was not going to be easy.

"USCV3, CAPCOM, URGENT," said Sue on the communications channel.

"Go ahead, USCV3."

"Eric has stopped breathing, and his pulse rate is dropping. We are trying to treat but finding it difficult to move."

"CAPCOM copies, we'll alert the ground crew. They are almost there."

Sue managed to turn over in her chair and saw that, thankfully, Christina had strapped the bag/valve mask to Eric's chair where she could reach it. If only the room would stop swimming, she thought, and she tried to focus on unstrapping the mask and putting it over Eric's face. She managed to get it roughly in place and tried a squeeze on the bag, but it wasn't effective. She couldn't easily get a good seal. She tried again, but her position wasn't optimal. Finally, on the third attempt, she managed to get a breath into him.

"Ok, it's working, just. How are you going, Christina?"

"Uuuh," was the reply. She heard the unzipping of a helmet and Christina retching behind her.

"Uhh, cleanup crew needed ... sorry," said Christina. She managed to swing her legs around and off her chair and stand beside it. "I need a minute for the world to stop spinning."

Suddenly there was a knock on the crew hatch, and the locks started to turn. Thirty seconds later, one of the rescue personnel entered.

"Ladies, you can relax now. We'll take over," said the responder.

"Great, he's not breathing, not sure for how long. I've given him a few breaths, SPO2 80, pulse 40," said Sue and collapsed back into her chair.

Suddenly the craft was full of people as they worked on Eric and extracted him.

13

Eric's death sent shock waves throughout the Astronaut Corp. His was the first death of a NASA Astronaut in service since the Columbia disaster in 2003. For such a risky venture, there have been surprisingly few deaths during missions. The event triggered an immediate review of the Boeing Starliner and the NASA Commercial Crew program. Fortunately, the SpaceX Dragon flights weren't put on hold, but the Starliner flights were held for 6 months.

Sue was devastated. After all, they had done to try and save Eric, he'd died during the descent. They'd debriefed the mission as a team, including Steve on the ISS, which she had led as deputy commander. NASA had provided counselling, which continued. Eric's wife, Marion, had thanked her for all she had done many times, but she still felt responsible.

When she'd arrived home, she had run to Jessica and Jerome and hugged them, kissed them and cried until Ron had finally peeled them away from her. They didn't know why she was so upset, which in turn, upset them. Ron had tried to help and understand, but he never really succeeded. Rather than the expected night of passion on her return, it was a night of sobbing.

Mike had been practising in the Dragon simulator when the news of the emergency came through. He and David immediately cancelled their practice and drove to the Astronaut Corps' offices, where other astronauts were gathering. They celebrated when the call came through that they had landed successfully. His classmates, Sue and Christina, were safe. Then came the urgent call from Sue about Eric, and about an hour later, they were called to a briefing where Alan Pointer had informed them that Eric had not survived. They'd been instructed as a group not to make comments to the press or on social media other than expressing condolences. A few experienced astronauts were selected to talk to the media. Others not assigned to missions or with relationships with the mission members were assigned to the families of Eric's mission team and the current members on the ISS to support the existing astronauts already supporting those families.

Mike had finally driven home, where Lisa was waiting for him.

"Are you ok?" Lisa asked after hugging him at the door.

"Yeah. It's a pretty random thing, getting hit by a meteoroid, and the shielding should protect us from most of those."

"Did you know the guy who died?"

"Not really. We hadn't been on any teams together. We've been training so hard that we don't see that many of the rest of the Corps."

"What about the others? Two of them were in your class, right?"

"Yep, I know Sue and Christina pretty well."

"Have you called them?"

"We've been asked not to for a day or so. They're still recovering from their mission too, and I suspect there's a few debriefs going on."

"Your mum called."

"I guess I'd better give her a call."

"Do you want a beer?"

"Thanks. How's your day been?" asked Mike.

"A bit crazy. We had a feed playing in the centre when the meteoroid hit. Kids were a bit upset, so we spent a lot of the day helping their teacher counsel them."

"That must have been hard."

"Yeah, not what I expected to be doing. It's so unlikely for that to happen."

"I know. We protect the capsule by flying the service module first so we don't have high-energy particles striking the capsule. But obviously, these came from an unusual angle."

"Are you worried about your flight?"

"I don't think it will be affected, they might postpone Starliner flights for a review, but that shouldn't affect the Dragon flights too much."

"But what about your flight being hit."

"No, I'm not worried. That has never happened before. We've had some minor showers on the ISS, but it's up there all the time. The chance of a capsule being hit has to be minuscule."

"Ok. It would be ok if you were worried."

"No, it's fine. I better ring my mum. She will be worried."

14

Monday, April 12, 2021

Mike's mum had been worried, and he knew she was still concerned as Mike sat inside the Crew Dragon vehicle on top of a Falcon 9 while it was fuelled with liquid oxygen and chilled kerosene. He had explained everything to her and that if anything went wrong, the capsule would be thrust away from the launch site before anyone even knew there was a problem. Yet he knew she would worry. Only natural, he thought. He was sitting on a bomb!

There wasn't much to do while they waited except to think, look out the windows, or to read or watch videos on his tablet. The windows mainly showed the blue sky of Florida, with vapour wafting by as the kerosene and oxygen were loaded, and the occasional passing cloud. The commander and pilot didn't have much to do either. They had some checklists to complete, but the entire flight was automated, and they would only need to intervene in extreme circumstances.

As Commander and Pilot, John and Andrew were seated in the two centre seats, with Mike and David in the outer seats. Their suits were connected to the spacecraft, and Mike felt very comfortable. There was about 100 kilograms of cargo on pallets under their chairs.

"CAPCOM, USCV7," was broadcast on the communications.

"USCV7, go ahead, CAPCOM," replied Andrew.

"We have about 10 minutes left in the fuelling cycle, then we'll have you guys on the way. All looks good from here."

"USCV7 Copies, 10 minutes. All green here too," replied Andrew.

"Ok, men, this is what we've trained for," said John. "You know your jobs. You know the systems. Now we put it into practice. Take some deep breaths, pray, meditate or do whatever you do."

Mike didn't pray, nor did he meditate. He played Coldplay. Bluetooth connected spacesuits. Cool!

"Go for launch."

Mike took some deep breaths. That call was at T-0:45. There would be some G forces coming. Nothing too bad. He could feel his pulse rate climbing.

"All tanks pressing."

The countdown was broadcast through their suit communications.

He felt the Falcon 9 engines ignite, the vehicle shake, and then a lurch as it was released. They were heading to space!

"Vehicle pitching down range."

Mike noticed some vibration, but not much. He could see some clouds passing and the sky darkening as they continued to climb into orbit.

"Stage 1 throttle back."

"Max Q," was the call on the communications marking the point of Maximum dynamic pressure on the vehicle, so the Falcon 9 throttles down briefly. They were around 14 km up in the atmosphere.

"Stage 1 throttle up."

Mike was going the fastest he ever had, and his velocity just kept increasing. The g-force he felt gradually increased as the fuel load burnt off.

At about two and a half minutes into the flight, "MECO" was heard on the communications channel as the main stage one engines were cut-off. Mike briefly felt the first effects of zero-G, but not for long, and the first stage separated. The engine on the second stage ignited about 90 kilometres above the earth. The first stage then returned to earth to land on a drone ship.

The second stage burn was gentler and lasted about 6 minutes until it too completed and separated, leaving the Crew Dragon and its trunk (the service module) to complete their journey to the International Space Station.

During the second stage burn, John asked, "How is everyone?"

"Great, no problems, great view," answered Mike. The others were similarly ok.

"Good. Everything looks ok with the Dragon. Once this burn is over, you are going to be in zero-G for a month, so enjoy. Make sure you've got your sick bags handy."

Great, thought Mike. This bit was not going to be so fun. He looked out the window. Currently, he could see the earth, but the details kept slowly shrinking. They were now passing over the Atlantic on their way to Europe. He could make out numerous ships below and complete weather systems. The colours were amazing, the blue of the ocean, the brilliant whites of the clouds, and he was starting to be able to see the green/brown of Western Africa and Europe in the distance. He also noticed that it seemed to be getting darker ahead.

"Looks like we are heading for a sunset soon," said Mike.

"Yeah, about 5 minutes," replied John. "You'll get used to them soon, with 18 a day. Still, take the opportunity to watch when you get the chance. Sunset and sunrise are spectacular."

Mike continued to study the earth as they continued to gain velocity and altitude as they chased down the International Space Stations (ISS). He could now see details of the coast, including Gibraltar. There was a lot of cloud over it, but as it got darker, the cities became clearer as lights came on. They crossed the terminator around the western Mediterranean. They continued in the sunlight for a few more minutes before plunging into the dark. Now it was the lights of the cities that stood out.

"Wait till we get to Asia. There will be so many lights then," remarked David on his second mission.

"I'm just thinking, all those people down there, going about their business, and most don't have a clue we are flying above them. ... Oh wow! Lightening!" exclaimed Mike.

"Yep, it puts things in perspective being up here. And wait till you see a big storm. That one is a baby!" replied John. "Standby for engine cut-off."

Mike continued to watch the lightning below. The g-force steadily reduced until it ceased with stage 2 cut-off. They then separated from Stage 2 and the trunk, and the Dragon continued to chase down the ISS. Now he was in near zero-G.

Mike turned his head to look at the commander and felt the cabin spin. They'd trained for this in the 'vomit comet', so he had a bit of an idea of what was coming. What he didn't know was how he would cope with the more prolonged exposure. However, they were all medicated for space adaption syndrome (aka motion sickness), so they didn't have any issues while in their spacesuits.

"Ok, everyone, remember your training, make slow movements, and keep your barf bags handy. Take the time to get used to this," instructed John. "You can leave your seats now if you wish. Just take it easy on the gymnastics."

Mike was happy to release his restraint belts and enjoyed the feeling of floating up out of his seat. He tucked a sick bag into his suit leg pocket. They were specially designed to hold the fluids and assist in clean-up with a built-in face cloth.

He floated up from his seat across the cabin to see the view out the opposite window. This time he was able to view space and the starfield. As he got closer to the window, he was able to see a quarter moon. It was beautiful and so clear. He could clearly see the craters and mountains. It was so different from what could be seen from the ground.

And so was the way he felt. All the fluids in his body were now floating in places they normally wouldn't. His stomach was slopping all over the place. He took some deep breaths to calm down and focussed on his pad, checking the mission timelines. Better to get a handle on managing the effects while medicated! For normal motion sickness, you try and focus on distant objects to help your brain understand the motion. In space, there were no physical cues, so it was actually best to focus on something close and remove any extraneous visual cues.

The crew didn't have a lot to do during their journey. The spacecraft was automated, so Mike continued to study the night sky, and he moved to the other side of the Dragon and joined Andrew, who was taking some photos of the dark side of Earth.

"How are you feeling?" Andrew asked him.

"Pretty good. I felt a bit queasy at the start, but I'm ok now."

"Yeah, you won't really feel it until we are off the meds."

"Wow, that is beautiful, that blue line."

"We are coming up on sunrise."

Mike could see a brighter red point in the line. It quickly grew in intensity.

Then it happened. One minute they were flying along in dark space. Then a shaft of light slammed into their window.

"Wow, that's bright," said Mike, closing his eyes.

"Yep, and it happens very suddenly," replied Andrew. "You shouldn't look at the sun directly, but the window coatings protect us from most of the energy."

Gradually the intensity of the sun increased, and the blue line of the atmosphere became brighter around the dark earth. At the same time, the brilliant sun began to dominate.

Mike enjoyed the sunrise while Andrew photographed it. He wasn't a big one for watching sunrises on earth, but this was something different. He and the earth were now separate. He was effectively watching an eclipse. He was no longer earth-bound.

"Ok, guys, we are coming up on our rest period soon. I suggest we have some chow, then try to get some sleep," John instructed.

Finally, after about a day, the spacecraft approached the ISS. While both spacecraft were travelling very quickly, their relative speed was quite low. The Dragon approached from below, went in front of the ISS, above it and then approached from behind. All complicated orbital dynamics and approach rules in order to limit accidents. Very, very slowly, the Dragon glided to the docking port. The final stage taking over an hour.

Mike hadn't really thought of space travel as boring, but during this trip, there hadn't been much to do except relax and enjoy. After a while, the novelty of watching the earth and the stars from orbit wore off. There was the new experience of eating in zero-G and using the small onboard bathroom. He was glad they actually had a toilet, and did not need to rely on adult diapers. Yet the process did require some practice.

And then, once they docked, there was yet more waiting while leak checks were performed and tests were undertaken to ensure there were no nasty contaminants around. It all made for a lot of reading and viewing time. There is only so much banter that the team can keep up. After all, they had been training together for 18 months.

Once they had docked, they did have the adventure of changing out of their flight suits into their mission apparel. It did make for some funny and awkward acrobatic performances as they all attempted to disrobe and then don their new day wear without the assistance of gravity. Andrew and Mike, as first-time astronauts, had the most fun, while John and David seemed to have effortlessly mastered using foot restraints. Clearly, this was a skill best learnt in space.

Eventually, John could report to the team that the hatch was opening. "Remember to smile, lots of cameras on us."

They all moved away from the hatch as it descended into the cabin space, which Oleg, a Russian crew member of the ISS, opened.

"Dobroye utro! My friends, welcome to the ISS," welcomed Oleg.

John, Andrew, Mike and David followed him through the International Docking Adapter into Node 2, also known as Harmony.

John entered, first greeting Robert Love, the current expedition commander from NASA, then Jeanette from ESA, and finally, Oleg and Anton from Russia. Each of them followed, welcoming each member in turn.

A few minutes later, the entire crew gathered in Node 2 for a video hook-up with the ground space officials and family members broadcast on NASA TV. It was a bit of a weird event, with each of the new members having brief conversations with friends, colleagues and family while the whole team was floating there, smiling for the camera.

When Mike's turn came, Lisa was the first person to call him.

"Hi Mike, it's Lisa. How are you liking zero-G?"

"Lisa, great to hear you. I'm still getting used to it. Just had a chance to float the longest distance yet. Awesome and weird at the same time."

"Mike, it's Clare, your mother. What was the launch like?"

"Hi, Mum. It was amazing. We get great views out of the capsule. The ride was smooth and great fun."

"Mike, it's your father. We are so proud of you for doing what you wanted to do, getting into space. Is it what you expected?"

"Hi, Dad. It is like nothing I've ever experienced. The view of the Earth is just something else, a totally different perspective. I don't think I expected that feeling."

"Mike, it's Lisa. How have you found eating?"

"Lisa, it has been interesting. The food for the flight was good. You have to watch what you do with fluids. I managed to cover my face in water the first time, which is a bit tricky because it just sticks in a blob to you."

"Mike, it's your mother again. Have you been able to wash?"

"Yes, Mum. It's basically a wipe-down process, and there's not a huge amount of privacy in the capsule, although there is a toilet. But I'm clean, Mum. Love you."

"Love you too, Michael."

"Mike, your father here. What did you do on the flight up?"

"Dad, I spent a lot of time watching out the window and saw my first sunrise from space. I spent a bit of time reading and watching movies. There's not much for us to do on the trip other than get used to zero-G. I'll see you later, Dad."

"Ok, son. Stay well."

"Mike, it's Lisa, Have a great time. I miss you. I love you. Have fun."

"Thanks, Lisa, I love you too, and I'll talk to you soon."

Mike sighed. He'd survived that bit of publicity. But it was also important for friends and family; fortunately, his chat wasn't too torturous.

After about half an hour, the event concluded with everyone having public chats with their family, friends, and some NASA officials. Then Robert, the ISS expedition commander, took them on a briefing tour so they could familiarise themselves with the actual layout and see the various experiments compared to the mock-ups in JSC.

One of the things that Mike noticed was the noise. Fans were running everywhere, cooling equipment and moving air around. And the smell took some getting used to, although now he'd been on the station for an hour, he wasn't noticing it so much. It wasn't bad, just different.

The view out of the cupola was jaw-dropping, with such a broad view, but they didn't have time to dwell there. He especially took note of the nodes with science experiments since that was his primary role, so he paid extra attention when touring Columbus, Destiny, and Kibo. One of the projects he would be working on was the Window Observational Research Facility (WORF) in the Destiny Module. He would also work on the Orbiting Carbon Observatory-3 (OCO-3). It was great to actually see those systems in place.

Mike wasn't quite so familiar with the Russian segment. The mock-up at JSC wasn't that detailed. He had once visited Star City near Moscow and received some basic training on systems there. He did notice it was more cramped and somewhat noisier. It got a bit crowded as they did the tour through that section, stopping at various consoles to orient themselves to the systems.

After their brief tour, the Dragon crew located their sleeping quarters to stow their gear. John as commander, and David, as replacement crew, were allocated ISS crew sleeping quarters. Mike and Andrew would sleep tethered in other nodes. Mike in Kibo and Andrew in Columbus. It meant a bit less privacy, but they did gain some space.

15

TUESDAY, APRIL 20, 2021

Mike had been on the ISS for a week, and things were becoming routine. He had got used to zero-G. Yes, he'd been sick, but it wasn't too bad. He was getting used to floating around and was now getting decent sleep.

The day started with breakfast as a crew in Node 1. Mike was getting used to the process of hydrating his meal. Today he decided to try scrambled eggs, which came in a packet, so he just needed to heat them. He also got pears and coffee, which he would drink through a straw!

"So, what are you up to today, Mike?" asked Robert.

"I think I'm stowing some of that cargo we brought up with us and then running an experiment in the WORF. But first, I've got a workout scheduled," replied Mike.

"How did you sleep, Mike?" asked Andrew.

"Pretty good. The earplugs help, and I didn't float off this time," replied Mike. The previous night he hadn't secured his sleeping bag properly and woke as he bumped into Andrew, 2 modules away in Columbus!

"Yeah, you're a nice guy and all, but let's not make a habit of sleeping together!"

Jeannette, a Scottish redhead with the European Space Agency, floated into the module and started finding some breakfast. "Morning," she said, "oh – Mike, we are working together on that cargo this morning, I believe."

"Hi Jeannette, yes we are. I'm glad you'll be with me. I think it will take me a while to locate all the lockers," replied Mike.

"Yes, we can be posties together," replied Jeannette.

"Posties?" asked Mike.

"Mailmen, people who deliver the post," replied Jeannette.

"Ok, sure, just hope they are addressed correctly!"

The others discussed their planned days running experiments and preparing for an upcoming spacewalk.

Mike floated from Node 1, known as Unity, through the port side hatch and into Node 3, or Tranquillity, module. He was scheduled for an hour's exercise and would start on the treadmill. He was required to take some medical measurements before starting, then he found his runners, and put them on, always fun in zero-G. Exercising on the ISS was the only activity that required shoes! Then he put on his treadmill harness, connected the tension straps, set up a video to watch, and started his run.

After his run, he continued his workout on the Advanced Resistive Exercise Device (ARED). This provided resistance, similar to lifting weights, but since they were weightless, NASA had developed this machine to help astronauts maintain muscle mass. Mike wondered what the plan was for the Artemis missions. They were planning to be away from earth for a month, so they would need some exercise equipment of some sort. He'd probably learn more as he started the training for that mission once he returned to earth.

After finishing his exercise, Mike moved to the nearby cupola and gazed at the Earth. Above the horizon, he could see the moon. From here, it looked small, quite different from viewing it from the Earth. Here, the Earth dominated the view. The moon was just a sideshow, a companion standing offstage. Mike grabbed a camera and took some photos of the moon to remember this moment.

He didn't have a lot of time. He needed to change, and then Jeanette would join him in the BEAM Module, which was attached to Node 3. There wasn't a lot of privacy on the ISS. This node contained the exercise equipment, the cupola and the toilet. So, it effectively operated as his change room since he didn't have allocated sleeping quarters. He quickly changed, wiping himself with the cleaning cloths, and hung his exercise clothes to dry. No wonder the place smelt like a locker room!

"Hi, Mike, you decent?" asked Jeanette as she entered Node 3.

"Yep, all done," replied Mike. "I probably need to grab a drink before we start."

"Ok, I'll join you, and we can look over these procedures."

"Cool."

They floated back into Node 1, and Mike started fossicking among the drink bags. "I'm just having a juice. What can I get you?" he asked.

"Apple juice will be fine, thanks."

"So, what is the plan?" asked Mike as he hydrated their drinks.

"Basically, we open up the freight bags that came up with you guys and put them into their long-term storage locations, mostly in the PMM, but a few things go to JEM and Zarya."

"Ok. I guess you get to be a postie often?"

"Yeah, each time a cargo or crew vessel arrives, we have to unpack the vehicle, then unpack each package. Everything is documented, so it's not hard. Just a bit tedious identifying everything and putting it in the right place. It's easy to store something in the wrong place, and then it's a bitch finding it again when we need it. How are you finding things after 2 weeks?" asked Jeanette as she sucked on her drink.

"Good. I'm starting to get into a rhythm, and my body has got used to this place. Well, mostly."

"And how's your girlfriend coping?"

"Lisa is doing well. I'm only away for a month, and we had longer separations during training. She works at JSC, so she understands what is going on. We had a good chat last night. In fact, she's got a call lined up for a STEM session with kids there tomorrow with me."

"That's sneaky – extra video time!"

"For her, maybe. I have to be the performing seal!"

Jeanette laughed, her long red hair falling back over her face. "Arggh, one thing I won't miss on earth is being able to control my hair!"

"That seems to be mainly a woman's issue here. All the guys are bald or almost."

"Yeah, we need some bloke to be a rebel and grow long hair."

"That's not the NASA way!"

"You guys need to relax a bit, and so do the Russians. I'm finished. Let's go deliver mail."

They placed their drinks in the trash bag, and Jeanette led the way back into Node 3. Mike followed, admiring the cute rear of his fellow astronaut as she floated ahead of him. Distracted, he forgot to slow his progress and ran into her as they got to the BEAM dock.

"Oops, sorry," he said as he head-butted her, and they sprawled against a wall at awkward angles.

"Hey, that's ok. If you want to get close, you only have to ask," she replied, her hand sliding down his back as she helped him find a foothold.

Mike smiled. "Do you have the checklist?" he asked. Relationships amongst crew were frowned upon, but he knew they had happened. He'd have to be careful.

"Sure, we can access it on this laptop. Do you want to call ground and let them know we are starting checklist 3 for the day."

"Ok, Jeanette."

"Just call me Jean."

"Ok, Jean." Mike moved over to the communications panel and keyed the mike. "ISS to CAPCOM on 2."

"Go ahead, ISS."

"Good morning, this is Mike with Jeanette. We are starting checklist 3 now."

"OK, Mike. Let us know if you have any issues," came the reply from the ground

"Sure will. ISS clear," replied Mike over the radio.

"Bring that down here, will you," requested Jeanette, "then it will be handy to get to. Just stick it to the wall here." She was referring to the communications device, which was on a roll of cable.

Mike moved down to the location of the BEAM, unfurling the communications cable and attaching the device near where they would work.

"Ok, what's step 1, Jean," asked Mike.

"Open M01-1111. That should be just inside the hatch," replied Jeanette.

"Ok, that shouldn't be too hard to find," said Mike. He entered into the BEAM, the Bigelow Expandable Activity Module, a module that expanded after being delivered to the ISS. It was originally sent to the ISS to test the concept and engineering. However, after a year on the station, it began to be used as part of the storage area since it was deemed safe for use. It was only around 4m by 3m in size, so not too big, but initially, when flown to space, it had been folded up into a 1.5m x 2m configuration.

Mike rotated as he floated in the centre of the module to locate the storage position. "Found it," he said and started untying the ties. "So, what is the first package?"

"We want SXC-001-001, which will go in the PMM, so give it to me."

The PMM, known as the Leonardo Permanent Multipurpose Module, was docked on the opposite port, forward of node 3. Jeanette floated across above the cupola into the PMM.

"OK, I've found a whole lot of SXC-001 packages. I just need to find SXC-001-001," said Mike as he carefully started removing the bags from the storage locker. He found the right one. "Ok, got it, here it comes," he said as he gently pushed it towards Jeanette. "Hope you are good at catch."

"Sure", she said, retrieving it. "You just have to get used to the ball not dropping in space. OK, now this goes in M02-1000, which is down the back here somewhere." The PMM was larger than the BEAM, being around 6m long and 4.5 in diameter. "Ok, SXC-001-002 also comes over here, but into a different location."

"How'd I guess that was next! Here it comes," said Mike as he sent that bag across the space between them.

They continued for a few more bags until they came across some items to go to the Russian Zarya module.

"We need 4 bags, SXC-001-007 through SXC-001-0011, that need to go to Zarya, so we can take 2 each," said Jeanette.

"Sure, I've got two of them. Let me find the other two," said Mike as he searched in the storage locker. "So, who is back home for you, Jean?"

"My parents and sister, in Glasgow. And my dog, Terry."

"What kind of dog?" asked Mike.

"Chocolate Labradoodle. He looks like a chocolate milkshake with curly hair."

"Where is he while you are up here?"

"Staying with my parents. I get to video chat with him, and he licks the screen. I miss him heaps."

"Aww, how cute. ... I found them. Here, have these 2 and lead on." Mike passed the bags to Jeanette and followed behind her, again admiring her physique. They floated slowly down Node 3, wrangling their bags, into Node 1, then turned to the back of the station and entered via the Pressurized Mating Adapter (PMA) into the Russian Functional Cargo

Block (FGB) known as Zarya. That was a tighter fit, so they needed to pass the bags through one at a time.

"I think we need the fourth locker on the starboard side if I've got my Russian correct," said Jeanette. "Yep, here it is," she said as she opened the latches to find a mostly empty compartment.

"I'm glad it's empty. International post, eh!" said Mike.

"Yes. Most of the Russian stores come up on the Progress vehicles, but I guess this was something urgent," she said as they put the bags into the lock and secured it. "Ok – race you back to the BEAM," she said as she pushed off, smiling back at him.

Mike also pushed off in an attempt to reach the adapter first, but Jeanette was too experienced and slipped through. Nimbly swinging her momentum around and back into Node 3. In comparison, Mike flew past the docking port for Node 3 within Node 1 and had to grab hold of a restraint to stop himself from sailing right through the US Lab. He pushed back and turned into Node 3.

Jeanette giggled. "You need more practice, Mike. Too much thrusting too quickly misses the mark. Slow, steady and smooth makes us happy," she said with a wink.

Mike blushed. This was a wild Scot!

"Can you update ground?" she asked. "I'll find the next 4 that go to the JEM. We've finished item 7."

"Sure," replied Mike. Clicking the microphone button, "ISS to CAP-COM on 2."

"Go ahead, ISS."

"We have completed item 7 on checklist 3. Starting item 8."

"Copy that. CAPCOM Clear."

Mike swung around the corner into the BEAM to discover Jeanette floating with her back to him, directly ahead as she sorted through the cargo bags. Having no time to grab hold of anything, he grazed into her from behind, grabbing her shoulder from behind.

"See, I said slower was better," she said, pushing back into him.

"Sorry, I forgot how small and tight this was," replied Mike remembering his appropriate relationship training. Everyone was in each other's space up here anyway, but he would need to be careful. He moved back into Node 3.

"Small and tight is comfy. I found the bags. Just 3 this time. But a longer trip, how about I take 2, and you lead. I like guys who take control. Do you remember the way?"

"I better. I sleep there," said Mike. He took the bag offered to him and pushed off through Node 3. Reaching Node 1, he turned forward and led them into the US Lab.

"That's good, keep it smooth, with gentle pushes," said Jeanette.

Mike swallowed. "Hi, Robert and David," he said as they passed them into the US Lab, working on an experiment. They entered Node 2 when he slowed. He saw Andrew and John working in the Columbus module, waved, and turned left into Kibo, the Japanese lab. He progressed to the end and then pushed up into the JEM, a logistic module. It was around 4m x 4m and quiet.

Jeanette entered after him, pushing the 2 storage bags ahead of her and running her hands up his back from his hips to his shoulders to slow herself. That was definitely outside the appropriate relationship guidelines, thought Mike.

"That was better," she said. "Good bedroom choice. Nice and quiet, but plenty of attachment points and padding. I sleep here sometimes."

"Then you can find it in the dark," said Mike. "Where do these bags go?"

"Umm, M03-2000 ... over here," she said, turning around. "Pass me yours."

After securing the bags, she turned back to him and kissed him. Mike broke away and pushed off, saying, "Race you back to the BEAM."

A couple of hours later, the crew all gathered in the Russian Service Module Zvezda for a Russian lunch. Most meals were eaten in Node 1, but occasionally they had meals together in the Russian segment.

"Thank you, Anton and Oleg, for hosting us for this meal. What do we have?" asked Robert.

"You are welcome. We have got some borscht and goulash for you all with some bread. Something different for you all," replied Anton.

Mike took one of the offered food packets, which had been warmed. It tasted good.

"So, Mike. You have good fun with Jean playing postie?" asked Anton with a wink.

"Umm, we certainly covered a lot of the station, and I improved my flying, not pushing too much," replied Mike.

"Yes, you keep smooth," said Anton.

"We had some packages for you guys, too," said Mike.

"Ahh, good, that should be parts for our WC," said Oleg.

"Oh, you've had problems?" asked Mike.

"Sometime sucker stops. Not good," said Oleg, shaking his head. "Should be on the worklist for tomorrow."

The lunch finished with Oleg and Anton telling them a Russian folk story. Then Mike spent the afternoon performing experiments in the Destiny Lab on the Window Observational Research Facility (WORF).

The NASA, Canadian and European crew had dinner in Node 1 while watching an episode of The Big Bang Theory. Suitable for a bunch of geeks!

After another training session and a video chat with his mum, Mike strung his sleeping bag up in the JEM, reading for a bit before dozing off to sleep.

He awoke to see Jeanette's face, surrounded by her red hair, in front of him.

"I was starting to wonder what I'd have to do to wake you," she said, "you sleep deeply. Let's see how your smooth thrusts work."

She pulled them together, wrapped her legs around him, and kissed him deeply. Mike was stuck in his sleeping bag. She had him pinned down. After their long deep kiss, she moved back.

In the dim light, he saw that she was wearing only her underwear. He unzipped the bag.

"Are you sure this is a good idea?" he asked.

"Honey, don't worry. No one will mind. A girl gets lonely with a bunch of men up here. People need to relax. They all get it."

She slipped her top off and slid into his sleeping bag.

"It's a bit tight in here, Jean," he said.

"Good, it'll help," she said. They embraced, with her legs wrapped around him. "I'll warn you that you'll need to go slow."

16

— • —

April 21, 2021, ISS

Mike and Jeanette woke early, and Jeanette returned to her quarters. Mike found Node 3 empty, so he took the opportunity to wash. He was halfway through his tour and had a day of science experiments on the WORF. There were a few days during his tour when he would be acting in his specialist role, so he needed to be on his game today. Yesterday had been a surprising distraction. Today would need focus.

He returned to the JEM, finished dressing, opened his laptop, and reviewed his daily checklist. He noticed an email from Lisa, which he guiltily read. She was missing him and knowing he had a busy science day, she wished him the best. Mike wrote a quick reply thanking her, telling her he'd let her know how it went. Then got back to his checklist review.

After breakfast, Mike headed for the Destiny Module. His primary task today would be to replace the hardware for the ISERV project operating in the Window Observational Research Facility (WORF). The WORF was located in front of the highest quality window in the ISS, and it hosted several projects that performed earth observations. ISERV was a modified commercially available telescope and digital camera. It was used to observe the earth, and obtain near-real-time data about disasters, humanitarian crises and environmental threats.

His first task was to set up a local laptop to access the task checklist, and Andrew joined him to assist.

"So, Mike, what are we doing today?" asked Andrew.

"Replacing the hardware for ISERV, basically an upgrade."

"That's the system used by USAID, correct?"

"Yep, a joint project called SERVIR run out of Marshall Space Centre, helping countries access earth observations, especially for disasters etc.," replied Mike.

"So, what's first?"

"Step 1 is that we find our new equipment. It looks like there are several packages in the PMM. If you want to bring the laptop, we can go find what we are looking for."

"Sure."

Mike and Andrew floated back into Node 1, turned into Node 3 and down into the PMM. They spent 20 minutes locating all the packages they required for the upgrade. Then they moved all their packages back to Destiny.

"Andrew, can you let Ground know we are taking the WORF offline as per Step 2, please."

While Andrew did that, Mike secured the packages around the WORF in a way that still let the crew move through the module. Some of the packages were bulky.

"Ok, Mike, we are GO for Step 2.1, which is to close the WORF bump shield," said Andrew.

Mike moved a lever on the left side of the WORF from the bottom to the top, which slid a protective screen across the window. "That's done," he said.

"Great, now I talk to Ground again for them to close the outer cover," Andrew said, picking up the communications mike. "Destiny on 2 for CAPCOM."

"Go ahead, Destiny," replied the ground controller.

"We have completed step 2.1 of the checklist, so we are ready for you to close the external cover."

"Copy that, Destiny. We are implementing now."

"Copy that," replied Andrew and the radio, then to Mike, "so we can go on with 2.2 by the looks of it, taking off the cover."

"Sure, there's a bag for it in the locker at the bottom, so let's retrieve that first."

Mike and Andrew opened the locker, located the bag, then unscrewed the cover and stowed it in the bag back in the locker.

They then proceeded to unpack and assemble the new optical system. Once they finished assembling the components according to the checklist, Andrew looked for the next item.

"Ok, 5.1, connect ISERV2 to external power and data port 2 on WORF," Andrew told Mike.

"Yep, we will now power it up and make sure the new one is working before we extract the old device. Hand me that power cable, will you?"

Andrew passed Mike a power cable tethered to the wall near him. David proceeded to plug it into the ISERV2 and then floated up to the top of the WORF to the connector panel, identified power port 2 and was about to insert the plug.

Jeanette floated by, "Are you boys having fun?"

"Yeah – we've been making good progress, just a bit bulky to move around," replied Mike.

"You have to be careful how you move in space, don't you, Mike?" said Jeanette, with a wink.

"We better keep on at this. We just did a power-up," said Mike.

"OK, boys, you better get a move on while things are up!" said Jeanette as she continued down into Node 1.

"Did you....?," quietly asked Andrew with raised eyebrows.

"She is very upfront, forthright, and knows her stuff," said Mike, focussing on the ISERV2.

"Obviously," replied Andrew. "Now, see if you can properly insert the data cables. Here's one for you."

The powerup test was completed ok, and Mike and Andrew proceeded to remove the existing equipment from the WORF. Having been in place for several years, some bolts were a bit hard to unscrew, but they eventually extracted the WORF from the facility, secured it, and then worked to install the new one. This was not as simple as the different shape of the device meant rearranging some existing elements within the WORF. This increased the likelihood of problems with other experiments, which is why the crew was there – to solve problems.

Finally, everything was in the correct location, and the ISERV2 was now connected to internal ports in the WORF.

"CAPCOM to Destiny on 2, for Mike," was heard over the communications.

Mike took the microphone from Andrew and replied, "Go ahead, CAPCOM, this is Mike."

"Thanks, Mike. We aren't getting a response from ISERV2. Could you please check the cabling and confirm using internal 2 ports."

"Copy that," replied Mike. To Andrew, he said, "back in I go."

To check these components, Mike had to enter the WORF cabinet and check the cables. He checked and re-seated the power, communications and video cables.

Extracting himself again from the WORF, Mike took the comms microphone and keyed it. "Destiny for CAPCOM on 2"

"Go ahead, Destiny."

"Yeah – I've double-checked those connections. They are good."

"Copy that, Mike. We will test again."

"Hey Mike, isn't it quieter here, like the fans in WORF aren't running?" asked Andrew.

"Yeah – maybe they are power cycling it."

"CAPCOM for Destiny on 2," they heard over the radio.

"Go for Destiny. This is Mike."

"Mike, we seem to have lost communication with the WORF avionics. Can you reset breaker N2-71."

"Copy that, N2-71," replied Mike. "Andrew, can you do that?"

"Sure," he said, moving down to the node's power supply panel. "well, that had tripped, resetting it, and it tripped again."

"Shit, that's not good," replied Mike. On the radio, he said, "Destiny for CAPCOM, that circuit breaker had tripped and will not reset."

"Copy that, Mike. Standby."

"What do you think is wrong?" asked Andrew.

"Might be the load, but that module tested ok on the external port. Maybe there is something wrong with that set of connections. The WORF has been here for a while," answered Mike.

"Ground for Mike, can you disconnect ISERV2 from internal 2 and attempt to reset N2-71 again, please."

"Copy that, disconnect ISERV2, reset N2-71," replied Mike. To Andrew, he said, "Back in I go. I'll just disconnect from the internal connector board."

Mike put his head and torso into the WORF, located the relevant cables and disconnected them.

Coming out again, he said to Andrew, "Go ahead and reset that breaker."

"Ok – switching."

There was a flash, and smoke wafted out, followed by the sounding of a fire alarm.

Mike pushed across the lab to grab a fire extinguisher. "Andrew, make sure that breaker is off. Get CAPCOM on the radio," he said.

"Shutting down ventilation in node 2," said Andrew.

Pushing back to the WORF, he located the vent for the avionics and discharged the extinguisher into the space.

"Destiny, CAPCOM on 2 Urgent," said Andrew on the radio.

"Destiny, Go."

"Engaging N2-71 triggered a flash and smoke from WORF. Mike has applied an extinguisher. Ventilation off. Muting alarm."

Andrew pressed the alarm mute button. By this time, Jeanette had appeared, handing Andrew and Mike masks.

"Shit, guys, what did you do? Don't burn my house down."

"We were problem-solving a problem with the WORF when it blew," replied Mike. "Great, that's not working for a while."

Robert appeared. "Sitrep," he requested.

Mike replied, "During problem solving on WORF power supply, the unit flashed and smoked. N2-71 is now off, extinguisher applied. Ventilation off. The fire appears out."

"Thanks, I'll talk to the ground," replied Robert, taking the radio mike. "Destiny to CAPCOM, Commander."

"Go ahead, commander."

"It appears that the fire on WORF is out. We are on masks, and ventilation in Node 2 is off."

"Copy that. If you are happy the fire is extinguished, then restart ventilation."

"Commander copies, restarting ventilation in Node 2." Replied Robert, nodding at Andrew, who switched it back on. The noise level in the section increased as the ventilation fans restarted.

"That was well handled, Mike and Andrew. Unfortunately, some of these older racks are starting to cause us issues like that," said Robert.

"Sorry we broke your gear," replied Mike.

"CAPCOM to Destiny, for Mike."

Mike took the communications device and replied, "Go ahead, CAP-COM."

"Mike, we want you guys to pick up at item 16, so that will be storing the old equipment."

"Copy that. Just give us a minute to rearrange stuff here," replied Mike.

Andrew and Mike spent the next hour securing the old equipment and closing up the WORF.

The failure of ISERV2 and WORF was frustrating for Mike. This was one of his significant activities for the mission, so for it to fail was not great. But he knew it wasn't his fault.

Over dinner, Robert asked if he knew what had gone wrong.

"I'm guessing a fault in the avionics system relating to the internal 2 connectors. The experiment tested ok on the external connectors, so it probably had something to do with that, but we won't really know until they swap out the avionics systems," replied Mike.

"And that probably won't happen for a year," said Robert. "Bummer for you. I guess that leaves a gap in your schedule."

"Oh – I can help him fill it," said Jeanette.

"I'm sure you can. We'll see what tomorrow's task list has in it!"

Mission Control did, in fact, find tasks for Mike to do, and Jeanette did help him fill his time.

17

FRIDAY, APRIL 30, 2021, HOUSTON.

The rest of the mission had progressed well, with an uneventful return flight home for John, Andrew, Mike and Jeanette completing her long mission, and David stayed for an extended mission.

Lisa had been at Cape Canaveral for their recovery. Mike was happy to see her but felt a bit awkward about what had happened with Jeanette. Really awkward when they met. He was happy that Jeanette would be returning to the UK shortly. It's not like he'd chased her, but he hadn't stopped her either.

After a day's rest and monitoring at the Cape, they were able to fly back to Houston, and now they were home. Mike still felt a bit dizzy when he moved suddenly, but otherwise, he felt pretty good. He knew he'd lost a bit of muscle tone, but it wasn't too bad.

Mike flopped down on the bed after dropping his bags.

"Wow, it's good to be home with a real bed," he said.

"I'll bet," said Lisa, dropping beside him and rolling to sit on top of him. "And no one to do this," she continued as she took off her top and leaned down to kiss him. "I missed you."

"I missed you too," Mike replied.

18

— ◆ —

MONDAY, MAY 10, 2021

Sue arrived early at JSC. Today was the first meeting for the Artemis 3 team, and, as commander, she wanted to be ready and in control. Both the active and backup crew would be present today and would train together over the next three years.

Sue entered the lobby of Building 4 South, took the lift up to level four, where the team would be based, found her workspace, and logged into her computer to check her email. As she had hoped, she appeared to be the first to arrive. A quick check of her email showed nothing urgent, so she walked down to the meeting room booked for their meeting. Everything looked in order. She set up her laptop, ensuring she could access the room displays.

Both Sue and Ann Williams, the backup commander, had already been working with the mission team for the last month in preparation for the gathering of the complete team, most of whom had been on other missions recently. Together they had worked out training plans for the next few months.

While Sue was checking her presentation, Ann arrived. "Good Morning Sue. Are you ready to kick this off?" she asked.

"I can't wait, but it's going to be a bit of a marathon, not a sprint," replied Sue.

"Yep, and just remember, don't take any shit from the men. Especially John. We are the commanders, and some of them won't like it."

"I think we'll be ok, I'll keep an eye on John, but he has the experience, same with Steve. Most of the rest are newbies."

"True, but we've all flown. John is much more traditional, so just be careful."

Just then, some of the crew members started to arrive.

"Morning, George, Christina and Julie," welcomed Sue. "Grab your seats. We'll do introductions soon."

"Ok, Sue, good to see you," said Christina. She smiled at Ann. While finding seats, the rest of the teams arrived and acknowledged each other.

"Ok. Welcome, everyone; grab a seat, and we will get started. We will go through introductions shortly," said Sue.

"As you all know, I'm Sue Bright, Primary team Commander for Artemis 3, and you will also know Ann Williams, Commander for the Backup crew. If you aren't planning to travel to the Moon, you're in the wrong room!"

Everyone laughed.

Sue continued, "We've been busy for the last month working on our training schedules. There's a lot we need to get up to speed on, and not all of it is fully defined as yet. We have Orion and the SLS pretty much locked down, as are the spacesuits, so we will focus on that training first. The Lunar Lander is under development. We will get an early look at those systems in the next month, but we won't have high-fidelity mock-ups for maybe three months. Mind you, we also have the opportunity to speak into those projects, which is fantastic.

"Ann and I have talked a lot about how we want to operate as crews, and we've decided that for the next 18 months or so, we will operate as 1 team. For scenario training, we will mix up the primary and backup teams so that we are all used to working with each other. That way, we can easily move people into the primary team if required. Closer to launch, we will strengthen the team dynamics by training in our own teams. The primary and backup teams will still travel separately from now on."

"I'd like to remind everyone that you all deserve your place here, and you are all recognised as capable and competent in your roles, whether you are on the primary or backup crews," said Ann. "I know all of us on the backup crew would like to be on the primary, but there are only 4 seats, and choices have been made. We need to become comfortable with that. If that becomes an issue for you, talk to me, your mentor, or counselling services.

"We all are on future flights, so we will get there. In the meantime, we need to focus on the NASA mission and the Artemis mission and do all we can to ensure the success of Artemis 3."

"Thanks, Ann," said Sue. "I'd like us all to go around the team and introduce ourselves, not just professionally, but as people. We are going to be spending a lot of time together over the next few years and may as well make sure our relationships start well. Some of us have been on training or missions together in the past, but I want us to start afresh.

"So, I'll start. I have a partner, Ron, who is an Electrical Engineer and also now works for NASA. We have two children, Jessica, who has just turned 5, and Jerome, who is 14 months old. My father, Paul, is an electrical engineer, and my mother, Sharon, is a paediatrician. I mostly grew up around St Louis, Missouri, but we moved around a lot.

"I studied aeronautical engineering at MIT before joining the US Navy, where I eventually became a test pilot, and I still have the rank of Lieutenant Commander. While I was there, I completed a Master of Science in Systems Engineering at the Naval Postgraduate School. I'm a member of the class of 2017, as are others here, and I've had one space flight to the ISS in Oct 2020 on the Starliner.

"When I get the chance, I love to be outdoors and go hiking and camping, but we haven't been able to do much of that over the last couple of years.

"Ok – who is next? – Christina!"

Christina turned to face everyone and started, "Hi, everyone. I'm Christina Pak. I'm also from the 2017 class. My parents are Ann, a nurse, and David, a doctor. They live in Los Angeles.

"I studied Biology, first at UC Berkeley and then at Standford. Prior to becoming an astronaut, I was working at NASA Ames.

"So far, I've had one flight in the Starliner to ISS in June 2020.

I'm from L.A., so I love surfing and reading."

"Thanks, Christina," said Sue. "Ann, could you introduce yourself."

"Sure, I'm Ann Williams, and I'm the Commander of the backup team.

"I joined NASA in 2009 from the Army, where I flew Hornets. I flew many sorties, and I'm glad I no longer have to kill people for a living.

"I grew up in New York, New York. My academic studies were in Mechanical Engineering. I like to know how things work!

"I've been to the ISS twice. First time for 6 months in 2019, so I know what a Soyuz is like. And I got to fly in the Starliner test flight for another visit.

"For a hobby, I race cars. I guess I like going fast.

"My partner Lucy and I have a little girl George who is 6 and loves turtles.

"I'm looking forward to leading the backup team and leading a future Artemis mission and seeing America back on the moon."

"Thanks, Ann," said Sue. "John, tell us about yourself."

"Thank you, Sue," said John. "I am Colonel John Packer, USA Air Force. I flew FA-18s for 7 years, including 2 campaigns.

"I'm from the lone star state, from a city called Abilene. As well as my Ma and Pa, I have 2 sisters, Grace and Maureen.

"I'm married to Alice, and we have a son Michael, 8 and a daughter Sally, 6.

"I recently flew to the ISS for the second time with Mike here on a Dragon. Prior to that, I flew in 2017 in a Soyuz. I definitely prefer the Dragon.

"When I get time, I love to go home an' ride my horse. I've dabbled in rodeo, but nowadays, I just watch.

"I'm really looking forward to getting out to the moon, and I hope I get a moon walk in a future mission. My job is to make sure we all get there and back safely as deputy commander and pilot."

"Ok, thanks, John. Let's wrap up the primary team with George," instructed Sue, turning his way.

"Thanks, Sue. I'm really looking forward to getting to space again after my ISS expedition in 2018. I'm George Scorby. Yep, I'm Canadian, from Ottawa.

"I'm an astrophysicist, so I'm Mission Specialist 1, and I'm still blown away that I get the opportunity to walk on the moon.

"My wife, Jean and I have 2 sons, Kevin, 12, and Nate, 10, and we love sailing together as a family."

"Maybe you can take us all out for a sail one weekend?" asked Sue.

"Sure, we'd love to," replied George.

"Ok, now for the rest of the backup crew, Steve, your turn," said Sue.

"I'm Lieutenant Commander Steve Davidson, US Navy. I also fly FA-18s.

"I have also been to the ISS for 6 months in 2017 and again in 2020 on the Starliner with Sue, but I stayed on the ISS for 3 months. I'm itching to get back to space. I'm Deputy Commander Pilot for the backup crew.

"My wife, Kate and I have a son Graham, and a daughter, Michelle, who are currently studying at college.

"When I get a chance, we like to go diving. Kate's a marine biologist.

"Thanks, Steve," said Sue, "Mike."

"The cream of the crop at the end! I'm Mike Trellis, and I'm backup Mission Specialist 1. I also am a member of the class of 2017, and I've only just returned from an expedition to the ISS on a Dragon with John. While there, I infamously managed to destroy the WORF facility, much to the ire of Trekkies around the world.

"I'm a geoscientist, so I'm really excited to be able to travel to the moon to study it, and I'm scheduled on Artemis 5, so I'm looking forward to discovering stuff George doesn't find.

"My partner, Lisa, and I love going camping and canoeing. We are planning a trip down the Grand Canyon in Autumn.

"Oh – I'm from Colorado Springs – it's way too humid here. Who thought Houston was a good place for Astronaut training?!"

"Haven't you got used to the humidity yet?" asked Sue. "Regardless, Julie, please return some decorum to our group."

"Hi all, I'm Julie Mclean, from Indiana. I've been with NASA since 2010, and I recently spent 6 months on ISS, returning with Sue on the Starliner.

"I'm backup Mission Specialist 2 and a biologist, so I'm ready to discover new life forms in Mike's sweat here. I'm used to the humid summers of Indiana!

"Angus and I are into paragliding, and we've taken up kiteboarding locally, so maybe we can race George!"

"Great, sounds like some team competition," said Sue. "OK – I think it's time to go through the schedule for the next couple of years."

Sue presented the schedule on the screen, and the team started to understand the training they would go through before the mission.

"As I said earlier," began Sue, "our initial training will be on the Orion since that is all locked down. We will also get some time in survival training and a geology refresher. We expect to be able to start training for the Lunar

Lander in about 3 months, which are all going to be new systems. We will all cross-train on all those systems, but the commanders and Mission Specialist 1 members will focus on the lander, while the deputy commanders and Mission Specialist 2 will focus on the Orion.

"We are going to be the first flying in these craft, so expect for there to be changes as we go, and if you see issues, speak up early. The timeline is tight, and we and the entire team need to be agile in the way we work. We will be a long way from home if things go wrong, so think about safety all the time and always bring forward concerns early."

"Ok, let's get into the details."

The team worked through the schedule for the next few weeks for the rest of the meeting, raising issues and conflicts.

19

SUNDAY, JULY 4 2021

The spray splashed on Sue's face as the yacht pieced another wave as they sailed into Galveston Bay. George had come through, and both primary and backup teams and their families were on a large yacht he had obtained for them for the day.

Everyone had got involved in rigging the yacht, with George and Jean showing them how to handle the halyards and manage the winches, and they had quickly trimmed the boat to sail.

Anna and Jane had taken on the task of catering for the 30 people on board with some help from some of the other families.

It promised to be a great day and was also shaping up as a fantastic team-building exercise.

Sue's daughter, Jessica, came running over to her. "Mommy," she said, pointing to port, "Did you see the birds?"

"Oh, not yet, let me see," said Sue. She could see some Brown Pelicans flying in formation near them. "Wow – they are Brown Pelicans."

"They've got funny yellow heads," said Jessica.

"Yes, they do. Are you having a good time?"

"Yes, I've been playing with George."

Sue looked at her with a concerned look until she remembered Ann's daughter was called George.

"There you are, Jessie. You found Mommy," said Ron, and he carefully walked over to them with Jerome. "Sue, can you take him for a while? George said I can take a turn on the tiller."

"Sure. Has he been ok?"

"Yep, he's fine. You know where to find me."

Meanwhile, Mike was in the stern of the boat, drinking a beer with John and Steve.

"So, where's Lisa, Mike?" asked John.

"Ahh, well," said Mike, pondering his response. "We broke up."

"Really, that's too bad. What happened?"

"I don't know. She said I wasn't committed, especially after the ISS trip. I don't know what she means, but I think she found someone else."

"You weren't playing around, were you?" asked Steve.

"No, I guess we just stopped wanting to be together."

"You haven't been visiting Scotland when we weren't watching, have you?" asked John.

"What? ... No", answered a flustered Mike. "Don't know what you mean."

"I know you and that Scottish girl got on well on the ISS. Maybe too well," said John.

"Oh man, you didn't?" said Steve.

"Sometimes things, you know, it's difficult," answered Mike.

"You did. Well, that's your answer. Lisa worked it out," said Steve.

"Yeah, well, can we just enjoy this beer and leave my love life out of it."

"Sure," said John, "just one thing I'll say just once. Don't you ever play around with anyone on this team. You hear? It messes up stuff that can't be controlled. You got that?"

"Ahh – yes, sir."

"Good, drink your beer."

Mike decided he wanted to escape this conversation, so he excused himself and made his way forward, leaning over the rail.

Christina came over to him. "Hi Mike, you look lonely. Where's Lisa?" she asked.

"Not here," he replied.

"Aww, that's a pity. Everything ok?"

"Yep, we just broke up last week."

"Oh, sorry to hear that. You guys were great together," said Christina.

"Yeah, well, looks like it's over, and back into single life," said Mike.

"It's not that bad. I survive!"

"No guys chasing you?"

"There's one or two at church, but nothing serious."

"You need to widen your pond," quipped Mike.

"Maybe, but I want a guy who loves God first, and they tend to hang around churches!"

"Ok," Mike said, not knowing what to do with that. "We all love God and Country!"

"Yeah, reciting the pledge isn't enough," said Christina.

"So, you want to marry a pastor?!"

"No, he doesn't have to be a pastor, but he does need to solidly share my faith that Jesus is my saviour. And he needs to put God first and seek to serve him in all he does. It's not going to work if he doesn't."

"So, you do that?" asked Mike, "Put God first and seek to serve him."

"Yes, I try to."

"But you're an astronaut. You do all the same things I do."

"I don't know about all the same things, Mike, but sure I do all the astronaut stuff. But I'm living the way Jesus wants me to while being an astronaut. Just like others do as accountants, teachers and mechanics."

"But why does that get you into heaven compared to someone like me?"

"It doesn't," answered Christina.

"What? Then why do it?"

"I don't do it to get into heaven. There's only one way to do that, to recognise that we have rejected God and, in faith, believe in Jesus' death to save us from our sins and in his resurrection. I serve God because I am saved, not to be saved."

"That doesn't make sense to me."

"Yes, I know."

Just then, Jessica came running over, followed by Sue.

"Have you seen the birds?" asked Jessica.

"Which birds?" asked Christina.

"Those ones," said Jessica, pointing to some ibis on a nearby island.

"Oh, wow, they are beautiful. Which ones are your favourites?" asked Christina, getting down to Jessica's level.

"The ones with the bags on their mouths," said Jessica, nodding.

"Oh, the pelicans, yes, and they are big, too, aren't they?"

"And they don't move their wings when they fly."

"No, they don't much."

"Are you guys having a good time?" asked Sue.

"Yeah – we are just having a chat," said Mike, "I see Ron has left you with the kids."

"He's having a go on the wheel. We are just on our way back to see him," answered Sue.

"How's Jerome going?" asked Christina. "I see he is walking."

"Yes, he up and around for sure. And starting to say things. Definitely a more challenging time for us. But it's fun," said Sue.

"Dadda," exclaimed Jerome.

"Hi there, little one," said Ron, bending down to pick up the toddler. "You don't seem to be worried by the moving boat."

"Hi, Ron," said Christina, and Mike nodded at him. "Sue was just telling us about his progress."

"Oh, yes, he is growing every day and keeping me busy. It's great we can all get out like this. I've never been out here."

"Yeah, I guess you need a boat to see this part of Texas!" said Mike.

"Well, we fly over it all the time," said Sue.

"Not quite the same thing!" responded Christina. "But it is amazing to see all the barge traffic in places."

"Yeah – that surprised me too," said Mike.

"Coming about," they heard George cry.

"Ok, Jessica, hold onto Mummy's hand," said Sue.

"Why?" asked Jessica.

"The boats turning, so you don't want to fall over, do you?"

"I'll be ok."

"Jessica, hold my hand, please."

"Aww, ok," replied Jessica, taking Sue's hand.

They all took hold of something as the boat quickly turned to port.

"We are going to drop the sails and motor into this cove and drop anchor for lunch," yelled George over the sound of the sails as they started to flap. "So, if we can get some volunteers to help manage the sails...."

The team busied themselves with getting the boat organised to anchor in the bay.

Later that evening, Mike found himself back at his empty house. It had been a good day with the team out on the boat. But it had been disturbing too.

Lisa leaving had been a loss. He actually missed her. He had thought things were going well, but obviously, she hadn't felt the same. He hadn't sought out anything with Jeanette, and they hadn't been in contact since then. He did see a lot of Sue at work, but there wasn't anything there. Maybe he was just focussing too much on work.

Maybe he should just try and get back together with Lisa.

And how weird is Christina, wanting some guy who is more into God than her? And how can being an astronaut be serving God? What sort of god wants an astronaut to serve it? Mike didn't even really believe in a supreme being. He wasn't an atheist as such, more agnostic. He knew he couldn't say there wasn't a higher being. If he died, he figured that was it. So, he wanted to have the best life he could now, and he figured that included Lisa.

Yep, he was going to have to woo Lisa back.

20

TUESDAY, JULY 13 2021

Mike collected his lunch order, a chicken enchilada, from the counter and turned around to locate where the others had sat. He found Christina sitting with George near a window and started walking that way. Julie joined him as he walked.

"Have you finished reading the Lunar Lander briefing yet, Mike?" asked George as Mike sat down.

"Mostly. It will be good to see the trainer tomorrow," replied Mike. "How about you guys?"

"I have," replied George. "It's not that different from the Starliner, just the lander part!"

"Since I'm not going in it, not a lot for me to learn. I just get to stay in the Orion," said Christina.

"Yeah – we'll have more room up there by the time I get there on Artemis 5," said Mike. "By then, we'll be using the Lunar Gateway."

"Yeah, I think I'll go stir crazy in just the Orion for 20 days, especially 11 days with just John," said Christina.

"Well, you'll have more space without Sue and me there and more space than we'll have on the lander," replied George with a cough. "Oh man, hope I'm not coming down with something. I think my throat is a bit sore."

"Yeah, you are sounding a bit hoarse, George. You should take it easy, oh – by the way, I can't make the game tonight, so you should have a rest," said Mike.

"Maybe I should. What are you up to?" asked George.

"Ahh – Lisa and I are going on a date."

"That's great", said Christina. "I didn't know you guys were getting back together."

"Well, we aren't yet, but she has agreed to date a bit. I think I was a bit of an idiot and ignored her a bit," said Mike.

"Yeah, I know I need to make sure I make time to be with Angus, or he gets upset," said Julie. "We have so much going on here. You basically have to plan the rest of your life outside NASA."

"And don't get distracted," said George, winking at Mike.

"Yeah, the schedule doesn't help, that's for sure," said Mike, taking a bite of his lunch and ignoring George.

"Well, it doesn't help me meet anyone either," said Christina. "Maybe we should get Sue and Ann to schedule some downtime in our schedule, you know – always be at JSC on Fridays and finish at 3pm or something."

"Not a bad idea," replied George, "Jean would love to see me a bit more."

"I'll raise it with her," said Christina.

"So, is anyone having a vacation this summer?" asked Mike, "It's already half over!"

"Yeah, I've got a week in the first week of August. We are all going back to Ottawa to visit family," said George. "The kids get to see their cousins."

"That'll be great," said Christina. "I'm going back to LA and see my folks that week."

"Hmm, I guess that's why there's not much on that week. Maybe I'll go back home too," said Mike.

"I'm waiting till later," said Julie. "It's too hot and humid back home right now."

"And it's not here?" asked Mike.

"It is, but if I take vacation time and go home, I want it to be pleasant. Anyway, Angus doesn't have time right now, so I'll just stay here."

The group continued eating their lunch and discussing plans.

Later that evening, Mike met Lisa at an Italian restaurant on the water's edge in Seabrook. He figured he needed to step up from their regular bar and grill haunts.

"Oh, this is nice," said Lisa as she walked up and gave him a kiss on the cheek. "How did you find out about this?"

"Hi. John at work recommended it."

"Well done, John!" said Lisa. "Hope the food is as good."

They entered through the front door and were greeted by the maître d'.

"Sir. Madam. Welcome to the Capri. Do you have a reservation?" he asked.

"Yes, in the name of Trellis," said Mike.

"Fantastic, yes, I see here a table for 2 on the balcony. Follow me." He led them through the villa-style building out to the waterfront to a table set on the balcony. "Georgio will see to your needs shortly."

"Wow, great views," said Lisa. "Would be a fantastic place for a wedding."

"Apparently, they do quite a few," replied Mike, aware he didn't want to push things too quickly. "And they are supposed to have a great Sunday brunch. I think that is when John often comes."

"Good evening. I am Georgio, your waiter this evening," said the waiter as he unrolled their napkins and placed them on their laps. "Here are your menus. Today for appetisers, we have some beautiful mussels and also, the scallops. I recommend the clam chowder for the soup, and for Entrée, the Snapper Pontchartrain and the Veal Chop are both excellent.

"Would you like anything to drink to start with?"

"Do you have some Moscato?" asked Lisa.

"Yes, ma'am. By the glass?" said the waiter.

"Yes, please," answered Lisa.

Mike ordered a Heineken.

After the waiter left, Lisa asked Mike, "So, how's the team going?"

"Pretty good. We all went for a sail together on the fourth, which was good, but I missed you not being there."

Lisa looked away.

"We are all getting ready to train on the new Lunar Lander," he quickly said, moving on. "In fact, we get to see the trainer tomorrow."

"Oh – I didn't know that was ready yet," said Lisa, turning back to him. "That's based on the Starliner, isn't it."

"Yes," he said smiling, "I really love that you know that!"

"Well, it's good we have something in common."

Just then, Georgio returned with their drinks and asked for their appetizer orders. Lisa ordered Bruschetta with smoked Salmon and Mike, the Mussel Marinara with white wine garlic sauce.

After the waiter left, Mike took a deep breath. Now was as good a time as any. He said, "Lisa, I'm sorry that you feel that we don't have much in common. I think we do, but I know that I've been distracted and didn't spend enough time with you and that that hurt you, and you felt ignored. Will you forgive me?"

Lisa looked at Mike, a bit surprised. She definitely wasn't expecting this so quickly. She replied, "Wow, you really have been thinking about us."

"Yes, and I really have missed you," replied Mike. "I was a fool. And the trip on the fourth really brought it home."

"So, you've been lonely, is that it?"

"Well, yes, that is part of it. But I also realised how well we fit together. Like the thing about the lander. You're smart. And you're beautiful, and I really enjoy being with you. I just took you for granted," said Mike.

"How do I know that things will change?" she asked.

"We were talking about this at lunch today, Julie, Christina, George and I. We all need to make more time for our boyfriends, girlfriends and partners, or in Christina's case, finding one. So we are asking Sue and Ann to schedule more time here at JSC regularly, so we can be around, especially on Fridays."

"That would be good. But how are you changing?" asked Lisa.

Their appetizers arrived. The waiter felt the tension in the air and quickly left.

"I'm not sure, Lisa. I can try and be more proactive and plan better to spend time with you. What do you think I should do?"

"It's not just time. You have been disinterested, not there since your ISS Mission. It's been like there is something better, and you aren't interested in me."

Mike slumped and focused on the mussels in front of him, picking at them. Lisa took the hint and started on her Bruschetta.

"Yes, OK, I've already said I'm sorry. I was an idiot, as John has told me," said Mike

"John told you that?"

"Yes, after we broke up. In fact, on the sailboat. I know that I took my eyes off you, and I wasn't thinking about you but being selfish. I'm sorry."

Lisa continued eating her food, looking out at the lake, pondering what Mike was saying.

"You slept with someone," she said, turning back and looking at him.

Mike froze. How did she know? What would she say?

"It didn't mean anything," he said.

"It did to me. Who?"

"On the ISS, one of the crew."

"There was only one woman on the crew!"

"I know. She came on to me strong. I couldn't stop her."

"So, she raped you?" said Lisa, getting upset.

"I'm sorry, no, I should have said no, I just...."

"Gave in," Lisa completed. "Well, that explains it."

"Please forgive me," pleaded Mike.

"I don't know if I can, and I definitely can't stay here," said Lisa, standing up, turning and leaving the restaurant.

Mike stared at his food, no longer hungry. He signalled Georgio and asked for the bill.

21

The next day the Artemis 3 primary and back crews gathered at the Space Vehicle Mock-up Facility (SVMF) in Building 9 of JSC. Today they were getting their first look at the Lunar Lander mock-up.

Sue addressed the team. "Ok, everyone, this is an exciting day as we get our first look at the Lunar Lander. I hope you all had a good sleep and are ready for this." She glanced across at Mike, who clearly had not slept well. "I want to introduce you to Peter Johnson, the project lead for the Lunar Lander, who will be in charge of today's activities."

"Howdy y'all," said Peter. "We are so excited for you to start using this mock-up of the Lunar Lander. This closely represents the hardware we are preparing for launch, and at the moment, that means the capsule, the ascent and the descent modules. It is based on the Starliner module used for the ISS, so you will recognize some elements.

"With me today is Jane Shultz, the Lead engineer on the Starliner, and she will be briefing you today. Jane..."

"Thank you, Peter," said Jane, a tall, dark-haired woman in her mid-thirties. "You will find the module similar to the Starliner craft. However, it is fitted out internally quite differently. Most of the systems onboard are to support life and communications, spacewalks and control systems.

"Let me take you inside. I'll take the primary team first since there won't be room for all of us in there." Jane led the primary team into the mock-up.

"You are looking a bit under the weather there, Mike," said Ann.

"Ahh, I didn't get a great night's sleep," answered Mike.

"How was your date with Lisa," asked Julie.

"Umm, it didn't go well," said Mike.

"Oh no, sorry to hear that," said Julie.

"Thanks."

"So, John's special restaurant didn't work?" asked Steve.

"It was great, and Lisa loved it. I'm the problem," said Mike.

"You tried," said Ann, "Maybe she will come around in a few days."

"Maybe," said Mike despondently.

"How about we focus on the task at hand," said Ann. "Who can tell me how long we can stay in the lander?"

"Life support limit is 10 days," said Steve.

"Correct, which is way longer than Starliner. Why?"

"Additional consumables in the service module," replied Mike.

"Also correct."

At this point, Jane walked over to the backup team, saying, "Thanks for waiting. You can come in now. We are just having a quick look first up, we will do some briefings, and then each team will get some longer periods in the mock-up after lunch."

The team followed Jane up the stairs into the lander.

"So, as you can see, we have the capsule situated on top of the service module with ascent capability, and the lander module, so you will be able to practice ingress and egress," said Jane.

"This lander only needs to support 2 crew members, and as you can see, the additional elements for managing suits do take up some space, as do the storage lockers for consumables which would not be required on the Starliner for trips to the ISS.

"The avionics and controls are identical to the Starliner, so you can reuse that training. However, the landing systems are going to be quite different, as is the performance of the stack, especially on the descent.

"What do y'all think?"

"Seems a bit less room than the Starliner, but for just 2 of us, it should be ok," said Mike.

"So where is the toilet in this vehicle?" asked Ann.

"It's here on the mid-deck, so you can access it in lunar gravity. As you know, the Starliner CST-100 does not have a toilet for flights to the ISS, but since the lunar mission has a 7-day component on the moon, one was required. While it will work in zero-G, it is optimized for low gravity," answered Jane.

"I see there are bunks in here as well as the chairs," commented Julie.

"Yes, since the crew will be in lunar gravity for most of the mission, we needed somewhere for the crew to sleep. You can't sleep in those chairs," said Jane. "So if you have had a bit of a look around, we will go join the others in the briefing room and get into the details."

Jane led the way out of the capsule.

Mike noted how high they were, a good 10 m above the ground. "Wow, you don't want to fall from up here," he said.

"Yes, please hold onto the rails," said Jane.

They made their way into the office space to the briefing room for their detailed discussions.

22

—◆—

Wednesday, July 28 2021

Ann and Mike settled into the Lunar Lander simulator. This was the fourth session they had undertaken training in the simulator. They were not in the mock-up, just sitting in front of the consoles and displays as they appeared in the Lander. Today they were simulating a landing, which would be automated in most circumstances. But they were training for those unusual circumstances.

Sam, their trainer, leaned in front of them. "You guys all set?" he asked. They both nodded.

"Comms check," said Sam over the comms channel.

"Commander, five by five," said Ann.

"Mission Specialist, five by five," said Mike.

"Great, starting you out 1 minute before deceleration burn. MARK."

The displays in front of Ann and Mike came to life, showing system status and trajectory relative to the moon, and they were currently in orbit.

"Everything looks nominal," said Ann.

"I agree," said Mike after studying the data. While he wasn't a pilot, he would still need to be able to operate the spacecraft if Ann was incapacitated.

"Descent main engine firing for deceleration burn," said Ann.

He had only been working closely with Ann for the last few weeks, and they were still getting used to each other's way of working.

"Burn completed, normal thruster activity, trajectory nominal," said Ann.

"Ahh … I concur," said Mike.

"Seven minutes to landing," said Ann.

"CAPCOM, Lander," said Mike on the radio.

"Go ahead, lander," replied Sam.

"CAPCOM, deceleration burn complete, trajectory nominal."

"We copy, go for landing."

"Copy that CAPCOM, go for landing," replied Mike.

Ann pressed a button to acknowledge the system query as to whether to proceed.

"Looks like our trajectory is off by a little," said Ann.

"I see that too. Looks like a thruster is overperforming," said Mike.

There was a piercing beep, with a button flashing on the console. "Guidance 1 fail," said Ann. "Selecting Guidance 2."

"Understood", said Mike. "CAPCOM, Lander, Guidance 1 system fail, we've selected Guidance 2. Also noting some error in trajectory."

"CAPCOM Copies,"

"Auto Land sequence error," said Ann. "Taking Manual control."

Again, Mike relayed this to CAPCOM.

"Are you able to correct the error?" asked Mike as Ann attempted to manually direct the lander.

"Almost. It's as if we are getting twice as much performance from the starboard thrusters. And now I have to slow our descent rate."

Another alarm sounded. Since Ann was busy manually flying, Mike reported the error. "RADAR Overload error," he said. "You've got to be kidding! However, LIDAR data still looks good."

"Maybe we'll get a computer overload error in a minute! Camera visual looks ok. I can make out the landing site," said Ann, referring to the similarity to the Apollo 11 landing errors.

"CAPCOM, RADAR overloaded, using LIDAR data, have visual," said Mike on the radio.

"CAPCOM Copies, you are still go."

Another alarm. "Pitch angle over 10 degrees," said Mike.

"Shit, that thruster is pushing us over," said Ann

"15 degrees," said Mike.

"ABORT," said Ann as she hit a red button, triggering the separation of the descent module and firing the ascent module's main engine. The system began correcting their adverse pitch angle and thrust them back into the appropriate lunar orbit.

"Simulation over", said Sam.

"You trying to simulate the Apollo 11 landing on us, Sam?" said Ann, "RADAR overload!"

"Hey, it can happen," replied Sam. "So, what do you think was wrong?"

"Multiple systems, Guidance, RADAR, and an overperforming thruster or system bug. Bloody thing was trying to tip us over," said Sue.

"Do you think you could have corrected it?" asked Sam.

"I thought I did have it, but then it's as if the thruster just went hard on," said Ann.

"Also correct. You made the correct decision to abort."

"Right", said Sam, "grab a drink, and we'll go again."

A little while later, Ann and Mike were again in the simulator, going through the landing sequence.

"Burn completed, normal thruster activity, trajectory nominal," said Ann.

"CAPCOM, deceleration burn complete, trajectory nominal," said Mike on the radio.

"CAPCOM copies."

"We are still looking good," said Ann, "No errors, everything nominal."

"Something will go wrong. It's a simulation," said Mike.

"Ahh – it looks like my display is frozen," said Ann, looking across at Mike's displays, "yes, confirmed, you have the controls."

"I have the controls," said Mike, swallowing.

"CAPCOM, Lander, commander's screen frozen. Mission Specialist has control."

"CAPCOM Copies."

"All appears nominal. I can see the landing site on the screen," said Mike. "Go, No Go for Landing."

"Lander, CAPCOM, Go for Landing"

"Go," said Ann.

Mike acknowledged the confirmation dialog on his screen to continue with landing.

"We seem to be drifting slightly," said Mike.

"Give it another 15 seconds," said Ann.

"Still drifting," said Mike.

"OK, then try to adjust it manually," said Ann.

Mike reached for the translation control and gently applied input to correct the error. The display showed that their trajectory was still off-nominal. He applied more input and was rewarded with a slight correction, but still not enough, so he applied more. Suddenly the trajectory passed through nominal, and they were now off course in the opposite direction.

"Damm, it appears I overcompensated. This is touchy," said Mike as he attempted to correct the error.

"Just be gentle. Small increments," said Ann.

"I'm trying," said Mike.

An alarm sounded. Mike found the alert on the display – a thruster was overheating. "Forward thruster overheating," said Mike.

"There must be something causing us to deviate. Try rotating us," said Ann.

"What, to reduce the work that thruster is doing?" said Mike, entering the input to trigger a 90-degree rotation of the craft.

"Yes," said Ann.

"Looks better," said Mike. "I spoke too soon. The error has also rotated 90 degrees."

"Descent engine firing," said Mike. "we are still drifting. Damn, we are over a crater. I'm going to roll again."

Mike rotated the craft another 90 degrees. "That's helping correct," he said. Applying input to help correct the drift.

An alarm sounded. This time it was the thruster failing.

And the simulation ceased.

"Sorry Mike, you crashed," said Sam. "Do you know why?"

"Some thruster problem," Said Mike.

"Yes, but you were working out rolling would help, but you slammed into a nearby mountain. You lost the bigger picture while problem-solving."

"I guess I should hit the abort if I have to take over and things start going wrong," said Mike.

"That's an option," said Ann, "and a valid one, especially if you can't keep it under control."

"Right, obviously piloting is not my thing," said Mike.

"And it's not supposed to be Mike," said Sam. "Remember, this is training for edge case stuff. Aborting the mission is quite reasonable. In fact, I'm pretty sure CAPCOM would have called for an abort before you got that far."

"It's ok, Mike. I don't expect you to be an outstanding pilot. That's not your job. In some ways, we are still working out some of the flight rules, and I suspect we probably found one," said Ann.

Mike still felt bad but got ready for the next simulation.

When Mike got home, he got himself a beer from the kitchen and collapsed on the lounge. It had been a rough day, with a number of simulations, and he had a long way to go to be ready.

Mike's mobile pinged with a message. It was from Lisa. She wanted to meet, and he didn't know if he could cope with seeing her now. He replied that he was tired and asked if they could meet the next day. At least he wouldn't have had a day in the simulator.

They organised to meet after work the next day at a well-known Pizzeria and Pub near Marina Bay.

23

—◆—

Thursday, July 29 2021

Mike drove into the Pub's parking lot to find it half full. He messaged Lisa to find out where she was. He received her reply as he entered the cosy atmosphere and went to the area she had indicated.

Lisa was sitting at a table for two in a quiet part of the pub, drinking a cider.

Mike sat down, saying, "Hi Lisa, how are you."

"Hi, I'm good. Did you have a better day?" she replied.

"Yeah, thanks. Yesterday was full of sims. I was whacked."

"That's good," she said.

A server appeared to take Mike's order.

"I'll just have a Bull Shark, and can we get some chips and salsa," said Mike. He came here fairly often, so he knew the beers.

"So, you wanted to talk?" Mike said to Lisa.

"Ahh, yes. Mike, that really hurt the other night to find out that you cheated on me. But thank you for being honest."

Mike suddenly became very interested in the texture of the table between them. "Yes, I'm sorry..." he began.

"I know you are sorry," interrupted Lisa, "I'm just very disappointed and hurt. Does she mean anything to you?"

"No, truly, I haven't seen or heard from her since the mission."

"And is there anyone else?" asked Lisa.

"No."

"Then, I realised how much I miss you, even though you hurt me, and I'd like us to try again, but slowly."

"I'd like that too," said Mike, surprised at her. He had hoped she might want to get back together but didn't really expect it.

Just then, Mike's beer and the chips turned up.

"Ok," said Mike, "so let's start by you telling me how things are going for you."

"Well, I'm staying with my friend Kelly, but that is getting a bit awkward, so I have been looking for a new place, which hasn't been fun."

"I guess it is a bit soon to move back in together," said Mike.

"A bit. I can probably wait a week or so before doing anything," said Lisa.

"So, what else has been happening?"

"Work has been ok. I'm working on a new learning tool for understanding orbits. We want to get the kids to try and set up a lunar orbit transiting from earth orbit," said Lisa.

"Wow, that's a big ask. The maths is really hard," said Mike.

"Yeah, well, we are trying to simplify it a lot, and it is for senior students," said Lisa. "Why was yesterday so tiring for you?"

"Ahh, I was in the lander simulator with Ann most of the day. It wasn't so bad when she was in control, but a number of times they failed her out, so I had to take control ... I'm not a pilot!" exclaimed Mike.

"So, you feel out of your depth?" asked Lisa.

"Totally. There's just too much going on."

"I'm sure you'll get better, and surely you are just the backup."

"I know. Like, I crashed the first time around, and we realised that it's probably better for me to abort if I'm in control and something starts going wrong, but that's a big call as we scrub the mission."

"Surely that is fair enough. If that much has gone wrong, you need to stay safe," said Lisa.

"Yes, that's true, but I still need to be able to control things if Ann is out of action."

"You've still got three years," said Lisa. "You can do it!"

"Yes, I know we've got time. I've missed this. You helping me process this stuff. Do you want to get dinner?" Mike asked as he ate some chips.

"Sure, how about we get one of those Tejas pizzas to share."

"Sounds good, said Mike.

24

WEDNESDAY, 4 AUGUST 2021

Sue sat at her breakfast table with Ron and Jessica. She had a later start today, so she could eat with the children.

"What do you want for breakfast, Jessica?" asked Sue.

"Rice Bubbles, please," said Jessica.

"Ok, here you are," said Sue, getting up to fetch the packet. "The milk is on the table. What are you doing at school today?"

"I think we are reading and playing games."

"Ok, that's good."

With Jerome in front of him, Ron walked in, saying, "Here he is, all clean and ready to eat."

He placed Jerome in a high chair.

"Great, little man, I've got something yummy for you," said Sue, putting his food in his bowl and placing his spoon in front of him. "There you go."

"Ta," said Jerome.

"Thank you, very polite," said Sue. "So, Ron, what do you think you'll do today."

"Well, playgroup with Jerome, and I hope to get some work done while he rests, but not much else. We might go to the shops if he isn't too tired. How about you?"

"We've got a review meeting on the mission with primary and backup teams and the spacecraft teams. Probably going to go for a couple of hours. And I've got a T-38 flight this afternoon."

"Mummy, will you be flying?" asked Jessica.

"Yes, I will," said Sue.

"Will you be away for long?" said Jessica.

"No honey, just an hour. I'm just practising."

"OK, that's good," said Jessica, going back to eating her breakfast.

"Don't forget we've got that appointment with Jerome's paediatrician tomorrow afternoon," said Ron.

"It's in my diary, so I will be there," said Sue. "Ok, Jessica, finish your breakfast and juice, and then get your things for school."

"Ok, mommy."

Jessica finished her breakfast, got out of her chair, and went to her room. Sue cleaned up their bowls and glasses and then helped Jerome with his food.

"Mommy, can you help me," cried Jessica down the stairs.

"I'm coming," replied Sue. "Ron, I'll let you finish up with Jerome."

"Ok," said Ron.

Sue went upstairs and helped Jessica do her hair and prepare her school bag. When they finished, she told Jessica to meet her in the kitchen.

Sue quickly readied herself for work, grabbed her laptop bag, and went back downstairs for Jessica.

"Ok, Miss, let's take you to school. Bye, Ron, love you," said Sue, kissing him.

Sue dropped Jessica off at the school and then drove to JSC.

George walked over to her desk as she sat down and logged in.

"Morning Sue. How are you?" he said.

"Hi George, I'm good. How are you?"

"I was wondering if we can have a chat privately?" said George.

"Sure, looks like the small meeting room is free. Let me make sure it isn't booked," said Sue as she opened up the room calendar. She was wondering what George wanted to talk about. "Yes, it's free. Let's go."

As they walked, she asked, "How's Jean and your family?"

"They are fine, thanks," replied George.

They entered the meeting room, and George closed the door behind them. Sue took her seat. "So, sit down, George. How can I help?" she said.

"Well, I'm sorry to tell you this, but it looks like I'm not going on the mission. I saw the flight surgeon this morning, and he has withdrawn my flight status," said George.

"Oh, George, I'm so sorry. Can you tell me what is happening?"

"You might remember me complaining about a sore throat earlier in the month? Well, it turns out to be more serious than a cold or COVID. It appears that I have thyroid cancer."

"I'm so sorry to hear that, George. How are you coping?"

"I'm in a daze. Apparently treatment is usually quite successful, and they think they've found it early. But I'm unhappy to lose the mission," said George, looking downcast.

"And how's Jean coping?"

"She is doing well, at least I think she is. We told the boys last night, which was hard."

"I'm sure it was, so what's the next step for you?" asked Sue.

"I'm seeing a surgeon tomorrow, so I'll know more then."

"Ok, so you can't fly on the mission. Do you still want to stay with the team, perhaps as CAPCOM? It might be good to still be around friends."

"I don't know," said George. "Thanks for the offer. I need to think about it - whether I want to stay close to the mission after missing out or do something else. The flight surgeon is talking with the Corps to organise some meetings about how to proceed, but I thought you should know."

"So, are you happy to share that with the team today, or for me too?"

"Yes, I thought you should know before the meeting."

"Ok, I guess Mike will move onto the primary team then."

"I guess so. He will do ok."

"Let me know if we can do anything for you or Jean and your family," said Sue, getting up and giving George a hug.

"Thanks, Sue, that means a lot," said George as they walked out of the meeting room.

Sue looked for the mission project leader, Callum, and Ann. They would need to move quickly before their project meeting in half an hour.

She met briefly with Callum and Ann, and they confirmed that they would move Mike into the Mission Specialist role on the primary team.

Mike was checking his emails when Ann walked up to his desk. "Mike," she said, "can we meet for 5 minutes, please."

"Sure," said Mike, quickly following as she power-walked to the meeting room. Had he done something wrong?

"Sit down," she said as she closed the door. "We don't have much time, and this is going to come as a bit of a shock."

Mike picked a seat and sat in it. Ann sat opposite.

"You are being moved up to the primary team. Unfortunately, George no longer has flight status. You will hear more in the meeting," Ann said.

"Oh, wow, umm," Mike's mind was reeling. "Is George ok?"

"Well, not totally, but he is expecting to recover. He will explain in the meeting. But we didn't want to surprise you with this in the meeting."

"No, I understand. Poor George. Is he staying on the team?"

"We don't know," said Ann. "It's too early. He only found out his status this morning, and Sue, Callum and I just decided to move you up to the primary. So, congratulations, I guess."

"Yeah, doesn't quite feel like a time for celebration," said Mike.

"No, probably not, but you will do well in that role. I know the sims have been hard, but they are supposed to be. You'll do great."

"Thanks, Ann."

"Ok. We better go to the review meeting. It starts in 3 minutes," said Ann.

They left the room to grab their notebooks for the meeting.

Sue walked into the conference room for their mission review meeting, with Ann following her. Mike had entered just before them.

Callum brought the meeting to order, saying, "Right, everyone, thanks for coming. As you know, this is a project flight consultancy for Artemis 3 to ensure that we all know what is going on and to identify any issues early, not a formal project review. However, any issues that are raised here will feed into the next formal review.

"Since most of the astronauts don't get to attend those reviews, this is a good time for you to understand the bigger picture and raise any issues you have. You can, of course, raise issues with your commanders or me at any time. Make sense?"

He looked around the room to make sure he was understood.

"OK, before we get into the agenda, we have some news that we have been processing just this morning," Callum continued. "I'm sad to inform you all that George needs to step down from the primary flight crew for medical reasons. He may stay in the project, but that decision has not yet been made. In light of this, Sue, Ann and I have met this morning, and we have moved Mike from the backup crew to the primary crew, effective immediately. The Corps will soon be identifying an astronaut to replace Mike on the backup team."

There was a murmur around the table.

"Can I speak?" asked George. Callum nodded, and George continued, "Folks, I'm very sad to be dropping out, but it appears that I have thyroid cancer, and I am about to start treatment. My flight surgeon has revoked my flight privileges. As Callum said, I might stay around on the project, but right now, my and my family's focus is to beat this thing."

"I think we all understand, George," said Callum. "And we wish you well, and I think I can speak for the team as a whole in saying that we, your NASA family, are here to help in any way we can.

"We will now move on to a brief overview of the general status before diving into more detail.

"Building of your Orion is progressing well and slightly ahead of schedule, as is the Space Launch System, which is on schedule with the production of your boosters. Our mission is not using the Gateway, so you aren't interested that it is ahead of schedule and may actually be in orbit at the time of your launch, which may give us some emergency contingencies we hadn't counted on. And we will update flight profiles to use those if available.

"The Design Review of the lander has been completed, and as you know, the high-resolution mock-up has been delivered. We will receive some updates as changes from the Design Review are implemented.

"Finally, the Lunar Terrain Vehicle has also just completed the Design Review, and we should start receiving training components in the next 6 months.

"So, let's start looking at these in detail."

25

— • —

Mike left the meeting during the lunch break. Life was great! He was now scheduled on Artemis 3 with a moon walk, and added to that, his relationship with Lisa was improving daily. In fact, she was meeting him for lunch.

"Mike, you coming down for lunch?" asked Christina.

"Sure, Lisa is meeting me there," replied Mike, "Is George coming?"

"I think he's left," said Julie, joining them.

"Ok, let's go," said Mike, heading towards the elevators.

As they rode the elevator down, Christina asked, "When did you find out, Mike?"

"Just before the meeting. That's why we were almost late."

"Wow, so what are you thinking?" asked Julie.

"It's great, for me anyway. Bad news for George, and I feel sorry for him," said Mike as they exited the elevator. "There's Lisa. Can you give me a few minutes, and we'll meet you at the table?"

"That's fine," said Christina as she and Julie walked to the cafeteria queue.

"Hi," said Lisa, and Mike walked over and she gave him a quick kiss. "You look happy!"

"Well, you are looking at the next man to walk on the moon!" said Mike.

"No way," said Lisa, giving him a hug. "What happened?"

"That's the sad bit, George is sick and can't fly, so I've been moved up."

"Is it bad?" asked Lisa.

"Possibly," said Mike, "I haven't spoken to him. Some sort of cancer, thyroid, I think. He seems to have left for the day, so I'll have to call him later."

"Wow, so what does that change?" asked Lisa.

"For the moment, not much, just the team I'm in, but we've been training together a lot, so that won't be a big deal. Actually, thinking about it, there probably won't be much change in my schedule, just more press!

"Are you ok to eat with Christina and Julie?"

"Yeah, sure, let's go get some food," said Lisa.

They proceeded to the food line, Mike getting a burger and salad, and Lisa a BLAT on Turkish bread. Mike located the others at a table in the middle of the room.

As they sat down, Christina said, "Hi, Lisa. So, did he tell you?"

"Hi. Yes, it's amazing for Mike," said Lisa.

"It's good to see you, Lisa. I haven't seen you for ages," said Julie.

"Yes, well, we've been through a bit of a rocky patch," said Lisa.

"Well, good to see you here," said Julie. "I think this guy needs something to keep him in the real world, or the Moon would be all there was for him!"

"I wouldn't say that," said Mike, "I have quite a love affair with Mars too."

"See!" said Julie.

"I try, but I guess it will be even harder now he is on the primary team," said Lisa.

"So, what is everyone up to on the weekend?" asked Mike.

"I'm heading back to LA to see my folks," said Christina. "I can surf with my friends and relax without thinking about the Moon!"

"That sounds great," Julie said. "Angus and I going to a Jazz Festival here in Houston. I'm really looking forward to it."

"We are flying up to Colorado Springs," said Mike. "Lisa hasn't met my folks, so it seems a good time. And I can tell them I'm going to the moon!"

"Oh no, I'm never going to hear the end of this," said Lisa with a groan.

26

—◆—

Thursday, 5 August 2021

The following afternoon Sue left JSC and headed to the rooms of their paediatrician, who was associated with NASA. There she was to meet Ron and Jerome.

As she drove, Sue thought about the reason for their visit. Jerome appeared to have very flexible limbs, and his skin was very loose. She had expected these issues to resolve as he got older, but that did not appear to be occurring, so they had consulted with their paediatrician, Dr Peter Bowers. Today they were meeting to receive some test results.

Sue pulled into the parking lot just as Ron opened the rear car door to extract Jerome from his car seat. She pulled into an empty space beside him.

"Hi," she said, getting out of the car.

Ron stood up with Jerome in his arms, saying, "Look who that is. Is that Mommy?"

"Yesth," said Jerome, squirming to push his arms out towards her.

"Hello, little man," she said, taking him from Ron and giving both of them a kiss.

Ron went to the back of the car to unload the stroller. "How was your day?" he asked.

"Good, thanks. Not as crazy as yesterday," answered Sue. "How was yours?"

"Pretty good, we've had a good morning, but you know that he is going to get grumpy now since it is his sleep time."

"Yes, well, he'll just have to sleep in his stroller," said Sue. "There weren't many times that worked for the appointment."

"OK, well, you put him in, and I'll grab the bag," said Ron.

"Hey Jerome, let's put you in here, and we'll go for a walk," said Sue, placing him in his stroller and strapping him in. Jerome wasn't too impressed by this.

"Amazing," said Sue, "we are actually early!"

"I know, but we aren't in the waiting room yet," said Ron. "Let's go."

They walked into the building and, in fact, did make the waiting room without any significant delays.

They didn't need to wait long before they were ushered into the doctor's room.

"Sue and Ron, how are you and Jerome?" asked Dr Bowers.

"We are all doing well, thanks," said Sue. "I hope you are well?"

"Yes, thank you. Well, let's just do a check-up on your little boy, and I think he is due for a vaccination shot, so I'll get our nurse to organise that on your way out," said Dr Bowers, looking at his screen. He then proceeded to examine Jerome.

"So, he hasn't had any problems since I saw him last?" asked Dr Bowers.

"No," said Ron, "he has been good."

"Great, well, all looks good today. The nurse will weigh and measure him, but I don't expect any problems. So here you go," the doctor said, passing Jerome back to Sue, who sat him in his stroller with a toy to play with.

The doctor sat down and typed some information into his computer. "Ok," he said, "we were a bit concerned about some possible hypermobility of joints and soft skin. Correct?"

"Yes, doctor," said Sue.

"As you know, Jerome is still very young, and he may still outgrow these issues. However, there is a possibility that he may have a connective tissue disorder. Have either of you any history of any diseases such as Ehlers-Danlos Syndrome or EDS, or Marfan's disease in your families?"

"I don't recall any in my family," said Sue.

"I don't either," said Ron.

"That's ok. I do suggest that you each have a talk with your extended family and see if anyone does recognise those conditions. I'll give you some pamphlets on them.

"Again, I don't want to alarm you. Both of those conditions can have related cardiac issues. Do either of you know of a history of cardiac problems in your family?"

"Ahh, I think my uncle had a heart attack, and my grandmother just collapsed and died one day," said Ron.

"I also had a grandparent have a heart attack," said Sue.

"I think we all have relatives who have had heart attacks. When you are talking to your families, ask about other cardiac conditions, things like holes in the heart or problems with the aorta. It's amazing what you find out when you ask. But again, don't worry. Most of these issues don't present until people are much older.

"To help keep all our minds at ease, I suggest we organise some basic cardiac checks for Jerome, which will pick up any irregularities that might be present. I don't expect any. For both of those two conditions, we won't be able to detect anything until he is in his teens at the earliest."

"Is there genetic testing that will help?" asked Sue.

"Possibly, however again, it is much too early to be able to properly diagnose.

"Jerome is walking around fairly well, isn't he. Let's get him up and walk around a little," said Dr Bowers.

Sue said to Jerome, "Hey, little man, let's get you out of your stroller."

Sue placed Jerome on the floor, and he promptly stood up and walked to Ron.

"Yes, clearly no problem there. So, if he has a form of EHS, it is mild," said the doctor.

Ron picked up Jerome and put him on his lap.

"If you are happy, I suggest we proceed as follows.

"First, I'll order a cardiac assessment, so I'll refer you to a cardiologist.

"Second, you both do some homework and talk to your families to get some history. Those brochures will give you some basic information.

"And, third, we'll come together again in a month or so and see what we find.

"Again, I want to counsel you both not to worry. If Jerome has something, then I believe it is mild. You will read some scary stuff on the internet. There are lots of similar conditions out there. You'll think Jerome has symptoms of all of them. He doesn't. Generally, for most of these diseases, there is a family history, and you would likely know about it already. Your parents or siblings would have it. Any questions?"

"Lots, probably," said Sue. "Is he in pain?"

"I don't think so," said the doctor.

"Is there anything we can do?" asked Ron.

"Until we know if there is anything wrong and what it is, I can't answer that. Generally, just look after him. Being careful of dislocations is about the only thing I'd watch out for.

"If there's nothing else, we will get him his vaccination, and we'll see each other in a month. Ok?"

"Ok, thank you, doctor," said Sue.

"Yes, thank you," said Ron.

After getting Jerome his vaccination and booking the next appointment, they walked to their cars.

"So, there's nothing like this in your family?" asked Ron.

"No, and NASA's medical probably would have shown it up," said Sue.

"True. I feel bad for him," said Ron.

"Don't worry, it may not even be a thing. He is still young. How about I pick up Jessica on the way home," said Sue.

"Ok, I'll take him home for a sleep. Maybe take Jessica for ice cream or something to give him some quiet," said Ron.

"Sure, some girl time!"

Sue waved bye, got in her car and drove to Jessica's school in time for the pickup run.

As she waited for Jessica, she pondered the situation with Jerome. It was strange that neither Ron nor she knew of any similar problems in their families. Maybe they'd just been hidden, or perhaps nobody knew. As she thought about it, a doubt grew. Maybe, just maybe, it was because Jerome wasn't Ron's son. Maybe Mike was his father after all? But surely NASA would have checked his medical history as much as it had hers. She couldn't really ask him. She would have to wait until Ron and her families were ruled out as a cause.

27

— • —

TUESDAY, OCTOBER 19 2021

Sue arrived at JSC slightly late after dropping Jessica off at school. It had been a difficult few days. Both she and Ron had finally finished talking with extended family members about medical issues. They had both failed to find anyone with anything like a connective tissue disorder. There was still a possibility Jerome had no problems, and also, possibly, there had just been a random mutation. Fortunately, Jerome's cardiac tests had shown nothing unusual. However, she was starting to wonder if she needed to talk to Mike, but she didn't want to open that can of worms if she didn't need to.

Sue locked her car and started walking towards Building 4 South.

"Morning, Sue," said Christina, walking over to her. "Looks like we are both running late."

"Oh! Hi Christina, I didn't see you there," said Sue looking around to locate Christina. "We're not late for anything important! I have kids. What's your excuse?"

"Umm, late night, talking with a friend."

"Well, I guess that's better than a late-night gaming or that you fell asleep reading a manual," said Sue. "Ready for the rendezvous training?"

"Yep, we just have to sit there. You guys have to find us!" said Christina, entering the building. "How is your family? I hope no one was sick, making you late."

"They are all fine. No, it was just the joy of getting 2 children ready in the morning."

They arrived at their floor.

"I'll see you later, Christina," said Sue, walking to her desk. Checking the clock, she just had enough time to grab a coffee and quickly check her emails before they needed to go to Building 16 and the System Engineering Simulator.

Half an hour later, the primary team, Sue, John, Mike and Christina, met in the elevator lobby.

"Ok, guys, let's go," said Sue as an elevator arrived, and they all entered. "Everyone ready for some crashes?"

"Sure, but only after you show us how it's done first," said Mike. "I don't want to earn a reputation for crashing landers."

"It's all learning," said John. "Better crashing now than in 2 years' time."

The team walked the 300 metres across to building 16 and entered the System Engineering Simulator.

They were welcomed by the manager, who led Sue and Mike to the Beta Dome, which was configured for their lander. John and Christina were taken to the Alpha Dome, configured for the Orion.

"How are you going, Mike?" asked Sue as she settled into the simulator.

"I'm good," said Mike, "How are you and your family."

"I'm good too, as are the family. Doing a bit of testing to check out a possible condition with Jerome, but it's probably nothing."

"Oh really," said Mike, "anything serious?"

"Hopefully not. He seems to have loose skin and hypermobility, which might suggest some future issues. But he is still young, and it's a bit difficult to be sure."

"Hypermobility? Is that where people are double-jointed?"

"Yes, that's part of it," said Sue. "Do you know anyone with that sort of thing?"

"Ahh, there was a friend at school who freaked us out with the strange things she could do. And one of my mother's cousins had some issues, and I think she kept dislocating her shoulder. He isn't dislocating a limb, is he?"

"No," said Sue, pondering this revelation. "He hasn't hurt himself yet. We've just noticed a few unusual things."

"Ok, that's good."

"Lander, this is Control for a comms check," came over their headsets. They and the Orion performed their communications checks.

"Right folks, we will be practising rendezvous of the Lunar Lander and the Orion Capsule, starting from nominal ascent from the lunar surface," said the controller over the communications. "This will include correct timing for launch, right through to rendezvous, with a bit of time compression, rendezvous and docking. Theoretically, that should all be automated. So, we will start with a clean run so you know what it's like.

"Initialising systems, Lander, you will start from T minus 3 minutes."

Sue and Mike grabbed their pads and located the relevant checklists and time.

"Lander, are you ready to proceed?" asked Control.

"Affirmative, at T minus 3 minutes," replied Mike over the communications.

"Control copies, clocks are running."

Both Mike and Sue started processing their checklists.

"Navigation is good. Systems all ok," said Sue.

"Comms, carrier lock with Orion good," said Mike.

"T minus 1 minute. Descent locks disengaged. Ascent module independent power," said Sue.

"Here we go," said Mike.

"8, 7, 6, 5, 4, 3, 2, 1, launch," said Sue. "Thrust nominal, navigation nominal."

"Compressing timeline next 5 minutes in 1," said Control.

"Do I have to speak really fast?" said Mike.

"Let's just pick up at T plus 6 when we get there. Everything is supposed to be nominal," said Sue.

"I think I can see Orion," said Mike.

"Copy that, Mike. We can see you," said Christina.

The Orion module grew from a pinprick of light to a larger blob to something they could make out its features as they chased it down. When they were about a kilometre away, the lander module rotated, so they were looking away from Orion and back at the moon and fired its main engine again to slow the approach towards the Orion. The lander flipped over again so they could see the Orion module out of their windows.

All the time, Sue and Mike monitored the systems and maintained continual dialogue with the controller and John and Christina in the Orion.

The Lander approached the Orion, travelling above it in orbit until it was about 50m ahead of it, again flipped over so the crew could see the Orion, and translated slowly down so that the Lander was in the same orbit ahead of the Orion. It then slowly approached the Orion module and successfully docked with it, all without either crew's intervention.

"Well, that was easy," said Mike," What do they need us for?"

"For when it all goes to shit," said Sue. "And you have to be able to handle the ascent and this docking without me if something happens to me. At least that's if you want to get home."

An hour later, they reset for their third run after taking a five-minute break to stretch. During the second run, Sue had needed to deal with a navigation error. This time Mike was in the hot seat.

"Lander, are you ready to proceed. During this simulation, the Commander is incapacitated," said Control on the communications channel.

"Lander copies. We are ready," said Mike.

"Orion, are you ready to proceed," said Control.

"Origin is ready," said Christina. "Just don't crash into us, Mike."

Mike took a deep breath.

"Control copies. Starting at T-3 minutes ... Mark."

Mike started going through the reduced checklist for the scenario where the Commander wasn't available. Usually, he would primarily cross-check Sue's checks with some of his own. This checklist hit all the big ticket items so one person could achieve it in the timeframe available.

"Navigation is good. Systems all ok, Comms, carrier lock with Orion good," said Mike. "T minus 1 minute. Descent locks disengaged. Ascent module independent power. All green."

"Control Copies all systems nominal," said Control.

"Orion nominal," said Christina.

"5, 4, 3, 2, 1, Launch," said Mike, "Thrust nominal, trajectory nominal." He was glad they had gotten through that stage.

"Compressing timeline, next 5 minutes in 1," said Control.

The view out of the window started changing rapidly.

"T plus 6 minutes," said Control.

Mike referred to his checklist. The next event was the flip before the next burn. He checked that the thrusters were armed and that navigation was still on track.

T plus 6 came. "Flipping over," said Mike. The image of the approaching Orion started moving up the window, and a view of the moon was displayed. A minute later the manoeuvre was completed.

"Flying tail first, all go for orbital insertion burn," said Mike. Shortly after, the main engine fired to slow them to a speed slightly faster than the Orion vehicle.

"Alarm, early engine cut-off, 10 seconds," said Mike. "Approving corrective burn."

He approved the correction displayed on his screen. As they passed it, he saw the Orion appear again in his window, and it continued to shrink. He checked his navigation display. They were now 2 kilometres past the vehicle.

Another burn recommendation appeared on his screen, which he approved, saying, "correction burn."

He was now 5 kilometres from the Orion in a much higher orbit. He needed to speed up and lower his orbit, but at least the vehicles weren't moving further apart.

Mike looked at his checklist and followed the checks necessary at this point.

"Control, the Lander has not yet established approach communications with Orion. I suspect that is due to the distance," said Mike.

"Affirmative, Lander. You will need to adjust your orbit with thrusters," said Control.

"Copy," said Mike.

The system was now presenting him with several options. He disregarded the main engine burn option as that was too dangerous, even this far away from the Orion. There were two thruster options. He selected the option with a longer thruster burn, figuring he was far enough away to slow down and correct if needed.

"Firing thrusters," said Mike. The Orion started approaching surprisingly quickly. However, the navigation status remained green. As the Lander approached within 1 kilometre of the Orion he received another suggested thruster firing which should slow them to an acceptable approach speed, which he accepted.

"Firing thrusters again", said Mike.

An alarm sounded. "Alarm, low pressure on forward thruster fuel," said Mike. He hoped he had enough to dock. He checked his other thruster fuel reserves, and they were ok.

Mike again performed his checklists, wiping sweat off his forehead.

"Approach Comms lock," he reported. That was good, the ship should now be able to automatically dock. He looked at the 'time to docking' display. 16 hours! The lander didn't have enough fuel for the forward thruster to approach faster.

"Lander, Control. I recommend active docking by Orion. Insufficient thruster fuel for a fast dock. Current ETA is 16 hours."

"Control, Lander, negative, your consumables are sufficient to allow for delayed docking with nil impact of mission timeline."

Mike dropped his head. That big thruster burn was obviously the wrong move.

"Skipping ahead 16 hours," said control.

The image of the Orion quickly came close until the time to the docking clock showed two minutes. Mike ran his checklist for docking and found no issues.

"Lander, go for docking," said Mike.

"Origin, go for docking," said Christina.

"Docking," said Mike, as he clicked the approval for docking button.

"Contact," said Mike, "Driving latches."

"Simulation concluded," said Control.

"So, do you know what you did wrong?" asked Sue.

"Yep, the thruster burn was too big. Either I should have gone with the main engine burn anyway, or the smaller, slower thruster burn. I used up too much forward thruster fuel slowing down," said Mike.

"Correct. I would have discussed with Control the main engine burn, and we might have done a slower one. Since you were stationary relative to Orion, we had time to work on the issue," said Sue. "This is what training is for!"

Mike got out of his chair to stretch. There was so much to learn and a complex system to be familiar with. It was all part of what it meant to be an astronaut, but sometimes he just wished he could focus on just the science again.

28

MONDAY, JULY 4 2022

For the second year, the Artemis III crews were on a yacht sailing from Kemah.

After treatment, George had again joined the team, this time as CAP-COM. He would be the voice of mission control to the astronauts on the mission, a role usually held by an astronaut. He and his family again were hosting the primary and backup crews for a day on the lakes near Houston.

This time Mike was joined by Lisa. After helping raise the sails, they settled down on the starboard forward deck.

"Wow, this is great," said Lisa.

"It will be even better when we get away from the built-up areas and see some wildlife," said Mike.

"Can we join you guys?" said Christina as she walked up to them with a friend.

"Sure, Christina," said Lisa. "I haven't met your friend."

"Oh, sorry," said Christina, "This is Graeme. Graeme, this is Mike and Lisa. Mike's on my crew, and Lisa works at Space Center Houston in Education."

They all greeted each other, and Christina and Graeme sat beside them.

"So, Graeme, what do you do day to day?" asked Lisa.

"I'm a mechatronics engineer working on underwater robotics," said Graeme.

"Oh, cool. Do you do any space-related stuff?" asked Mike.

"Our company has in the past, but currently, we get more work in the ocean."

"Christina, how did you guys meet?" asked Lisa.

"We are both in the same small group at our church and realised we both are geeks and started having some in-depth discussions. But Biology and Mechatronics are quite different!" said Christina.

"A bit like the Scribes and Pharisees working together," said Graeme.

Lisa and Mike both looked at him as though he was speaking Klingon.

"Sorry," said Mike, "Who?"

"You know, the Scribes and Pharisees in Jesus' day were both students of the Law, but the Scribes were more about writing the law and interpreting it, while the Pharisees were more a political group," said Graeme.

"Ahh, no, I don't know anything about that," said Mike.

"Umm, ok, then, umm, we just both like science, but different bits!" said Graeme, flustered.

"What have you guys been doing over the weekend?" asked Christina.

"We went to this great concert at the NRG Stadium, The Priceless Donkeys. So cool," said Lisa.

"Wow, never heard of them," said Christina. "What type of music do they play?"

"RnB, come Techno Funk, with a heavy metal twist," said Lisa.

"I have no idea what that would sound like," said Christina. "So, what did you do yesterday?"

"We stayed at the Crowne Plaza near the stadium, so we didn't have to drive and checked out this morning, so we had a romantic locked-in weekend. I'm so tired I just want to lie here all day long," said Lisa. "So, have you guys been spicing things up on the weekend?"

"Ahh, we had a nice picnic on Saturday at Alexander Deussen Park, and after church yesterday, we had lunch with Graeme's family," said Christina.

Jumping in before Lisa said anything else embarrassing, Mike asked, "How long have you guys been going out?"

"A couple of months," said Christina. "Yesterday was the first time I met Graeme's family. They live over in Sugar Land."

"That sounds great. I'm going to go and get us some sodas. Graeme, you want to come and grab something?" said Mike.

"Sure," said Graeme, joining Mike as they walked to the stern. "Lisa is pretty direct, isn't she?!"

"Umm, I think she is still a bit drunk," said Mike. "You must be pretty special. Christina hasn't had a boyfriend in all the years I've known her."

"Really? I'm surprised," said Graeme. "But we have just clicked. I only moved over this side of town this year."

"So, you must be a missionary man," said Mike.

"Huh? Sorry?" said Graeme.

"Just the way she was talking last year about finding a guy passionate about God."

"Well, I am passionate about God and Jesus. But I wouldn't call myself a missionary," said Graeme.

Mike sorted through the icebox for some sodas. "Well, I'm glad that makes you guys happy," he said.

"It's not just about being happy," said Graeme. "It's about being the people God created us to be and being His presence in the world."

"So, you are saying that God is here because you are here."

"God is always here, but He has called those who love Him to show others what He is like. Jesus talks about his people shining as lights and not hiding our lights under a cover. So hopefully, Christina and I can show something of who God is by who we are," said Graeme as they walked back. "Hi, ladies, here are your drinks. What you been talking about?"

"You, hot boy," said Lisa.

"Ahh, right, silly question," said Graeme.

"Hi guys, ready to be invaded by my tribe?" said Sue, walking down the yacht to them. Jerome was walking in front of her, and Jessica was behind, followed by Ron.

"Hello, Jessica," said Christina. "Are you ready to see birds again today?"

"No."

"You're not ready?"

"Birds are boring," said Jessica. "I want to see dolphins."

"Okay, I guess we might see dolphins," said Christina.

"Wow, Jerome has grown," said Mike. "How's he doing?"

"He is doing great. He still has hypermobility, and we are still trying to understand why and if anything else is happening. But otherwise, he is good."

"Hey, Jessica, what's that over there," said Lisa, pointing off the starboard bow at a dark shape in the water and a puff of steam.

"Where?" said Jessica.

"Come here and follow where I'm pointing," said Lisa. Jessica came over to her and looked down her arm.

"You have pretty hands," said Jessica.

"Thank you! Mike likes them too," she said, winking at Mike. "So, can you see? Oh, there's another one!"

"Is that a sea monster?" said Jessica.

"No honey, I think that's a dolphin," said Ron. "Well spotted. I'm Ron."

"Thanks, Ron. I'm Lisa, Mike's partner."

"Hi, Lisa. You are good with kids," said Ron.

"I should be, I'm with them every day, but they are usually somewhat older than Jessica," said Lisa. "I'm in education at the Space Centre."

"So, Sue, do you need to do more medical testing with Jerome?" asked Christina.

"Probably, but some potential issues won't show up until he is older. They think it is genetic, but we haven't really tracked down anything like it in our families. However, apparently, there is always a chance of a genetic mutation happening randomly," said Sue.

"Does it concern you much?" asked Christina.

"We don't worry too much about it," said Ron. "We can't do anything about it. There are just some things we will need to watch out for as he gets older. So where are these dolphins going, Jessica?"

A while later, Lisa and Mike were alone at the boat's bow as it cut through the water of Trinity Bay. Lisa was leaning out, with Mike holding the rails behind her, with his body pressed against her.

"I want a baby," said Lisa.

"Of course you do," said Mike, laughing.

"No, really, I want to have a baby with you now."

"Ah, ok. Are you sure we are ready?" asked Mike.

"I love you. You love me. We just had a weekend of great sex. And I want one of those beautiful children."

"Right. I think you might be a bit drunk, Lisa."

"No, I want a child. Don't you."

"Sure. I just hadn't thought about having one now."

"If we have one now, we'll be over all the sleepless nights before your mission."

"Wow, you have been thinking about this!"

"Only a bit, but yes."

"Umm, OK, I haven't. Can I give it some thought?" said Mike.

"Yes, but not too long, or you'll have a baby waking you the night before you launch."

"Ok," said Mike.

Lisa turned around and kissed him.

An hour or so later, the yacht anchored in a protected location and lunch was served.

Lisa was busy chatting with Christina, so Mike joined George as they ate.

"You are looking well, George," said Mike.

"Thanks. After the surgery to remove my thyroid, there wasn't much need for radiotherapy, so all I really need are hormone tablets. I will get a check soon, but we aren't expecting anything unusual," said George.

"That's great. Does that mean you can fly again?"

"Not sure. If I'm stable, maybe. We'll see. How are you going?" said George.

"I'm doing ok. Lots of training, as you know. Got training on the Lunar Buggy soon."

"That will be so cool. It's good to see Lisa here."

"Yeah."

"How are things going for you guys?" asked George.

"Good. Good. Apparently very good."

"That's good, but you sound surprised!"

"Well, it seems Lisa wants a baby. I think all the kids here today has pushed some buttons," said Mike.

"But you weren't thinking about that."

"Not really. I've been focussed on the mission."

"Kids are great, buddy. You just have time before the mission. Are you ready to settle down with Lisa?" said George.

"I think so. We get on well."

"Well, you should know you want to settle down with her before having kids."

"I know. I just haven't thought much about it or much about having kids," said Mike.

"It is a lot different, having a family, but still good," said George. "I better go and check how Jean's going feeding everyone."

"Thanks, George, for the food and the talk."

"You are welcome, Mike," said George leaving and heading into the cabin.

29

— . —

TUESDAY, JULY 4 2023

A year later, Mike and Lisa missed what had now become the annual Artemis 3 crew sailing day. The previous afternoon Lisa had given birth to a beautiful daughter who they named Jasmine.

The year had become a blur with the constant training on equipment, practising lunar walks, refining procedures for spacecraft docking, and many, many project meetings. More recently, there had been additional pressure as NASA required them to engage more often in publicity events.

The schedule of landing the first woman and the next man on the moon in 2024 was clearly linked to the US presidential election cycle, and there was increasing pressure on NASA to complete the mission as early in the year as possible.

The NASA mission also wasn't the only Lunar landing mission being undertaken. The Chinese also were attempting to put a crew on the Moon's surface, and it appeared that they were trying to get there before the NASA team. Although the NASA Artemis mission included other country partners, such as Canada and the European Space Agency, the Chinese were not a part of it. So this also meant that the US administration applied pressure on NASA to complete the mission early in 2024.

The last six months had also meant a busy time for Mike at home as he and Lisa prepared for the birth of their first child. Mike and Lisa had spent several weekends shuttling between the local Home Depot and their house in Brook Forest. The whole place was painted white internally, so they decided to repaint and decorate the nursery in a toned-down shade of yellow. Then they had decided that the existing beige carpet wasn't right, so they ended up replacing all the carpet in the house with a modern charcoal colour. Lisa then decided she didn't like the fan-light combination in the room, which was quite a dark brown. Then the Venetian blinds didn't look right, so they replaced all the blinds in the bedrooms. Then they decided that they needed to renovate the guest bedroom so that it would be acceptable when the family came to stay. Then Lisa decided that the laundry would not be up to the task, and they replaced all their white goods, including the refrigerator, which almost led to a kitchen renovation, but Mike finally needed to call a stop to the work before they required a second mortgage!

Mike held his daughter in his arms and looked down at her small beautiful face as Lisa rested in her bed in the hospital. Her fingers were so small and tiny. She was so perfect. He didn't want to put her down.

Mike's cell phone rang.

"Who is it?" asked Lisa.

"I don't know. I thought you were asleep. Here, take Jasmine, and I'll look," said Mike, handing the baby carefully to Lisa. He then quickly took his phone from his pocket and answered.

"Hi. This is Mike."

"Hi Mike, this is Sue, we are all out on the lake, and we heard about your new daughter. Congratulations."

"Thanks, Sue. I'll put you on speaker with Lisa."

"Hi, Lisa, congratulations."

"Thank you, Sue," said Lisa.

"What's her name?" asked Sue.

"We've named her Jasmine," said Mike.

"That's a pretty name," said Sue. "And everything has gone ok."

"Yes, thanks," said Lisa. "We are all well."

"Great. Well, we are all missing you both. Jessica has decided dolphins are boring this year, so we are on the lookout for alligators. Let us know if we can help, and remember, we don't want to see Mike at work for 2 weeks. Bye," said Sue.

"Thanks, Sue. See you," said Mike, hanging up. "I can't remember the last time I had 2 week vacation."

30

TUESDAY, APRIL 30 2024

The last 9 months had been busy for the Artemis 3 crews, but they had been hectic for Mike. All had started well, but it was not long after returning to work after his paternity leave that he began to feel perpetually tired. That lasted for 4 months until Jasmine finally started sleeping until dawn. Then there just had been the ongoing effort of maintaining a family and looking after a baby.

Everyone had had a busy year, with the team cycling through the various simulators, training on system updates, additional team building trips, psychological and medical evaluations, and an increased rate of media events.

Six months previously, the Space Launch System (SLS) had launched the Lunar lander to the moon, and it was currently in lunar orbit waiting for them. A SpaceX Heavy launch had placed a rover at their landing side two months ago. Now in just 2 weeks, Artemis 3 would launch to the moon from Cape Canaveral on an SLS stack.

Today the primary and backup crews were beginning their 14-day isolation, as had been the case for all NASA manned flights since the days of the Apollo missions, to minimise the risk of astronauts becoming sick during a mission with minimal medical assistance. Today would be the last time the crew members could touch and hold their loved ones for about 6 weeks. Since the COVID-19 pandemic, restrictions had been tightened so that family members could no longer have even limited contact during the quarantine.

Both crews and their families arrived at the Astronaut Quarantine Facility at JSC to say their farewells. There was also a small media contingent present to witness the event. The crew had been joined by senior project staff and the medical and training staff who would join the crew in quarantine.

Sue stepped up to the small dais and addressed the small crowd. "After several years of training and preparation, we are now ready to start our mission of putting the first woman and the next man on the moon. God willing, I hope to be that woman," she said.

"Today, we begin our quarantine in preparation for our launch," Sue continued. "This will be the last time we will be able to kiss, touch, and hug our loved ones until we return in about six weeks. That will be hard, but it is a price we are all prepared to make in this historic endeavour.

"This will be an emotional time for our families, so we ask the media to respect our privacy. Each of the crew will pose for photos with their families and as the primary and backup crews. Then we would ask for privacy as the crew and families have their last private moments before starting quarantine. We will not be taking questions.

"For the family members, I want to thank you for the deprivation you are about to endure. We know that the next few weeks will not be easy, and the NASA family is there to help you. Please lean on your Family Liaisons. They are astronauts and are there to help you, see to your needs, and handle all the logistics. They can answer your questions. Thank you again for your support for my crew."

Sue stepped down from the dais and joined Ron, Jessica, now 9 years old and Jerome, a 4-year-old, and her parents, Paul and Sharon. As commander of the primary crew, her photo was first. A NASA media liaison helped arrange everyone for the photos, and then there was the whirr and click of the press and NASA photographers.

As the rest of the crew members had their photos taken, Sue and her family stepped to one side.

"Are we really not going to see you for a long time?" asked Jerome.

"Yes, honey," said Sue, "but we'll be able to talk on the computer, so you'll be able to see me."

"But that means I won't be able to hug you," he said with a pout.

"I'll hug you instead," said Jessica.

"Aww, that's lovely, Jessica," said Sharon, Sue's mother. "And we'll be here too."

"Mom, thank you again for helping Ron with the children," said Sue.

"How could we not help! And we'll try and give Ron some space, too," said Sharon.

"Ron and I have a project to work on together as well," said Paul, Sue's father.

"You do? That's news to me," said Sue.

"We were just talking about it last night," said Ron. "We are going to make the whole house smart. I've been wanting to do it for ages. How can we go wrong with two electrical engineers?"

"But Daddy worked with high-power equipment," said Sue.

"Not a problem, it's all electrons," said Paul.

"Well, don't go crazy. I don't want to chant 13 passwords to turn on the bedroom light," Sue exclaimed.

"Don't worry, it'll be simple and easy," said Ron.

At that point, Sue needed to join the primary crew for a photo.

After their crew photo, Mike returned to Lisa, Jasmine, his parents, John and Clare, and Lisa's parents, Tammy and Karl.

"I say, Mike, little Jasmine is very flexible. Maybe it is just a baby thing, but her legs and knees seem very loose," said Clare.

"Yes, I've noticed that too," said Tammy. "Maybe you should have a chat with your paediatrician."

"I guess I can talk with him next week during her check-up," said Lisa. "We weren't able to get an appointment before Mike went into quarantine."

"I'm sure it's nothing to worry about," said Mike. "It looks like the media are leaving now, so I think we need to start saying our goodbyes. Remember, we'll be able to talk online all the time, even when I'm on the moon."

"You be safe now, Michael," said his mother, giving him a hug.

"Yes, don't take any unnecessary risks, son," said Mike's father, John. "Make us proud."

"I will, both of you."

Mike said goodbye to Lisa's parents and then took her and Jasmine in his arms, kissing them both.

"I'm going to miss you both," he said.

"And we will miss you," said Lisa. "Stay safe. Remember, we love you very much."

"And I love you both too. I'm sorry we can't be together again until I return. They just can't risk infecting us in these times."

"It's ok," said Lisa. "We will be able to see each other at least before you launch. And we'll be able to video conference."

"I know," said Mike.

"Ok. Everyone, time for the crew to leave," called Sue from near the door.

"Goodbye. Look after Jasmine for me," said Mike to Lisa, giving them one last kiss and hug. "I'll talk to you tonight."

Mike waved to his and Lisa's parent and then joined the rest of the crew as they entered the facility.

31

The crew and those quarantining with them got settled into the facility. In fact, there were two groups, the primary crew and the backup crew, and they were isolated from each other.

Mike found his room simple yet adequate. He had his own en-suite, and the room seemed quiet, so he should be able to get some good sleep.

He unpacked his belongings. It was mostly stuff to get through the next 2 weeks here and in Florida. He could take very little with him on the mission itself, and all the clothing for the mission was supplied. He had a few family photos and books, two thinner ones he would keep for the mission. While he often read on tablets, he occasionally liked to read a physical book for a change.

A while later, Mike met up with Sue, John and Christina in the lounge for coffee.

"Is everyone's room ok?" asked Sue.

"Can't complain," said Mike, "basic but functional. Same as last time." The others all agreed.

"Well, you know we get our own chef, so the food should be good," said John. "Better than eating Russian food all the time."

"Some flavour could be good," said Christina.

"Ahh – that's right. None of you have launched from Kazakhstan, have you," said John. "You don't know what you are missing!"

"Thank God we have manned launch capability," said Mike. For many years the USA had to rely on the Russian space program to launch their astronauts until the first manned SpaceX Cygnus and Boeing Starliner missions in 2020. This meant astronauts served out their quarantine in Space City near Moscow and in Kazakhstan.

"Did you guys hear that the Chinese launched this morning?" said John.

"That's their lunar mission, isn't it?" asked Christina.

"Yeah," replied John. "They must be spending huge amounts on their space program since they are still building their space station."

"So, they got to orbit safely?" asked Sue.

"As far as I know," said John. "I guess they start their transit to Lunar orbit soon."

"Wow, I'm glad I'm not on that mission. They are pushing very hard and fast, trying to beat us," said Mike.

"I'm sure we'll get briefed soon," said Sue. "We've got 30 mins to get over to the simulators for today's exercise. I'll meet you outside in 10 minutes."

Even though the crew were quarantined, the simulators and training facilities were managed as part of the quarantine zone so they could continue training as long as possible.

The Chinese space program to reach the Moon had been of growing concern to the Artemis mission, and there was an increased level of security around the facilities. The likelihood of the two missions being on the Moon simultaneously was triggering no end of meetings and risk analysis.

China had been seeking to explore the Moon since 2004. They had been progressively working toward a similar target as the USA. They had successfully soft landed on the Moon in 2013 and landed rovers on the far side of the moon in 2019. It was probably not just a coincidence they had just launched as the USA crew entered their quarantine. If they were successful, the Chinese would have the next human walking on the Moon.

The crew spent several hours simulating the process of undocking the lunar lander from the Orion. George, as CAPCOM, had been training with both primary and backup crews during the last year to ensure they worked well together.

The crew eventually returned to the quarantine facility for a late lunch.

As the crew sat down, the facility staff brought in their lunch, lasagne and salad.

"Wow, smells fantastic," said Christina. "I'm hungry."

"Yeah, it's been a busy morning," said Sue. "I'm glad we've only got a briefing this afternoon. Tomorrow's full launch rehearsal is going to be a long day."

"And probably very boring," said Mike.

"Hopefully," said John.

The rehearsal would involve the complete Mission Control team at Johnson Space Center and the Launch Control Center at Kennedy and test procedures. In another week, they would execute another rehearsal, this time with the crew in the launch vehicle in Florida, in their flight space suits which would include fuelling activities and checks. Tomorrow's rehearsal would be the last time the testing team could throw in unexpected problems.

"That scenario today was pretty rough," said Christina. "I doubt there is much chance of survival given that much damage."

The scenario they had encountered was an undocking failure which led to catastrophic damage to the Orion.

"Yeah, a bit nasty giving us that one this week!" said Mike.

"Well, it does make you think," said Sue. "This mission is not risk-free."

There was silence as they each pondered this. John broke it. "Maybe that's why they gave it to us, so we would ponder the consequences."

Mike blew out a long sigh between his teeth. "I guess I really don't want to think about it. Lisa and I have spoken about what might happen, of course. I know that she and Jasmine would be ok. But, ..."

"I don't want anything like that to happen," said Sue. "And I don't want to miss my kid's growing up."

"I'm not worried. I won't know what is going on," said John.

"So, you don't believe in any afterlife?" asked Christina.

"No, ma'am. This is all there is," said John.

"I guess you feel differently, Christina," said Mike.

"Yes. I believe we are made for more. That we go on living in a different way when we die," said Christina.

"In heaven or hell," said Mike.

"Yes. My view of heaven is probably different from what you think, though."

"In what way?" said John.

"I think we'll have new bodies, in some way, and live in God's presence in a city here on Earth. And we won't be just floating around as angels with wings doing nothing, but we will have a purpose. What, I'm not sure, probably managing or looking after something, maybe creation."

"Yeah, that's not what I think of when someone says 'heaven'," said Mike.

"I know, right?" said Christina. "We all tend to think it is floating around above the clouds singing hymns or something. But that isn't what the Bible actually says. Have a read of the last two chapters of the Book of Revelation, chapters 21 and 22."

"Na, once you're dead, there's nothing," said John. "I'm going to check my email. See you in an hour for the briefing." John stood up and left for his room.

"Interesting idea, Christina. I'm going to check my email, too," said Sue.

"I think you scared them," said Mike after Sue and John had left.

"Well, what do you think, Mike?" asked Christina.

"It's a different idea. I can't imagine eternity singing!" he replied. "I tell you what. I'll read that stuff and let you know."

"Great. Now I guess we better check our messages!" said Christina.

An hour later, the crew met in the briefing room. The curtains across the windows to the other briefing room where the backup crew were located were open.

Callum Rogers, the mission project leader, sat at the front of the room with a microphone so the backup crew could hear him.

"Afternoon, all. Hopefully, everyone in the other room can hear me. Ok, yes, that appears to be the case," said Callum. "So, let's get started."

"Everything is running pretty much to schedule. The SLS preparation is on track with the Orion stacked on the launch pad. The lander is in Lunar orbit, and the systems are nominal. The rover has been delivered to the landing site and is operational and ready. Even the Gateway, which we won't use, is on station and available for communications support and as a refuge if required.

"Launch Control and Mission Control are both operational and fully staffed. We will implement the final full system simulation tomorrow with the aim of testing command, communications and response systems. We will discuss this further a bit later.

"As you are aware, the China National Space Administration (CNSA) launched a mission to the Moon this morning. We expect them to perform their trans-lunar injection burn sometime in the next 12 hours. If they are successful, they will be the first non-Americans to walk on the Moon.

"Security services have become aware of some chatter about possible sabotage attempts of Artemis 3 by China. It is possible that they do not want us to succeed if they fail. And, unfortunately, we do expect them to fail since they appear to have skipped any testing phases and proceeded straight to a manned lunar launch.

"As you are already aware, NASA has already increased security at our facilities. These are now being increased here and at Kennedy, and an exclusion zone has been implemented around the launch complex.

"Increased cyber-attacks against NASA facilities have been detected and mitigated.

"If the Chinese mission is successful, we expect them to have returned by the time you launch, although there is a possibility that their return to Earth may overlap with your lunar transfer. NASA is reaching out to the CNSA to ensure that our transfer orbits do not intersect.

"Any questions about any of that?"

"Sure. Is the chatter credible?" asked John.

"Yes, however, we don't think they have a feasible plan," said Callum. "Work is being done to understand what the actual threat may be. At the moment, I think you will just need to trust that everything possible is being done to protect our mission."

"How confident are we that the cyber-attacks have been thwarted?" asked Sue.

"The team is very confident," replied Callum. "However, attacks do continue, and additional protective measures are being put in place."

"So, there may be a successful attack? In fact, there may have been an undetected successful attack?" said Mike.

"Yes, that is possible," said Callum. "But it is unlikely. Just a reminder not to use any of your devices on any unsecured networks, such as a cell network."

"Is the Gateway a serious option for us?" asked Christina.

"Yes, if required," said Callum. "It is provisioned and operational, and your orbital parameters are compatible with a rendezvous if required. It would act as a lifeboat, and we would launch additional consumables while we organise a rescue."

The Gateway was removed from the mission plans in 2020 when there was some doubt whether it would be ready for the mission and to simplify the mission. Less docking manoeuvres were required due to this change.

There weren't any more questions, so Callum continued, "For tomorrow's rehearsal, there will be some press around, but not a lot. We will have some social media influencers visiting as well. Remember to be friendly. They will probably have a few questions, but they know not to come near you.

"That should do you all for today. Relax, have a good dinner and sleep, and we'll see what fun gets thrown at us tomorrow!"

Everyone got up and left the briefing rooms. Mike returned to his quarters and sat down at his desk. It was a bit early to call Lisa and the kids, so he had a bit of time. Remembering his discussion with Christina, he looked up Revelation on Google and discovered a website called BibleGateway that had lots of different bible versions. He was surprised there were so many. He started with Chapter 21. The language was weird to Mike, with strange imagery. But yes, it was definitely talking about heaven as a city. And it seemed that it would be beautiful and good. It sounded like an excellent place for those God liked, but it talked about putting some people in a fiery lake of burning sulphur. That was not something that agreed with Mike. If there was a God, wasn't he supposed to love everyone?

Mike returned to the Google search page and noticed some videos from something called the Bible Project. He played a segment and noticed it was graphically explaining the book. He found the bit on chapters 21 and 22. He saw that this vision of heaven was different from what he expected. He might watch the videos in full later. More likely, he would need to chat with Christina. There was a lot that he read that made no sense. Obviously, he didn't have the context to understand it!

Mike pondered what he actually thought would happen if he died. As a scientist, he'd always tended towards the same view that John had espoused.

He hadn't been that worried about his last flight. Yes, there had been risk, but flights to the ISS had become commonplace. But, a manned mission to the Moon hadn't been completed since 1972. Growing up, his family had been fairly nominal Christian. His mother went to some church things, especially when he was younger, but they rarely went as he got older.

Most of the Christians he had met had insisted that the Earth was only ten thousand years old, which strongly conflicted with the science he had learnt as a geologist. But he quite liked the idea of living forever and not ceasing to exist when he died. But that was a bit hard to align with his scientific training. So, he tended to be agnostic about it all. Mike wondered how Christina reconciled her faith and science.

32

―•―

Saturday, May 4 2024

The final simulation rehearsal was indeed a long day. The test team threw multiple failures for the team to work through on the SLS, the service module and the Orion itself, plus a weather delay. They all could be solved, so they finally launched in their assigned launch window, but it had achieved the object of the test, testing the command and communication capabilities of the whole project team.

Their first weekend of quarantine did not have a lot of scheduled activities. There was some family time scheduled, a medical workup and some time in the gym, but there was still lots of time to rest and relax.

Mike had just returned to his room after his medical check-up when Christina dropped by.

"I'm going out for a run. Do you want to come?" she asked.

"Sure, give me a few minutes to change," Mike replied.

"Ok, I'll meet you in the foyer."

A few minutes later, Mike and Christina met up at the entrance.

"Where were you planning on running?" Mike asked as they stretched.

"I was thinking of running down Linkage and Second Street to Little Joe and coming back between the buildings," said Christina. "That will be about 2 miles."

"Lead the way," said Mike.

Christina led them down Fifth street to Linkage Road, and the heat hadn't started to build up too much. They turned into Second Street, past the Mission Control building, then down to the park housing the Saturn V and Little Joe II, a purpose-built rocket used to test the Apollo capsule abort system.

She then led them back via the parkland in the centre of the campus, slowing down and stopping to stretch at one of the ponds.

"Not too strenuous," said Christina.

"No, barely warmed up," said Mike as he stretched his hamstrings. "I had a look at that Bible passage on heaven the other day."

"You did? Great. What did you think?"

"Well, I can see what you mean about heaven being on earth, but the whole thing was pretty weird and confusing. I'm guessing there's lots of imagery in there."

"Yeah, it probably wasn't the best place to send you to read the bible for the first time. It is a special writing style that uses a lot of symbolism, and you need to understand a lot of the rest of the Bible to make sense of things."

"It got me thinking. How do you reconcile your faith with science? Most Christians I've met in the past believe that the world is only ten thousand years old. I can't believe that. It doesn't fit with the science I've learned."

"I can understand that. And I don't follow the young earth creation theories. I think the Bible was written to tell us about God and why we are here, not how the Earth was created," said Christina.

"So, you don't think the world was created in 6 days?" asked Mike.

"Not necessarily. I think God could have done that, but I think it is more likely that the creation story in the Bible is trying to communicate that God did create man, and He wants a special relationship with us. One that was much different to the way societies around the people of Israel thought at the time Genesis was written."

"So, you don't think Christianity has anything to do with science?" said Mike.

"I wouldn't say that. But I would say that the Bible isn't a science textbook! Lots of scientists have been Christians and investigated the world precisely because the God they see in the Bible is rational, and they wanted to understand how He had designed the world. They expected to be able to understand it. Not all belief systems allow such a concept."

"Hmm, let's continue back before I cool down too much," said Mike.

They started to jog back to the quarantine facility.

"I like the idea of not ceasing to exist when I die," said Mike, "but I'm still not sure about this God thing."

"That's ok," said Christina. "Why don't you read one of the books about Jesus. Maybe the book written by Luke in the Bible. Or watch the Jesus Film, or there's a TV series called The Chosen which presents that material. The Christian view of eternal life is that you need to believe and trust in Jesus to receive it, so you need to understand who he is to do so."

"I'll think about it. Maybe I'll watch something. I'm getting sick of all these manuals I'm reading."

"I know, and memos and briefings, and perpetual reports! I think you'd like The Chosen. It's a drama of the people who met Jesus, so quite different, but very well done."

"Ok, I'm going to have a shower. See you at lunch," said Mike as they arrived at the facility.

33

TUESDAY, MAY 7 2024

Sue placed the final items into her luggage. They would soon drive out to Ellington Field and fly their T-38s to Johnson Space Center. She was looking forward to flying, and the weather was clear, so it should be a nice flight.

Ron was flying with Jessica, Jerome, and Sue's parents on a NASA charter flight later in the day to stay in accommodation near the launch site.

With a week to go before launch, everything was starting to feel very real. Tomorrow would be a full-dress rehearsal right up to the final hold before launch. Her crew seemed to be handling things well, although Mike had seemed a bit more distracted than usual. He had been spending a lot of time talking with Christina. She hoped that there wasn't something more going on there that she might need to deal with during the flight itself. She would chat with John about it and maybe get him to speak with Mike.

Sue zipped up her luggage and checked the room to ensure she hadn't left anything. Then she picked up her bags and headed out to the foyer.

There she met the rest of her crew, and they all piled into a minivan for the 20-minute drive to Ellington Field. The backup crew would follow them.

"I hope everyone is ready to fly," she said.

Everyone nodded.

"It looks like a beautiful day," said John. "Pity there are storms in Florida."

"Not unusual," said Sue. "Christina, you are flying with me."

"Great, time for girl talk!" said Christina.

"Well, Mike, looks like we get to have some special time together," said John.

"Fantastic, I need your advice on eyebrow plucking," said Mike.

"You start talking eyebrows, and I'm pulling G," said John.

The team continued their drive to Ellington Field. They entered the hangar and headed to the offices to receive weather briefings and plan and submit their flight plans.

Forty minutes later, they had donned their flight suits and were heading to check out their aircraft. Their luggage would fly in a Gulfstream with some of the mission team.

Sue and Christina walked to their T-38, and Sue spoke with the crew chief, checking the paperwork and performing a walk-around. Christina climbed up to the rear seat, with the assistance of a crew member, and got herself seated. All the astronauts flew these aircraft regularly, so she was quite familiar with it.

Sue finished her checks and was assisted to the front cockpit seat. They checked their communications and performed their pre-flight checks.

Sue looked across and saw that John in his aircraft was ready, as were the 2 jets for the backup crew. They would fly as 2 flights of 2 aircraft.

"Are you ready to fly?" asked Sue of Christina over the communication circuit.

"Sure am," said Christina.

Sue confirmed that John and the other jets were ready and contacted the tower for clearance. They then taxied out to the runway.

"Are your parents flying out to Florida today?" Sue asked.

"Yes, they are going straight there. In fact, I think they may have landed already. They had an early start," said Christina.

"Mine are on the charter today. I guess you'll be glad to see them, if only from a distance."

"I sure will, although I spent a few days with them a couple of weeks ago, so it hasn't been too long."

"Ok, we are cleared for take-off. Ready?"

"Go."

The first two T-38s proceeded down the runway as a flight, took off, and banked out over the bay heading to the Gulf.

Once they had reached altitude and settled into their flight, Sue said, "You and Mike are spending a lot of time chatting lately."

"Yes. I think that the last simulated full system rehearsal made him think about life a bit. We've been chatting a bit about life, death, heaven, Jesus etc."

"Oh, ok. You don't think he wants to get close to you, then?"

"What, Mike? No."

"He's been known to play around. Trust me."

"I'm sure. I think he was interested once, but he seems much more settled with Lisa these days."

"Hmm, I hope so. You don't think he is spooked, do you?"

"I don't think so. I think that scenario just made things a bit more real. It did for me!"

"That's true. I did have a long chat with Ron that night," said Sue. And she had. That hadn't been the intention of the scenario, but it had really made the whole crew think about the risks of the mission.

Sue became occupied in the process of changing their flight's course and altitude to go around a storm front they were approaching.

Once they had settled back into cruise mode, Christine asked, "How has your family been coping with you being away?"

"Jessica has been pretty good, and she has gone through it before. She is excited about me going to the Moon, and her class has been doing a project on the Lunar mission.

"But it is all new for Jerome, and he misses me, and since he is only four, he doesn't really understand."

"That must be hard," said Christina.

"Yes, but Ron and our parents are helping out a lot."

Unexpectedly, Sue was informed by Air Traffic Control that they would be shortly joined by a flight of four Air Force F/A-18s to escort them on the rest of the flight. A minute later, they were joined by the Air Force jets, two on each side.

Sue was appointed flight leader. However, the Air Force flight leader informed her that they needed to deviate from their flight path and avoid built-up areas. They wanted her to stay out over the ocean and fly around Key West. However, that would have required refuelling, which in turn would have extended their flight time, and they decided to make random course changes as they traversed Florida.

"What on earth is going on?" asked Christina.

"I don't know, but no one is telling us over the air," said Sue. "I gather our security posture has changed. I think I see a mix of anti-aircraft and ground attack weapons loaded on those aircraft. Mind you, they are probably the local alert flight, so it could be just their normal weapon load."

Sue's workload increased as she was flight leader, and Christina took over communications as they flew over the Gulf and then crossed the coast. Air Traffic Control gave them a band of altitudes and cleared a swathe of the state of Florida ahead of them and the other NASA flight. They changed direction every few minutes so that no one could predict their flight track. That was an exercise keeping six aircraft in formation, especially with the different flight characteristics of the two aircraft.

However, they crossed the coast of the Atlantic without incident and flew to Kennedy Space Centre.

As they approached, they noticed numerous military helicopters patrolling around the runway and military vehicles stationed on the ground.

They landed, with the F/A-18s shadowing them to touch down before streaking away from them to land at the nearby military airport. They were greeted on the aircraft apron by yet more armed vehicles, and they were escorted quickly to their waiting minivan.

Sue asked their driver what was going on as they waited for John and Mike to join them.

"Good question," he said. "About half an hour ago, our security status changed, and all these guys appeared. Apparently, you will get a briefing when we get to the Astronaut centre."

John and Mike joined them, and they departed, escorted by armed vehicles.

Arriving at the Astronaut Facility centre, they went to the briefing room where they met by Callum, the Artemis 3 project leader.

"Callum, what is going on?" asked Sue as they entered.

"First of all, I'm glad to say that all of you, the backup crew, and your families are safe," said Callum.

"Just after you left Houston, Intelligence services flagged a credible threat to the Artemis 3 mission. At the same time, NASA noted an increase in cyber-attacks on our facilities. We took immediate action to protect our facilities and the flights of you and your families. The threat also triggered an increased level of readiness by US defence services and, of course, NASA's.

"Your families are safely on the ground and currently being escorted here by the National Guard. We are currently rearranging their accommodation in case they were targets, and the FBI is deploying protective details for them.

"However, just before you landed, we were informed that the current threat appeared to have eased, and a direct attack is now unlikely to occur. Even so, we are reviewing security arrangements and will likely increase our security."

"Are our families aware of what is happening?" asked Mike.

"Yes, to some extent. F/A-16s flying next to their aircraft was a bit of a giveaway! We will be briefing the family liaisons shortly so they will update the families when they arrive at their accommodation," said Callum.

"Were the cyber-attacks successful," asked John.

"We have also noted no compromise of any of our Artemis systems. We did have a problem with one or two public-facing systems," answered Callum.

"Are we still proceeding with the rehearsal?" asked John.

"Yes, but we will mix up the timeline a bit from the published times," said Callum. "We are asking all personnel to be ready to start up to 2 hours earlier. The actual start time will be published internally at 0700 tomorrow. You will be informed at 1900 tonight, but that information is confidential. Your families will depart their accommodation at randomised times earlier than planned.

"Unfortunately, we aren't so easily able to move our launch windows, so we are looking at ways to further reduce security risks for the launch."

"Do we know who is doing this?" asked Christina.

"Not exactly, but we suspect China," said Callum. "Any further questions?"

There were none, so they dispersed to their rooms to unpack.

Sue received a call from Ron

"Hi Sue, are you ok?" he asked.

"Yes, we are fine, just had a bit of extra formation flying practice with the US Air Force," said Sue.

"We are all ok, too. Jessica was really excited to see the jets out the windows and all the fuss we got when we arrived. I don't think she has realised why those things happened."

"Probably better she doesn't know, but there will probably be stuff on the news. It wasn't exactly subtle. Maybe I should have a talk with her."

"Ok, I'll get her," said Ron.

There was a pause, and Sue thought about how to help her daughter understand without frightening her.

"Hi, Mum, have you seen the rocket yet?" said Jessica.

"Hi, darling. We can see it from a distance. We'll get close to it tomorrow. How did you find your flight?" said Sue.

"It was so cool, with fighter jets flying beside us. I thought it might have been you!"

Sue laughed. "No, not this time. We had some fly with us too. The government thought we might need some extra protection."

"Why, Mum? Is someone trying to hurt us?"

"Well, they think someone might want to stop our Lunar mission. Do you remember how during the Apollo era, it was a race between the Soviets and America to get to the Moon first?"

"Yes," said Jessica.

"Well, it is sort of the same thing now. Someone else wants to beat us there," said Sue.

"You mean China," said Jessica.

Hmm, not getting much past this child, Sue thought. "That is one possibility. There are others, such as Russia, India or even countries like North Korea or Iran. We don't know for sure."

"So, will you be safe?" asked Jessica.

"As safe as we can be. Ok?"

"Yes. When will we see you?"

"You'll see me tomorrow morning during the dress rehearsal, and I'll be in my space suit!" said Sue.

"That will be funny."

"Yes, I'll see you then. I love you."

"I love you too, Mum. Bye."

34

—·—

WEDNESDAY, MAY 8 2024

Mike sat in his orange crew survival system suit as technicians sealed up his helmet and began the pressure test to ensure its seals were working correctly. They had started their day about 45 minutes earlier than initially planned. Extra escort vehicles had accompanied them during the drive to the complex, and military helicopters were visibly patrolling the area. Lisa was upset by the extra security measures, but he had managed to calm her down. She was probably waiting for him outside the building with Jasmine to wave to him before they drove out to the launch vehicle.

The rehearsal was an important event. It allowed testing of all the procedures they would use in a week's time during the launch and was designed to show any problems now rather than during the actual launch.

Mike's suit testing was completed, and his helmet was opened and removed. He would carry it to the Orion capsule, where he would again don it.

Mike looked around the white room as he waited for the rest of the crew to finish their leak checks. John had already finished and was chatting with his technician. It was a historic room with astronauts from Gemini, Apollo and Space Shuttle eras and now the Commercial Crew program all going through a similar exercise. Strange to think he'd be making history in a couple of weeks, hopefully walking on the moon. Daunting really.

"Right, folks," said George, their CAPCOM, who was with them for the ride to the spacecraft. "It's time to head out. Remember to smile for the cameras!"

George led the four of them with their technicians out of the preparation room, down a corridor and out to the car park outside, where their families were waiting, watched by a gaggle of media. In a week, this would be the last look their families and the world would have of them, other than via NASA cameras, before returning from the moon three to four weeks later.

They each walked up and stood a couple of metres away from their families. Lisa was holding Jasmine; it was the first time Mike hadn't seen them for a few days.

"Hi, Honey. Are you ok?" said Mike.

"Yes, we're fine. We are being well looked after," said Lisa.

"Great, this is where we get to say meaningful things with the world watching on."

"I know, a bit daunting."

"Yeah," said Mike. "Another reason we do a rehearsal! Look around, get used to it, then it won't be so strange next week!

"Is Jasmine ok?"

"Yes," said Lisa. "She slept ok last night. We are in a suite with my parents, so they are helping to look after her."

"Ok folks, time to go," said George.

"Love you," said Mike, "talk to you tonight."

"Love you too," said Lisa.

Mike turned around and followed Sue and John into the bus, with Christina following behind.

The technicians assisted them into their seats, connecting up their umbilicals to provide cooling. Mike looked out at the mass of media behind the families; this was just a rehearsal! Next time it would be for real. He realised that he needed to think about what he would say to Lisa in a week when they did this for real.

"Right folks, no more press until we come back so you can relax a bit, but there will be cameras on most of the time," said George.

"You are doing a good job, George," said Sue. "Thank you!"

"You are welcome. I'm just disappointed not to be flying with you."

"Are you getting my flight?" asked Mike.

"Still not sure, Mike. Not quite on flight status yet. I suspect it will be a later flight," said George.

"You'll be there for longer then," said Mike.

"True. And probably have less media attention."

The bus started its drive out to the Launch Pad 39B. Soon they were driving next to the massive track on which the crawler moves the SLS and Orion spacecraft. Each time Mike visited Cape Kennedy, he was impressed by its scale. Everything was big. The roads were big. The buildings were big, such as the Vehicle Assembly Building, the world's largest single-storey building. The towers were big. The tanks and storage were big, with systems to dump millions of litres of water on launchpads in seconds. And the rockets were big.

And they were driving out to one of the biggest, the Space Launch System. Just the core stage was 64.6 metres high and 8.4 metres in diameter. Then there were the boosters attached to it, plus the second stage plus the Orion, its service modules and the escape tower on top, being over 111 metres above the ground. The height of a 30-storey building.

The launch vehicle was visible in the distance, next to its service tower.

"There she is", said John.

"It already looks big," said Christina.

Mike noted the helicopters buzzing the area. There were definitely more than usual, and there seemed to be ongoing security concerns.

A few minutes later, they drew up next to the tower at Launch Pad 39B. As Mike exited the bus, he looked up at the rocket. He struggled to see the top. It was a magnificent site. Gantries accessed the smooth white rocket at various levels. The two 17-storey boosters were attached on each side of the core, suspended between them.

"Impressive, isn't it," said George to Mike.

"Sure is," said Mike, still staring at the launch vehicle.

"Ok, guys," said George to the crew. "I'll head back to the control room. Time for you to ride on up to the Orion. Talk to you soon. Have a good day."

George turned back to the bus. The rest of them, with their technicians, walked to the tower lift that would carry them to the top. They had all ridden the elevator or a similar one in the past. The wire netting surround let the occupants view the environs and the rocket as they ascended. Despite the wide view around them, today, the crew was focused on the SLS in front of them. In a week, it would already be partially fuelled, with vapours escaping and systems running. Today it was relatively quiet. There was no need to risk loading fuel, just to offload it again, so the rehearsal was 'dry'.

Mike watched the different components pass as the lift climbed the 30 storeys. The 5 segments of the solid boosters. The long vast body of the core booster seemed to go on forever. Then the Launch Vehicle Stage Adapter narrowed the diameter of the vehicle. The second propulsion stage passed them, another adapter, the Orion service module, and finally, they arrived at the Orion crew module with the launch abort system on top.

The door opened, and the crew and technicians exited and walked down the gantry to the Orion, in order, with Sue leading, followed by John, Mike, and finally, Christina. They had practised this procedure many times, so they were very familiar with the process of getting into their seats, so it was not long until Mike was in his, lying on his back in his seat. He was in a sitting position, even though he was on his back, and his legs were supported. He was beside Christina and below the commander, Sue.

It was an odd position to be in, but the team had been fully briefed on the reasons for the strange orientation. The main reason was safety. The position best protected the crew in the event of a rough landing, especially their backs. Astronauts' spines lengthened during zero-G, and additional care had been taken to protect them during re-entry. Being in a sitting position was close to the position the human body naturally assumes in zero-G.

Mike took some deep breaths and relaxed as the technician strapped him in and connected his umbilical supplying cooling, air and fluids. The suit he was in could protect him and keep him alive for up to six days in an emergency.

"Commander to crew, comm check," said Sue over the communications in Mike's ear.

"Pilot, check. I read you 5 by 5," said John.

"Mission 1, check," said Mike.

"Mission 2, check," said Christina.

"Reading you all 5 by 5," said Sue. "Orion, CAPCOM, Comms check."

"CAPCOM, Orion, reading you 5 by 5," said George in the control room.

"Orion copies, reading you 5 by 5 also. We are in our seats and ready for hatch closure."

"CAPCOM copies you, Orion. Stand by."

Mike could relax now. He and Christina had very little to do until they left the capsule again. It was all Sue and John's show today.

He looked around. They had not had much time in the actual flight vehicle. Everything appeared to be in the same position as the trainer mock-up, at least all the items with which he might need to interact.

Mike took out his tablet to read as he listened to the rehearsal proceed. So many of the systems were automated that even Sue and John didn't have much to do. However, they did have to follow along with the checklists. He thought about his own personal checklists that he needed to complete before the launch in a week.

The most important items on his list revolved around his family. Making sure Lisa and Jasmine were okay and that his parents and other family were prepared. He was also thinking about what would happen if things went wrong. It was probably a bit late to start thinking about what would happen if he died. There had been philosophical discussions during their early training, as well as occasional talks with NASA psychologists during regular check-ups, but for some reason, he hadn't really thought that deeply about it until the last few weeks. So that was the topic of his reading material.

He was also concerned about Jasmine. Medical tests suggested that she did indeed have some sort of hyper-mobility issue. It was difficult to tell because she still was so young. Mike was concerned that she might have problems later in life and that she might have inherited the condition from him, although none of his immediate family had such issues. It was odd that Sue's son had something similar. Maybe it was an environmental thing.

Mike was reading when he heard the call on the Communications channel.

"CAPCOM, Orion. BUZZARD."

"Orion copies, BUZZARD," said John.

They all acted immediately and closed their helmets, putting their suits into pressurized mode.

"CAPCOM, Orion, abort system armed. This is not a drill."

"Orion copies abort system armed."

What the hell is going on, thought Mike. BUZZARD was the mission's emergency alert code. For the escape system to be armed without the core being fuelled was unusual. It meant that there was some threat that might require them to be evacuated using the launch abort system.

Mike looked at his tablet and switched to a mission communications page used to communicate details too complex for the communications channel. There was a post about a security threat.

"Sue, check your communications page," said Mike.

There had been multiple breaches of the air and sea exclusion zone around the launch site. Security forces were dealing with them, with lethal force authorised.

"Looks like our friends are trying to play with us again," said John.

They had just come to a Go/No Go decision in the rehearsal countdown, and the Range controller had to say No, which put the count into a hold. They had a nominal 2-hour launch window, so the issue should be able to be resolved. It was concerning that there had been such incidents two days in a row.

"Is everything else nominal?" asked Mike.

"Yes, everything was proceeding very smoothly. There's a storm cell on the radar, but we are still in acceptable launch parameters," said Sue.

"What is the point of this?" asked Christina. "Do they really want to actually stop us or just harass us?"

"I don't know," said John. "Harassment seems most likely, although it sounds like that has gone to the next level today."

"Maybe they are probing us to see what our responses will be," said Sue.

"Could be," said John.

"CAPCOM, Orion, Range intrusions have been turned back or neutralised. We have some search and rescue going on in the range, so we will continue to hold in BUZZARD for at least 30 minutes."

"Orion copies, thanks."

"Hmm, neutralised, with search and rescue. That got real serious," said Mike.

"Sounds like it," said John.

"I guess we'll be on the news for all the wrong reasons," said Christina.

"Yeah, well, sounds like we can relax for a bit," said Sue.

Right, thought Mike. Relax in a pressurised suit with my feet above my head. He took a sip from his drink straw. He didn't want to be in here any longer than he needed to. It was comfortable enough, he thought, but not relaxing.

35

—·—

Sue checked the system status. They were still in the hold period during the rehearsal, and the abort system was still armed. She consulted her tablet and checked the communications page. The search and rescue operation was continuing.

"Orion, CAPCOM," she called on the communication channel, "are we cleared yet to stand down from BUZZARD?'

"Negative, Sue, not until the range is clear. Shouldn't be too much longer," said George as CAPCOM.

"Is everyone doing ok?" Sue asked the crew. All replied in the affirmative.

The security threats were unnerving. They had trained endlessly for system failures and risks relating to the mission. There wasn't much they could do about external security threats, so there hadn't been much training about that. She realised that she should raise that in the event debrief and made a note on her tablet.

Sue didn't have a plan for this scenario, and that was stressful. The organisation did appear to have plans that were being activated. Still, she wasn't sure whether this was just good planning for possible risks during a range incursion or a broader security strategy.

So, she was worried for herself, the crew and the mission. Added to this, she was worried about the safety of her family. They were all on the site right now if something were to happen. Sure, they were a distance away, but still in range of an attack.

Sue hadn't really considered something happening to Ron, Jessica and Jerome. She was the one with the high-risk job, and they'd talked about the possibility of her not returning. This was different.

And she couldn't even give them a hug.

A tear rolled down the side of her face into her ear.

Crying in a sealed space suit wasn't ideal. She blinked her tears away.

Sue noted something else for the debrief – additional counselling and more time with family.

"CAPCOM, Orion, you can stand down from BUZZARD."

"Orion copies that, thanks," replied Sue.

"Thought you'd like that," continued George. "Just letting you know that all personnel and visitors are safe and well. We'll be lifting the hold in 2 minutes."

"Copy," said Sue as she opened her helmet. To her crew, "so did everyone copy that you can open your helmets, and I can see that the abort system has been disarmed."

A chorus of copy followed, and the crew settled back into the rehearsal. With the resumption of the countdown, Sue and John would once again be more occupied with their checklists.

36

TUESDAY, MAY 14 2024

After the rehearsal, the crew were given more opportunities to spend time with their families, which they appreciated.

No country claimed responsibility for the range intrusions, although everyone assumed it was China. The military presence around Cape Canaveral increased, and more US Navy ships were moved to the area and even into the Atlantic along their expected ground track.

It happened early in the morning. A satellite in low earth orbit exploded, damaging a dozen nearby satellites. Most of them were communication or earth observation satellites.

The purpose of destroying them was unclear. There was, of course, an apology from the Chinese owners. They claimed that there had been a power supply disruption which led to an explosion of their fuel supply. Experts thought this was unlikely siting that the fuels used aren't known to be explosive.

Mike waved at Lisa as she walked towards him. She was holding Jasmine. Mike sat at an outdoor table at the Astronaut's accommodation, and Lisa sat opposite him. They were allowed to sit opposite each other but not to touch or get too close to avoid infecting Mike with anything.

"Hi, how are you?" asked Mike.

"Good. Jasmine's been sleeping well, so I feel human," said Lisa.

"Great, she looks well."

'Yep, she just had a feed, so she will probably sleep. Are you ready for tomorrow?"

"Pretty much, as long as both of you are safe," said Mike.

"Are they expecting any more problems?" asked Lisa.

"Not really, but who can tell. Do you feel safe?"

"Yes, they are moving us again today, which is a bit of a pain, but they say we'll stay at the next place for a week or so."

"I guess that makes sense. I'm sorry about this. I didn't expect you guys to be at risk."

"It's not your fault, Mike. Who would have thought someone would want to stop a launch to the Moon?"

"I know, it's nuts. But access to resources on the Moon and having a presence there is seen as very strategic. Some countries want to make sure they are there and there early. Heck, isn't that why we are going?"

"What about exploration?" asked Lisa.

"Well, we're exploring to gain access to resources, even if those resources are so we can be on the Moon long term. It's all about resources, as has been the case on Earth forever. Obviously, someone, probably China, but it could also be India or Russia, don't want us there."

"Should we leave?" asked Lisa.

"You are probably just as safe here. They would have to give you protection if you went home, anyway," said Mike.

"I can't believe this is happening," said Lisa, crying.

"I know. I'm sorry," said Mike, reaching across to hold her hand. "We'll be ok.

"On the bright side, everything is going really well with the mission itself."

"Well, that's good," said Lisa, drying her eyes. "Are you ready?"

"As much as I can be. What do you think happens when we die?"

"Ah," gasped Lisa, startled by this leap of thought. "Umm, I don't know. We go to heaven?"

"Why? And what does that mean?"

"I don't know, I haven't thought about it much. That's where good people go when they die. It's a nice place."

"But are we good people?"

"Yes, of course we are. We aren't murderers, or thieves, or idiots terrorising astronauts!"

"I don't know if we are good enough. Both Buddhism and Hinduism say it is really hard to get to nirvana. Now I've looked into it; it seems even Christianity says that being good isn't enough to get to heaven."

"What are you saying, Mike?" asked Lisa angrily, "Are you saying if you die up there, we won't see you again, even in heaven?"

"Maybe."

"That's nuts! Of course, we will meet again in heaven. That's what everyone says."

"What? Couldn't there just be nothing? That's the atheist view."

"Why do you bring this up now, Mike?"

"I'm sorry to upset you. We had a simulation last week where we failed. Sue and I would have died. It got me thinking, and I've been chatting with Christina a bit about it. I don't think I'm ready to die."

"You're not going to die, Mike."

"I might. There is a reasonable possibility of me not returning from this trip alive."

"We knew that. That hasn't changed. What's changed is I'm not so sure what will happen when I die. I used to think nothing happened, but then I wasn't particularly focused on the issue!"

Lisa took a deep breath. "Ok, so you are thinking about the meaning of life. I guess I can understand that."

"I know it's a bit late. I'll send you links to some of the stuff I've been reading and watching. Maybe that will help you to know where I'm coming from."

"Ok," said Lisa. "I'll have a look at them."

"Something else that concerns me is Jasmine and that she might have inherited something from me."

"I think she's going to be fine," said Lisa.

"I hope so, and I know if she does have something, it won't be an issue until she is older, but still, it is worrying."

"I was talking to Ron the other day about their son Jerome. He says it gets easier as you get used to the idea as time goes on. It's strange that Jerome and Jasmine both seem to have something similar."

"Yeah, weird. Maybe it is something environmental, or maybe it is just more common than you think."

"Maybe you should chat to Sue about her experience."

"Probably," said Mike.

They spent another twenty minutes talking about family and what they had been up to. When the time came for Lisa and Jasmine to leave, Mike was able to kiss and hug them briefly.

37

Meanwhile, in another part of the gardens surrounding the house, Sue was meeting up with Ron, Jessica and Jerome at another table. She hugged and kissed them all, and the children excitedly told her about their adventures on the Space Coast.

"Hey, kids," said Ron, "why don't you play next to us here for a bit while our Mum and I talk."

"How are you feeling?" Ron asked Sue.

"Good, although I still worry about you guys being safe."

"We are fine. They are looking after us well. They are even moving us today. I don't even know where."

"I always knew I was taking risks, but I never expected it to put my family in harm's way."

"Hey, Sue. It's ok. I don't think they want to harm us. They just don't want you to get to the Moon before them."

"I know, and the failure of the recent Chinese mission doesn't help. At least their crew is safe," said Sue.

"We never trained for attacks on our mission. That was pretty naïve, wasn't it?"

"Idealistic, maybe."

"Is everyone coping ok?"

"We are fine. We just have some extra escorts. The kids don't even notice."

"That's good. And my folks aren't worried?"

"No, not really. They are more worried about the mission itself."

"Mum, are you excited to be going to the Moon," asked Jessica.

"Yes, I am. Nobody has walked on the moon since 1972, that 52 years ago."

"That's a long time. That was Apollo 17, wasn't it."

"Yes, it was, honey. In a week or so, I'll be able to look down and see their landing site."

"Are you going to be safe?"

"I think so. We are doing the best we can to be safe," said Sue.

"But it is dangerous," said Jessica.

"Yes, but so is climbing up a cliff face or diving to the bottom of the ocean. But we manage the risks."

"I want you to come back, Mum."

"I will, and I'll bring you a moon rock."

Jessica's eyes almost exploded in excitement.

38

WEDNESDAY, MAY 15 2024

Sue settled back into her chair in the Orion capsule. The events of a week ago had been repeated, but this time her comments to Ron and their children were more sincere. She had paid extra attention during the pressure checks and smiled extra hard at the cameras. No longer was this practice or training. This was the real deal. She was leading the next manned mission to land on the moon!

She looked across to see John being assisted into his seat. It would take about twenty minutes to get everyone seated and cabled in. During that time, she would review briefing documents and the general status screen until John was ready, and then they would start working on checklists. In fact, they would be running checklists until they exited this capsule back on earth in 4 weeks. Even when they were sleeping!

She looked out her windows. Both John and her had windows they could use for navigation if required. The sky was bright Florida Blue, with a few clouds. The scheduled launch was at 1130, so before the afternoon thunderstorms began. This had meant an early morning for the crew, but that was ok, as most would have had trouble sleeping. They'd had the traditional NASA astronaut breakfast of whatever they wanted, but most had kept it simple. No one on this flight was a rookie.

Sue watched a chopper pass by the launch pad, and she could see a flight of fighters orbiting the area. That was different from her last launch. Last time there had been security, but this time they were almost on a war footing. The number of visitors had been culled, and those who had come had been thoroughly checked.

She heard Mike being helped into his chair, and she turned to her tablet and reviewed the briefing documents. She looked across at John in his bright orange survival suit. He was still sorting out his work area and making himself comfortable. Everything had to go in the right place and be properly secured to be accessible when needed. It would be no use if it had fallen to the back of the spacecraft or was floating out of reach.

There was nothing unexpected in the briefing. The weather was still looking good, and a couple of minor technical issues were being worked. The security threat hadn't changed markedly, there were a couple of extra VIPs who had decided to attend at the last minute, and a couple of members of the mission control shift had called in sick and were being replaced. Nothing remarkable.

"Sue, you ready?" asked John.

"Sure, I am just reading the latest briefing," said Sue, swiping her tablet to display checklist 1 dot 0. "Nothing unusual in the latest briefing. The weather is still fine. There are a couple of minor fuelling hiccups, but nothing that should be a problem. And a couple of guys on the mission control shift called in sick."

"Ok, so the president didn't come?"

"No. She's not quite as enthusiastic as the last one for the mission. But the VP is here."

"I'm surprised we didn't see him when suiting up," said John.

"Ok, let me clarify, 'will be here'. He arrives in about twenty minutes.

"Mike, are you with us?"

"Yep, but I'm still getting settled. Christina is coming in now."

"Ok, thanks," said Sue. "John, let's start 1 dot 0."

Sue toggled the switch that enabled communication to launch control. "Launch control, this is Orion. How do you read?"

"Orion, Launch control, reading you 5 by 5. Good morning. What's your status?"

"Command and Pilot operational, starting checklist 1 dot 0," said Sue.

"Copy that. Mission Control, how do you read Orion?"

"Launch Control, this is Mission Control, reading you and Orion loud and clear. We are ready to start checklist 1.0 on the mission to place the first woman and the next man on the Moon."

Sue sighed. She was going to keep hearing that phrase a lot. Mission Control statements were often carefully crafted as much for public consumption as for managing the missions. All the communications were live-streamed on NASA TV. They'd even practised some of the statements in simulations.

"Hi all, I'm plugged in now," said Christina on the internal communications channel.

"Great," said Sue. "You and Mike continue to get settled back there, and we'll proceed with 1 dot 1."

Most of John and Sue's activities were simply monitoring steps. Occasionally they initiated actions on board, but so much was automated or managed by mission control. With their helmets still open, they could occasionally hear systems in the spacecraft being initiated. The life support systems were now being activated prior to the hatch closure. From then on, they would rely on the Orion's systems and service module to provide all they needed to live for the next 4 weeks.

As Sue and John worked on their checklist, Mike started to relax in his seat. He had finished getting settled, and he'd checked that his tablet was working and that his survival suit was correctly connected to the Orion systems. Until they reached orbit, he and Christine were basically along for the ride. They had no access to controls from their seats, and all they could access were their own suits. Their tablets and snacks were stowed in their pockets, and they could access drinks from the suit's drinking straw.

Mike took a deep breath and sighed. It had been an early and busy morning, and the NASA traditions had been followed, starting with the astronaut breakfast. He'd kept it simple with eggs and bacon and a juice. He would have loved a steak but knew he would regret it later.

Lisa and Jasmine had been joined by his parents to farewell him as they exited the suit room for their walk to the bus. They'd all wished him well, and they had exchanged greetings of love. It was frustrating to stand just 2 metres away from Lisa and Jasmine and not to be able to hug and kiss them, but protocols were protocols. They couldn't risk the crew getting sick on their four week voyage.

Now, here they were, literally sitting on top of a bomb. Around 1100 tonnes of liquid hydrogen and oxygen were below them, plus two boosters, each with 630 tonnes of solid propellant. Time to close the hatch in case they had to get out of here in a hurry!

"Hatch sealed, arming escape system," said Sue.

Well, at least they could get away now, thought Mike. But now they had 4 weeks locked in the same tin can, well, this one and the lander.

Mike glimpsed out of Sue's windows as a helicopter flew past. He had a very limited view from his position. He could also see a bit out of the pilot's windows, and the crew ingress hatch had a small window in it as well, but that currently opened into the same access arm they had walked along to enter the Orion capsule.

He pulled out his tablet and started reading. He had a good hour before anything interesting was expected to happen. After the intrusion into the exclusion zone during the rehearsal, the exclusion zone itself had been expanded, and the US Navy and Air Force patrolled those areas. Of course, this led to more intrusions as boats and planes wandered into normally legal areas. They usually turned around when greeted by military force!

39

Mike was startled by the call on the communications circuit. He'd actually fallen asleep. That had happened occasionally during a few simulations in the Orion.

"... T minus 30. Go for item 3 dot 2."

"Copy 3 dot 2," said Sue on the communications.

"Mike, you are back with us," said John.

"I guess I didn't get as much sleep as I thought," said Mike.

"That's fine. It's not like there's anything for you to do. Hey, I'm bored!" said John.

"Well, things are starting to pick up now," said Sue. "They are fuelling stage 2 and the service module."

"Was it this noisy in here last week?" asked Christina.

"There are a few more noises, and I suspect that relates to fuelling. The internal sounds seem to be about the same," said Sue.

"Sounds pretty similar to the SpaceX Falcon sounds, so I guess so," said Mike, stretching in his chair.

"Anything interesting happen while I was dozing?"

"No," said Sue.

Sue and John then got occupied with their checklists, with Mike and Christina following them.

All but two of the connecting arms from the tower had been withdrawn, and the remaining ones were topping off fuel levels.

Mike took some deep breaths to relax. So many things had to go right to get them to the Moon. But then all the redundancy and testing reduced that risk. They were only the second crew to fly on top of an SLS stack. These were built from leftover components from the space shuttle era, so many of the components had a verified safety history. This was only the third launch of an SLS and only the second with people on board.

He wondered how Lisa and his family were coping. At least there didn't seem to be any significant security threats today.

Mike checked his tablet. The briefings looked normal. He noticed new emails and quickly scanned the index. Seeing one from Lisa, he opened it.

Hi Mike,

Just a quick note as we watch the launch. All looks good. Our parents are excited, and the liaison is keeping us well-informed. It is so exciting.

Stay safe, my love.

Love, Lisa.

Mike quickly wrote a reply

Lisa,

All good here too. Even had a snooze!

Give Jasmine a hug, and my parents too!

I love you and Jasmine so much.

Mike.

40

—·—

Sue looked out through the window through which sunlight was pouring.

One minute.

A beautiful day, so there were no local weather problems, although they expected some winds around 30,000 feet.

She went back to scanning instruments. Everything was automated, and there wasn't much that she or John could actually do at this stage of the flight. The most important function they could perform would be to initiate an abort. Even then, it was more likely that automated systems would detect a life-threatening issue before they could and trigger it before they even knew what was happening.

"Everyone all secure and ready with shields down?" she asked the crew.

"Yes," said John.

"Yes," said Mike.

"Yes," said Christina.

"Orion. CAPCOM. Crew secure and ready for launch," said Sue.

"Orion, copy. God's speed."

The crew could not hear the flight control loop, so their only knowledge of what was going on came from CAPCOM.

"CAPCOM, Orion, T minus 30, you are Go."

"Copy, Go for launch," responded Sue.

"John, are you still happy with the vehicle," Sue asked.

"Affirmative. Everything is in the green," said John.

Sue changed her display to show data relating to the SLS stack, while John had Orion systems and the flight profile displayed.

Sue took a deep breath. Everything still looked ok.

"Ok, folks, here we go. Christina, you got a prayer?" said Sue.

"Jesus, keep us safe through the fire," said Christina.

"10 seconds," said CAPCOM over the communications channel.

"You have control," she said.

"I have control," said John.

They felt vibrations start as turbines spun up a hundred meters below them and a muffled boom as the engines ignited.

The shaking increased, and then she felt a push into her seat as they started their ascent.

Sue continued to scan the displays, keeping her hands not far from the abort lever. John might have notional control, but either of them could abort.

"Tower cleared," said CAPCOM.

The vibrations and noise levels increased as the stack gained speed and climbed. The velocity slowly increased as the amount of fuel burnt off.

It was definitely a lively ride as Sue felt the rocket rebalancing, and she noted the gimbal angles of the rocket engines.

The roar of the rocket engines diminished as she felt the vehicle roll. The roar of the atmosphere against the outside of the capsule began to be the dominant noise as they pushed through the dense atmosphere.

The craft began to pitch over to speed them into orbit. It wasn't just a matter of getting them up high in altitude; they also needed to gain speed to get into orbit.

"Max Q," came the call from CAPCOM.

The noise of the wind and the shaking of the craft increased as they passed through the zone of maximum dynamic pressure on the craft.

"Status?" requested Sue.

"Everything is nominal," said John.

The wind noise continued to increase as they sped towards space. Sue was glad to note that the vibrations had decreased.

"Standby for booster separation," said John.

"Booster separation," came the call from CAPCOM seconds later.

Sue was pushed further into her seat as the four RS-24 main engines in the core stage throttled up. She ran her mental checklist of all she needed to be concerned about. The SLS was operating normally, their trajectory was nominal, the Orion and its service module were performing normally, and all the crew were ok. She was about to lose the Launch Abort System. Any aborts after this would be from some sort of orbit.

"John, you OK for LAS jettison," she asked.

"Yes," said John as he concentrated on his displays.

They didn't have to do anything. The jettison would just happen.

"LAS jettison," came the call from CAPCOM. Now, if something went wrong, the AJ10 rocket in the European Service Module and control thrusters would separate them from the core stage, and they would either land in Europe or enter an orbit and then splash down in the Pacific Ocean.

The ride was smoother now, and the noise level reduced as the atmosphere thinned out. Time to check on the crew.

"Mike and Christina, all ok with you guys?"

"Beautiful massage," grunted Mike.

"Wonderful," said Christina.

Nobody liked speaking much under multiple G, and they didn't have the benefit of the G suits they would typically wear in a fighter jet, but then the forces weren't as great either.

"We've got about 4 minutes to MECO," said John. MECO was Main Engine Cutoff. The performance of the rocket system improved as they approached MECO, so their highest g-force of around 4g would be felt at that time.

Sue switched her display to show the Interim Cryogenic Propulsion Stage (ICPS) status. It all looked good, and it would be the next stage to fire to perform the Trans Lunar Injection.

"The ICPS looks good," said Sue. "How's everything looking, John."

"Everything is right on target. All our systems are green. We are still Go."

"Orion, CAPCOM. All is looking good here," Sue reported on the communications.

"Copy that, Orion. We also see everything as nominal. Just on 2 minutes to MECO."

"Roger," replied Sue.

A couple of minutes later, Sue warned the crew, "MECO, followed by separation, this might be a bit of a slam."

The noise from the engines reduced even further and the g-force diminished as the engines throttled back.

"MECO," came the call from CAPCOM, just as the charges fired to separate the Core stage from the ICPS and Orion, slamming the crew hard into their chairs.

"Yep, that's like being hit in the back with a baseball bat," said Mike, recalling comments made by NASA Astronaut Bob Behnken after the first crewed launch of the SpaceX Crew Dragon in 2020.

"CAPCOM, Orion. Welcome to orbit. Go ahead and open your visors."

"Roger, Wilco," said Sue on the communications.

All the members opened their visors.

"Wow, that was wild," said Mike.

"Yes, it was quite lively," said John.

"Noisier than I expected," said Christina.

"I'm happy it went so well. So, we have 15 minutes until the next burn.

41

An hour and a half later, Mike once again strapped himself into his seat. They'd spent the time since launch checking systems and some critical supplies. It had been their first time in the Orion in zero-G, and they were only the second crew to fly in one. Although there was almost twice as much volume than the Apollo Capsules, they were still relatively confined. Four people living for 4 weeks in a moderate-sized bedroom!

They were coming up on the next major burn, the Trans Lunar Injection burn, which would raise their orbit's apogee towards the moon. It would then only take a smaller burn using the Orion's service module rocket to enter into their lunar orbit. Then they just needed to rendezvous with the lander, transfer to it and descend to the surface, wander around there for a week, launch back up into orbit, rendezvous again with the Orion and then leave orbit and head back to Earth. Nothing to it, really!

Mike relaxed in his chair and drank from his suit's drinking straw. The last 45 minutes had been busy as he and Christina checked out the supplies. They didn't want to put themselves on a week-long return orbit only to discover that their food supply had somehow spoilt or that the toilet wasn't working. Of course, there were contingencies in place if either of those things did happen, but no one wanted to start the journey without confirming all these things were ok.

"How are you feeling?" Mike asked Christina.

"Pretty good, considering we were just doing somersaults and hanging upside down checking out stuff," she said.

"I know what you mean. I actually feel worse now I'm strapped in than free-floating," said Mike. He assumed that he had somehow adjusted to the movement he perceived when the fluid in his inner ear moved, whereas he could not move so easily when strapped in. However, he also knew that after a couple of days, his brain would ignore those signals, and he would no longer feel dizzy.

Mike looked out the windows in front of Sue. He could make out the Earth below in their current orientation. It looked beautiful. It also seemed to be growing bigger. Actually, it was growing more prominent as they fell towards it. The Orion was in a highly elliptical orbit with quite a high apogee (highest point) and a low perigee (closest point), and the upcoming burn would significantly raise that apogee.

Retrieving his tablet from his suit leg pocket, Mike checked his emails. Seeing one from Lisa, he opened it. There was a spectacular photo of the launch of the SLS, with Lisa and his parents watching the launch. It had clearly been taken by a professional.

Hi Mike,

Watching the launch was amazing. This photo almost captures it! We are all so proud of you and the team. Have a great trip.

Love, Lisa and Jasmine.

He quickly found a photo that he had taken not long after they had left their seats. It showed one of Earth's oceans glistening in the sunlight draped with white clouds.

He emailed it to Lisa.

Lisa

Looking forward to spending some time with you on the ocean like this when we return. I booked us a cruise on the Caribbean a month after I return. Nothing to do but eat, party and be tourists. Surprise!

Love Mike.

"CAPCOM for Orion. 30 seconds until manoeuvre," came the call on the Communications system.

"Everyone ready as we re-orientate before the burn?" asked Sue.

Everyone replied in the affirmative.

"Copy that Ground. We are ready," said Sue on the communications channel.

Seconds later, they heard the jets fire causing the vehicle to change orientation, ready for the next burn. They were on the end of a reasonably long stick, with the Orion Capsule at the top, followed by their 4-metre-long service module based on the European Automated Transfer Vehicle. It was mated to the 5-metre-long Interim Cryogenic Propulsion Stage, essentially the upper stage of a Delta IV. So, the spacecraft was about 13 metres long. That stick had to be correctly oriented so they would be heading for the moon when the ICPS main engine fired again.

Mike watched as John and Sue checked the displays in front of them, ensuring everything was as expected. They looked calm and practised.

Sue looked down the checklist. They had about five minutes until the Trans Lunar Injection (TLI). She took a deep breath as she felt the tension in her stomach. If something went wrong with this burn, it would be at least 2 days before they would return to earth. They were about to be only the second group of humans to leave Low Earth Orbit since the days of Apollo, and only the Artemis 2 crew had proceeded them.

"Ok guys," she said to her crew mates. "Has anyone got any concerns?"

"Oh no, I forgot my bird!" said Christina, deadpan.

"Don't worry, CAPCOM will look after it," said Mike, recognising the Space Force show reference. They all laughed.

"It all looks good to me," said John.

"Lead us on, Sue," said Christina.

"CAPCOM, Orion, please close your visors," they head on the communications circuit.

"Copy that, CAPCOM," said Sue in reply.

The crew all closed up their helmets and reported their status to Sue.

She noted John working through the pre-TLI checklist. Once everyone's visors were closed, she reported the fact to CAPCOM.

Was there anything she had missed? Were they ready? All she could do was trust that the thousands of people involved in the Project at NASA and ESA had done their jobs well. She hoped that was enough.

What the hell, she thought. It couldn't hurt. "Christina, got a TLI prayer?" she said.

"Sure," said Christina. "Jesus, thanks for the NASA team that got us this far. Keep us safe as we go check out your creation of the Moon."

"Amen," said Mike, which surprised Sue.

"Orion, you are go for TLI," said the CAPCOM.

"Copy that, George. We'll be back for our sail on Independence day."

"Sure thing. I'll stock up the galley. God's speed," said George as CAPCOM.

"30 seconds," said John.

Sue and John worked through the final checklist together, ensuring they were ready, knowing full well that Mission Control was seeing the same data.

The thrusters on the ICPS were now firing regularly to ensure the fuel stayed in the lower end of the tanks and was pressurised.

"We are go for TLI," said Sue on the communications channel.

They didn't need to actually command anything, and they only needed to take control in the case of an emergency.

"Sit back and relax, everyone," she said. Putting her head back against her headrest in preparation for the increase in g-force.

"5, 4, 3, 2, 1, ignition," called John.

Sue felt the g-force increase and push her into her seat. It was quite a pleasant feeling after the last reasonably short period of weightlessness. She watched the display and monitored the control jet firings that kept the stack pointing in the right direction.

So far, so good, but she would wait until the end of the burn to celebrate. The problem with simulating endless failure scenarios is that they all passed through her mind as options as their time approached.

"Primary Injection pump pressures dropping. We have switched to secondary," said John.

Ok, thought Sue, that's not great, but survivable. "Well, that's why we have backups," she said.

"Orion, we see reduced pressures on the primary injection pump, with the secondary in use. We are still go with that, and trajectory is nominal," said CAPCOM.

"Roger, we saw that too," said Sue on the communications channel.

"Anything else looking off?" Sue asked John.

"A couple of thrusters on the ICPS aren't quite performing in spec, but the Orion thrusters are being used to compensate," said John.

"Hmm, that's two strikes for the ICPS. It is its last flight!" said Sue. "Let me know if anything else causes an issue."

The next Artemis flight would use the Exploration Upper Stage instead of the ICPS, with improved performance and new hardware.

The rest of the TLI burn proceeded without incident.

"Burn complete, standby for stage separate," said John.

Sue braced herself. Stage separations were relatively violent, with charges forcing the Orion vehicle and the ICPS apart.

"Burn data looks good, and your trajectory is nominal," reported CAPCOM.

The separation charges fired, and once again, Sue felt like she'd been hit in the back with a baseball bat.

"Looks like good separation," said John. "The ICPS is adjusting its orbit slightly as expected".

The ICPS would fly with them to the moon, launching several CubeSats during its orbit and then entering into an orbit around the sun after passing by the moon.

"Orion, you are cleared for post-burn activities and preparation for rest," said CAPCOM.

"Roger that. We are looking forward to some dinner and sleep," said Sue on the communications.

"Ok, guys, time to go through the post-burn checklists and get this cabin ready for dinner and sleep," said Sue.

They all opened their visors and started unbuckling their restraints. The next hour would seem them remove their survival suits, disassemble their chairs and stow them to make the best use of the cabin space.

42

— ◆ —

THURSDAY, MAY 16, 2024

Sue woke up early in her sleeping bag suspended in the Orion Capsule. It was a strange feeling to be weightless, and she was momentarily disorientated. She checked her watch. Only about half an hour before their scheduled wake-up. Not too bad.

She looked up at the displays above her. No alarms were displayed, and it had been configured to be minimally distracting during their sleep period, so only essential information was shown. She quietly pulled out her tablet from where she had stowed it on charge. She checked her messages, and there were a lot! But nothing marked urgent, which was good.

Sue opened an email from Ron, which included photos of him with Jessica and Jerome watching the launch. He said they had all had a great time, and Jessica was excited to have a mum going to the Moon. There had been no more security problems, and they had finally got back to the hotel and got some sleep.

She replied that she had slept okay and all was going well and included a selfie she had taken out the window with the Earth in the background.

Scanning the other emails, she noted a security briefing update and opened it. It reported some attempted breaches of exclusion zones during the launch. Most appeared to be harmless, but two, in particular, were of concern. A security review of workers who had been at NASA sites during the last 6 months had also revealed several suspicious workers who had worked in assembly areas. One had associations with suspects from other incidents. The particular pieces of flight hardware involved included the ICPS and the Lunar Lander. Sue wondered if the issues with the ICPS were actually the result of sabotage, although they weren't very successful. It was concerning that the Lunar Lander might have problems. However, that was still a few days away.

Sue noticed Christina had also woken up. She smiled at her, and Christina smiled back and gave her a thumbs-up. There was still a little while until the official wake-up music, so she would let the others sleep.

Checking her schedule for the day, she saw that she had the first exercise session for the day not long after breakfast. It was going to be interesting to see how well the four of them were going to be able to work in the volume of the Orion capsule. They had some maintenance tasks to perform, but few scientific tasks, and they weren't going to be overly busy during their transit time. Keeping people from becoming bored while living on top of each other was going to be a real issue that Sue would have to manage over the coming weeks.

Suddenly "Together" by King and Country started playing on the vehicle's speakers. It was one of Christina's song choices. Mike and John started to stir while Sue and Christina got out of their sleeping bags and began rolling them up and stowing them.

"How'd you sleep, Christina?" asked Sue.

"Pretty good, thanks, until Mike started snoring!" replied Christina.

"I don't snore," said Mike as he started to unzip his bag.

"Well, you do in space," said Sue.

"And you have this cute little warble at the end of your breath," said John.

"Now I know I don't snore," said Mike. "I slept really well. Are we ready for breakfast yet?"

"Well, once everyone has had their hygiene break and we've stowed everything, John and I need to run a system check, and while we are doing that, you and Christina can cook breakfast!" said Sue. "So, excuse me while I visit the waste extraction facility."

It was one of the significant compromises in the capsule. While they did have a small cubicle for the space toilet, there wasn't a tremendous amount of volume and not much privacy, especially if the exercise equipment, located next to it, was in use. Their current plan was to use a couple of the sleep bags strung across the capsule to create a barrier to separate the toilet and exercise area from the rest of the cabin. The crew rearranged two sleep bags into this arrangement and stowed the others.

Thirty minutes later, the crew joined together for breakfast. Mike and Christina had hydrated the requested meals and drinks. The food was the same as that flown on the International Space Station (ISS), so they were all quite familiar with it.

"Is everyone ready for their first full day in space on Orion?" Sue asked.

"Should be great fun," said Mike.

"I'm glad you say that, Mike," said Sue, "since I think we will need to make it fun to get through it. One advantage Apollo had over us is that they had way more stuff they had to do to manage their vehicle to keep them busy."

"I don't know what you guys are worrying about," said John. "Christina and I are in Orion for the duration! There will only be so many photos we can take!"

"How did everyone think the privacy shield worked?" Sue asked.

"It's OK", said Christina, "and better than nothing, but you are still quite exposed. I'm not sure there will be enough space there to exercise in."

"As Christina said, it is better than nothing," said Mike. "I think we'll have to see how we go with the exercise mode."

"I agree," said Sue. "Something you guys may not have caught up on yet is that there have been some security developments. There were a couple of serious attempts to breach exclusion zones yesterday that were defeated. They have also identified some suspicious workers on the project, including one who had access to the ICPS and the Lander."

"Whoa," said Mike. "That's not great."

"Does that explain our issues yesterday?" asked Christina.

"It might play into it, but I don't know," said Sue. "And we currently don't know how much access this person had. I'm guessing we'll have to perform extra checkouts on the Lander after we dock."

"Has there been any change to our mission?" asked Christina.

"Not yet. I think we'll know more in the next day or so. For now. I think we need to focus on our jobs and get into lunar orbit safely.

"First up, we have exercise time for me, then Christina, John and finally Mike. Mike, you also have a chat with the flight surgeon before your exercise session. John, you've got some tests to run on flight systems this morning, so we should be kept fairly busy."

Sue spent an hour undertaking various exercises as prescribed. A mix of strength and cardio workouts. They didn't have the treadmill that the station had, but they did have a device that gave them resistance training and something like a bike to pedal.

After that, she cleaned up and changed out of her exercise clothes into her operational clothes while Christina started her exercise routine.

Leaving the exercise area, Sue found John deep in conversation with mission control on his headset and Mike floating in the back of the capsule reading something on his tablet. Sue floated to the water dispenser near Mike and filled her drinking bag with water.

"How was the workout?" Mike asked her.

"Good. Everything seemed to work ok," said Sue.

"I'm glad you are functioning well," said Mike with a smile.

"I was talking about the equipment," said Sue thumping him on the shoulder, which immediately caused her to fly across the capsule. Mike had his feet in a restraint, so he just wobbled around where he was. Sue pushed herself back to where Mike was and found a foot restraint for herself.

"Are you catching up on your emails?" she asked.

"Yeah. Lisa is seeing the Paediatrician today about Jasmine," said Mike.

"Is everything ok with her?"

"Nothing major, but it seems she might have a genetic thing to do with hypermobility," said Mike.

"Really," said Sue. "Jerome has a hypermobility issue too!"

"Wow, that's a coincide... Are you ok, Sue?" asked Mike as the colour had drained from Sue's face. That niggling pebble in her shoe had just become a full-grown boulder.

"Umm, yes," she said, taking a deep breath. Whispering so the others couldn't hear. "Mike, it may not be a coincidence."

"What might not be?" he asked, wondering why she was whispering.

"Well, remember when Ron was away that time, and we slept together. That was just before I found out I was pregnant," said Sue.

"What?!" Mike exclaimed.

"Shh," said Sue.

"You mean to say that Jerome might be my son?"

"It's possible, even probable, given this news," said Sue.

"Did you know?" asked Mike. "Didn't you suspect?"

"Nothing firm. I just had the odd thought, but Ron loves Jerome."

"Wow," said Mike, a bit dazed. "What do we do."

"Nothing," said Sue. "We definitely can't do anything from here. I'd prefer things to just keep going the way they are."

"Well, I guess I can understand that, but it might become a bit obvious as they get older and if they both have similar issues," said Mike.

"Please, let's just keep it to ourselves for now. It'll be very hard for us to talk privately up here anyway until we enter the lunar lander."

"Ok, as long as we are ok," said Mike.

"We are fine," said Sue. She hoped so.

43

— • —

SATURDAY, MAY 18 2024

The moon was growing large in the cabin windows.

With the Outbound Powered Fly-By burn due, the crew rearranged the cabin, stowing equipment and putting the chairs back into place. Fortunately, they didn't need to don their survival suits for this burn, and they would not need to do that again until they docked with the lunar lander.

It was 2 days since Mike had discovered that Sue's son Jerome may be his son. He'd never considered that as a possibility. Sue was right. There wasn't much they could do about it right now. Mike and Sue couldn't even easily discuss it. Lisa would be devastated.

Affairs between astronauts weren't uncommon, especially once more women were in the corps. But they were discouraged.

Why hadn't he picked up on the similarities between Jasmine's and Jerome's conditions? He probably had just not paid enough attention to what was going on for Sue and Ron with Jerome.

"Mike, are you going to screw that in?" asked Christina. Mike realised he was holding the powered screwdriver and had forgotten to screw in the bolt.

"Sorry, drifted off there," said Mike as he worked to secure her chair. It was a relatively simple operation, but without gravity, it required 2 people to position everything, and Sue and John had just finished securing their own chairs in place.

"Anything you want to talk about?" said Christina.

"No, just pondering some stuff at home," said Mike.

"It can be hard being so far away."

"Yeah. How's Graeme going?" he asked her.

"He seems to be doing okay. Can you give me the driver, and I'll secure this side?"

"Sure," he said, passing her the drill.

"His work is fairly busy, so he gets quite involved with it, which is good," said Christina.

Finishing her chair, they moved on to Mike's. As usual, lining up the first bolt was always the hardest!

"Have you had a talk with Lisa recently?" Christina asked Mike.

"Not for a day or so. We are scheduled for a video conference in a couple of hours," said Mike. "I guess she's watching the burn, maybe at Mission Control, although that might be a bit hard with Jasmine."

"So, is she worried about it?"

"I don't think so. She hasn't said much about it. Is Graeme?"

"Graeme?! No, not at all," said Christina. "He seems to have almost absolute faith in NASA and thinks we will be fine."

"Maybe it's his faith in God," said Mike.

"Yes, that too. But he just doesn't expect things to go wrong, even though Apollo 13 would be one of his favourite movies!"

"Ok, that chair seems secure, so we both should be snug during the burn," said Mike.

Sue strapped herself into her seat beside John and ensured that her suit umbilical was connected correctly. The Outbound Powered Fly-By was one of the mission's major burns, which would change their orbit from earth-centric to lunar-centric, and stop them from being in a free return trajectory. Basically, as they passed by the Moon, they would initiate a burn which would place them into a highly elliptical near rectilinear halo orbit (NRHO) orbit of the moon. The same sort of orbit that the Gateway was in. They would need another burn in about three hours to complete putting them into the correct orbit, 1,600 km from the Moon at its closest and 70,000 km from the Moon's surface at its furthest and an orbital period of around 7 days.

The orbit was called a halo orbit because it mapped out what looked like a halo around the Moon as seen from Earth. This would be the orbit the Gateway used, and it didn't require much energy to maintain. It also meant the spacecraft was always visible from Earth, allowing for continuous communication. It also provided continuous visibility of the Lunar South Pole, where all the missions would be based.

However, they weren't planning to rendezvous with the Gateway, even though it was now on station. The Lunar Lander was in orbit for this mission, and they would rendezvous with it. If something went wrong with the Orion, they would use the Gateway.

"How is she looking, John?" Sue asked.

"Everything looks nominal," replied John. "Let's start the pre-burn checklist."

Sue informed Mission Control that they were working the checklist, and they proceeded to check the status of the Orion systems and the cabin configuration.

"Christina and Mike, are you guys secure in your seats and seats configured?" Sue asked.

"Roger," said Christina.

"All good," said Mike.

After another ten minutes of checking, Sue said, "Ok, guys. Does anyone have any concerns before we initiate the burn?"

"Are there any further security issues," asked Christina.

"Not at this time. There may be issues related to the Lander, so we will need to take extra care when checking it out," said Sue.

"Ok, I'm happy," said Christina.

"So am I," said Mike.

"Everything looks good, and I'm happy also," said John.

"Right then, I'll tell Mission Control we are ready to proceed," said Sue.

"Orion for Mission Control, we are ready to proceed with the Outbound Powered Fly-By," said Sue on the communications channel.

"Copy that, Orion, stand-bye for GO/NOGO. In the meantime, please proceed with the pitch over manoeuvre," said George as CAPCOM.

"Roger, Wilco," replied Sue.

John commanded the system to pitch the spacecraft over 180 degrees so that they would be travelling 'backwards' with the service module facing their direction of travel so that its rocket engines could slow them down. It had two systems, a Space Shuttle Orbital Manoeuvring System (OMS) from the Space Shuttle Program and eight R-4D-11 thrusters, which could produce the same amount of force if required as a backup.

Sue watched as the moon filled their windows. Their view panned across its surface as they raced towards it.

"Are you seeing this, Mike?" she asked.

"I sure am," Mike replied. "It's beautiful."

The grey-brown surface passed before their eyes, with the stark contrasts from shadow to light marking the ridges, valleys and craters below.

An enormous crater passed before them, and they, in silence, studied the barren landscape on which Sue and Mike would soon walk.

And then, the more startling image appeared before them.

There is the distance hung the blue, white and brown planet they called Earth. They could see the white swirls of clouds across the blue seas, with the occasional patch of brown or green land.

"Wow," said Christina.

"That is breathtaking," said John.

Sue retrieved a camera and took photos out her window.

"We've all seen the photos," she said, "but it is something else to see the Earth from here like that."

"Orion, I see you have a beautiful view of home," said CAPCOM.

"Yes, and you guys better take care of it while we are away," said Sue.

"Roger, Wilco, and you are go for your burn as scheduled."

"Copy that Mission Control. Go for Out Bound Powered Fly-By," said Sue.

"Ok, guys, we've got 10 minutes until the burn, so relax and watch the view," said John.

Sue checked their checklist and confirmed that they had no further actions due for almost 10 minutes, quickly reviewed the system status panel and then spent some time gazing out the window.

It was amazing to consider that that small blue ball, surrounded by the black nothingness of space, was the home of over 8 billion people. There were 8 people on the ISS and 4 on the Orion. That was all of humanity; out her window, she could see half of the solar system and the dazzling stars of millions of other star systems and galaxies. But humans lived in the 9 cubic metres of the Orion and on and around the small ball. She put up her hand and noted that she could indeed block them out with a finger.

Sue shivered. She was a long, long way away from home. From her family. From everything she knew. She closed her eyes and took a deep breath. Now was not the time to ponder the meaning of life or the fragility of their situation. If she was thinking about this...

"Hey, guys, what are you all thinking? I know that view is making me think," she said.

"Yeah, we are so far from home," said Christina.

"But we are safe," said Sue.

"It does make you think, though," said Mike. "We are all alone out here."

"Yes," said John, "but it is what we trained for. And so many people have thought about all that could go wrong and worked out solutions."

"We all know all the failure modes and what we have to do to survive. We are just about to start a different set of those. We've trained for them. We know what to do. And everything is working well," said Sue.

"Yes, we have trained. It's a bit different when you look out the window, though," said Christina.

Sue looked at the mission clock and said, "Ok, this is it. We have 2 minutes until the burn. Are you all ok to proceed?"

"Yes, ma'am," said John with conviction.

Taking a deep breath, Christina closed her eyes, mouthed a few words, and then replied, "Yes, I'm ready. It's what we are here for."

"The Moon is what we are here for," said Mike. "Let's go orbit it. I want to go for a walk!"

"Ok, here comes the burn," said Sue. She and John proceeded with the rest of their checklist and confirmed the commanded trajectory change.

The g-force was a shock after 3 days of zero-G. Sue felt dizzy as her brain tried to interpret signals it hadn't had for 3 days. She closed her eyes and breathed through it, quickly opening them again to keep monitoring the spacecraft signals.

"The burn looks nominal," said John.

There was a bit of vibration as the burn continued using the OMS. Sue was pleased it wasn't the shaking that was apparent during the Apollo burns.

The view of the lunar surface through the window increased, and the level of detail they could make out increased as they got closer.

Yes, thought Sue, in a week, I'll be walking somewhere down there. It looked very inhospitable, and indeed it was!

And then, after a few minutes, the burn was finished. Sue and John checked their displays which showed everything was working as expected and that the Orbital Maneuvering System (OMS) had been made safe.

"Orion, this is Houston. Telemetry from that burn shows everything nominal. You are okay to proceed with the pitch over."

"Copy that, Houston, that was a nice smooth burn for us," said Sue. "We will initiate the pitch shortly."

The manoeuvre would again orient them to be flying head first, with the Orion end of the stack pointing in the direction of travel.

Once orientated 'properly', the crew could leave their seats and partake of their lunch.

44

—— • ——

SUNDAY, MAY 19, 2024

The burn regularising the orbit three hours later had been successful, and the Orion was now chasing down the Lunar Lander orbiting just ahead of them. What had been a pinprick of light had now become a distinct shape after they had completed a sleep period.

The lander had been one of the fastest-developed elements of the mission. Commercial contracts for development had only been initiated in 2019, with three proposals being developed simultaneously from Blue Origin, Dynetics and SpaceX. The Dynetics concept ended up being the selected system.

The spacecraft they were approaching was odd looking. It was essentially a girder with a cylindrical habitat in the middle and two gold spheres on each side of the habitat, storing fuel. Below the two spheres, on either side of the habitat, were 4 engines on each side. Towards the end of the descent, the outer two fuel tanks would be disconnected and dumped, reducing the landing and take-off mass. Solar panels would roll out of the top of the habitat after landing.

Sue and John were busy working through checklists for the approach. Christina and Mike were busy undertaking housekeeping activities to maintain systems in the Orion. The commander and pilot chairs were still set up after the burn. Mike and Christina's chairs had been partially folded to give more room in the cabin.

"Ok, everyone," said Sue, floating out of her chair and turning to see the rest of the crew. "We are coming up on the time to dock, so it's time to don our survival suits again. After that, Mike and Christina, can you please reassemble your chairs. Have you finished the housekeeping tasks?"

"Just about done. We need about ten minutes to finish," said Christina.

"That should be fine," said Sue. "John and I can suit up first while you do that."

Forty minutes later, the crew were again in their survival suits and strapped into their chairs.

Mike chewed on his snack bar as he opened his tablet to check his email. Once again, he and Christina were passengers watching on from the back seat while Sue and John flew the craft. The crew had gotten into a rhythm the last few days. But apart from checklists, exercises, meals, and occasional manoeuvre, there hadn't been much to break the monotony. This particular event would take about 4 hours to complete, and then they would all be busy as they checked out the lander. Most of that work would fall on Sue and himself, which would be a nice change for Mike.

He opened an email from Lisa. It included a photo of her and Jasmine at a playgroup, with Jasmine sitting and playing with some blocks.

Hi Mike,

We went to the playgroup today, and Jasmine seemed to really enjoy being with the other babies. She tries to play with the older kids too, but she can't keep up.

I think your folks got the idea I wanted more space for myself, so they've gone to New Orleans for a few days, so it is just us in the house, which feels weird, but I am enjoying time to myself when Jasmine is asleep. But I miss you!

I'm looking forward to our call later.

Love, Lisa.

Mike smiled as he looked at the photo of Jasmine. He looked across at Christina.

"Christina, look at this," he said to her. He maximised the photo and passed the tablet to her.

"Aww, isn't she cute!" said Christina.

"You got a baby photo?" asked Sue.

"Yeah, I'll show you later," said Mike. "They went to JSC playgroup, and Jasmine was chasing the older kids."

"That's great. Is Lisa taking Jasmine to Space Family Education?" asked Sue, referring to the JSC preschool program.

"Yes, two days a week when she is working," said Mike.

"It's a great program. Ron cared for our kids at home most of the time, but we used them to give him a break, especially as they got older," said Sue.

Mike retrieved his tablet from Christina and wrote a reply to Lisa, telling her of his exciting activities in preparation for docking with the lander and letting her know he was looking forward to their call. There was no privacy on the Orion, but it would still be good to hear her voice.

He was really looking forward to spending time with his family full time in three weeks. The quarantine had meant he had had minimal contact with them for over three weeks. Jasmine grew up so quickly that he could already see changes and behaviours on video that he had not witnessed first-hand, which was hard. Who would have thought having a child would change his thinking so much!

Next, Mike displayed his personal task list, reviewing processes he would need to perform during the rest of the day. The major ones would relate to the hatch opening to the Lander and the Lander checkout procedures. The team on the ground had sent up additional procedures that they wanted to be carried out due to the heightened security posture. Some of the tasks involved less familiar activities, and since Sue was busy commanding the mission, it was up to him to become familiar with these procedures. So, he had a couple of hours of reading and video-watching to keep him busy.

45

— • —

The Lander hung in space 40 metres away from them. The Orion had flawlessly navigated automatically to this position. In fact, the entire docking sequence was expected to be automatic. Sue and John were there to monitor and take over if something unexpected happened. This was the first docking of an Orion and the Lunar Lander, so it was a test flight.

Sue read out the checklist items as John checked them, and she double-checked. In some ways, it was overkill, with automated systems already continuously monitoring systems and the data being streamed back to mission control, where teams were also examining the same systems. Yet, it was a test flight, no one had performed this docking before, and if something went wrong, they were a long way from help! So, they manually double-checked the systems.

"Houston, Orion, we have completed item 30 dot 2, and we are ready for docking," Sue said on the communications circuit.

"Copy that, Orion, standby," came the reply from George as CAP-COM.

"Does anyone have any concerns about the docking," Sue asked the crew.

"No," said Mike. The others likewise had no concerns.

"Great. The lander looks ok from what we can see from here. Solar panels are deployed. Hopefully, we get the go in a minute."

"Orion, you are go for Item 30 dot 3 and docking to the Lunar Lander," came the call from Mission Control.

"Copy that. Go for 30 dot 3," replied Sue on the communications channel.

"Here we go, guys. John, approve the docking sequence," said Sue.

John pressed a button on the display, and shortly afterwards, the thrusters fired, moving the Orion closer to the Lander.

Twenty minutes later, the Orion had moved to within 5 metres of the Lander. Once again, they were holding steady, and once again, they had a Go/NoGo decision and proceeded. All was going well.

As they closed the final few metres, Sue felt confident that they would be docked very soon.

Then as they got closer, there was a series of over-corrections that the automated system could not correct.

As they got within one metre of the lander, their docking probe was off target by 10 centimetres.

"I'm aborting," said John.

"I concur," said Sue. John pressed the abort button, and thrusters fired, moving them back to the 40-metre holding location where again thrusters fired to keep them in position.

"Mission Control, this is Orion. We aborted docking as we were outside mission parameters," said Sue on the communications.

"Copy that, Orion. We saw that. Give us a few minutes as we review the data," said CAPCOM.

"Those thruster firings as we got close were a bit overcooked," said John.

"We'll try again, and if it still can't dock, we will go manual," said Sue. "They only had the Artemis II rendezvous to qualify the Orion systems, so we knew there might be issues."

"Orion, CAPCOM, just to let you guys know, we are adjusting some of the thruster settings slightly to attempt to compensate. I think we all saw that the thruster firing close to the Lander was a bit too energetic. We have that in work, and we will attempt another docking soon."

"Copy that CAPCOM," said Sue. "That correlates to what we saw." Sue took a drink from her drinking straw. Talking to the crew, she said, "Ok, time for a rest, anyone following any sports?

"The Yankees hit three home runs yesterday," said John.

"Do you follow the Yankees?" asked Christina

"No, but they did it!" said John.

"The French Tennis Open is just starting, and Dominic Thiem is expected to win," said Christina.

"What, Nadal won't?" said Mike with mock incredulity.

"He can't keep winning it forever," said Christina.

"He's a superman," said Mike.

"He'll need a wheelchair soon," said John. "I reckon Alexander Albon is going to win the Formula One championship this year. He just won the Spanish Grand Prix, and he'll probably win the Monaco GP this weekend."

"I thought you'd be more IndyCar fan than an F1 fan," said Mike.

"I like the best, and F1 is the best of the best!" replied John.

"Orion from CAPCOM, we are ready to proceed with another automated docking attempt. Restart from Checklist 30 dot 3."

Sue replied, "Copy that, Houston, starting from 30 dot 3." To the crew, she said, "OK, game time for us. When you are ready, John."

Once again, John approved the approach, thrusters on the Orion fired, and they started approaching the Lander.

"I think Pierre Gasly will actually win the championship," said Christina.

"Which one?" asked Mike.

"Formula One, of course."

"You follow F1?" said Mike.

"Sure," she replied. "Graeme and I watch it all the time. John's right. It is the best motorsport!."

The docking progressed smoothly, and twenty minutes later, they were floating 5 metres from the lander.

"Here we are again. Everything looks ok to me. John?" said Sue.

"I agree. All green to me."

"Houston, we are now at 30 dot 8. Do we have a GO for docking?" Sue asked on the communications channel.

"That's affirmative for 30 dot 8," replied the CAPCOM.

"I hope this works this time," said Sue.

As the Orion approached the Lander, the thruster firings were noticeably less energetic.

"This is looking much better," said John. "It's not fighting itself."

"I agree," said Sue. Then on the communications channel, "Houston, we think this approach is much better."

"Copy that, Orion. Our guys are fairly happy too."

Five minutes later, they successfully had soft capture and received permission to drive the docking latch. Once they had a hard dock, they began to pressurise the vestibule. That would take 40 minutes.

"Mike, go ahead with the docking hatch preparations.

Mike unstrapped himself from his seat and floated up to the docking hatch, carefully managing his umbilical since they were all still wearing their survival suits due to the test-flight nature of their mission.

Most of his activities related to rearranging the items stowed around the hatch to ensure that it could be safely opened.

Eventually, the pressure in the vestibule stabilised. Houston reported that the Lander's environmental systems had been activated, and the crew were asked to close their visors while Sue and Mike opened the hatches and tested the air.

Sue joined Mike at the hatch, and Mike handed her one of the testing devices. He then began to turn the handle, with allowed the hatch to open. An event that causes at least mild anxiety on any spacecraft. If something is wrong, then you could lose your atmosphere. But due to an abundance of caution, the crew were already in their survival suits if something did go wrong.

"Hatch is open," reported Mike on the communications channel. He slowly swung it into the open position and secured it.

"Entering the vestibule," reported Sue as she pulled herself into the small space between the craft. She took a measurement of the air quality. "The air is ok in here."

Sue proceeded to the hatch of the Lander, which not long ago had been exposed to space, and this was one of the reasons they conducted air testing. Residue from the Lander or Orion thrusters could remain on the exposed parts of the Lander hatch or the outer face of the Orion hatch.

"Air quality test results are ok in the Orion as well," reported Mike.

"No alarms on the Orion environmental systems either," reported John.

"Houston," said Sue on the communications channel. "All gas tests are clear. I'm opening the Lander hatch."

"Copy that," replied CAPCOM.

Sue braced herself and turned the handle on the Lander's hatch. After a few turns, she gently pushed it into the craft and latched it out of the way.

"Hatch open. Follow me in, Mike."

Mike followed Sue in. Sue went to a console using her headlamp to see and turned on the internal lights. Then they both proceeded to take air samples in various locations.

Once the tests had passed, Mike took his tablet from his knee pocket and displayed their checklist. It had been extended, so they now not only needed to check out basic systems but also several non-critical systems to ensure that they were working optimally.

"This is going to take us hours," Mike said.

"I know," Sue replied, "and so does Mission Control. What we don't finish today, we will do tomorrow."

"A pity the others can't help," said Mike.

"I know, but many of these are the more obscure systems they haven't trained on, so it is up to you and me."

"Right. So, first is a basic system check, so that shouldn't take us too long."

An hour later, the basic systems had been confirmed to be working correctly in the Lander, and Sue and Mike returned to the Orion for a break.

"Ok, everyone, we can remove our survival suits. Mission Control is happy that we should be safe. Then we get to eat before Mike and I tackle more of this monster checklist," said Sue.

"That's great," said Christina. "I was getting sick of this suit. I really would not like to spend 6 days in it."

The survival suit was designed to keep the crew alive in several scenarios, including loss of cabin pressure. This was good, except it was a bit like being in a super-sized nappy since it catered for all their bodily functions for those 6 days. Breathing, drinking, eating, and waste management were all functions of the suit. So, for an astronaut to don and doff them required discretion from the rest of the crew.

The crew worked through the process of doffing their suits as elegantly and discreetly as they could and then observed a meal break. Christina took on the role of cook since she had had little to do all day and hydrated and heated the various food selections and drinks while the others finished doffing their suits and arranging them around the cabin to dry.

Christina passed a lasagne meal to John, a turkey wrap to Sue, a burrito to Mike, and Christina herself had Mexican scrambled eggs.

"Does everything look ok in there?" asked John, pointing at the lander.

"From what we've seen, everything looks ok," said Sue. "However, we have a long list of checks to go through. It's much longer than planned, so they really want to make sure everything looks ok."

"I don't know about you," said Mike, "but if I was sabotaging the mission, I wouldn't do it somewhere you could easily see it."

"Which means you probably won't find anything," said Christina.

"I understand what you are saying," said Sue, "however, we still need to check these systems. The team on the ground have tried to work out the minimal set that will ensure our survival and give us confidence in the systems. They have been testing automated systems before we arrived."

"It will be nice to have a bit more room to spread out in for a while," said Christina.

"Yeah, I'll finally be able to get some sleep without listening to Mike's snoring drone on all night," said John.

"Talk for yourself," said Sue. "I'm supposed to bunk with him in the Lander! I think for the next couple of nights, we are having girl's night in the Lander!"

"Great idea. I'll get movies and chocolate," said Christina.

"That's not fair!" said John. "That leaves me with the chainsaw here."

"I don't snore!" said Mike emphatically.

"It's decided then. Girls' night in the lander tonight," said Sue.

After eating their lunch and spending some time checking on their messages, the crew returned to the Lander checkout activities. This primarily involved Sue and Mike, but Christina and John were involved in the procedures as well.

There was a bit of space in the lander since it was designed for four crew members, so their habitable volume had roughly doubled.

Now that they could work in a shirt-sleeve environment again, Sue and Mike could proceed faster through the checklist. They first needed to check all the consumables and accessible equipment to ensure they were undamaged. Christina and John managed the checklists while Sue and Mike located lockers, opened them, checked the content and restowed the items.

They completed the day's work finding nothing unusual.

"As expected, we found nothing," said Sue. "Tomorrow, we will check out the airlock and also check system compartments. I suspect, with the level of checking that occurs prior to launch, that we will once again find nothing. In fact, the suspects should not have had access to the system compartments at all.

"Since Mission Control is happy with our plans to occupy the Lander, I suggest we return to the Orion. We will each get 20 minutes alone in the Lander for some private communication with our family. Then Christina and I will occupy it for girl's night!"

"You got the beer and pizza, Mike?" asked John.

"It seems we can do pizza, but I think you'll have to make do with Cranberry juice," replied Mike.

"Where's a Russian when you need one," said John. "They would at least have Vodka!"

The crew returned to the Orion capsule.

When it came time for Mike's call, he was able to talk to Lisa.

Mike strapped his tablet to a locker door and floated in front of it. After a minute, an image of Lisa holding Jasmine appeared.

"Hi, Lisa. Hi Jasmine. It's so good to see you and chat privately," he said, waving.

"Hi! Say hi to daddy," said Lisa, waving Jasmine's hand like a puppet.

"We are," started Mike.

"Are you there?" said Lisa.

"We are going to have some lag, so we'll have to do the whole OVER thing," said Mike.

"Oh, OK," said Lisa. "It does seem worse than last time we talked. How has your day gone? OVER."

"It has gone really well, but it's been busy. But a big benefit is that we now have twice as much space to live in and a private space if we need it. In fact, we could use the airlock as well. Everything is working well. How are you guys? OVER."

"We are well. Jasmine had another fun day at playgroup. Your folks just got back, so you can talk to them in a few minutes. It's been good to have some time to ourselves, but I won't mind their help with Jasmine."

Mike smiled. "I know what you mean about time to yourself. This is the first time I've been by myself since we left earth. You can't even consider the toilet to be private because they are just on the other side of the panel, and there is often someone exercising above you. So being in here talking to you is a luxury!"

"So, will you be sleeping in there with Sue?" Lisa asked. Mike thought she had a bit of a strange look on her face.

"Not at the moment. Sue and Christina are having a girl's night in there tonight, so John and I are having beer and pizza and watching sports or something."

"They let you have beer up there?"

"Sure, we just have to blow in the breathalyser before doing anything," Mike said, laughing.

"I can see that happening, not! I'll call your folks in," Lisa said. "John and Clare, come in and join us."

Mike's parents entered the image.

"Hi, Mum and Dad. There's a bit of a lag between us due to the distance. I'm in the lander, which means I've got all this space to myself – see," he said, pushing off from the wall down the length of the lander and performing a somersault on his way back.

"It's great we can see you, and we can talk more privately," said Mike's father, John. "How are you going?"

"I'm going well, it was a bit boring until we opened the hatch to the lander, but since then, I've been very busy with the checkouts," said Mike.

"And everything is working properly there? The Chinese haven't messed with it?" asked his mother.

"No, Mum. Everything is looking good. We are doing extra checks, but everything is in the right place and working properly."

"That Asian woman isn't a spy, is she?" his mother asked.

"You mean Christina? No, Mum, she is an American, born in L.A. And her family is from Korea, not China. I've known her for years. She is fine."

"You never can tell. I don't trust them," Clare said.

"How long until you land?" asked Lisa.

Mike smiled, knowing that she knew exactly when that would be. "We have another six days before the landing. So once we finish the checkouts, we don't have a lot to do before we start the landing work. We've got some supplies to transfer, but that won't take that long. There's a lot of waiting on this mission."

"Why is that?" asked John.

"It's all to do with the orbits. The one we are in now is the same that the Gateway will be in. It doesn't use much fuel to maintain, and it also always maintains line of sight with Earth, which is good for communication. Unfortunately, it is also almost a 7-day orbit, so we have lots of time to wait. There's a couple of experiments that we can do, plus some photography, but most of our time will be taken up with exercise!"

"That's right, I remember you explaining it a couple of years ago," said John.

"Ok, Mum and Dad. Can I have some time with just Lisa before I finish? Thanks for saying hi, and staying with Lisa. I love you both."

"Ok. Keep well, Mike," said Clare.

"Yes, son, look after yourself. We love you too," said John. After some waves, they left the room.

"There's a bit of angst down here about the Chinese interfering with the mission, at least on TV. That's why your mother is worried," said Lisa.

"I guess I understand. We are checking things, but there is no sign of any problems," said Mike.

"That's good. I miss you."

"I miss you too. They say I snore."

"You do."

"No! I don't snore. You never said I snore."

"But you do, not loudly. And only when you are on your back."

"I guess in space, I'm always on my back! Nobody complained during the last mission."

"Weren't you at one end of the station last time?"

"I guess so. But no one complained."

"Who would be close enough to hear you? You'll be on the Moon in a week, and you can lie on your side."

"Ok – I have to go. It's Sue's turn in a minute. I love you all, and I'll chat with you again tomorrow," he said, waving.

"Ok – we love you too. Bye!"

Mike closed the call on his tablet, removed it from the strapping, and pushed off to head to the Orion. As he approached the airlock door, he noticed a small slip of plastic poking out from behind a panel. He took a closer look. He surveyed the area. The panel had environmental systems behind it, and they had not removed it during their checks so far. That was concerning.

He pushed himself through the hatch into the airlock and the docking hatches. He located Sue and went over to her.

"Sue, your turn." He said, and turned around and went back into the Lander to wait for her.

"Hey Mike, are you going to let me have some privacy?" Sue asked as she floated in.

"Sure, but let me show you something first." Mike pointed at the plastic poking out from the panel.

"Ok, that's a bit strange. Let's talk to ground," said Sue.

Sue pushed off to a nearby communications panel. "Lander, Houston for CAPCOM, private."

"Houston copies, go channel two," replied the CAPCOM.

Sue changed to channel two. "Lander for Houston on two."

"Go ahead, Sue."

"We've found a small flap of plastic trapped under panel C-22-D. It might be nothing, but Mike and I think we should check it out."

"Copy that, Sue. Could you guys take some photos and send them to us, and then standby."

"Sure. While you are looking at them, I'll have my call home."

"Copy that. CAPCOM free of channel two."

Mike used his tablet to take photos of the panel, especially of the tab of plastic.

"That panel relates to the airlock, doesn't it?" asked Mike.

"From memory, yes," replied Sue.

"Ok, I've got those photos, and I'll send them to CAPCOM. You go and have your call," said Mike, and he pushed himself through the airlock and into the Orion.

"What's going on?" asked John.

"We found some plastic sticking out from behind an environmental systems panel. We think it relates to the airlock. I'm just sending photos to CAPCOM for them to look at," said Mike.

Sue moved into the middle of the Lander cabin and located some footholds, and started the call home.

Ron answered, "Hi. Is everything ok? We were expecting your call 10 minutes ago."

"All is fine. We just found something that needs investigation, so I had to chat with Mission Control about it. How are you guys?"

"We are fine. Hey Jessica, Jerome, come and say hi to your mum," said Ron.

"Hey, mummy," said Jerome, waving and running over to the laptop that Ron was using for the call."

"Hey, my lovely. It's so good to see you. How about you go back and sit with Daddy," said Sue.

Jerome backed away, and Sue could see Jessica sitting beside Ron.

"Hi, Jessica, my love. It's so good to see you too," said Sue.

"Hi, Mum. Can you do any tricks?"

"Of course, I can. Hang on while I put this tablet somewhere." Sue then floated in front of the camera and performed some somersaults.

"It looks like you have lots of room in there," said Ron.

"Yes, we've more than doubled the volume of the Orion. Christina and I are going to have a girls' night in here tonight. I just realised that this is the first time I've been alone for almost a week!"

"Are you coming home soon, Mummy?" asked Jerome.

"I'll be away a while yet," said Sue. "But we can talk again."

"Have you seen the moon yet?" asked Jessica.

"Oh yes, it was really big and beautiful as we passed it. Right now, we are going away from it. We joined up with the Lander, and that's where I am now," said Sue. "What have you two been doing?"

"I've been to Sally's birthday party. We went swimming and played games, and I ate too much," said Jessica.

"I've been playing trains with Daddy," said Jerome. "We had a blue one, and a green one and the green one hit the blue one; this one went over the bridge and hill and came down and then everything went poof."

"Wow," said Sue energetically, "that sounds like fun."

"And we're going to do it again tomorrow," said Jerome.

"We might, said Ron, "or we might do something else. How about you two say good night to your Mum, and she and I will have a little talk."

"Good night, Mummy," said Jerome.

"Good night, my little man," said Sue.

"Good night, Mummy," said Jessica.

"Sweet dreams, my lovely," said Sue.

The children got up and left the room.

"Are they going ok," asked Sue.

"Yes, they are. They miss you, but they are coping. They are used to it now," said Ron.

"And how are you going?"

"I'm ok. It's a bit tiring. It's better when they are at school or daycare. I miss you too."

"You know my parents would love to help you if you need it."

"No, it's fine. Tomorrow is a school day."

"But you'll need help once school ends," said Sue.

"I'll think about it."

"Ok, well, I better have a chat to Mission Control about this issue. I love you and miss you," said Sue.

"I love you too. Be careful. Bye"

"Bye." Sue ended the call. She missed them all desperately, but her job was keeping the crew safe, and they needed to deal with this new discovery.

46

— · —

Mission Control decided that following up in the plastic behind the panel could wait until the morning. Christina and Sue moved their sleeping bags into Lander, and once they prepared their meals in the Orion, they both moved into the Lander. The Lander's toilet and food preparation systems had not yet been activated and were reserved for Lander operations, so they had to use the Orion's systems.

"Wow, there is so much room in here compared to the Orion," said Christina.

"I know," said Sue. "There's not the need for an aerodynamic shape, so it is basically a cylinder. And the airlock gives extra space to get privacy."

"What do you want to do for girl's night? Watch a movie?" asked Christina.

"Well, facials are out. Drinking is out. We could play games or trivia," said Sue

"Or Karaoke."

"No way. I'm not singing."

"Well, food is pretty limited, but I did grab some chocolate. So Chick Flick?" said Christina.

"And chat."

"Of course, chat," said Christina. "How was your call home?"

"Good. Ron seems a bit tired looking after the kids, and the kids are missing me, but they seem fine," said Sue.

"Is Ron getting any help with the kids?"

"No. He is relying on childcare, but I encouraged him to get his parents down to help for the holidays."

"But he isn't interested?"

"You know guys. They are independent or want to be seen to be. And I'm not sure Ron wants his mother around the place for a couple of weeks!" said Sue.

"I can understand that. I'm not sure I'd want my folks around for 2 weeks."

"How's Graeme doing?"

"He's good. Busy working, so he is pretty well distracted. I spoke to my parents too, and they are just worried about me!"

"Parents are the worst," said Sue. "Mine are worried too. Even though they are both quite academic and understand a fair bit of what is happening on the missions, they still worry. I guess I would worry too if Jessica or Jerome were on this mission instead of me!"

"They can't control it, so they worry. If I wasn't here, they'd be worried about Graeme and me. If I wasn't going out with Graeme, they would be worried I was single. You can't win!"

"Yep," said Sue with a laugh. "Got to love parents! What do you want to watch?"

"Well, there's Pride & Prejudice, Me before You, About Time, ..."

"Crazy Rich Asians, Mystic Pizza, Breakfast at Tiffany's, ..."

"Don't forget Pretty Woman and Mamma Mia."

"And Beaches, Letters to Juliet, Bridget Jones' diary."

"Too many choices," said Christina. "Let's watch Crazy Rich Asians."

"I was actually thinking About Time."

"Yep, sure. English works for me!"

"I'm glad someone thought a mini projector and screen would be a good item to pack," said Sue.

"In fact, we've got 2, one on the Orion and one on the Lander."

"That's right. Must have been the psychologists figuring we'd need a movie night," said Sue, floating to the storage locker containing the screen and projector. She passed the screen to Christina and began connecting and securing the projector.

"Probably the best place to secure the screen is in the entry to the control area," Sue instructed Christina.

The screen was similar to the one first flown to the ISS in 2015, and it flattened as Christina took it out of its storage tube and unrolled it. She then tethered it to the walls forming the entrance to the cockpit area of the lander.

"Maybe just put some music on while we eat," suggested Christina. "I think I want to set up my sleeping bag to watch a movie, and our meal will get cold."

"Good idea," said Sue, starting a playlist. "Are you coping ok sharing the cabin with the guys?"

"Yeah. A few awkward moments, but we knew that would happen. I haven't noticed too many stares."

"Same for me, although I've seen Mike watching me a bit too much."

"Is that going to be a problem?" asked Christina. "You have a week or so alone together on the surface."

"It should be ok. We have some history, so it's probably Mike daydreaming."

"You and Mike have history?"

"Not a lot," said Sue. "But we did get together once during training."

"Weren't you and Ron together then?"

"I don't know about you, Christina, but relationships wax and wane, and ours had waned a lot."

"But still, it's crossing a line with a teammate."

"Yes, but we had finalised our neutral buoyancy tank training, and we got drunk. We know we crossed the line, and it only happened once."

"Why are you telling me this, Sue?" Christina asked, surprised that her commander would share such detail with her.

"I don't know, Christina," Sue replied. "I guess I want to know if you've noticed anything."

"No, nothing. I used to get looks from him, but he is much more settled with Lisa these days."

"Yes, he is. But it's more complicated than that, but you can't mention this to anyone!" said Sue, looking directly at Christina.

"As long as it doesn't endanger the mission, sure."

"It doesn't. Mike might be Jerome's father. In fact, since Jerome and Jessica have the same genetic disorder, it is almost definite."

"No – you are kidding!" exclaimed Christina.

"It looks like it, but we only worked that out a day or so ago."

"Wow – that is heavy. You guys need to sort that out before your descent."

"I guess we do. I don't know how."

"We need to find a reason for you and Mike to be alone for a while, and I need to keep John busy."

"Or I order John to leave us alone," said Sue.

"That might make him suspicious. I think you should just tell John that you guys need to talk through some Lunar landing issues in light of the China attacks. And I suggest that you actually do talk a bit about the impact that has on the mission while you meet with Mike."

"Not a bad idea. Maybe you should be commanding."

"I've been told I have wisdom."

"Maybe you do. If you've finished your meal, I suggest we set up our sleeping bags and get the movie started. I love a good time travel romance!

47

MONDAY, MAY 20, 2024

The next day, with guidance from Mission Control, Sue and Mike began investigating the plastic sticking out from behind the airlock environmental panel.

"So, Mike, Ground want us to open the panel above the one we are interested in and use the endoscope inspection camera to look around in case there are any surprises," said Sue as they began their inspection. Christina and John had remained in the Orion on instruction from Mission control in case there were problems.

"What?! They are worried it's booby-trapped?" asked Mike.

"Well, they want to make sure it isn't."

"Right, well, can't say I'd think of putting one of these cameras on board," said Mike.

"They are pretty cheap and work with our tablets. They are cheaper and easier to use than the fiberscope they had on the ISS. You should find it in Locker J2."

Mike moved over to the locker and opened it. "What is the satchel id?"

"2658-1," replied Sue.

Mike spent a few minutes searching the locker before finding the item. Opening the satchel, he found a semi-rigid endoscope inspection camera they could connect to by WiFi from their tablet.

"OK, so we have the camera. Which panel do they want us to open?" asked Mike.

"The one above," replied Sue. They worked to unscrew the panel. Once they had that detached, Mike turned on the camera, and Sue connected her tablet to it by WiFi and shared it with Mission Control so they could see the results.

"Mission Control want us to capture images of the panel, including the edges, to see if there is anything that might detect the panel being opened," said Sue.

"Makes sense, I suppose. Hopefully, we can get a fairly clear view," said Mike as he directed the camera into the next compartment. It took a few goes to get the curve on the cable correct. "How does that look?"

"That actually shows quite a lot. Let me take a photo," said Sue. "I'm pretty sure nothing is touching the panel in the middle, from what I can see, so we will probably need to focus on the edges."

"I'm thinking we are going to have to take off other panels all around," said Mike.

"Let's see how much you can get to. One side is against the airlock, so probably not so easy to access."

"Ok, I'll run across the top if you can record it," said Mike. Slowly he moved the camera across the top of the panel. He had to view the camera output on Sue's tablet, and it took a while to learn how to manage the camera properly.

After an hour, they had finally photographed all the internal edges of the panel and were working to resecure the surrounding panel cover. At the same time, Mission Control analysed their photos and videos.

"Mike, while we have time, can we talk about Jerome and Jasmine?" asked Sue.

Mike swallowed. He'd been dreading this discussion, but they couldn't really avoid it. "Sure," he said.

"So how sure are you that Jasmine has hypermobility?" asked Sue.

"Not very. The Paediatrician only just started considering it, so we haven't had any tests done," said Mike.

"And I can tell you, nothing will be very conclusive until she is much older!" said Sue.

"Oh, that is unhelpful. Are there any genetic tests?"

"Not really. There are advances all the time. But for Jerome, there are too many things it could be, so they just want him to get older, and they'll deal with the symptoms as they present. Do you have any relatives with hypermobility?" said Sue.

"No. One of my Mum's cousins has a problem with shoulder dislocation, but our doctor dismissed that. Actually, you asked me that a couple of years ago. Have you been thinking Jerome is mine all along?"

"Sort of. I knew it was possible."

"Didn't you use any protection?"

"Did you?" asked Sue indignantly.

"I was drunk!"

"So was I!"

"But you're the one who can get pregnant!" replied Mike.

"And Ron and I were trying to get pregnant!"

"Shit."

"I know."

"We had sex once, and you got pregnant. How unlucky is that."

"It happens."

"Not that often."

"It's a one in 20 chance, but a bit age dependent."

"Shit. So, Ron doesn't know?"

"No," replied Sue. "And I don't want him to know unless he needs to."

"Ok."

"Is this going to be a problem for us on this mission?"

"I don't think so."

"So, you don't think I've trapped you, and you don't feel like you have to sleep with me?" Sue asked.

"Those are quite different things. No, I don't think you've trapped me. And no, I'm not looking to hook up with you. That was a different time, and I'm sorry. But Lisa and I are happy together, and I don't want to mess that up," said Mike.

"So, you aren't attracted to me."

"I didn't say that. I just said I don't want to get together with you. Do you?"

Sue paused. She hadn't thought about it. "Of course not. Ron and I are happy. Happier than we were then. We need to stay professional."

"So, we stay friends, colleagues, and parents together," said Mike.

"The last is not proven, and I'm not looking for your involvement in Jerome's life," said Sue. "Do you think Lisa will notice?"

"Maybe, but Ron has just as much of a chance of realising."

"True. After this mission, we probably aren't going to be on the same mission again, so we won't be working that closely together."

"Right, we'll just be doing interviews together until we die!"

"Ahh, right. If you think you can't work with me for the landing, tell me, and we'll work something out."

"It's not going to be a problem for me," said Mike.

"Okay, then. We move forward. Let's get a drink and snacks from the Orion since we are still waiting," said Sue.

A while later, they were given the go-ahead to remove the cover of the suspect compartment. The plastic hanging out turned out to be part of a tag for a cable.

"That's weird," said Mike. "The cables are normally far enough away so the labels don't get caught. It's probably worthwhile following it."

"Sure," said Sue.

Mike carefully followed the cable and discovered it unconnected at one end. "It looks like this cable has been disconnected. Everything else appears ok. Let's talk to Mission Control."

Sue moved over to the communications station, took the microphone and called, "Mission Control, this is Lander."

"Go ahead, Lander," came the reply.

"It appears the plastic stuck in the cover was the tag for a disconnected cable."

"Copy that. Can you provide us with the code for the cable, please," CAPCOM replied.

Sue provided the code to the CAPCOM.

"OK, give us a few minutes to locate that cable information and to get some advice," said CAPCOM.

"I'm going to get a snack," said Mike, and he headed back into the Orion.

"I'll join you," said Sue.

In the Orion, they updated John and Christina as they organised and ate their snacks and drinks. The Mission Control called requesting them to reconnect the cable and providing instructions in an email.

When Sue and Mike were back in the lander, Mike asked, "do they say what the cable does?"

"Yes, it has something to do with airlock pressurisation. However, there are a couple of redundancies, so we are to check those out after we've reconnected this, and then they want to test cycle the airlock with us in the Orion."

"Sounds like a plan," said Mike.

Four hours later, they had completed all the checking, and the ground team had tested the airlock.

As the crew ate their evening meal, they considered the impact of this potential sabotage.

"It doesn't seem a very useful attack," said John. "All it would have done is meant that a backup system was used."

"Maybe the hope was that the mission would be scrubbed," said Sue. "If we had tested that system after undocking, as planned, we probably would have scrubbed. We would not have had the time to make the repair, and Mission Control would be forced to scrub."

"Yeah, they wouldn't let us go with a system failure like that," said Mike. "That's the only thing that makes sense."

48

— ◆ —

The next day, a Tuesday, was designated as a rest day. So apart from their exercise regime, the crew had time off. They could now spread out more into the combined complex and get time alone.

The crew spent Wednesday and Thursday checking out the Lander as planned and configuring it for operations.

Finally, Friday arrived. They had the morning free of scheduled work, apart from the daily exercise requirements.

Mike woke in the Lander. He and John had slept in here last night. Surprisingly John was still asleep, and Mike rarely woke before the others. He extracted himself from the sleeping bag and pushed himself to the control section of the lander, which had the best windows, and studied the heavens laid out before him.

They were heading back to the Moon in their orbit, and it was growing larger. The sun was ever-present in their view from this orbit. And looking out into the 'dark', he could see millions of stars and galaxies everywhere. The view was mesmerising as he looked out into the Milky Way. And then, looking away from the Sun, he could see the Earth, the blue-green jewel, floating in space. Home for every other human! Even the six on the ISS orbited only just above that jewel.

"Stunning, isn't it," said John, floating up behind Mike.

"Morning, John. I didn't hear you wake up," said Mike, slightly startled. "It is an amazing view."

"The amount of space in here, and I guess the dividers for this control area make good acoustic baffles, so you can actually get privacy in here," said John. "You and Sue are going to be in luxury compared to a four-person crew and compared to what Christina and I will have to put up with while you are gone."

"The limitations of re-entry are a pain!" replied Mike.

"What's your favourite bit of the sky?" asked John.

"This bit with the Earth in it!" said Mike.

"Yeah, that is up there. On the ISS, I used to love watching the Moon, but from here, I do tend to watch the Earth," said John. "Are you ready for your lunar descent tomorrow?"

"Can't wait. This week has been slow once we sorted out those issues with the Lander."

"I know. This week-long orbit that the Gateway will be in is a pain operationally."

"I agree. I know it is low cost to maintain and stays in the sun and in view of Earth, but a week is a long time," said Mike.

"Wait till we have to rendezvous dock, transfer, undock and then change orbits, roughly 4 hours after your ascent. That is going to be a busy day!"

"I know," said Mike, "but we've practised for it. Just you guys be ready for us!"

"Are you ready to spend a week alone with Sue?" asked John.

"Yeah, sure. We get on well. And we are going to be busy. You guys are going to get bored!"

"That's what the exercise machines are for!" replied John. "Seriously, are you ready?"

"Absolutely. It's what we've been training for."

"You aren't worried by this terrorism crap?"

"Not really," replied Mike, turning away from the window. "There's enough risk without it. But I think we'll be fine. We've trained for just about every scenario imaginable.

"Are you ready for a week with Christina?"

"Yeah, we are planning a chess tournament!" replied John.

"Really! I didn't realise you both were so into chess."

"We both play a bit, but we've been studying. We won't just be playing ourselves. We've got games lined up, a couple of NASA clubs, and a couple of schools."

"Wow, I had totally missed the fact you guys were doing that," said Mike.

"We've got to do something during the week you are on the moon," said John, launching himself back up to the docking port. "We can't just exercise all week. I think it is time to disturb the sleeping beauties."

"I might watch the heavens a bit longer," said Mike turning back to the window.

He gazed down at the Moon. It looked different because a lot of the surface he could see was the part that faced away from the Earth. The features were less familiar. Even though he had studied maps and photos of the Moon, it still looked unfamiliar. For one thing, the far side didn't have the darker patches known as seas that were actually lava flows. There were a lot more smaller impact craters. There were theories, of course, as to why this difference existed, but it was one of the areas of research that Mike and other scientists would study while on the Moon.

In many ways, the training and preparation for the Moon landing had overshadowed the scientific work that he would conduct on the Moon. The focus had been getting there and getting home, similar to the way it had been for Apollo 11. For Mike, Artemis 4 would have been a better mission scientifically, but being the next man to walk on the Moon since Apollo 17, 52 years earlier, was certainly a thrill.

"It's a great view," said Christina approaching the window behind Mike.

"Wow, you are the second person to surprise me this morning," said Mike. "I didn't hear a thing."

"Yeah, I'm jealous of how much space you guys have."

"I was just talking to John about that."

"The Moon looks so different from this side, doesn't it?" said Christina, studying the view out the window.

"Yep, one of the mysteries we need to solve."

"God has made an amazing universe."

"I'm still not sure I'm sold on the concept of a creator God," said Mike, turning to look at Christina.

"But you haven't discounted it?"

"No."

"Ok, how about something simpler. Have you come to any conclusion about who Jesus is?"

"From what I've been reading, it seems reasonable to conclude he was a historical person. And he said good stuff."

"What about his claims to be God?" asked Christina. "Don't they demand a decision that he was either correct, or mad, or worse?"

"I'm not so sure he made such claims," said Mike, feeling a bit uncomfortable. He wasn't sure and hadn't spent much time thinking about this lately.

"Ok, I'll send you a few links," said Christina. "My view is that what he said was understood by his contemporaries to mean that he was claiming to be God, which was heresy to the Jews, so they wanted to kill him."

"I don't have much time. I'll have to look at them," said Mike. He really didn't think he'd have much time.

"Mike, we are doing pretty crazy stuff here. I really think it's important for you to work out who you think Jesus is and the consequence of that before the landing."

"You are worried about us."

"Yes," said Christina. "All this China stuff only increases our risk. I want you to be really prepared if something happens."

Mike took a deep breath. "Ok, I'll have a look, maybe later this morning if you can send me that info ASAP."

"Sure. I don't want to pressure you, but I think it is important."

"Ok. You keep safe too. You and John aren't out of the woods yourselves."

"True. But I am eternally safe."

That was a strange expression, Mike thought. "I'm going to get some breakfast."

"Sounds good."

They both floated back through the docking adapter to the Orion.

After breakfast, Mike checked his email and replied to some from Lisa and his family. Then he noticed an email from Christina containing some links to information. One was a video from a course called Alpha and a video called 'Who is Jesus?' Since they had good connectivity on the Orion in this orbit, he decided to watch it while still on the Orion. The other links included some books by C.S. Lewis, John Dickson,, and a guy called Josh McDowell. He downloaded the books and other web pages to look at later, put in his earbuds and settled back to watch the video.

The video was well done and challenged a few of his preconceptions. The main presenter mentioned Christina's argument that Jesus was either a fool, mad or God, and referred to C.S. Lewis. Mike hadn't watched the Narnia movies, but he had heard of them. He hadn't read all of the Bible, but he had read some of the stories about Jesus. But he didn't remember Jesus claiming to be God. But there were a few times he was surprised at how other characters in the story reacted to the statement that Jesus had made. He needed to investigate further.

The crew gathered for their last meal together as an entire crew for a week in the Orion. After they had all prepared their meals, Sue got all their attention. "Today is a momentous day for us as a crew as we split into two. Remember, we are doing this whole mission as a crew. Mike and I could not do the moonwalks if it were not for you, John, and Christina. I wish we could all do the landing, but as you know, that is not the plan. I want this meal to be a celebration of what we have done in this mission so far and a chance to look forward to the next two weeks during the landing and return."

"It is truly an honor to be with you both on this journey," said John. "Yes, we will be disappointed to miss out on the landing, but we will have other opportunities. We are part of Man's return to the Moon, and that is something we are all committed to."

"I want to thank both of you, Sue and John, for leading us," said Mike, picking up on the spirit of the meal. "It has not all been easy, but you have kept cool heads and guided us well."

"And I want to bless both of you, Sue and Mike, as you travel down the surface," said Christina. "You have both trained for this. You have been well chosen. I know there's a bit of politics involved, but you are also both great examples of who NASA is. I pray that God will guide and protect you both."

"Thank you all," said Sue. "Let's eat."

The crew had decided to have pizza for this meal. It wasn't quite the same as grabbing a piece of pizza from a tray since everyone had their own food satchel, but they all had the same pizza selections, Pepperoni, and a Mushroom.

'Who's got the Chili sauce?" asked John.

"I've got it," said Mike. He'd been spicing up his mushroom pizza. One drawback of zero-G is that flavour is diminished due to fluid movement in the head. Mike was finding he wanted more spice on just about everything. He passed the sauce to John.

"I'm going sweet chilli on the mushroom, myself," said Christina. "Have you guys got any special meals planned for your time on the Moon?"

"Not really," said Sue. "We have the standard provisions, even though we have some gravity, so I don't know about Mike, but I was just going to play it by ear!"

"Me too," said Mike. "Maybe ice cream after the first walk?"

"I think that would be the least we can do," said Sue.

The crew continued to banter as they ate their lunch.

Once they finished their lunch, Sue and Mike coordinated with Mission Control as they officially moved to the Lander, moving their limited belongings across to the Lander and stowing them there.

Since this was the first mission and effectively a test, both crews donned their survival suits before undocking in case of an unexpected issue.

Sue and Mike, together with the ground, fully activated the life support systems on the Lander and performed final system checkouts.

Finally, in the mid-afternoon, John and Christina farewelled Sue and Mike, the Lander crew. Then the hatches of both vehicles were sealed, leak checks performed, and the docking vestibule decompressed.

John then undocked the Orion capsule from the Lander and manoeuvred it about 100 m away and into a position so that they would not be affected by the thruster firing of the Lander and out of its planned path the next day. Sue monitored the Lander systems, but the only action required was to counteract a small amount of movement gained during undocking.

Sue and Mike were about to spend their first night in the Lander alone.

49

— • —

Saturday, May 25, 2024

Sue awoke in her sleeping bag in the Lander. The Lander was quieter than the Orion, possibly partly due to its bigger volume, so she had slept better than in the Orion.

The previous night she and Mike had prepared their dinner, using their food preparation area for the first time, and also christened their waste management facilities. Then they hung their sleeping bags and got some much-needed rest after a busy afternoon.

Today would be an interesting day. They would descend towards the Moon and land on it. It would take most of the day, with them first entering into a lower lunar orbit and then descending to their landing. There would be three main burns, including their powered descent. The following week would be busy for Mike and herself. Tomorrow would be the first moonwalk, and another the next day. Then they would have a rest day, which means they would be doing a fair bit of cleaning! Then 2 more days of walks, and on the last day, they would ascend back into lunar orbit and rendezvous with the Orion.

Retrieving her tablet, Sue checked her messages. There was nothing urgent, and the latest status report showed everything normal, so there were no pressing issues to process.

Sue unzipped her bag and floated out of it, unhooking one end and attaching both ends to the same attachment point. She unzipped it so it could air-dry, then moved down to the control area to gaze out the windows.

As expected, the Moon filled the view out the windows as they rushed towards it. She could almost make out their landing site near the Lunar South Pole.

Tomorrow she would be walking down there, she was certain. She wondered how she would feel.

Earth was in view too, and she wondered what Ron, Jessica and Jerome would be doing right now. Probably eating breakfast. Jessica was growing up so quickly and reminded Sue of herself as a child. Very inquisitive and confident.

Was she overconfident in being certain she would be walking on the Moon tomorrow? After all, a lot had to go right today for them to get there. Yet, she was confident that the NASA teams had done their jobs properly. She also didn't think there had been any more attempts of sabotage. She knew she could perform her job. She and Mike had trained for all the scenarios anyone could come up with, so she knew they were ready.

Sue heard Mike's tablet start playing his alarm sound, and a groaning noise emanated from his sleeping bag.

"Time to get up Mike. Big day today," she said.

"Go away," came a muffled cry from his bag.

"Well, I'm going to start making noise. There's a beautiful Moon outside!"

"Maybe we should go take a look at it," said Mike, unzipping his sleeping bag.

"Since we are so close, might as well," replied Sue.

Sue started getting ready for her daily ablutions. Another convenience of the Lander is that there was a bit more privacy than the Orion, but only a bit.

Mike grabbed a drink bottle and headed to the control area himself, gazing out at the vista. The Moon now dominated, but he could still see the Earth, millions of stars and galaxies, and the Sun.

After a few minutes of gazing at the view, Mike retrieved his tablet and checked his messages. Lisa had sent some photos of herself and Jasmine, and his parents. It was great to see life progressing normally while he was orbiting the Moon.

Mike took some photos of the Moon and Earth and sent some of them to Lisa, telling her he missed her.

It was strange. A few years ago, he would have been intoxicated with the thought of spending a week alone with Sue with nowhere to go. Now all he could think about was Lisa and Jasmine! He'd do anything for Jasmine. It was odd that he didn't think that way about Jerome. But why should he? He didn't even know for sure that he was his son. But still, shouldn't he have the same bond?

He stared out at the Moon. It was a geological mystery. It was huge and close. One side was pockmarked with craters, the other with recent volcanic activity. Why?

He looked across at the Earth and caught a glimpse of the Orion capsule. Here they were, in two small capsules so far from the only planet they knew of that supported life. And it looked tiny against the vast expanse of planets, stars and galaxies. No wonder people worshipped gods. If a being created all this, then it was worthy of worship. Maybe Christina was right in worshipping a creator God. What flummoxed Mike was that such a being would intervene in the lives of men, let alone come as a baby and then die on a cross. It didn't make sense. Except, he'd do the same for Jasmine. Maybe love did make sense of it all.

"Ground for Lander," came the message on the speakers.

Since Sue was occupied, Mike moved to the nearest communications station and keyed the microphone. "Lander copies you, Good morning, Go ahead."

"Good morning, Mike. We hope you had a good night. We just wanted to make sure you both are up and getting ready for your big day."

"Thanks, Houston. We are both awake and making our preparations for the day."

"Fantastic. Christina and John are also up on the Orion. We will configure a loop for communications in about an hour."

Two hours later, both crews had finished their breakfast meals and cleaned up. Sue and Mike had now secured loose items in the cabin and strapped themselves in their seats, ready for the first deceleration burn to place them in a much lower orbit. This and a shorter burn in about 2 hours would put them into an orbit about 200 kilometres above the lunar surface. The burns had to be precisely timed.

"You know," said Mike as he settled into his seat, "I'm still amazed at how Apollo managed to do these tasks with the equipment they had. Even for us, if our burn is not performed at the right time and for the right amount of thrust, we will end up in the wrong orbit, and then we might not be able to get back. We have multiple high-capacity computers, and my smartwatch has more capacity than the Apollo lander systems."

"It is amazing, isn't it. I think it's even amazing today that we can navigate so precisely. Think how easy it will be in the future once we get some positioning and communication satellites in Lunar orbit," replied Sue.

"Lander, this is Houston on the loop. We are ready for item 45 dot 5."

"Roger, Houston, beginning item 45 dot 5," said Mike on the communications channel.

"Ok, so we are essentially performing a system check," said Sue. For the next five minutes, she read through the checklist, identified the relevant display and ensured each system was correctly configured.

"Houston, Lander, we have completed item 45 dot 5," reported Mike on the radio.

"Lander, we copy. We've got a Go/No-Go poll in three minutes."

"Copy that, Houston," replied Mike.

"Hmm, I guess we were a bit close for that one," said Sue, checking the timeline. "I think they started us late. Are you aware of any issues?"

"No, we've still got twenty minutes to the burn, so there is contingency. I gather there was nothing in the commander briefing?" asked Mike.

"Nothing to do with this. There was a bit higher than expected solar activity, but I haven't noticed any comms issues."

"Orion, Houston, on the loop, are you go for the burn?"

"Houston, Orion is go for Lander burn," said John on the radio.

"Lander, Houston, on the loop, are you go for the burn?"

"Houston, we are go for the burn," said Sue on the radio.

"CAPCOM copies, you are go for the burn, stand by," said George as CAPCOM in Houston. "Flight Director has approved the burn, Lander. You are go for item 45 dot 6."

"Lander copies, Go for burn, performing item 45 dot 6," replied Mike on the radio.

Sue commanded the execution of the burn, and a timer on the screen displayed the remaining time to ignition.

"Houston, Lander, T minus 17 minutes 30 seconds to burn ... MARK," said Mike on the radio. It was a fairly pointless exercise since all data was being streamed back to Houston. However, it was a NASA tradition providing a crude backup in case of telemetry loss and some context for recordings when reviewed.

"Time to relax for a bit," said Mike.

"Not really going to happen," said Sue.

"At least we can talk about something else for a bit."

"Lander, Orion, on the loop," said John on the radio.

"Orion, Lander, go ahead," said Mike.

"We wanted to wish you guys the best. Christina and I both wish we were with you. We'll be watching from above," said John."

"Thanks, guys. We know we'll have you angels watching us while we are down there," said Sue.

"Now they can get back to their exercise regime," said Mike. "The way this mission is organised never really made sense to me. They could have just as easily landed with us since future missions will have four members landing. At least if the Gateway had been in use, then they could have done a reasonable amount of science."

"Political funding compromises, and a bit of over-cautious planning, I think," said Sue, running through a few system status pages on her display.

"I think someone just thought, 'Hey, they did it for Apollo, so we have to do it.'"

"Personally, I think they don't want to leave capsules unmanned yet," said Sue.

"You are probably right, but it doesn't make sense since we have lots of unmanned missions."

"Did you get any messages from Lisa?" asked Sue, changing the topic.

"Yeah, mostly just some photos, which was nice. I sent a couple of the local landscapes to her!"

"Local landscape! You can say that tomorrow. Today it is a great vacuum!"

"I did send a photo of the Orion," said Mike sounding hurt.

They started to hear some new sounds, and the Lander's systems prepared for the burn. The thrusters were firing a bit more often as the vehicle was precisely orientated, and the fuel was settled in the tanks.

"Did you get any messages?" asked Mike.

"My mother sent me an email wishing me the best. I suspect Ron hasn't had time. Let me check," said Sue. She checked her tablet and discovered a message from Ron and another from Jessica. "Actually, Jessica and Ron have written. Let me have a read."

Jessica had taken a selfie with Jerome and said she loved her mother. Ron said they were all watching and hoping all went well, and that he loved her and then had a selfie of all three of them.

"They are all well and send their love. They are so cute. I miss them," said Sue.

"Yep, I miss Lisa and Jerome too. Just think – we'll see them in 2 weeks!" said Mike.

The vehicle shook as the Lander engines fired for the first time, slowing them and lowering their orbit.

Mike looked across at Sue as she studied the displays. "A bit rougher than the simulations," he said.

"A bit, but we are the first humans in one of these craft."

A year earlier, a version of the lander without crew quarters had been tested to ensure systems operated as expected.

"Houston, Lander. All systems green, getting some vibration, otherwise all good," reported Mike on the communications channel.

"Lander, we copy that. Your trajectory is nominal. One minute left in the burn."

"The Orion is starting to move away a lot faster now," said Mike, "or perhaps I should say we are moving away a lot faster."

"A pity I won't get to fly this thing," said Sue. "I'd love to feel how it actually responds."

"I bet it would be as touchy as hell. You know what the simulator was like." Both had trained to manually control the Lander, and Sue could land it manually if necessary. However, it was improbable that they would need to do so. The most that was expected was some correction of inputs for the landing site, which would be implemented by the computers.

"And that's the end of the burn," said Sue.

"Houston, Lander, our burn is complete," said Mike on the radio.

"Copy that, Lander. You are GO for 45 dot 8."

"Roger and Wilco, 45 dot 8 in work," replied Mike.

Sue and Mike worked through the next item on the checklist, ensuring the systems were made safe.

"All done," said Sue. "That was too easy!"

"Well, it was the easy bit," said Mike. "Houston, Lander, 45 dot 8 completed."

"We copy that, Mike. You both can leave your seats now and reconfigure the cabin. Tracking shows you are on nominal course."

"We copy that. Thank you."

"A pity that the landing, the hard part, is at the end of the day," said Sue. "I'll want a snooze this afternoon before that. I'm getting a coffee. You want snacks?"

"Sure", said Mike. The burn that had just been completed would lower their orbit. Another one would circularise it in a couple of hours, so they were basically 200 kilometres above the lunar surface. Then, about 2 hours later, they would perform the landing burn.

They unstrapped their seat harness and floated to the food dispensing area to prepare their coffees and other snacks.

The pressure in the Lander cabin was being reduced to the same pressure that the xEMU suits operate at, 4.5 psi. This meant that the amount of oxygen was being increased as well. The lower pressure, however, water boils at around 70 deg C, so their coffees were not as hot as usual.

"Hmm, a bit lukewarm, isn't it," said Mike.

"Yep, but at least the ice cream will stay cold!"

"I was thinking about Jerome," said Mike.

"Umm, go on."

"So, you haven't had any doubts in the past that he was Ron's?"

"Only a little before he was born, but he looks like Ron," said Sue. "Until I heard about Jasmine, I hadn't given it another thought."

"OK. I was thinking it would be good to get a test."

"What?! Why? Does it matter that much to you?" asked Sue, surprised.

"It would clear things up and might help with the children's treatments if we know they are related."

"But then both Ron and Lisa would find out," said Sue with a look of horror. "I don't want that."

"I think we can handle it."

"You might be able to, but I'm not sure I can. At least you weren't in a relationship."

"But it will clear things up," said Mike.

"I don't want to talk about this," said Sue, turning away. "Let's focus on the suit preparation."

"But it is important," said Mike, moving in front of her.

"Mike, I don't want to discuss it. Move on," said Sue, her face reddening.

Mike acquiesced and took his coffee and snack over to his spacesuit. They were scheduled to perform some preparation activities on the suits to prepare them for their first moonwalk the next day.

50

— ◆ —

They spent the next couple of hours prepping their xEMU suits for the moonwalk the next day and definitely not discussing Jerome. Sue was annoyed that Mike now wanted to talk about her son. There was no way she was going to disclose to Ron that she and Mike had hooked up while he had been away years ago. She only envisioned disaster doing that.

They returned to their chairs briefly for the circularising burn that put the Lander into an orbit at roughly 200 kilometres about the lunar surface.

During their lunch, Mike judiciously avoided any discussion about Jerome, and they had a scheduled rest period after lunch to be ready for the landing. Sue managed to catnap and felt rested as they once again strapped themselves into seats to begin their checklists for the landing sequence.

"Are you ready to do this?" asked Mike.

"I sure am. It's taken long enough to get here. Are you ready?" replied Sue.

"Bring it on," said Mike.

After talking to Mission Control, they verified that the lander systems were correctly configured. Once again, the process would be almost entirely automated. However, Sue would need to designate and refine the exact landing spot as they approached the surface. She could take over control and manually land if required, but only under certain emergency conditions.

"Lander, Houston," came the call from George as CAPCOM in Mission Control. He was rostered on for all the significant events of the mission.

"Go ahead, Houston," replied Mike.

"Mike, we have a GO for you guys to proceed with item 50 dot 7. Godspeed."

"Houston, we copy that," replied Mike. To Sue, he said, "Time for your speech, and don't forget to smile!"

"Houston, this is Orion, on the loop for Lander," said John on the communications circuit.

"Proceed, Orion," replied CAPCOM.

"Sue and Mike, we wish you Godspeed and a safe landing. We'll be watching and the first to see you land."

"Orion, Lander, thank you, John and Christina, for your wishes. We will give you a wave," replied Sue. Despite them being the closest humans, it was virtually impossible to locate the Orion against the background of stars. But they knew they were there. It had been good to hear their voices. Unlike the days of Apollo, they didn't have much of a role to play until they rendezvoused again in a week.

Sue took a deep breath. She was now on script. The first part of item 50.7 was actually a speech! On the communications circuit, she said, "Houston, Lander."

"Lander, go ahead," came the reply about three seconds later. Sue looked at the camera facing them.

"As we initiate this landing, we continue Man's exploration of our solar system, particularly our Moon. We continue the work done fifty years ago by the brave men of the Apollo program. In Artemis, we extend the boundaries of the men and women of Earth by working towards the ongoing presence of men and women living and working on the Moon. America and our partners in the Artemis Accord will learn how to live here on the Moon, access her resources, and travel to Mars."

Sue paused to allow any urgent communications to be sent and then continued, "Mike and I are proud to be on this journey as the first woman and next man to land on and walk on the Moon's surface, preparing the way for many to follow. We thank the Artemis project team for all the work that has been done to get us to this point. We are ready for this next small step."

"Houston copies, Lander, and look forward to working with you over this next week as we once again step onto the Moon," said George.

"Lander copies and we are proceeding with item 50 dot 8," replied Mike.

Ten minutes later, the countdown on their screens showed T minus 00:04:03 as the call came from Houston: "Lander, you are go for the burn."

Mike replied, "Houston, we copy and are executing."

"Do you have any issues we need to consider?" asked Sue.

"No, all looks good to me. You?"

"I'm good. We've now had two burns, so everything seems to be working properly, so probably no sabotage there."

"Oh, I wish you hadn't brought that up. But regardless, there is redundancy, so I'm happy."

Once again, noises of the rocket system preparations were heard in the cabin, and thruster firings became more common as the fuel in the tanks settled to the bottom. Otherwise, the lack of gravity would mean that fuel would not be at the bottom of the tanks where the feed tube was when the engines were ignited, meaning the rocket engine would not work or would not work properly. This could lead to the destruction of the engines.

"Orientation looks good, pressures are good, all systems green. I think we are landing," said Sue.

"Houston, we are still looking good for landing," said Mike on the radio.

"Lander, we concur. We are still go. Flight sends their best wishes."

"Copy that, Houston."

During the last ten seconds of the countdown, the thrusters were firing almost continuously, and the whine of the fuel pumps could be heard. Just before zero, the engines began their start-up sequence, and a T plus zero, Mike and Sue felt the comforting force of acceleration push them back into their seats.

"And here we go," said Sue. "All systems nominal, thrust on all engines nominal and stable, thrust increasing in 5 seconds."

The acceleration that Sue and Mike felt now increased again to the maximum. It was the third time that day that their bodies had felt something that resembled gravity. The whole spacecraft shook as the engines decelerated them from their orbital speed, and they began their descent.

Gradually, they transitioned from orbital flight to descent, and the engines throttled back as they fell towards the lunar surface.

"Lander, Houston, all systems look good, and tracking is nominal."

"We copy that, Houston," said Mike.

"We just lost an engine, it is restarting, and the others in its pod are compensating," reported Sue.

"Lander, we see your engine out. Otherwise nominal." Said CAPCOM on the radio.

"Can you see the landing zone yet?" asked Mike.

"Only just. Still a bit high and fast," said Sue.

"Hmm, some of our data communications have lost lock, and are re-establishing, said Mike.

"That engine has relit," said Sue.

"Houston, Lander, we appear to have some communication dropouts. We are still nominal, with all engines operational," reported Mike on the radio.

"Lander, we copy. We've got the data we need. We just lost video for a short while."

"Copy that, Houston."

"I'm able to see the landing site now," said Sue. "We are still too high to designate."

Mike looked down towards his feet. There were windows located there so they could see the surface during the descent. It took him a few moments to find the geographical features of their landing site next to a large crater called Shackelton Crater. It was precisely where it had been during simulations.

"Ok, I see it too," Mike said. "Confirming landing system is tracking the same location."

"I agree," said Sue.

"Houston, Lander, we have a landing site in view, and the landing system is tracking the correct location. Going hot mics," said Mike. Their microphones would now be activated whenever either of them spoke.

"5000 metres at 200 metres per second," said Sue.

"All systems green," said Mike.

"4000 at 120, on target", reported Sue.

An alarm sounded.

"Radar Altimeter error. LIDAR is ok.," said Mike.

"Seriously?" said Sue. "3000 at 80, on target." Apollo 11 had problems relating to radar, she hadn't actually expected any, but they had practised for them.

"Tracking is nominal. You are looking good," said CAPCOM on the radio.

"Radar Altimeter has now reset and looking good," said Mike.

"2000 at 50, on target."

"1000 at 30, on target."

The grey lunar landscape was now indeed rushing up before them, and they could make out great detail, but they didn't have time to admire it. In fact, they were both very familiar with the landscape after countless simulations. One of the benefits that the Artemis 3 crew had over the Apollo crews was the wealth of imagery and data on the Moon accumulated over recent decades.

"800 at 20, on target. I'm picking this spot," Sue said, pointing to a location on her screen with a flashing icon.

Mike looked at his display and the area around the icon. It appeared flat, without any large boulders, and not too far from the crater edge, yet in sunlight, which they needed for their solar power cells. "Yes, I concur," he said.

Sue confirmed their selection, and they immediately felt a slight shift in the direction of the lander as thrusters fired to align them with that location.

"500 at 10, on target, four engines out," said Sue. The engine shutdowns were expected as fewer engines were required to slow their progress and hover if needed. Landing using rockets was a tricky business, often requiring a rocket's last-minute firing since the rocket engines' power means the rocket can't hover. However, the lander was designed such that a smaller number of its engines would allow hovering on the Moon if required and a gentle landing.

"400 at 8," said Sue.

"Lander, Houston, you are GO for landing," came the call on the radio.

"Roger, Wilco, Houston," replied Mike.

"300 at 5, on target. I'm still happy with the site," said Sue.

"Yep, LIDAR only shows a 2-degree slope," said Mike.

"200 at 4. On target, proceeding."

"All systems are still green," said Mike.

"100 at 2, on target."

Sue took a deep breath. This was it. They would be on the lunar surface in less than a minute.

"50 at 1, on target, site looks clear, proceeding."

Mike looked out the window and checked the landing area visually.

"25, all system green, kicking up dust," said Sue. And boy, was she right. They'd have to rely on the radar.

Sue counted down the last 10 metres, one at a time, monitoring that the craft stayed level.

"0, engine shutdown," said Sue.

"All engines showing shutdown, fuel valves closed."

"Houston, Shackelton Base, we have landed!"

"Shackelton, Houston, congratulations and welcome to the Moon!"

— • —

51

Sue and Mike remained in their chairs, feeling the lower lunar gravity, and monitored the safing of the Lander's rockets. Their landing site appeared to be stable, so there did not appear to be a need for an emergency abort ascent. There was not much they could see outside as the dust they had disturbed was still settling to the surface.

"That went well," said Mike.

"Yes. About the only issue was the RADAR Altimeter," replied Sue.

"I'm sure we'll hear an explanation, but I bet someone was playing a joke on us."

"We've got a slight slope, but I don't think it will worry us too much. Did you get an idea how far we are from the crater rim?" Sue asked.

"Roughly 500 metres, I think. We are pretty much in the perfect spot as per our plans."

"The systems all look good. We've got lots of fuel, and the solar panels are now feedings us power again. I think we are in for a good week," said Sue.

"Shackelton, this is Houston," called George as CAPCOM on the radio.

"Houston, this is Shackelton. Go ahead," said Sue.

"Everything looks good to us. You are GO to leave your seats, get some dinner and prepare for your rest time. Hopefully, you'll be able to see the view in an hour."

"Copy that, Houston. We would like to congratulate the team on an almost perfect landing. We are ready to get some shut-eye and have a look outside tomorrow," said Sue.

"Thank you, Sue. You guys enjoy some well-earnt rest," replied CAP-COM.

Sue and Mike unstrapped themselves and, for the first time in 2 weeks, did not immediately begin to float away from their chairs.

"Remember to take it easy standing up," said Sue, as she carefully ventured standing up herself. "The room is now definitely spinning."

"I had noticed that a bit as I looked around," said Mike, still in his chair.

"Well, my bladder is urging me forward, so I'm going to be the first to use a toilet on the Moon."

"Sure, go ahead. I'll let Mission Control know," said Mike.

A bit humiliating, thought Sue. Yet historic. In zero-G, body fluids went to all strange places, and now they were in gravity again, those fluids were returning to their usual locations. Just as they would for a landing on Earth, both she and Mike had consumed additional fluids before the landing to help ensure that they did not pass out due to low blood pressure.

The toilet Sue would use was essentially the same as used on the Orion and the International Space station since the Lander needed to support zero-G and low gravity operations. That meant essentially a low-level suction device for this need. At least they had been able to test and train on this equipment on Earth, which was not really possible with the zero-G operations.

But it was still better than adult diapers. They were still used in some short-duration space suits, even the xEMUs.

Meanwhile, Mike was able to stand up, and he began walking around the cabin, checking that stowed equipment had not come loose during the landing. He located his sleeping bag and placed it on his bunk. Yes, they had bunks for the period they were on the lunar surface. They could have used these spaces for sleeping while in orbit, but they both had preferred to hang their sleeping bags in the open. A crew of four would constrain that option in the future.

Mike bent down to pick up a bag he had dropped and almost fell over into the lockers.

"Are you ok, Mike," asked Sue as she re-entered the cabin.

"Yes, I just lost my balance there," he said, straightening up and swaying as he fought to keep his balance.

"Tomorrow might be fun in the suits," said Sue.

"Hopefully, a night's sleep will help. I guess the extra time in orbit has not been helpful compared to the Apollo experience."

"I don't think it has helped," replied Sue. "At least we have chairs and a table to sit at to eat now! Why don't you clean up while I prepare some food. Do you want to choose yours?"

Since they were to be on the surface for almost a week, the Lander had to work in both zero-G and low-gravity environments. Sue unlatched the folding table against one wall of the cabin. There were two fold-down chairs and another two stools located in lockers which they could use with the table

"Sure," said Mike, heading to their toilet. "You pick."

Sue walked over to their food preparation area and steadied herself against the wall. She took care to carefully look at what she was doing. They had trained to counter the effects of Space Adaption Sickness (SAS). She needed to be careful to trust only what she could see. The rest of her body was giving her conflicting messages about her orientation.

She selected two meals, placed them in the warmer, and set the time and power settings. She then chose two drink packs and filled them with water. Then she got some cutlery and put them on the table. The Moon's low gravity meant that they could eat normally, and several meals had been prepared so they could be fully opened and eaten on a plate if they so desired.

She slowly walked over to the observation windows while she waited for the food to heat. Outside, the dust was slowly settling, and she could see the crater rim and the surface beneath them. The lighting was stark, as expected, and the dust was like a haze. It looked surprisingly like the deserts in which they had trained, except there was no blue sky. At the horizon, the view went from a bright surface to the darkest black. The long shadows cast by various features likewise were black.

Mike returned to the cabin and walked over to the window. "That's amazing," he said. "The dust is settling quickly, and I really want to get a closer look at that crater rim."

"It's close enough that we can go tomorrow," said Sue. "Dinner is ready."

"This could be fun," said Mike. "We might end up wearing dinner. I've already hit my head twice on the ceiling in the toilet."

"We should be right, just no rapid movements and no food fights!"

They walked to the table, which really meant, they stepped. Both of them misjudged the distance and overshot. The lower gravity meant that they spent longer in the air between steps.

"Whoa, overshoot," said Mike. "This will take a bit of getting used to." He took one of the seats. "What have we got?"

"I thought roast turkey was a good choice for a first meal on the Moon. It smells pretty good."

"Yep, it tastes good, too," said Mike after his first bite. "Hey, I can taste the food! I haven't really been able to for the last 2 weeks!"

"The fluids in your sinus must have settled. That's a bit quicker than expected."

"Well, I'm happy about it. Food without taste is boring."

"I agree," said Sue. "I wonder what the Chinese think about our landing."

"I reckon they will be really, really unhappy, especially after the failure of their mission."

"I don't think I'd like to be part of the CNSA project team. They must be getting a grilling."

"You have to admit, though," said Mike as he examined his vegetables, "that they have come a long way in a short time, and they are doing everything by themselves, whereas we are working with our partners."

"It is amazing how far they've come in the last 20 years, and I'm pretty sure they are spending more than NASA."

"Actually, I'm not so sure about that. The reports I've seen still put their spending at around half ours."

"Then, they are getting a lot of bang for their buck! It is only 21 years since China put their first man into orbit."

"You know, we got stuck in a rut, which the commercial space program helped break. They have been very motivated and learnt quickly, and they haven't had stupid political interference stuffing up their programs, at least not often."

"Hmm," said Sue. "We need to finish prepping our suits ready for tomorrow."

"Is that the only major task on the checklists before we rest?"

"Yes. Not sure how I'm going to sleep, though."

"I don't know, I'm pretty tired. It's been a long busy day."

"Yep, it will be nice to hit the pillow. An actual pillow and actually lie down."

"Yeah – that will be different," said Mike, finishing his meal. "So, what's the task with the suits?"

"Basically, we need to set them in the correct orientation for tomorrow, ensure the charging is happening, and check consumables. It's all in the checklist."

"Great, it shouldn't take long. Then I can chat with Lisa and do some reading."

"Sounds like a plan. Ron should have Jessica and Jerome ready to chat with me in about an hour."

They both disposed of their meal trays and grabbed their pads to work through the checklist items.

An hour later, Mike climbed into his sleeping bunk, pulled the curtain for privacy, and put on his earbuds, ready to chat with Lisa. The prep work on the suits had gone smoothly, as expected, and they had a couple of hours before they were expected to sleep. Time to talk with friends and family and relax.

There was just enough room for him to be able to sit in the bunk space. He set up his tablet in front of himself and started the call with Lisa. There would be a bit of a lag, as the Orion was acting as a communications gateway since it could always see the Earth and their location on the Moon.

"Hi Mike, so good to see you," said Lisa, waving.

"Hi, honey, good to see you too. Have you had a good day?"

There was a pause, and Mike watched Lisa wait for him to respond.

"Yes, we've all been watching you guys and especially the landing. It all looked to go perfectly."

"It was almost perfect, but it has been a long, busy day. I'm looking forward to relaxing."

"Are you coping ok there?"

"Yeah. Takes a bit to get used to gravity again, but we both enjoyed actually smelling our food!"

"That's great. We all went to Ron and Sue's house to watch the landing, and we had a grill together. It was good to see everyone and to be together, especially during the landing."

Mike had heard rumours this might happen, but Sue hadn't mentioned anything. Perhaps Ron hadn't told her!

"That would have been good."

"Yes, and I had a chat with Ron about Jerome's hypermobility. It was good to get some perspective on how Jerome has been going. Maybe it won't be as bad as I was thinking. Ron was a bit surprised that Jasmine may have the same condition since it is pretty rare."

"Oh really," said Mike, swallowing. "Well, we don't know if it is the same thing yet."

"I know, but it was still good to hear how they had coped. So, can we see out a window?" said Lisa, holding up Jasmine.

"Umm, sure, let me get out of here," said Mike, opening his bunk curtain and stepping out of it. "I have to remember that I can't just float there. I hope I remember that when I wake up tomorrow."

Mike walked over to the main window and stood so Lisa and Jasmine could see the moonscape over his shoulder.

"Wow, that is amazing."

"Yes," said Mike, turning to look out the window and switching to use the camera on the other side of the pad. "The dust has cleared now, so we can see everything very well. I want to go over to that patch over there on the rim tomorrow. There appear to be different colours, so that should mean different rock types, which will be interesting."

"Oh wow, that is an even better view. Can you see that, Jasmine? That is where Daddy is."

Mike switched back to the selfie camera and waved at his young daughter. "How are you, my lovely girl?"

"She is doing really well, but I think she is ready to sleep now," said Lisa.

"Fair enough. Are you getting enough sleep?"

"Yes, and your parents have been great, especially Clare. And she is sleeping through until about four now, so I get about six hours of sleep uninterrupted."

"That's great. I'm sorry I haven't been there much in the last month. She has really grown a lot!"

"Just don't make a habit of it! Are you ready for your walk tomorrow?"

"I can't wait. Hopefully, I'll sleep tonight. The chance to actually walk on the Moon and explore it! We aren't far from a permanently shadowed spot, so we might even find water tomorrow."

"Wow. You have worked so hard for this. I'm so excited for you."

"Where are you going to watch it from?" Mike asked.

"The project team have invited us to Mission Control, and they are feeding us nearby. So, we will get to see the feed in real-time."

"Great. But I guess you won't be there the whole 8 hours?"

"No, probably the first 4 or so. I think Jasmine needs to go to bed now. She is getting restless. Have a good sleep and a great walk tomorrow. We love you."

"Ok – I love you both too." They waved and threw kisses at each other, and then Lisa closed the call.

Mike went back to his bunk, noting that Sue was on a call with someone.

He checked his emails and responded to a few, as well as his social media, and then settled in to read. He'd been reading an ebook called 'Is Jesus History' by an Australian historian, John Dickson. Mike had not spent much time understanding history, so it was fascinating to understand a bit about how ancient texts are treated academically and how much historical evidence there is about Jesus.

52

SUNDAY, MAY 26, 2024

Sue awoke lying in her bunk. Actually, lying on something! Not just floating. It was different. With the lower gravity, she tended to bounce more,
too.

She had slept surprisingly well and woke a little before the official
wake-up time. She stretched and grabbed her pad from its charging place,
having a quick look at incoming messages. There were a bunch of operational messages which she would need to read soon. She also had a couple
of personal messages, but nothing urgent. It wasn't surprising, they were
operating in the same time zone as Houston, so Ron would have been
asleep while she was.

Sue unzipped her bunk curtain, swung out, put her feet down on the
floor, and carefully stood up. They needed to be careful since actions taken
with the same force used on earth would probably put her into the ceiling,
which wasn't that high anyway. In fact, that was a downside of being in
gravity. It wasn't so easy to stretch. In zero-G, she would just orientate in a
different direction to stretch. The area they used for exercise had a bit more
space, with a lower floor and higher ceiling, so she moved down there to
perform some stretches.

Just as Sue finished these, the wake-up music started, Walking on the
Moon by The Police. Each day Mission Control played a wakeup song

related to the day's activities, and on this mission, they had been digitally triggered rather than broadcast. The tradition started with Gemini 6 when Hello Dolly was played and had become a bit of fun between Mission Control and the crews.

As the song played, Sue headed back to the front of the craft. Meanwhile, Mike sleepily emerged from his bunk.

"Morning Sue, ready to go walking on the Moon?" asked Mike.

"I sure am," said Sue. "Did you sleep well?"

"Very well. Nice to lie down!"

"I agree. Just watch out for the low ceiling!" she said as Mike started stretching.

Sue looked out the observation window to see a sparkling lunar rover sitting there.

"Our ride has arrived," she said.

"Cool," said Mike. "I didn't fancy walking everywhere."

As the music stopped, Sue reached for a communications microphone. "Good morning, Houston. We are both ready to go walking on the Moon today!"

"Good morning, Sue. Good to hear. I hope you both slept well," said the CAPCOM.

"Yes, we both enjoyed lying down for a change."

"Great. We have nothing urgent for you. Give us a call when you are ready with your medical data."

The surgeon was always interested in their medical data, but even more so while they were on the Moon. During the night, the pressure in the cabin had been gradually reduced to 8 PSI and the proportion of oxygen increased. This had been done to help shorten their pre-breathe procedures to use their suits. The new xEMU suits also helped by beginning operations at 8 PSI and gradually reducing pressure to 4 PSI with a pure oxygen environment. The lower pressure assisted with mobility. However, without any pre-breathing of oxygen, the nitrogen would still bubble out of their blood at the lower pressure and cause decompression sickness. So, they started the day with medical tests.

The tests weren't anything too tricky, blood pressure, oxygenation, pulse, breathing rates, and temperature. They also applied ECG pads which would remain on them during the spacewalks. Once they had completed these, the data was transmitted to the ground, and they both had private discussions with the surgeon.

Sue read through her outstanding operational messages while Mike had his discussion with the flight surgeon. Everything was to be expected. A few final changes to procedures and some timing adjustments. The security briefing contained no surprises, and everything looked good for their first full day on the lunar surface.

Mike finished his discussions and joined Sue. "Time for some breakfast?" he said.

"Sure," said Sue.

"What do you want?" Mike asked.

"Eggs, scrambled if there are any. And some flatbread, and Apple juice, thanks."

Mike grabbed these, a Mexican omelette and an orange juice for himself and started heating and adding water as required while Sue finished her reading.

"Anything I need to know in the briefings?" he asked.

"No. Everything is as expected, just some tweaking of some times, but nothing that you'll notice!"

"So, when do we start the pre-breathe?"

"In about 30 minutes. I gather SURGEON was happy with you?"

"Yep, no problems. Yourself?"

"Everything was good," said Sue.

"I don't know, all this training and no problems to fix!" said Mike as he passed Sue her breakfast, and they sat at the fold-out table.

"Hey, don't complain. I'm sure we'll have problems during the walk. No one's done this for 50 years!"

"Do we have an order of tasks for the walk? I want to know when we get to go see that outcrop."

"I did pass on your request, and it's on the list. As expected, we have a few housekeeping and test tasks around here first, and, of course, speeches. I think it's the second destination for today's drive."

"Great! I can't wait to do some actual geology! You can have the speeches! Is it 'great leap for woman kind' this time?"

"Nothing so droll."

"Shackelton, this is Orion, Good Morning," said John over the communications channel.

"Good morning, Orion. How are you guys?" replied Sue.

"We are well, Sue. Just watching you guys recede below us as we float around."

"Great, John. We enjoyed a night lying in our bunks, and we are sitting down eating our breakfast on plates!"

"Ahh yes, but you can't perform a triple axel with a quadruple somersault."

"I'll try one later during our walk if you like. Or maybe I'll get Mike to do one!"

"Ok, we will watch. Have a great day, guys, and a fantastic walk."

"Thanks, John. You guys keep safe."

"I'm glad I'm down here and not them. I'd be really frustrated staying on the Orion," said Mike.

"Well, it's good you aren't there. And they've known for years, so they are prepared for their role."

"True. We've still got 15 minutes before we start the procedure. I'm going to clean up," said Mike.

The pre-breathe process required each of them to perform ten minutes of strenuous exercise while breathing pure oxygen, then breathe pure oxygen through a mask for the next hour before entering their suits. Once they entered their suits and performed leak checks etc., they would be able to leave the craft. This was much faster than the previous space suit requirements, which required 2 hours and 20 minutes of pre-breathe procedures.

Sue, as commander, began first, with Mike reporting the completion of the steps in the procedure to Mission Control. Once she had finished her ten minutes of exercise, Mike climbed onto the exercise device for his ten minutes. They then spent the next hour wearing the oxygen masks while they finished preparations for their walk, changed into the special garments they wore in the suits and completed items on their checklists.

"Shackelton, Houston. We are ready for you to proceed to the airlock. We are turning on the cameras. So, the first step is to enter the airlock and close the hatch."

"Roger and Wilco, Houston. We are proceeding to the airlock," replied Sue.

They disconnected their oxygen masks and proceeded into the airlock, a relatively constrained space. There they reconnected their oxygen masks, and Mike closed the hatch. The turning on of the cameras indicated that the media event had begun in earnest.

"Houston, we are in the airlock, masks transferred, and the hatch is sealed," said Sue.

While the airlock atmosphere was changed to pure oxygen, they had a bit of time to kill as they continued their pre-breathe on their oxygen masks. Rather than operate the entire vehicle with pure oxygen, this was only done in the airlock so they could safely ingress into the suits without having to wear the masks. Sue decided to read some of her personal messages that she hadn't had time to read earlier. She noticed that one had recently arrived from Ron and opened it.

Ron expressed his surprise that Mike and Lisa's daughter may also have a hypermobility condition. He didn't remember Sue ever telling him about it, and he found out about it when Lisa visited their house the day before. This worried Sue. She had been concerned that Ron might get curious as to why two children of their team members have the same medical condition.

Sue wrote a quick reply, saying she was preparing for the moonwalk and that they would have to discuss the matter later. She also commented that she had only recently heard about it herself, and it was early days in the medical investigation for Jasmine, and it may be something else entirely.

"Did you know Lisa and Ron talked about Jasmine's hypermobility yesterday?" she abruptly asked Mike.

"Yes, said Mike through his oxygen mask, "She mentioned it last night but didn't make much of it."

"Well, Ron is surprised and curious. He is going to ask questions."

"Don't worry about it, Sue. The testing may yet show it to be something else entirely."

"That's what I told him. But you and I know that isn't going to be the case, don't we?"

"No, we don't. Not for sure. Don't worry about it. We definitely can't do anything about it from here to improve things, but we could make things worse."

"He is going to work it out, Mike."

"No, he's not."

"He is already asking me why I haven't told him."

"And what did you say?"

"That I'd only recently heard about it myself."

"There you go, that's fine, and it's true. And Jasmine might just have whatever my cousin has. If you want to know, we can do the tests."

"We might have to now!" replied Sue.

"Shackelton, Houston," came the call on the radio.

Sue grabbed the microphone. "Go ahead, Houston."

"Sue, your pre-breathe time is up, and the airlock is now pure oxygen. We have a green light for you both to proceed with entering your suits."

"Copy that, Houston," replied Sue.

The xEMU suits had a rigid upper torso with a hatch on the back, with the portable life support systems (PLSS) in a pack attached to the hatch. The suits were arranged in such a way so that Sue and Mike could enter by lifting themselves up using a bar located above the suits and then lower themselves, legs first, into the suits through the hatch. Since they had trained to perform this manoeuvre in 1 g on Earth, it was much easier in $1/6^{th}$ g on the Moon.

It was possible that these suits could be accessed by a suit port rather than using an airlock. But it had been decided not to attempt to use that technology this early in the Artemis program. Such an arrangement would have meant that the suit was already exposed to a hard vacuum, with only the hatch and system pack entering the spacecraft.

Sue and Mike lowered their feet into their own suits, climbing in through the hatch in the upper back of the suit. Once they connected up their cooling circuits for their undergarments, they were then able to put their arms into the sleeves. They each then needed to assist each other fit and tighten their shoulder harness, fit and seal their gloves, and activate their suits.

It took them about ten minutes, which was better than the older suits. They had practised the process many times during training, and apart from the reduced gravity, the process went well.

Before closing their suit hatches, Sue and Mike needed to perform system checks. They could communicate with their suits in a similar way that people could command their internet-connected home devices.

"OK, EMU," said Sue to her suit. "Perform system check."

"Welcome, Sue. Initiating system check with the hatch open," said the suit. Sue could hear Mike performing the same sequence with his suit.

The status of her suit, including consumables, power and communications, was displayed on her suit's heads-up display. It also currently displayed the system check status.

"Sue, all systems are nominal," reported the suit.

An overview of Mike's suit's status appeared on the right of her display, but without detail to not confuse the occupant.

"Ok, EMU, display Mike's suit's status detail."

"Displaying Mike's suit status," replied the suit. A popup window displayed details of Mike's suit status. Everything looked good to Sue.

"OK, EMU. Close Mike's suit status display." The pop-up closed." OK EMU, display checklist 1." A window on the left opened, displaying the initial checklist.

"Mike, are you ready for suit hatch closure?" said Sue. The suit automatically routed the audio to Mike's suit and the Lander's speakers.

"Yes, I am, Sue."

"Ok, I'll chat with Houston."

"Houston, this is EMU 1 for a comms check." The suit automatically identified this as a call to Mission Control and routed it via the Lander's communications system to Houston."

"EMU 1, reading you loud and clear."

"Mission Control, EMU 1 copies you loud and clear," said Sue.

"Houston, this is EMU 2 for comms check," said Mike.

"EMU 2, we are reading you loud and clear as well, Mike."

"Houston, EMU 2 copies you loud and clear."

"Houston, EMU 1, we are ready for suit hatch close on your GO."

"Copy that EMU 1. We are GO for suit hatch closure for EMU 1 and 2," replied George as CAPCOM.

"Houston, Roger and Wilco," replied Sue. She turned her back to Mike so he could close the hatch, and Mike reached up and brought the pack and hatch door closed.

"Ok, EMU, lock hatch," said Sue.

"Hatch is closed and locked. Checking seal," replied the suit.

"Thanks, Mike, your turn," said Sue, turning around so that she could close Mike's suit. "Houston, EMU 1 suit hatch closed."

"Copy that, EMU 1, we see that," replied George.

Sue closed Mike's suit hatch, and soon he too reported his suit hatch closed to Mission Control.

"Suit pressure check completed, OK," reported the suit. Sue noted that Mike's suit icon soon also changed to show a good pressure check.

"Houston, EMU 2 suit hatch closed," said Mike on the comms.

"Copy that EMU 2," said CAPCOM.

"Are you all comfortable, Mike?" Sue asked.

"Yes," said Mike, "that was easier than on Earth. Let's get outside."

"Mission Control, EMU 1 requesting go for depress of the airlock."

"Stand by, Sue," replied George.

"Yep, that'd be right. Now I get an itch on my cheek," said Mike.

"Just be careful you don't blind yourself trying to scratch it," said Sue. They had all found ways to alleviate itches, and cramps for that matter, in the suits, but ones on the head were the most dangerous. Not that there were many pointed objects within the helmet, but trying to scratch tended to put heads in odd positions.

"All good. All done, and I can see," replied Mike.

"EMU 1, you are GO for airlock depress," called CAPCOM.

"Houston, copy GO for airlock depress," replied Sue. She moved to the airlock control panel and commanded the depressurisation of the airlock. During this process's first stage, the atmosphere is pumped into storage bottles until the pressure is about 2psi, and then the rest of the gas is expelled to space.

As the pressure in the airlock gradually decreased, Sue's suit expanded slightly and slowly became more rigid. The new suits had new shoulder, waist and hip joints to enable better movement and new glove technology to allow better dexterity. The first test of the suit was on the International Space Station (ISS) in 2021, and it had only been in regular use there during the last 2 years. Astronauts had found it to be much easier to work in, and it fitted a much wider range of body sizes than previous suits. However, Sue and Mike had only twice practised in these suits in low vacuum.

"Ok, Mike, while we wait, let's go through the next steps. Once we depressurise, I move to the hatch and open it. I turn around and exit down the ladder backwards. Before I reach the bottom, you come to the hatch and look down at me, allowing your cameras to see me. I step onto the surface and say my speech. Houston congratulates me, blah blah. Ok, so far?"

"Sure – you exit, get the limelight."

"That's about it. Then you come back into the airlock, turn around, exit backwards down the ladder, close the airlock hatch for dust control, and proceed down the ladder. I step back a couple of metres to give you space and allow my cameras to see you. You step on the surface and say your stuff, Mission control says their stuff, we high five, and then we get on doing a vehicle check. Sound good."

"All good. Do you want me to select any particular filter on my camera?"

"Oh – funny man," said Sue sarcastically.

"I don't know, I thought bunny ears would look good!" said Mike.

"Why not the Martian one with the UFO?"

"That's a great idea. It would have all the conspiracy nuts going crazy. Where is the filter setting in this camera setup?"

"While you find that, I'll review my speech notes", said Sue. She configured her Heads Up Display (HUD) to display them to one side, replacing the checklist once she quickly reviewed upcoming items. Everything on the list had to do with egress, so not an issue, as Sue knew the process well.

The speech had been carefully constructed with the NASA media team. Technically, Sue had written the first draft, but it had been massaged and tightened, with the message tuned, like an ad for the Super Bowl. It was a big deal, historically, being the first humans on the Moon since 1972 and for Sue to be the first woman on the Moon, ever. They had rehearsed this part of the trip almost as much as any other.

Sue paused to think about this as they continued to wait for the airlock to depressurize. It had been a long journey for her to get to this point. Years of study and training. The whole process of being selected to be an astronaut, then the training for the ISS mission, and now the Artemis mission training. She would have been happy to be chosen for any lunar mission, let alone the first manned landing in 52 years. And it had been a very long time for NASA. Who would have thought in 1972 that it would be more than 50 years until someone walked on the Moon again? But politics and derailed NASA manned programs had seen the focus be on low Earth orbit, with Spacelab, then the Space Shuttle and the ISS. It had taken the start of commercial space launches and the threat of China's space program to bring about the Artemis program. So, these next twenty minutes would be memorable, historical, even.

"This is pretty big, isn't it, Mike?" Sue said.

"Yes," said Mike, "but don't get overwhelmed by it."

"I know, but it has taken a lot of work by a lot of people to get to this point."

"True, and for us to be the two people actually here is a bit mind-boggling."

"Sue, the airlock is performing the final depressurisation," stated Sue's suit.

Sue once again scanned through the speech. It was short, and she already had it memorised.

The airlock hatch status light switched to yellow, indicating pressure was low enough to be safely opened.

"OK, Mike. It looks like we are ready. Are you ready?" Sue asked.

"Sure, take a giant leap."

That was Mike keeping things light!

"Mission Control, Shackelton. We are ready for the airlock hatch opening," said Sue.

"Copy that, Shackelton. We are ready for hatch opening and EMU 1 egress."

"Houston, setting open mike," said Sue. "Ok, EMU, enable open mike on EMU 1 and EMU 2."

"Open mike enabled on EMU 1 and EMU 2," replied the suit.

Sue initiated the latch unlock sequence and spun the hatch wheel, withdrawing the locking latches. She then pulled the hatch door. She could hear a very faint hiss as the last remaining gasses in the airlock escaped out of the hatch, and it became easier for her to pull the hatch door into the airlock on its hinge.

"Mission Control. Hatch is open."

She stepped back to one side to swing the hatch out of the way. Once the hatch was secured, Sue turned around and faced into the airlock.

"Mission Control. Hatch is secured. Proceeding with egress for EMU 1," said Sue.

"See you on the surface, Mike," said Sue, waving. She grasped handles around the hatch opening, bent forward and extended her right leg out of the hatch, searching for the top run of the ladder. It took her a few moments, but she found it, put her weight onto her right leg, and lifted her left leg out of the hatch. They had practised this manoeuvre on Earth in analogue environments, but it was actually much easier on the Moon.

"I have both feet on the ladder. It was much easier than in training, I'm glad to say!" said Sue.

Carefully, she took a step down to the next ladder rung, which allowed her to move her body out of the hatchway. "I'm out of the hatch completely," she reported.

Mike moved towards the hatch. "It still didn't look that elegant," he replied.

"Descending the ladder," said Sue, and she carefully located each ladder rung below her and stepped down. The new suit helmets at least did allow good visibility towards the ground, and she could just make out the rungs. After a few minutes, she reached the ladder's last step. "Mike, are you in position?"

"I am, and it's a great view!"

"I can see a bit of dust on these ladder rungs. I'm stepping down onto the surface now. It is not too big a step," said Sue.

Sue carefully stepped down onto the surface with one foot and then added the other. She carefully stepped back and, looking at the Lander, said, "Mission Control, as we step once again onto the Moon, we share the goals of all humankind, women and men, of all colours and creeds, to explore the Universe in which we live. I thank the team of many thousands of men and women from the United States and partner Artemis countries who have enabled us to make this giant leap."

A few seconds later, George, as CAPCOM, replied, "Sue, we celebrate the accomplishments of you and your team on this historic day as the first woman and next man walk on the Lunar surface. We in Mission Control and all the Artemis Partners wish you a safe and productive exploration."

"Copy that Mission Control. I'm stepping away from the ladder now to let Mike come down," said Sue. She took a few careful steps away from the Lander and turned around to view it. "Mike, you are ok to descend. Mobility is pretty good in this suit."

"Copy that, Sue," replied Mike. He backed back into the airlock and turned around to exit the hatch backwards. As Sue had, he held the handles around the hatch and searched for the ladder steps. Finding them, he stepped down a rung and located the external handles. "I'm on the ladder. Closing the hatch," he reported

Mike leaned into the airlock and pulled the hatch door towards him, latching it closed to stop dust from accumulating.

"Hatch closed. I'm descending the ladder," he reported. The suit's mobility was good, even though it was still operating at the higher pressure.

Mike reached the surface and turned around. "Mission Control, stepping again on the Moon, we continue the exploration conducted by the Apollo team. As I gaze across this lunar surface and beyond to the Sun, the Earth and the stars and galaxies above, I look forward to continuing the scientific study of the universe God has given us."

Mike surprised himself. The last few words about the universe being given by God had not been part of the script. It just came out of his mouth as he gazed across the lunar surface and out into space. He felt small, humble and amazed.

"Ahh, Mike, we look forward to following as you study this region of the Moon over the next week. You are fulfilling the NASA vision to discover and expand knowledge for the benefit of humanity."

"Thank you, Mission Control," said Mike. He then walked forward to join Sue. "I agree with you, Sue. Mobility is good in this suit. So, it's on with the checklist?"

"Sure is," replied Sue. They would spend the next 15 minutes performing external checks on the Lander and deploying systems from it.

Once they had completed the checklist and reported their findings to Mission Control, Sue and Mike were cleared to proceed to the lunar rover. It had autonomously driven to the Lander while they slept during the night. It had been parked a distance away from the landing site so that it wasn't impacted by debris blown up by the landing. Although it was close, it was still 100m from the Lander in case of a sudden abort. This allowed Sue and Mike to have a proper walk on the surface.

53

—·—

Mike found walking on the Moon easier than expected, even after all their simulated training. The pressure in the suit was still a bit high, so it felt puffy, but all the joints worked well.

So he was surprised when he tripped and fell forward. He managed to get his arms out to break his fall, which meant he bounced slightly. While his backpack wasn't as heavy as those that the Apollo astronauts wore, it still wasn't light.

"Mike, are you ok?" asked Sue.

"Yeah, I guess I didn't see a rock. Give me a minute while I get up." The suit's flexibility allowed Mike to kneel and then stand up, compared to the strange bouncing antics that the Apollo astronauts had to perform. Yet it was still more of a balancing act in a lower gravity environment than he was used to.

Once standing upright, he instructed his suit to perform a system check. This was a bit of overkill since pressure, temperature etc., were constantly being monitored.

Once he had confirmed his suit was ok and Mission Control was happy, they continued their walk to the rover.

"I guess I'll be all over social media by now," Mike said.

"You are just lucky that you weren't in front of me at the time. They'll just have long-distance shots from the Lander," replied Sue with a laugh. "You will have some extra suit cleaning to do when we return."

"You'd think as a geologist I'd be looking at the ground all the time and not miss my step, but the landscape and view is just amazing."

"You mean moonscape," said Sue.

"Sure, I meant moonscape. It is very stark, isn't it?"

"Yes, especially in full sunlight."

"Look at that shadowed area over on our left," said Mike, stopping and pointing. "To me, it is just totally black. I can't make out any detail at all from this distance."

"Neither can I," said Sue.

"I have established contact with the rover," stated Mike's suit. "All systems are nominal." Some additional data appeared on Mike's HUD.

"Let's move on," said Sue.

After a few more minutes of walking, they arrived at the rover, placed their equipment in its locker, and sat in their seats, applying their safety harnesses.

"Mission Control, we are situated in the rover and ready to proceed," said Sue.

"Copy that, Sue. You are ready to proceed to within 50 metres of the crater rim as per the mission plan and to reassess," replied George as CAPCOM.

"All systems are green, proceeding to the rim," said Sue. She slowly accelerated the rover and directed it towards the waypoint shown in her HUD. She started out slowly to get a feel for how the rover behaved.

"Traction appears to be good," said Sue. "I'll perform some figure eights to get a feel for the steering." She drove to some clear ground, turned to the left with the steering locked, and then turned again to the right to find the steering lock. "The rover appears to be behaving as I expected. Continuing to our destination."

"Well, that was fun," said Mike. "Want to try some doughnuts?"

"You can later," said Sue. "Keep an eye out for boulders or hidden holes."

"Looks clear to me at the moment," said Mike. He looked around behind them. "We aren't kicking up too much dust at this speed."

"Ok. I'll increase speed a bit. The shadows here are quite long, so I'll avoid them. They are so black we wouldn't see much in them until we were upon it."

Sue navigated between boulders and their shadows, finding a path to their destination near the crater rim.

"The view is just amazing," said Mike. "In fact, just stop for a minute. We are higher than the Lander and have a view back down on it."

Sue slowed the rover and turned it so they could more easily view back to the landing site. It was only about half a kilometre away, yet the odd-looking Lander was clearly dwarfed by the landscape around it. There were several other craters nearby, meaning several ridges rose up nearby.

"It's a big place," said Sue.

"It sure is," replied Mike. "And the big shadows around here give it an eerie feel."

"OK, let's keep going. There will be better views further up on the rim anyway." Sue turned the rover around and continued the climb.

As the incline got steeper, the rover had some difficulty with traction, spinning its wheels in the loose regolith. A few times, Sue needed to back up and attempt a less direct route.

After about 15 minutes, they decided they were as close as they could get, around 65 metres from the rim, which was acceptable in the mission parameters.

"Mission Control, we are parking the rover and ready to walk to the rim. We are approximately 65 metres from the rim," said Sue.

Several seconds later came the response from Mission Control, "Copy that, Sue. A reminder to connect your safety lines."

"Roger, Wilco."

Sue and Mike removed their harness and stepped out of the Lander. Mike slipped on the steep surface, grabbing onto the Lander for support.

"Whoa, it is slippery," he said, digging his boot into the ground. "I suggest we take the walking poles."

"Sounds like a good idea," replied Sue.

Mike opened a locker on the back of the rover and removed four walking poles. They each would also carry a satchel of equipment.

Once they both had their equipment satchels secured to their suits and had their walking poles handy, they attached the safety lines to each other. They each unspooled from separate high locations on the rover, and Sue and Mike would need to take care not to get the lines tangled.

"OK," said Sue, "do you see any risky areas we need to avoid?"

"Nothing specific. It all looks fairly consistent and stable. But who knows, there's no erosion, and nothing else walking around, so only lunar quakes and meteorites to trigger any movement," said Mike.

"Right, so we may as well just take the most direct route then. Let's go," said Sue.

Sue and Mike began walking up the outer side of the Shackelton crater, digging their boots into the loose regolith and using their poles to maintain their balance, walking a couple of metres apart to ensure they didn't accidentally pierce each other's suits with the poles.

"Wow, this is a bit of a workout after 2 weeks in zero-G," said Mike, puffing.

"I know, it is, isn't it. The lower gravity doesn't quite compensate for the weight of our suits and gear and the slipperiness of the ground."

"Sue, this is Houston," came a call on the radio.

"Go ahead, Houston," said Sue.

"Surgeon would like you both to slow your work rate a bit, and maybe take a break."

"Copy that," said Sue. "Mike, let's take a break and admire the view."

They both stopped, carefully looked around, and had a drink. They had climbed over half the distance from the rover to the rim. They looked down on the rover and, even further away, could identify the Lander, the only signs of mankind in their view, apart from the Earth itself.

While they were watching, Mike caught a brief glimpse of a flash on the horizon and then what looked like a dust cloud. "Did you see that?" he asked, pointing in the direction.

"No, what was it?" asked Sue.

"It looked like a meteorite hit. See the dust cloud."

"Oh, ok, yeah, I can just make it out."

Checking his HUD details, Mike called Mission Control. "Mission Control, this is Mike. I think I just saw a meteorite impact towards the horizon on a bearing of 35 degrees. We can see what looks like a cloud of dust and a flash caught my attention. It should be on my camera feed."

"Copy that, Mike. We will check out the recording."

"Hopefully, it isn't part of a meteor cloud," said Sue. "Let's keep going, but a bit slower."

They turned back around and continued their climb. Gradually, they got closer to the rim until, at last, they could see over it.

"Wow, what a view," said Mike, as they could see over the top. "It is so wide! It is so dark at the bottom that I can't see it."

The Shackelton crater has a diameter of 20 kilometres and is 4 kilometres deep, but since it is permanently in shadow, it is not easy to see the bottom of the crater.

Sue and Mike were finally able to stand at the peak. The inner wall sloped away at around 30 degrees.

As they looked around, Sue said, "It's amazing that we are the first humans to see this crater with our own eyes."

"Isn't it beautiful? I wouldn't mind seeing one that is lit, though," said Mike.

They began to take measurements with the instruments they had brought. One small experiment would stay on the site to monitor the crater, and Mike unpacked it and set it down, confirming with Mission Control that they had data feed and good power.

Mike stepped away from the experiments and, checking the clock on his HUD, noticed that half an hour had passed since they arrived on the rim. He looked around the crater while Sue finished her task. Only about a sixth of the rim was lit, including the portion they were on, and the rest was dark but slightly illuminated by scattered light. The bottom of the crater was not visible below them, but he could see some of the slope below him, which looked reasonably smooth with the occasional boulder and even the odd small crater.

Mike looked up and studied the stars above him. He suddenly felt himself falling.

54

— · —

Startled, Mike looked down to see that the rim had collapsed around him, and rubble was falling down the crater's inner slope.

His safety link jerked tight and quickly slowed him. Seconds later, he saw Sue swinging backwards towards him on her safety line.

"Sue, you're going to hit me," he managed to say as he put out his arms in an attempt to soften the blow. If he didn't, the back of her system pack would hit his visor, not something he wanted to experience in space.

Mike managed to push against Sue's backpack and cushion the blow without injury, and they started swinging together.

"What happened?" asked Sue.

"The rim gave way. I had no warning," said Mike.

"Sue, Mike, are you ok?" asked George in Mission Control.

"Yes," replied Sue, "all are systems are ok. We are both just startled and happy for the safety lines. There was a landslide, and we both got trapped in it."

"Copy that. We will prepare to use the rover to drag you out once you are ready," replied George.

Mike looked up. They were only a few metres from the rim. A section of the crater's wall had slipped, and there was a small section with very steep sides. He and Sue were against that very steep incline. "Sue, I suspect that pulling up the safety lines will further destabilise the rim above us, especially since the lines will be rubbing against it. I think we would be better to ascend the lines."

Sue looked around. "I see what you mean," she said, "but that is really hard for us to do. I think we should try using the rover to get us out."

"We are going to have to do it slowly," said Mike.

"Yep, sure," said Sue. "Let's move so we are standing against the wall."

They rearranged themselves so they could walk up the side of the crater as they were pulled out.

"Mission Control, we are ready for you to begin extraction. We would like you to do so slowly and stop and check with us after each metre. We are concerned that the rim above us may further slip."

"Sue, we copy and agree. Your first move should start in 15 seconds," replied George.

Sue and Mike braced themselves and tried to separate. They felt a tug and could slowly walk up the crater side about 1 metre and then stop. A bit of loose material fell down the slope.

"That was ok, not too much debris," said Sue.

"Yup, better than I expected," said Mike. "But the surface we are on is still slipping a bit."

"Yes, I noticed," replied Sue. "Mission Control. That worked well. We notice some slippage of the surface we are on but little debris from above. We are ready for the next move."

"Copy that, Sue. The next haul should start in 15 seconds," replied Mission Control.

Once again, they felt their safety line tug them upwards, and they continued to walk up the crater side. Mike noted that the cables were biting deeper into the crater's rim.

"Mission Control, that was good. We are ready to go again," said Sue after the attempt ended.

"Sue, and Mike, unfortunately, that attempt ended with the rover's wheels spinning, so we are losing traction. Are you able to pull yourselves out from your location?" asked George as CAPCOM.

"What do you think, Mike?" asked Sue.

"I guess we could try climbing it. The safety line is too thin to pull ourselves up on. But then it should retract unless it is caught on the rim, and then we could tug on it and lock it off. It should be doable."

"Ok, why don't you try that."

"Right, let me step up and see if I can free my line from yours at the rim."

Mike carefully took a step up the side of the crater, taking pressure off his safety line and flicking it to free it from the crevice it had made above them. After several attempts, it came free, and the line retracted and became taut again.

"Well, that bit worked, so I'll try climbing," said Mike.

Leaning forward to steady himself on the crater side, Mike took careful steps up the hill. The weight of the equipment on his back pushed him forward, so it wasn't hard to hold that position. He carefully dug his boot into the hill each time he took a step, and after three steps, he gave the safety line a tug to lock it.

After a few cycles of this, Mike's head was level with the rim. A few more steps and he could climb over the edge, although a fair amount of material was falling down the slope. He quickly moved away from the edge.

"Ok, I've made it up," said Mike. "The last bit breaks up a bit, but it wasn't too hard."

"Yeah, I noticed all the rubbish coming down at me," said Sue. "I'll start up now."

Mike carefully stood up, moved a few metres around the rim, keeping clear of the edge, and watched Sue climb up, using the same process he had used.

Once she had reached the top, they both moved back away from the rim and consulted.

"Clearly, the crater rims aren't all that stable," said Sue.

"That appears so, but I noticed no sign of failure before the slip," said Mike.

"Mission Control, we are both safe now, and all systems are nominal. I think we need to review our procedures for work on the crater rims and safety equipment."

"Sue, we copy that, and the team is currently looking at our mission plan. We would like you both to return to the rover and sit down for a 10-minute rest, please," said George.

"Roger and Wilco," said Sue.

They both turned and started walking down the outer wall of the crater to their rover.

"Well, that's a pity. I think we lost that experiment we set up," said Mike.

"Yeah, and I think all we learned is that the rim is not that stable!"

"And we got some photos and learned using the rover to retrieve us is only partially effective," said Mike.

They reached the rover and detached their safety lines. Then they both climbed into their seats.

"Time for a snack, I think," said Mike. "Choices, choices." He sucked on his one feeding tube.

"Yep, I'd love a nice cake right now," said Sue.

"A beer is what I'd like," said Mike.

"Sue, this is Mission Control. Mics are hot," came the call on comms.

Mike and Sue looked at each other through their helmets and laughed.

"Copy that, Mission Control," replied Sue. "OK, EMU, disable open mic on EMU 1 and EMU 2."

"Open Mic is disabled on EMU 1 and EMU 2," replied the suit.

"Ok Mike, are you feeling ok?" asked Sue.

"Yep, my heart rate has calmed down now. I don't think I bruised anything bouncing around. How about you?"

"Pretty much the same. Thanks for catching me. I'm not sure what would have happened if we had hit like that."

"Nothing good, I think," replied Mike. "I still want that beer."

55

After their short rest, Sue and Mike drove the rover to the outcrop that Mike had earlier identified. There, Mike collected samples while Sue took photos and observed.

Sue was glad that this part of the walk was going smoothly and that there was little risk compared to the rim walk. She watched Mike as he focused on the outcrop and examined the different rock structures.

"What do you think it is?" Sue asked.

"I'm pretty sure it is anorthosite. There was less volcanic activity in this region," said Mike. "I'll break off a section for a sample."

Mike proceeded to gather the tools necessary to break off a piece of the outcrop.

Sue watched as Mike expertly identified a split point in the rock, placed the chisel there, and then struck the chisel with a hammer. It only took one blow, and the rock fractured, with a portion falling off the front. Sue retrieved a sample bag, scanned its code, and held it out for Mike to place the sample in it. Her suit automatically noted the sample location, and Sue attached a photo of the sample area.

As Mike collected other samples, Sue gazed across the moonscape. It was desolate and stark, and the shadows hardly moved. She was actually here, walking on the moon, the first woman ever to do so. That was mind-blowing. And it had not been easy. She'd been one of the few women studying aeronautic engineering, and when she joined the US Navy, she had been one of even fewer women. Others had broken the ground, but it was never easy. In fact, she had found it much easier in NASA. Maybe it was part of the changing times. After all, NASA wanted a woman on the Moon, and she had been surprised that someone from her class had been selected for this mission and not a more experienced astronaut.

"Sue, you have one hour of consumables remaining," reported her suit.

"Ok, EMU, I acknowledge the warning," said Sue. She checked the status of Mike's suit, and he would soon get the same warning. "Mike, we have an hour of consumables left, so we should finish up here and return to the Lander."

"Ok, I've got what I want from here. I guess we used up more oxygen climbing out of that crater than was planned," said Mike, picking up his sample bags.

"Yes, the mission plan had us out for another hour, at least," said Sue. "Mission Control, we have received the one hour consumable warning on our suits, and we are preparing to return to the Lander."

"Sue, we copy that," replied George. "The team would like you to deploy the seismology experiment on your return journey, and that should only consume five minutes. We will forgo the testing. If there are problems, we will correct them on the next walk."

"We copy that, Mission Control," said Sue. "Mike, hop in once you've secured those samples." She considered giving Mike an opportunity to drive. However, he would need to set up the experiment, so it would be faster for her to remain the driver.

Sue sat back in the command seat for the rover and initiated the auto-mated checklist. She noted that the rover battery levels were slightly lower than expected but still within acceptable bounds.

"Mission Control, I'm seeing lower than expected battery levels on the rover. Do you guys understand why?" asked Sue.

"Stand by, Sue," said George.

Mike sat down in his seat and began strapping himself in. Sue completed securing her restraints.

"Sue, this is CAPCOM. We believe the battery was depleted more than expected when attempting to pull you out of the crater."

"Copy that," said Sue. She should still have plenty of power to return to the Lander.

"OK, EMU, show me a route to the seismic experiment location and then to the Lander."

Her suit displayed the route. It was almost a straight line, with only a slight diversion to the experiment location. Of course, this didn't account for terrain and shadows en route.

"Mission Control, we are proceeding to the seismic experiment location," said Sue. She checked that Mike was secured and turned the rover around to return in the direction of the Lander, which meant a gentle descent. She accelerated towards the experiment spot, weaving around the occasional boulder.

"When we get there, I'll retrieve the experiment and deploy it while you video and take photographs if that's ok with you?" said Mike.

"Sounds like a plan. It shouldn't take too long if we don't need to test it," said Sue. She was concerned about their oxygen use since once they returned to the Lander. They still needed to stow samples, clean the dust off themselves and get back into the airlock, and all those things took time. The drive itself, without a stop, would take ten minutes. They both had an emergency reserve of one hour of oxygen, but she really needed to avoid using the contingency.

"That looks like the experiment site at that outcrop over there," said Mike, pointing to his right. "I need to try and secure the experiment to the rock itself, so try and stop on the top side of the outcrop."

"Sure," said Sue. She identified what looked like a safe route around to the top of the small outcrop. It had been chosen because there was what appeared to be uncovered rock on the top of the outcrop, so even placing the experiment would meet the minimum requirements for a successful experiment.

Sue slowed the rover, navigated to the outcrop's top, and parked. "Mike, you have five minutes to deploy the experiment. If you can't screw in the probe, we will just have to place it. We may get time to revisit this later. OK EMU, set a five-minute timer and display on EMU 1 and EMU 2."

"Five-minute timer activated," replied Sue's suit.

"Roger," said Mike, unstrapping himself, stepping out of the rover and walking to the stowage area. There he released the seismic experiment from its transport clips. It was essentially a box with legs, a solar panel and a communications dish, both currently furled. Mike picked it up and carried it over to the intended location.

"Sue, can you please bring me the drill," he asked.

He placed the experiment on the ground and ensured it was orientated correctly. The box's surface had solar panels on most sides, and Mike would soon unfurl another panel which would be effective for about a third of the lunar day.

Sue gave Mike the drill, and he attempted to secure one of the feet with a screw. The first one went in easily, however, the second one took longer.

"Two minutes remaining," reported the suit.

"Right, I'll deploy the communications dish," said Mike. He removed the latch securing the dish in a folded configuration, and it unfurled.

"And now I'm deploying the solar panel," said Mike as he unlatched the panel's clip, and it unfurled.

"Mission Control, the seismic experiment is deployed with two screws in place on the two rear feet."

"Copy that, Mike. We have basic comms to the unit and will test it out and align the comms. Sue, please proceed to the Lander," said George as CAPCOM.

Sue and Mike both returned to the rover and secured themselves once again.

"I think we'll be back here," said Mike. "It wouldn't take long to screw in the other feet."

"I guess we'll see how the planning goes," said Sue. "It looks like our power will be ok to get back to the Lander. What're our consumables like?"

"Ahh, it looks like you have 45 minutes, and I have 49 minutes."

"Ok, so, our focus when we arrive is to first secure the samples, then proceed with dust clean off. I don't think there is anything we need to do with the rover.

"Mission Control, are there any tasks you need us to perform on the rover on our arrival other than the removal of samples and ourselves?"

"Standby, Sue. I will check," replied George.

"If we allow five minutes for this drive and ten minutes to sort out the samples, that gives us thirty minutes for dust cleaning and entry, which should be just enough," said Sue.

Sue heard a beep, and a warning was displayed on her suit display. It was related to a motor on the rover overheating. "Houston, I just got an over-temperature alarm on the left rear motor on the rover. I'm slowing our speed to see if that helps. Our timeline would appear to be tight."

"Copy that, Sue. I can also confirm you have no other activities relating to the rover once you arrive. We will monitor the drive temperature," replied George.

"I just pulled up the temperatures on the drives, and that temp has stabilised and is dropping since you slowed down," said Mike. "So, I think we are ok. It will just take an extra couple of minutes to get to the Lander."

"Sue, this is CAPCOM. We agree with Mike's assessment. You should be able to proceed at your current speed."

"Copy Houston," said Sue as she continued driving to the Lander, which wasn't that far away.

They continued to bounce across the surface, but now at a slower pace. Looking at her suit HUD, it appeared that they would arrive with 36 minutes to get into the airlock. Tight but doable if nothing else went wrong.

"Mike, we will have to be super-efficient putting things away when we get there. Do you have any ideas for optimization?"

"Perhaps we skip the double check on the bag location. The guys at home can check our videos for mistakes.," said Mike.

"That sounds good. Mission Control, did you hear Mike's suggestion?"

"Sue, this is CAPCOM, we did, and operations concur. We'll check your video streams afterwards."

"Great," said Sue. "Mission Control, any other suggestions?"

"Yes, Sue," replied George as CAPCOM. "We want you to skip the rover shutdown checklist from item 3 on. We will manage remotely."

"Copy that. Skip all items from item three on the rover shutdown checklist."

"Good copy," said George. "We may also have a few changes during your dust cleaning."

"Ok, thanks, Houston," said Sue. They were approaching the Lander. She needed to park close enough that it was not too far to carry equipment and samples yet far enough away to ensure that the rover would not get shaded by the Lander. She located a position on one side of it that looked good. It would not be shaded for weeks, yet it was close to the Lander. If the folks in Houston wanted it further away, they could remotely drive it.

She pulled into the spot and executed the first two items on the rover shutdown checklist: turn off the engine and put on the handbrake!

"Time to get out Mike. Houston, I've executed steps 1 and 2 of the shut-down checklist. We are exiting the rover and beginning sample transfer," said Sue as she unbuckled her harness.

Both Mike and Sue walked to the back of the vehicle. "Mike, why don't you handle the samples, and I'll put the equipment away," she said.

"Sounds like a plan. Just remember to get the things and storage bin in camera view," Mike replied.

"Shouldn't be too hard," said Sue. There were two sets of cameras on her suit, one on two on her helmet (giving a 3D capacity) and another on her chest. It would be difficult for an object not to be visible on a camera.

For the next five minutes, Mike and Sue worked hard, transferring the lunar samples and equipment to suitable storage lockers, occasionally requesting the appropriate location from the mission control team. Sue had to connect some of the equipment to power supplies in their storage location. Their suits automatically scanned QR codes on the sample bags, equipment and storage locations, so they both just needed to look at the code on the equipment or sample and the code on the storage bin to automatically associate them.

Sue finished her task and checked the quantity of consumables she had left. "Mike, I've got 29 minutes remaining. I'm going to start on my dust clean-up."

"That's fine, I just have to close these bins and close up the rover storage bins, and I'll join you," said Mike. "I still have 33 minutes."

Lunar dust was a significant issue that needed to be addressed. The regolith became extremely fine and is very damaging and abrasive. It will stick to almost everything. It can cause equipment failures, and worse, it can harm the astronauts' health, causing lung damage and even entering their bloodstream.

"Great," said Sue. She walked to the Lander and started climbing up the ladder. She arrived at the small porch area outside the airlock. Reaching into the airlock, she opened a nearby compartment and removed a sticky pad, which she placed on the floor of the porch. She then stood on the pad. She retrieved another device attached to a cable from the same locker. She closed the door of the airlock and plugged in the device, which produced an electrostatic field, to a power outlet in the porch area.

Sue stamped her feet and saw some dust slowly collect on the sticky pad. She began waving the device over her arms and hands. The concept is that the device directs an electron beam at the target, causing the target object to gain a negative charge, and the negatively charged dust particles on the object's surface are repelled. The device projected a low-powered laser at the same location as the beam so the user could correctly target it. The process had been developed by the University of Colorado at Boulder, and Sue was happy that she did not need to brush down her entire suit. Mike would need to use the device on her back, but she could start without his assistance.

A few minutes later, Mike joined her on the porch. Sue handed him the device, and he resumed working down her suit from her head to her toes. The hope was that the dust would gently fall as it was repelled from the suit.

It took Mike ten minutes to complete the cleaning of Sue's suit. During this time, she considered the plan for their entry into the airlock and discussed this with Mission Control. Sue then moved closer to the airlock hatch and began cleaning Mike's suit. An appreciable amount of dust was gathering on the sticky pad. Their fall over the crater's edge had not helped since they had effectively been lying in the dirt, and more had fallen down on them.

It would be helpful, Sue thought, for future missions if proposed suit locks could be included in the airlock design so that the astronauts could climb out of their suits into a pressurised environment and not interact with the outside of their spacesuit at all. At the moment, it was virtually impossible to eliminate the dust from their living environment; in fact, there probably was already dust in the airlock.

As Sue scanned the back of Mike's suit with the device, she noticed some damage at the back of the shoulders. "Mike," she said, "we need to check out the back right shoulder of your suit before your next walk. It looks a bit scuffed."

"OK," said Mike, "I seem to remember bouncing off something there during the fall."

"Mission Control, can we please schedule additional suit check-out time to investigate damage to Mike's suit on the back of his right shoulder."

"Sue, we heard that exchange and checked out your video feed. The team are analysing your video and are updating the suit checkout checklist,' replied CAPCOM.

Sue wasn't overly concerned. The damage looked minimal, and clearly, there had been no compromise to the suit's integrity, but they did have another three walks scheduled, and she did not want to see those plans disrupted. There wasn't much they could do to fix the fabric of a suit, and they were designed to be hardy.

Once they finished the cleaning, they both entered the airlock, and Mike closed the airlock hatch.

"Mission Control hatch closed," reported Sue. She had five minutes left of consumables without needing to access her emergency supply.

"We confirm that, Sue."

"Repressurizing," announced Sue. She and Mike connected each other's suits to the Lander's supplies.

"That was a bit close," said Mike.

"I agree. We, or Mission Control, should have noticed our lower con-sumable levels earlier."

"True, but that is also why the suits are programmed to warn us," replied Mike.

"Let's start the checklists," said Sue. They had a two hour pressurisation process to go through to get back to Lander pressure, as well as checkouts of their suits while they waited. At least once they were able to remove their helmets, they would be able to eat some snacks that they had placed there just for that purpose.

"Ok, so Item 1 dot 1 is 'start pressurisation', which we have in work. Item 1 dot 2 is 'connect suit umbilicals', which is complete, and Item 1 dot 3 is to secure tools from our belts," said Sue.

The long day had not yet finished.

56

— • —

Three hours later, Sue and Mike were finally relaxing in the Lander, eating their evening meal. It was a relief to finally finish the checklists and to be no longer on an open mike with Mission Control, as was the case in the suits.

"That was quite a first moonwalk," said Mike.

"Understatement of the year, Mike," said Sue. "That landslip was crazy."

"But it wasn't something we hadn't planned for," said Mike.

"True. But still, we probably shouldn't have gone there on the first walk."

"You know it is one of the key mission objectives. We had to go there on the first walk in case we abort. We survived."

"And we showed that we need a better rescue system."

"I won't disagree with you there."

"I'm looking forward to talking to Ron later. I guess you are talking to Lisa?"

"I sure am. Don't forget we just did something nobody has done for fifty years. It's really amazing, and I'm sure that's what Lisa will focus on."

"I know, the later events sort of swamped all that history-making stuff."

"I wonder what else happened today?"

"I'm sure a lot of people were born, died, got new jobs, got fired, got married. All on the day we walked on the Moon!"

"Yeah, I guess that might be how they remember it."

They spent a bit of time eating.

"Were you frightened at all today?" asked Mike.

"Frightened, no. Surprised. Yes. Some fear response, especially when we fell. What about you, Mike?"

"Falling, definitely. I was happy those lines were in place. And then, when we were bouncing off each other, I was worried about our helmets."

"It would take a heavy whack to crack them," said Sue.

"Well, I was looking to head butt your backpack, and I didn't like the odds of that working out well."

"It probably would have only cracked without leaking. Mind you that would be the mission over!"

Mike finished his meal in thought. "Do you want some fruit or pudding?"

"What pudding is there?"

"How about ice cream. I think we deserve a treat."

"Sounds good."

Mike fished out two ice creams from their kitchen freezer store and handed one to Sue. He opened his and took a spoonful.

"I guess Lisa probably would have been concerned," said Mike. "I gather she would have been watching it live."

"I'd expect so. We don't really know what they saw or were told."

"I'm sure the team would have managed them well. They were all together, at least for the first part."

"Well, I guess we'll find out in ten minutes when our calls are scheduled. I still think we have done amazing things today, and we should focus on that," said Mike.

"I agree. It's been amazing."

Mike finished off his ice cream and packed away his rubbish. He then began setting up for his call with Lisa. Sue began preparing for her call. They would sit at distant ends of the crew area for privacy.

The call from Lisa came through, and Mike arranged his camera, put his headset on, and answered.

"Hi Honey, good to see you," said Mike.

"Mike, I'm so glad you are ok. Did you get hurt at all?"

"Lisa, I'm fine, no injuries. We were safe at all times and didn't slip all that far. It was always a possibility, and we had trained for this sort of thing."

"It looked scary. We didn't know what was going on."

"It took us a bit by surprise, but we had the safety lines on in case this sort of thing happened. I'm sure the guys would have explained that."

"Yes, they did, but it was still scary. And then when you had to rush back at the end, that was tense."

"Yes, we had to move at the end, but we were still safe. We were avoiding needing to use our emergency consumables. It was all controlled. No need for you to worry."

"How's Jasmine?"

"She's great, but she misses you."

"And I miss her. Has she done anything new?"

"She is trying to stand a bit more, grabbing hold of things and trying to walk. I've got a video I'll send you."

"Oh wow, that's great. She is growing so quickly!"

"How is Sue after today?"

"She is fine, although it has been tiring. And we are up for a walk again tomorrow, so there's lots of preparation stuff to do."

"Are you both getting on ok?" asked Lisa.

"Yes, we get on fine. How are my parents coping?"

"They were so proud of you during the start of the walk. Later they were worried, as I was, but now everything has calmed down, they seem to be ok."

"I hope Mum didn't get too upset during our incident."

"John kept her calm. And the family liaisons were great in helping us understand what was happening."

"That's good. So, is there anything else happening that I need to worry about?"

"No, we are all well. Everything is under control. Are you ready for tomorrow's walk?"

"As much as we can be. My suit got a bit abraided in the fall, but nothing anyone seems concerned about. I'm pretty tired, so looking forward to some sleep. Lying down rather than just floating is a nice change."

"Ok, well, I'll let you get some rest. Have a great walk tomorrow. We will be watching. We all love you."

"Thanks, Lisa. I love you too. Give Jasmine a hug for me. Bye," said Mike, blowing Lisa a kiss.

Mike put his laptop away, collapsed onto his bunk after an exhausting day, and immediately fell asleep.

57

MONDAY, MAY 27, 2024

It had been a long, exhausting yet fulfilling day, thought Sue, as she finally sat down in the Lunar Lander after having exited their xEMU space suits for the second time and left them in the airlock.

It had been a relatively uneventful day. She and Mike had once again donned their space suits and spent eight hours on the Moon's surface. After reprovisioning their lunar rover, they had first visited the seismic experiment they had hurriedly set up the day before and finished securing it properly and performing some validation tests.

They then drove past the Lander and away in the opposite direction and installed a lunar laser ranging experiment target. This target was an improved version of the reflectors placed on the Moon during the Apollo missions. They were still in use and helped scientists track the Moon's orbit and were also used to provide information on the lunar interior.

The rest of the walk consisted of collecting samples from several locations and taking photos and videos.

They had even had time to double-check the stowage of items from the previous walk since they had had to work so quickly.

That was how they were supposed to go, thought Sue. As planned, with no surprises!

Sue sat back in her chair and savoured her coffee. During the walk, they were limited to water and the food supplement supplied in their suits. Not particularly exciting foods!

Mike was in the Lander's bathroom, washing. Even though a shower would work on the Moon, they didn't have the water supply to support one.

Sue cast the vision of Mike washing himself from her mind and pondered their mission. They had now completed roughly half of their mission objectives. Tomorrow was a 'rest' day, but it still included significant tasks relating to their suits in preparation for their third and fourth walks and maintenance tasks around the Lander. They also had medical tests to perform. It was a rest day because they only had about six hours of scheduled tasks to perform instead of 12!

Even now, they had about an hour to clean up after their walk, have some snacks before a media event, eat dinner, and then spend some time talking with family and friends.

Sue opened her email on her tablet. There were a couple of mission status updates she quickly cast her eye over. She saw nothing unexpected in the summaries. Quickly, she read an overview of their upcoming media event and then took the opportunity to read some emails from family and friends on her personal tablet. The private communications were handled on a separate network from the NASA operations and required a different device for security reasons.

A few work colleagues and family friends had sent messages of congratulations after the previous day's walk. She quickly replied to a few close friends and family members. She would try to respond to the others during their downtime tomorrow.

Ron had sent an email of a couple of family photos with Jessica, Jerome, and Ron at NASA Mission Control watching the walk. Looking at the picture, Sue realised how much she missed them.

Sue checked the time. She still had half an hour before they needed to prepare for the media event. She went to the communications panel and configured a private call to the Orion.

"Orion, this is Sue," she said.

After a brief pause, John replied, "Sue, this is Orion. Good to hear from you. How can we help?"

"Hi, John. Good to hear your voice. I was hoping to spend a few minutes of girl time chatting with Christina if I could. I set this up as a private call," said Sue.

"Sure thing, let me patch you through to Christina's headset."

Sue waited while John did this.

"Hi, Sue," said Christina, "this was unexpected!"

"Hi, Christina. I know. I had a few minutes and wanted some girl time. I figured you would have time to talk."

"Absolutely. We have way too much free time up here. How are you going."

"I'm good. Tired though. Having a rest day tomorrow will be great. With only two of us here, we have to do everything, Lander ops and look after our suits and do the walks. It is pretty intense."

"I'm sure it is. Have you had any news from home?"

"Yes. I spoke with Ron last night, and I just got his email with a couple of photos of him, Jessica and Jerome watching the walk yesterday. They look very good, so I guess they were done by a NASA photographer."

"Was Ron ok after yesterday's walk?"

"Yes. He was a bit worried but glad I was safe. We chatted a bit about it."

"I bet that fall was scary," said Christina.

"It got my heart racing. Mike and I were about the same distance out on our safety ropes, so we were banging into each out. Fortunately, he grabbed hold of me, so we didn't bounce anymore. I think he was worried about cracking his helmet on my backpack, which would not have been great!"

"Wow, that would have been frightening!"

"Our training kicked in, and once we stopped swinging around, it wasn't too bad, but I think the whole safety line setup needs to be rethought."

"But at least you had them. Did you have a good rest overnight?"

"Mostly. We must have got a bit of dust into the cabin. I was able to smell something like gunpowder. I think we kept most of it in the airlock, though. It kept me awake a bit. And thinking about the kids."

"How are they going?"

"They seem to be doing great," said Sue. "They were on the video call after the landing. We are going to talk again tomorrow during our rest time. Jessica might join Ron tonight. I know she is really engaged in what we are doing and watching everything. Apparently, she wasn't worried at all about our fall. She knew we had safety systems!"

"Ha, ha, trusting girl!" laughed Christina.

"Yes, she is a bit, but she did know we had safety lines, and wasn't worried. It's a bit different when you are falling, even when you know you have a safety line!"

"I'm sure. Are you guys getting on ok? It can get pretty intense with just two of you stuck in a tin can. I know John and I have got on each other's nerves occasionally."

"Nothing too bad. Mike has given me space, and, as I said, we have been busy! Speaking of busy, we both better get ready for this upcoming media event."

"Ok, I'll talk with you then. Bye."

"See you." Sue closed the connection. And started preparing for the media event, setting up the camera. Mike joined her, setting up the extra lighting.

"Have you seen the updated briefing for the event," asked Sue.

"Yes. The fall was something we had trained for, and our safety systems worked as expected. We felt safe at all times."

"That sounds like what was said. Do you have any issues with that?"

"No," said Mike. "It is basically the truth. I do think we will do things differently next time, though."

"That's fine, and there is nothing wrong with learning."

"Absolutely not. I'm glad today's walk went smoothly, and we get a break tomorrow," said Mike.

"I am looking forward to a rest. I've planned a video call with the whole family in the morning."

"I've got one with Lisa, Jasmine and my parents as well."

"Have you got any more news on Jasmine?"

"No, you know how these things go. Slowly."

"True. Ron hasn't mentioned it again."

"That's good," said Mike. "I don't think it is going to be an issue."

"Shackelton, this is Mission Control. Are you ready to test the video feed?" came the call on the communications system.

They needed to focus on testing the configuration for the media event.

58

— • —

Tuesday, May 28, 2024

Mike yawned and stretched. They had had an extra hour in their sleep period, and he had needed it. Even though today would only be a half rest day, the pace was set to be slower so they could relax.

He grabbed his pad and checked the system status. Everything appeared to be green, and he had no urgent messages, which was promising. The wake-up music would start in just two minutes, so he had slept through most of the extra sleep period.

Two minutes later, the wake-up music started playing, and he heard Sue stir in the bunk below him.

"Good morning," he said, swinging his legs over the edge and jumping down from his bunk. "I hope you slept well. I did."

"I sure did, and I needed it," said Sue, sitting up in her bunk, her T-shirt clinging to her shapely body. Mike noticed and averted his gaze. He'd always found Sue attractive and couldn't afford any missteps during the mission. That would complicate things.

He walked to the bathroom, fetched his washer, and cleaned his face. When he returned to the main cabin, Sue was up, stretching and checking the Lander systems.

"I can't see any changes to our daily schedule, which is good," said Sue. "And I haven't seen any issues with the Lander overnight, which is fantastic."

"So, we still have an hour before anything is scheduled?"

"Correct. And that will just be medical. Why don't you finish your cleanup and change while I check in with Mission Control. I gather you aren't planning any exercise today?"

"Nope. I've had quite enough exercise on those walks," he said. Even though they'd only been in space for a week, it was amazing how quickly their bodies had adapted to zero-G and how much of a workout the lunar walks had been.

Half an hour later, they cleaned up and sat down for breakfast. Mike started with some oatmeal and orange juice.

"I gather you have the first call at 0900?" he asked.

"And yours is at 1000. We'll use the media camera setup from last night for these calls, so our families will have a great view, but we have less flexibility in moving things around."

"So, the other person just hangs down the other end of the Lander with earbuds in?"

"I think so. Maybe we can say hi to each other's family at the beginning of the calls."

"Sure," said Mike, savouring his cereal. "You know, it is good to be able to taste flavours again. However, I suspect these are a bit overdone. We might need to have lunar meals which are more like earth flavours than the ones they use for the ISS with extra strong spices."

"I've noticed that too, now that my sinuses have settled down."

"I'm surprised no one thought of it, or maybe someone did, and some-one else decided it didn't matter!"

"It's all part of the learning process," said Sue. "What are you planning to do in your downtime?"

"Probably a bit of reading, and maybe I'll watch one of the programs that I've downloaded. And probably some emails. What about you, Sue?"

"Similar. I do have a bunch of personal emails I need to read and respond to. But I'll mainly watch a movie, I think. That will get me through until lunch. Just time to unwind."

"And it's mostly suit prep this afternoon?"

"And a few housekeeping chores, but fairly light stuff." Sue got up and placed their hot meals in the food warmer. "Do you want coffee?" she asked Mike.

'Yeah, the usual. It's great that someone did realise that we could use cups up here rather than having to use the drinking bags."

"And plates, even if they are paper." There wasn't enough water to wash plates etc. They had to be careful washing the cups not to use too much water.

Sue took the warmed food and their drinks and placed them on their small table.

"Thank you, Sue. Do you have a paper and slippers for me as well?"

"A paper! Who reads a paper these days? And you can get your own slippers!"

Just then, an alarm sounded, and the lighting was reduced.

Sue walked over to the monitoring panel and acknowledged the alarm. "It looks like one of our battery banks just went offline. There was a temperature excursion."

"That's not great," said Mike, moving to the control area.

Sue picked up the communication microphone. "Houston, this is Shackleton. We have a battery issue."

"Copy that, Sue," came the response from Mission Control. "We've seen the issue, and the team here is checking it out. Standby."

"It looks like we've had a bunch of lights, fans, and a number of science and auxiliary systems powered off," said Mike as he examined the system status. "The battery temperature began spiking when we woke up. The system should be able to cope with us turning on a few extra lights and heating our food."

"How are the temps now?" asked Sue.

"The failed set of batteries' temperature is dropping, which is great. The other 2 sets are ok, but they are on the warm side."

"Is the failed set on the sun side?" asked Sue.

"Yes, I think so. So maybe we have an insulation issue? The solar panels are providing a constant twelve kilowatt hours, so the batteries are really only trickle charging and supporting the occasional higher energy use."

"Shackelton, Houston," came the call on the radio.

"Go ahead, Houston," said Sue.

"Sue, we've looked at the data, and we think it is an environmental issue. We want to re-enable the battery before it cools down too much to prevent thermal shock, and we will monitor it. Are you ok with that?"

Sue looked at Mike. He shrugged. "We don't know any better!" he said.

"Houston, we are happy with that. Let us know if we can do anything."

"Ok, Sue. We will also move most of the load to the other two battery sets."

"Copy that, Houston," replied Sue. To Mike, she said, "It looks like they agree it is something to do with the sunny side of the craft."

"Yeah, but why now? They've re-enabled it. I guess we watch the temperatures."

The lights came back on, and they could hear fans starting and systems restarting in the Lander.

"We better finish our breakfast, and I have to get ready for my family video call," said Sue, sitting back down to eat her breakfast. "Houston can monitor the systems. It's our morning off."

Mike sat for a moment, watching the battery temperatures and then returned to the table to finish his breakfast, which had cooled during the interruption.

"Can't say that life is boring on the Moon," he said.

"I can't imagine anyone saying that!" replied Sue. "But as long as Houston has it under control, I have the morning off, and I'm going to enjoy it. What are you going to be watching this morning?"

"Christina got me watching this series, 'The Chosen'."

"I haven't heard of that."

"It's a dramatization about Jesus and his disciples. It's actually quite good."

"I didn't take you for a religious type."

"I wouldn't either, but this mission has made me think, you know? We could die, and what does that mean? Do we cease to exist? Do we reincarnate? Do we go to heaven? I figured we just go to heaven, but talking with Christina, it seems I was being a bit simplistic. Now I'm not so sure."

"So, you didn't think this through before the mission?" asked Sue incredulously.

"Well, I think I just thought God would work it out. I haven't been that bad, so I should be fine. Now I don't think he works that way. Now I suspect no one is good enough to go to heaven."

"Come on. You aren't bad. I'd understand it if you were a murderer, but you are a good guy."

"But what is God's standard. If there is an all-knowing, creator God who is all good, then why would he tolerate people around him who aren't perfect, who are a bit bad. And I'm not perfect. I cheated on Lisa."

"I cheated on Ron. You weren't with Lisa then.

"Ahh, this was another time. I cheated on Lisa. I'm not perfect."

Sue looked at him with surprise. "That means no one can go to heaven!"

"I think that's the point. Jesus makes it possible in some way for those who follow him to go to heaven. At least, that's what Christina says. She says that Jesus' death made it possible for those who follow him to be made perfect and acceptable to God, so he will tolerate them in heaven."

"And that is in this TV program?"

"Not exactly," said Mike. "It brings to life some of the characters that are written about in some of the books of the Bible. They are a bit more understandable. You see them as real people with real problems, struggling with life, and trying to understand who Jesus is."

"I still don't think now is the time to rethink your core beliefs," said Sue.

"Probably not, but it is what it is."

"Maybe you should decide one way or the other before our next walk. I don't want you second-guessing yourself tomorrow. Maybe talk to Christina during our downtime if that will help."

"I don't think it's been a problem, but sure, I can chat with Christina," said Mike. "Have you finished your meal? I'll stick these in the trash."

Mike took their finished meal trays and disposed of them in the trash bag.

The morning proceeded as planned. Sue held her video conference with her family, and Mike took the opportunity to have a chat with Christina on the Orion. She also had a day off.

After they established the call and exchanged pleasantries, Mike explained Sue's concerns and asked Christina, "What are the core beliefs I'd need to hold to be with God in heaven when I die?"

"It's pretty simple," said Christina. "Recognise that God is God, and you can't meet his standards, that is, you are sinful and keep rejecting his leadership, and take control yourself. Believe that Jesus, as both God and man, died on the Cross, paying the penalty for your sin to make you right before God and that God raised Jesus from the dead and made him Lord, or King over us. And recognise that Jesus is ruler over your life, submitting yourself to His rule. If you do so, God will mark you as His by placing his Spirit in you to help you. You become part of his family. In most Christian traditions, baptism would be held for you to publicly announce those beliefs, together with the symbolic washing away of sins."

"Is that all there is to being a Christian?"

"Well, there are a lot of implications around that submitting to Jesus, bit. A believer becomes part of the community or family of believers, and there are teachings on how to love each other in that community and how to show love to those around us. To grow in understanding, it is advisable to read the Bible and understand Jesus' teachings. Putting God and Jesus first and honouring God changes your perspective a lot.

"But the fundamentals are being prepared to say 'Jesus is Lord, or Ruler or King', and mean it, especially of your own life. It is one thing to say God is in control of all things, and quite another to say 'Jesus is Lord, and runs my life!"

"Is that all there is to it, saying "Jesus is Lord"?"

"Yes, it is as simple and as hard as that. Making Him ruler of your life and handing over the reins isn't that easy. As is recognising that you are sinful and unable to meet His standards and that you need to make him Lord."

"How do you know what Jesus wants you to do if you have submitted to him?" Mike asked.

"Very good question. I don't sit around praying for God to tell me whether to get out of bed. He has placed his Spirit in me, and he prompts and guides me, if I'm listening. There is also guidance in the Bible, both from Jesus' teachings and the understanding that his followers gained, as well as the interactions God had with his people before Jesus came.

"So, I try to understand Jesus' teaching and try and apply them, which deals with a lot of issues. I seek Jesus' guidance, especially for bigger, obvious decisions, and I get advice from other Christians in my community. But I still get things wrong. And I still sin and need to repent and ask God's forgiveness."

"It doesn't sound so easy."

"Well, it is, and it isn't. God doesn't just provide a way to follow Him, but also helps you do it. I should also warn you that following Jesus is not always easy. There can be suffering. Making Jesus Lord goes against the normal ways of this world, and this can bring conflict. But God promises to be with us through that suffering. After all, many of Jesus' followers were themselves killed."

"Okay, then. That's scary."

"Not really any more scary than walking on the Moon!

"Mike. Let me ask you a question right now. Are you ready to make Jesus the ruler of your life?"

"Umm, that puts me on the spot. I don't know."

"That's fine. What is stopping you?"

"Hmm. Good question. I don't think I have a problem with believing that Jesus existed. I'm not so sure that he was God, but there seems to be a fair bit of evidence that he wasn't your average human. But I think the real sticking point right now would be if I want to submit to his rule."

"That's fair enough. It sounds like you need to think about it. If there are other questions you need me to answer, please ask. If you do decide that you do want to follow Jesus, then you can pray to Jesus, recognise that you haven't been following him and can't live up to his requirements and you need his forgiveness and that you now want to follow him and recognise he is in charge and ask Him to take control. You don't need to pray that with someone else. But if you do pray that, please let me know so I can help you, ok?"

"Sure, I do need to think."

"One more thing, would you be happy for me to pray for you right now?"

"Ahh, I guess so."

"It probably seems weird to you, I know.

"Jesus, please help Mike understand who you are. I pray that you help him understand his sin and rebellion against you, and your love and forgiveness that you have for him, and the offer of a whole life with you. In Jesus' name, I pray. Amen."

"Thank you, Christina. That was strange yet comforting. I'll talk to you later."

While Sue continued her video conference, Mike sat and pondered what Christina had said and the other things he had read and watched about Jesus. He laughed as he considered how many other astronauts had had spiritual encounters in lunar orbit or on the Moon. And here he was thinking about a man wandering around Israel, preaching and healing people more than 2000 years earlier. Was this man really God? And was he prepared to follow him and put his life under his control instead of his own?

After fifteen minutes, Mike had not reached a conclusion, but it was time for his video conference with Lisa and his parents. Then he watched his videos and pondered some more. He was happy with the historical evidence that Jesus existed and that the scriptures were accurate. His discussions with Christina had dealt with his scientific hesitations. He was left with deciding he really believed that God did exist and that Jesus was his Son and died for him, and for that matter, that anyone needed to die for him. He definitely knew he wasn't perfect.

Just before their lunch, they packed up the video equipment.

After storing the video equipment, Sue and Mike selected their midday meals and placed them in the meal heater.

"How was your morning?" asked Mike.

"Great, thanks. We had a great chat. The kids loved chatting and seeing the views out the window. It was great to have a whole hour talking with them. And having some downtime watching a movie was great. How about you?"

"Good. I had a chat with Christina, then had my video conference with Lisa and my folks. It was good to have one-on-one time with Lisa during that."

"Did your chat with Christina help?"

"She was able to crystalize my thinking a bit, so I know where I need to focus."

"But it sounds like you haven't made a decision yet."

"No, not yet. Tell me, do you think you could let someone else make your decisions for you?"

"No, well, maybe. I guess I would let Ron do so in some cases. Why?"

"Actually, that's a good thought. Why? There's this concept of giving control or rule of your life to Jesus. I don't fully get it, and I'm not sure how much many Christians actually do it. Actually, I guess maybe it isn't that unusual now I think about it. I have to follow what you tell me to do, and NASA for that matter, so I guess it isn't an alien concept."

"But that is under particular circumstances. I'm not telling you what to read, or what to do on Sunday, or what to eat. Sounds a bit like a cult."

"Hmm. But we've worked with Christina for years. Do you think she is in a cult?"

"No," said Sue, thinking. "I would not say that about her. She is a very balanced and caring person. I don't always agree with her views or how she spends her free time."

"Exactly, she is different, but sort of in an attractive way."

The meal warmer chimed, and Mike removed their meals. They sat down at the table.

"I would have real issues letting someone else make my decisions for me. I see the ability to make decisions as a core part of who I am," said Sue.

"I agree," said Mike. "But we see Christina make decisions all the time, so I don't think it is quite that simple. It seems to be more of a consultative process and following guidelines. I know I've made some stupid choices in my life. In some ways, being an astronaut has put some limitations on me, which have curtailed my excesses, eventually. Perhaps Christians have something similar."

"Hmm. Have you seen the updated work lists for this afternoon? They've added a few items relating to batteries, and I think there are some extra tasks related to that tomorrow on our walk," said Sue, changing the topic.

"No, I haven't looked. I guess we will get briefed after lunch."

After their lunch, they had a briefing with Mission Control, including John and Christina on the Orion, reviewing the mission progress and status of the vehicles. The battery set that had overheated was indeed causing some concerns, and activities had been prepared to try and mitigate any further issues. The activities for the moonwalks remained as planned, with minor changes to free up some time for the battery work. It appeared that the Orion was performing well, and apart from boredom, so were its crew.

After the briefing, Sue and Mike worked through the checklist relating to the battery system changes. The ground team had made minor changes to the power management system to move the load from the problematic battery system earlier. The crew were needed to migrate the system to the new software and properly power on and off systems.

Then Sue and Mike began several hours of work checking and reconditioning their space suits for the next two moonwalks. To avoid contamination from the lunar dust, they both had to wear head-to-toe suits, like a onesie but made more of a paper-like material, plus gloves, googles and masks.

Working on the suits, first Sue's, then Mike's, they carefully inspected them for damage, taking lots of photos. They replaced some consumables and also cleaned the suits, especially around the seals, to minimise wear issues there. Suit system tests were run, and the helmets were carefully cleaned inside and out.

The only damage of note was on Mike's suit, on his right shoulder on the back. There had been some abrasion there during the fall, and Mission Control provided them with some instructions to cover the area to protect it from further damage.

There was also a minor dent on Mike's suit backpack near the shoulder area, and conducted an internal visual inspection of the systems, finding nothing of consequence.

Finally, they could leave the airlock after carefully wiping down their overalls before exiting and then carefully removing and disposing of them just outside the airlock door. All in an effort to minimise lunar dust intrusion. However, there was once again the burnt gunpowder smell in the cabin that was associated with the Moon dust.

After their evening meal, they reviewed their procedures for the next day and then had a couple of hours of personal time before their scheduled sleep period.

59

— • —

Mike bent down to pick up the clip he had just dropped, something that would not have been at all remotely possible in the Apollo-era spacesuit. For Mike, it was just a bit uncomfortable and a little awkward to see directly down, so he had to step back a little.

Sue and Mike were arranging a shade sail over part of their lander to help with the thermal management of the Lander. The sunlight side of the Lander was around 120 degrees Celsius, while the shaded side approached minus 173 degrees Celsius. The orientation in which they had landed meant that one of the battery sets was constantly hot, causing some ongoing issues. They were using a first aid thermal blanket to shade the area of the Lander. The plan was to remove the shade before they launched.

Mike used the clip to attach the sail to one of the panels of the Lander, finishing their activity to install it. Sue took some pictures and confirmed that they had completed the task with Missions Control while he turned and looked out across the lunar surface.

There were several hills nearby, caused by the multiple craters in the region of the pole. The nearest was that of Shackelton Crater. He could make out the nearby crater walls of Shoemaker, Faustini and Slater craters. The low angle of incidence of the sunlight cast long stark shadows, creating a dramatic landscape. The Apollo landing sites had all been within about twenty degrees of the equator, with well-lit locations. Here there was much more drama in the scenery.

After a few minutes, Mission Control reported that the sail was working well, and battery temperatures had returned to manageable levels.

Sue and Mike loaded equipment onto their vehicle and set off to their first location for experiments. Today they would once again enter the Shackelton Crater. However, this time it would be a planned, controlled entry. They would descend about one hundred metres into a constantly shaded area. While nowhere near the crater's floor, it was hoped that the material they would gather would contain some traces of water. It was possible future missions would descend further into the crater. However, such a journey would require additional protective measures, such as an enclosed rover capable of driving down the crater's steep walls.

Sue and Mike settled in for the drive. This time, Mike was at the controls.

"It looks like we are ahead of schedule," said Sue. "That work for the battery finished ahead of time, which means we might get some more time in the crater."

"That's great," said Mike. "I'll be interested to see what the regolith looks like in that permanently shaded part of the crater. It's possible that it's never been heated since the crater impact."

"You are going to descend first, correct?" asked Sue.

"Yes, and then you will follow if my descent goes ok."

"People really don't think of rock climbing when they think of moon-walks, do they?"

"They will after today!" said Mike. They had practised this procedure a lot in training, and he had done a fair amount of rock climbing to be familiar with the process, but they were in space suits, in a vacuum, in low gravity, on the Moon. All sorts of things could go wrong. Just the lower gravity meant that he would bounce more as he descended. Also, the ropes would not be as taught, so some of the systems may not work as expected.

Due to this risk, they would also use the safety restraint system they used on the first walk.

After a ten minute drive, they arrived at the crater rim. They offloaded their equipment.

This time they would use the rover as their anchor point for the descent, not just as a safety restraint. Mike and Sue proceeded to prepare their ropes and carabiners, just as they would have for a rock climb on earth. They could wear an additional harness around their suit, but one was already built into them, with attachment points around their waists.

They set up for each of them to rappel into the crater

"If you are ready, I'll let Mission Control know we are ready to descend," said Sue.

"Yep, I think we've got everything," said Mike.

"Mission Control, we are ready for Mike to descend into Shackleton Crater," said Sue.

"Copy that, Sue, we are watching, have a safe climb."

"Roger, Wilco, Mission Control," said Sue.

Starting cautiously but with increasing speed, Mike descended into the crater. The walls of the crater were angled about 30 degrees, and the surface was loose, which would make climbing out more work.

Once Mike reached the end of his rope, Sue started her rappel into the crater.

"Rock," said Sue as she dislodged some rocks. Fortunately, Mike had moved a few metres to the right of the descent to try and avoid any rocks that Sue would dislodge. A bunch of stones cascaded past him.

A few minutes later, Sue arrived next to Mike in the crater. It was permanently shaded in this part of the crater and very cold, around -190 deg C! Not a place where they wanted to spend a lot of time.

"Ok, that wasn't too bad," said Sue.

"And take a look at the star field above," said Mike. The lack of sunlight made the stars appear even brighter.

"Wow, that is beautiful," said Sue, admiring the view and taking some photos. Since she had her camera out, she took pictures of the surface around them.

"Let's move over to the area on the left that we haven't trampled and take some samples," said Mike. They moved over to that area and took some surface and deeper core samples, sealing them in tubes.

Then they took some surface samples and placed them in a small portable experiment that heated the sample and used a spectrograph to analyse it.

"This will be interesting," said Mike as he waited for the result.

"It's only the primary reason we landed at the South Pole," said Sue.

"Hmm, well, that is interesting," said Mike, looking at the results.

Sue looked at the display, reading the same results. "Yes, definitely interesting."

"Mike, can you please repeat the experiment after a calibration to confirm the results," said CAPCOM.

"Copy that, clearing test cell and calibrating," said Mike. While he waited for that to occur, he collected another sample of the regolith, which was fairly loose in that area.

"Adding the sample now," said Mike.

"I bet it's the same," said Sue.

"Probably, but one test wouldn't be very scientific, would it," said Mike.

The results appeared. Mike smiled. "Houston, the results confirm that water is detected in the sample."

"Copy that, Mike. That's a great result."

"I'm glad our visit here wasn't a wasted trip," said Sue.

"I reckon water is a bonus," said Mike.

After taking some more samples, they climbed back out of the crater. Mike belayed Sue while she climbed up, and then she set up to belay Mike from the top.

Reaching the top, they both sat on the rim for a few moments, resting and taking in the view. They could see part of the Earth on the horizon.

"No one else has ever seen this view," said Sue.

"Well, that's changed since everyone can see our camera feeds!"

"But that's not the same thing as being here and seeing it, is it?"

"No, there's something about feeling the regolith under my suit and the vast nothingness above that makes it real," said Mike.

"How big was the asteroid that created this crater?" asked Sue.

"Probably about 1.5 kilometres," said Mike. "At least that is the likely size."

"That's crazy."

"It was a couple of billion years ago!"

"Still, the power that was unleashed is amazing, and the crater is still here, pretty much unchanged all these years later."

"Makes you feel small, doesn't it?"

"Yes, but also proud that we are here."

"Hey, Sue and Mike, we hate to break up the moment, but it's time for you guys to pack up that site and move on to the next activity," said the CAPCOM.

"Copy that, Houston", said Sue.

They both climbed off the crater's edge, retrieving their climbing ropes and packing up their climbing gear.

Fifteen minutes later, they were back aboard the rover, driving to their next site, an unusual-looking rock outcrop.

"Looks easy compared to our last job," said Mike.

"Sure, just remember we are in space suits, in a vacuum, on the Moon. But otherwise, easy!" replied Sue.

"It's all relative. So, I take some samples while you take photos."

"Umm, stereoscopic video and also a lidar scan."

"Which we need to do first."

"Yes, do you want to work out the best place to set it up, while I unpack the equipment."

"Yes, Ma'am," replied Mike. He unbuckled, stepped out of the rover, and walked around the outcrop, which protruded about 8 metres out from the hillside, and was about 3 metres high. Roughly the size of a small house.

"Sue, I think we will need to scan from two positions to do this properly." The outcrop extended several metres, like a headland into the ocean, surrounded by sea on three sides.

Sue carried over the lidar and tripod to him. "Ok, so about 45 degrees from the face on the left and right. Maybe we should do 3."

"If we have time, that would be even better."

"Houston, we are thinking of taking three LIDAR scans here. Do you concur, and do we have time for that?" asked Sue.

"Sue, the team is discussing that now. The limitation is the time. Go ahead and set up the LIDAR on the tripod, and we will confirm locations shortly."

"Copy that, Houston," said Sue. "Hmm, we must be a bit tighter on time than I thought," said Sue.

Mike set up the tripod, locking the legs into place, while Sue retrieved the LIDAR from its storage container and then secured it to the tripod.

"Sue, Houston, we are happy for you to take three scans."

"Great, Houston, we will set up the first one now, on the left, about 10 degrees away from the facial plan of the outcrop."

"Copy that, Sue," replied the CAPCOM.

Mike carried the equipment to the first location. Sue aligned the LIDAR, and then they both retreated to the rover and triggered the scan.

Once completed, they replaced the LIDAR with the stereoscopic camera and photographed the same scene.

They repeated this two more times, with the LIDAR and camera, directly in front of the outcrop, and the last time with them to the right of the outcrop.

"Now it's time for me to get busy with my hammer," said Mike, fetching it from the rover.

He walked up closer to the outcrop. "There appear to be a couple of different rock layers in this outcrop. I see a good amount of anorthosite. I'll get samples of the 2 visible types before me."

Mike stepped up to the outcrop and struck part of it with his hammer, causing it to break off. He handed it to Sue, who had followed him. She placed it in a sample bag, scanning its QR code.

They worked their way around the outcrop, with Sue recording Mike's actions on her cameras so that the location of the samples could be documented.

Mike walked around to the far side of the outcrop, looking up at the rock face as he walked, intensely concentrating on the features. Stepping on some loose rock, he slipped, attempting to keep his balance, he swung around and fell backwards against the rock wall.

A couple of warnings were immediately illuminated on Mike's screen.

"Oops," he said, "that was a bit clumsy." As he righted himself, Mike checked the warnings. "I've got a high G warning on my suit, which makes sense, and it appears a rear camera got damaged. Sue, could you please inspect my backpack."

As he stepped away from the wall, Sue walked up behind him and closely inspected the unit.

"There's a bit of an indentation here at the top but no perforation. The CO_2 sublimator appears ok. We will need to perform a full checkout when we return. Keep an eye on your warnings.

"Houston, are you happy for us to proceed?"

"Yes, Sue, the team have been checking Mike's suit systems and are happy for you to continue at this time," replied CAPCOM.

"Ok, Mike," said Sue, "any more samples around here?"

"This area over here looks like something different is happening, so let's take a sample from there and then continue onto our next site. Who knew a rock wall could be so dangerous?!"

"As I said before, everything here is dangerous."

Mike walked over to the area he was interested in and struck it with his hammer, breaking off a sample, which Sue duly placed in a sample bag and documented.

"Ok, time for a picnic, isn't it?" asked Mike.

"Did you pack the cake?" asked Sue.

"Sorry – just liquid supplements for you today."

They placed the samples in the rover's storage and sat down in their seats to rest and consume some of their liquid meal.

The rest of the walk progressed normally, with more sample collection and stowing of samples when they returned to the Lander. Their post-walk suit checks took longer as they carefully inspected Mike's suit for internal damage after the fall. Under the direction of Mission Control, they performed extra tests and inspections, but they did not find anything of concern.

After a meal and completing preparations for their final walk the next day, Mike was able to talk to Lisa just before their rest period started. He initiated the call.

"Hi Lisa, sorry I'm late. We spent extra time checking my suit."

"Hi Mike, sorry, Jasmine isn't happy and has been screaming most of the day."

"Oh, that's not good. Do you know why?"

"Of course, I don't know why. Don't you think I would fix whatever is wrong?" replied Lisa angrily.

"Hey, it can't be that bad. I've had a tough day too."

"Tough day – you fell against a cliff, Mike. Try spending a day with a screaming baby, and see how you cope."

"It sounds like you've had a tough day. Are my parents still there?"

"No, they went to Houston to give me some space."

"Ok, can I see her?"

"I just put her down."

"I'm sorry I can't help. I should be home in 10 days."

Lisa took a breath and replied, "I know. Today has been hard. This is the quietest she has been."

"Maybe I should let you rest while she is quiet. I've got to turn in soon."

"Are you ready for your last walk?"

"Yes. We didn't find anything wrong with the suit. It's strange to say, but things are getting routine now. It would be strange doing a month-long mission here."

Mike heard Jasmine start crying in the background.

"There she goes again," said Lisa. "She just won't stop. I've got to go." She closed the connection.

Mike stared at the screen for a moment. Lisa wasn't coping as well as he had thought. He emailed their family liaison and told them about the situation. Maybe they could help out by organising dinner or something. Or contact his parents. He felt helpless.

Unfortunately, life kept going on, even if he was creating history on the moon. He couldn't even control himself, let alone things happening hundreds of thousands of miles away. But he knew someone who could.

He thought about that for a minute, then initiated a private call to Christina. It was time to make a decision.

60

—–·—–

THURSDAY, MAY 30, 2024

This was it, their final day on the Moon. Sue was happy with how the mission had gone. There had been a few hiccups, but nothing that they weren't trained to handle. They had made history and well and truly met their mission objectives. Today's walk had all the 'nice to do' tasks, such as locating some of the recent landers and examining them, and taking samples from the same location for analysis on earth.

Standing by the observation window, she checked her messages while waiting for Mike to finish his morning ablutions. The window gave her a sense of expanse, necessary when they spent a lot of time in the relatively small lander.

There were a few messages relating to later parts of the mission that she would need to read later, and one from the media team wanting to start scheduling interviews after their return. That one she'd leave for the return journey. There was one involving a risk analysis on Mike's suit. She read the executive overview and noted that the risk had increased slightly but was still considered acceptable.

Finally, there was a security assessment about increased tensions with China. A security review had found evidence of more espionage by China within NASA, this time relating to space suit production.

Sue walked across to the system's display for the Lander. Everything was operating normally, and the battery temperatures had reduced on the problematic cells.

Satisfied that all was well, Sue walked to her bunk and fetched her personal tablet. She checked her private email and found lots of messages from friends. Most importantly, Ron had uploaded some photos of Jessica and Jerome. They were photos of typical kids doing typical stuff that typical kids do. But their mum was on the Moon!

Sue quickly typed a reply, commenting on their activities and saying she loved them. Then she took a selfie and sent it to Ron so they would have it when they woke up.

Mike had finished his morning wash, so it was her time to prepare for the day ahead.

A bit over an hour and a half later, after eating breakfast, Mike and Sue worked through the now very familiar process of preparing for their fourth EVA on the Moon. Mission Control had run extra tests on Mike's suit, and they could find no issues of concern, so they were currently 'go' for the walk. They carefully checked their suits, cross-checking their work.

They both entered their suits via their rear hatches and assisted each other with their gloves, sealing each other's hatches before the depressurisation of the airlock began.

It was a chance for them to physically rest and review procedures and checklists, and Sue took the opportunity to review the walk's procedures.

"Mike, we will be visiting the PRIME-1 landing site first today, then working our way back here via a couple of sites VIPER performed tests at," said Sue.

PRIME-1 was a lander that drilled into the surface of the Moon and tested for volatiles. VIPER was a mobile rover that performed similar tests in various locations around the South Pole.

Sue continued, "Our main mission is to retrieve the samples those missions made and take our own samples where possible. We are also to photograph PRIME-1. Today's drive will be the longest we have performed."

"That sounds all correct to me," said Mike. "It looks like a nice day for a drive on the Moon. Not a cloud to be seen."

"Thanks for that weather forecast, Mike. Have you got any concerns?"

"Not as long as the rover works correctly. I don't fancy a long walk home."

"I am pretty sure we won't have to worry about that," said Sue. "However, we can walk it if we have to."

"I'm more worried about being able to locate the VIPER sites, but that's not really a safety issue unless we take too long."

"I guess we will find out. Is your suit checking out ok?"

"There are no warnings, and I had a brief look at the logs, and nothing looks unusual. But I'll let the guys at Mission Control keep an eye on that."

"Please avoid any rock walls today, Mike, ok?"

"Sure. Our last moonwalk. Do you have any outstanding wish list items we need to cross off?"

"Playing tennis might have been fun, but we don't have anything like a racket. Getting an earthrise photo would be good, but we haven't been in the right place at the right time. Attempting a long jump would be fun, but the risk assessment was just too high."

"Really? I didn't hear about that."

"We could probably have worked up a learning process that would have reduced the risk, start with small jumps etc. The big concern was not being able to estimate the landing area and managing the landing without damage to the craft or occupant."

"So, they were worried that you might crash land."

"Yes. They are planning on doing some experiments on a later flight with more resources around to help confirm modelling and improve our training so we can properly learn how to jump to deal with things like crevasses."

"So, we can take some small hops instead, then."

"I think some gentle leaps when we return to the Lander would be fairly low risk and informative."

They sat waiting for a few more minutes, reviewing checklists and pondering the activities ahead.

Once the airlock depressurisation had been completed, they exited the Lander and began loading it with the equipment required for the day's work.

As Sue worked, she took little snatches of time to gaze at the moonscape before her. It was barren and lifeless, with stark lighting, yet at the same time, beautiful.

During one of these brief pauses, Mike walked up beside her and commented, "The view is stunning, isn't it? We are very fortunate to be here to see it."

"Yes, it is, and yes, we are. How many items do you have left to retrieve?"

"Three, what about you."

"Just two, so we should be on our way in five minutes."

"Sounds good," said Mike.

Sue walked over to the Lander and found the next storage location indicated on her checklist on her display. After opening it, she located the required equipment. In this instance, it was a trowel for sample gathering. She checked the checklist and noted that the next item was also in the same stowage bin, a pick, also used for gathering samples. She scanned both items, closed the storage pod, and carried them to the rover, finding their new storage location and securing them there. They would remain on the rover after they left rather than weighing down the Lander, which would not be reused.

"Mission Control, I've finished my checklist item 7.1," said Sue.

"Copy that, Sue," replied George as CAPCOM.

Her next task was to prepare the rover. She performed a walk-around inspection, looking for damage and open storage pods. Finding nothing out of place, she took her seat at the controls and began buckling up her safety harness.

Meanwhile, Mike finished his tasks, reported his completion to Mission Control, and took his seat in the rover.

Sue started activating the rover systems. "Let me know when you are secure, Mike."

"Sure thing. How much charge have we got?"

"Plenty, batteries are over 90%. The wonders of solar power with permanent sunlight."

Mike carefully secured his last harness strap. "Right, I am now secure," he said.

Sue looked across at him and checked that his straps were correctly locked. "I confirm you are secure."

Mike checked Sue's straps and reported, "I confirm that you, too, are secure."

"Mission Control, rover departing landing site for PRIME-1," Sue called on the radio.

"We copy that, Sue, have a good drive."

Driving the rover was relatively easy, although they often stopped and discussed the safest path to take to their destination. Rocks and small craters meant that their path was not a straight line, and although route planning had been performed in advance, they still needed to fine-tune the route to allow for conditions that were not apparent to the planners.

Today there was a large patch of boulders over several hundred metres. The planned route worked well until they came to a section with a sharp half-metre drop that had not shown up during the mapping process, possibly due to the shadows cast by the boulders. This required them to backtrack and find an alternate route.

The first alternate path they tried was too narrow to pass through, and they progressed to the following likely route. This one was safe to pass through, and after a few extra turns, they could rejoin their original course.

They exited the boulder field and continued to drive to the lander site.

"Are you able to see it yet?" asked Sue.

"Not really," replied Mike, "but I see an occasional sun reflection from that direction, so that must be it."

"Well, that's hopeful. We just have to skirt around this crevasse, and once we are over that rise ahead, we should have a clear view."

The route led them up the hillside around a crevasse that formed a gully. It wasn't particularly wide, yet they would not be able to drive over it, so they must go around.

"Hmm, pity we can't fly there. It would be more direct," said Mike

"Yeah, well, there aren't any plans for a space hopper-type craft anytime soon, but there are definitely limitations for a rover here," said Sue.

"That would be cool," said Mike.

"Yes, it would. In the meantime, we just enjoy the scenery, which isn't bad!"

A thought about the Chinese lunar project occurred to Sue. However, she couldn't mention it since they were on an open channel with a live public broadcast. The Chinese had recently tested a lander that attempted to fly around on the surface. Its design was very similar to the one being researched by NASA.

That thought reminded her of the recent security report regarding Chinese espionage of the NASA suit development. She hoped that they had just looked and hadn't sabotaged any of their suits in any way.

But Sue couldn't dwell on those thoughts. She needed to focus on the task at hand, driving the rover.

They completed their detour around the crevasse and climbed over the small hill. Sue stopped the rover as they reached their highest elevation and looked down on the plain below.

"There it is," said Mike, pointing towards the small man-made lander in the primarily grey moonscape. It was pretty strange, with it being the only geometrically regular structure they could see, and they were still about 1 kilometre from it.

"It looks like we can drive straight to it from here," said Sue. "Time to take some pictures for context."

This was one of the planned activities, and they unstrapped themselves and retrieved the tripod and camera equipment to take some high-quality images of the scene.

Mike took the role of photographer. They even took some selfies, with mission control controlling the camera remotely.

After 15 minutes, they packed up the photographic equipment and continued the drive to the lander.

As they approached the PRIME-1 lander, Sue slowed the rover to reduce the amount of lunar dust they raised as the rover drove. They parked about 50 metres from the lander, unstrapped themselves, and got their photographic and sample retrieval equipment.

"First thing is to perform a photographic survey," said Sue as they placed their equipment bags on the surface. She handed Mike a camera and took another one herself. As planned, they walked around the Lander in opposite directions, photographing it as they went. When roughly opposite, each posed for photos of the scene for historical records.

"It's strange thinking people will look back at these photos in a hundred years or more," said Mike.

"I know, but we do it now with the Apollo photos," said Sue. "This is the first robotic lander visited by astronauts!"

It was historic and time for Mike to make more history.

61

Mike was about to perform the first sample return from a lander on a planet or Moon other than the Earth.

PRIME-1 had not been designed for sample return. The samples that had been gathered by its drill and analysed had simply been disposed of onto the surface. Mike could clearly see the sample pile under the lander.

The mission team had decided it was worth gathering the samples, even though samples from different depths would be mixed up. So, Mike needed to gently sweep the sample pile into a storage container.

Simple, thought Mike, but he knew from his training that it wasn't that simple. He only had one go at this.

First, he had to kneel next to the pile, fighting against the pressure in the suit. Then he placed a special specimen capture trowel up against the sample pile. Then he carefully swept the sample onto the trowel. It worked. The sample pile didn't collapse, and he now had most of the sample on the trowel.

Next, he needed to carefully transfer the sample into the sample container. Mike needed to move smoothly and not make sudden movements or knock the sample, as that would likely cause him to lose much of it.

His training paid off, the sample was safely stored, and he could breathe easily again.

He took a couple of deep breaths and looked out at the scene around him. It was still amazing to be here. The small lander, with its white, blue, grey and gold surfaces and black solar panels, contrasted with the wild, untouched, grey-brown of the lunar surface around it.

He'd spent many years preparing for this mission, and here he was on the last EVA before returning home to Earth.

Enough pondering, thought Mike. His next task was to take his own core sample. This would be taken as close to the lander as possible.

The drill Mike would use would be powered by the rover, which required Sue to drive the rover closer and to pull a cable to Mike's location. While Sue did this, Mike set up the stand and placed the drill onto it. He would need to hold the drill while operating it to provide mass so it would bite into the rock. The core would be pretty small but valuable.

Sue brought the cable over to him. They had taken several such samples on two of their walks, so he was confident of success.

"Are you happy with my location here, Sue?"

"It looks as good as any to me. I can't see any dangers, and you aren't too close to the lander if you slip."

During their last drill, Mike was dragged halfway around the rig as he lost grip on the surface. He had allowed a bit extra room in case it happened again so he didn't get flung into the lander.

"Mission Control, we are ready to commence drilling. Are we go?" asked Mike.

"Copy that, Mike. We are go for you to proceed."

Mike was excited to drill another core. What he had seen of the two previous cores was fascinating, and he knew years of research would be performed on just this core, expanding their knowledge of the Moon.

He switched the drill unit onto standby, and it performed system checks with all lights turning green. It was a relatively simple unit with some power management and an electric motor that drove the drill head. It also had some communications circuits, so essential information was sent to his suit to be displayed on his HUD. Mike checked the data presented.

"Ok, Sue, ready to proceed."

"Copy that."

Mike checked his boot positions and checked that they weren't slipping and braced himself for the rotation that would be imparted by the drill.

"Starting drill," he said, initiating the drill at a low speed.

The drill started spinning, and he pushed it down into the ground. The drill bit and slowly started to descend. They were only drilling a one metre core, so not that deep.

After a minute, the drill started encountering more resistance, so Mike increased the drill's power. This was expected. So was the temperature increase in the drive unit. In a vacuum, the only way to remove heat is radiation. He expected he would need to stop in a few minutes and let the motor cool before resuming.

"We are progressing well," said Mike on the radio. "I think we will only require one break."

Mike kept an eye on the temperature while ensuring the drill stayed aligned.

Suddenly there was a bright flash, and Mike felt stabbing pain in both his legs. Simultaneously alarms sounded as the pressure in his suit dropped.

What had happened? He pressed the stop button on the drill, but it was no longer running. He saw a glob of bright red stuff float in an arc from below the drill mount, falling to the grey surface. He heard the increasing whistle of oxygen as his suit tried to compensate for the pressure drop.

"Sue, I have a problem, suit rupture, pain in my legs. I think I'm bleeding," he said. He started to feel faint and fell backwards, which helped him not feel so faint. He suspected he needed at least one tourniquet, but there was no way he or Sue could apply one.

"Mike, talk to me. What happened?" said Sue. Rushing to his side.

"I don't know. I think the drill exploded."

Mike thought through what he could do. Perhaps they could stem the air loss, but Sue couldn't stop the blood loss.

"Sue, tape around my legs," he said. He was starting to feel faint again, his vision narrowing. Was this the end? "Lisa, Jasmine, Mum, Dad, I love you all." Mike took a breath, "Jesus loves you too. I'm sorry."

62

— • —

"Mike, Mike, talk to me," said Sue. She shook him, no response. She grabbed a roll of tape on her waistband and started to tape as hard as she could around Mike's upper legs. There was blood streaming out.

"Sue, Mike's blood pressure is plummeting, his heart rate is rising quickly, and his oxygen sats are low," said the CAPCOM.

"Copy," said Sue, out of habit more than anything else. Mike was dying. He was bleeding out and running out of oxygen.

"I am trying to seal his suit legs with tape. There are large gashes to both legs with blood flowing from both."

"Copy that, Sue," said CAPCOM.

She tore off the tape and started taping his other leg. He must have severed both femoral arteries. He needed tourniquets fast, and the tape wasn't going to do it. It still took her over a minute to tape around both his legs, and finally, his suit pressure stabilised.

"I've taped around his suit, which seems to have sealed it. For now, I'm going to try and make some tourniquets for both legs."

"Copy that, Sue."

She raced to the rover and grabbed two tie-down straps for holding equipment onto the rover. She wrapped one around Mike's upper left thigh, pulled the strap through the rachet and tightened it as much as she could. She then did the same thing on his right thigh.

"His oxygenation is better but still low at 90%, his blood pressure has stabilised, but again it is low at 75/44, and he is tachycardic, with his pulse being 140. SURGEON wants to speak to you."

"Go for SURGEON," said Sue, and she applied more tape around the suit tears.

"Sue, Mike is in critical condition. If he makes it back to the lander, he will need lots of fluids, including plasma. Then he will likely need a double leg amputation because you aren't going to be able to repair the laceration to his femoral arteries. If he made it back to earth orbit, it is doubtful he would survive the landing. This is not a survivable injury, given our mission parameters.

"According to Mike's wishes and our protocols, I am instructing you that Mike is Not For Resuscitation. You are not to perform any heroic efforts to save him. Do you understand?"

Sue sagged as she bent over Mike's inert form. They had had multiple scenario training sessions to develop plans for what would happen in this sort of circumstance. But it was different when there was a real live person, colleague, and friend dying in front of you.

"Copy, Mike is NFR," replied Sue in a strained voice.

She understood what was happening medically. Mike had had a decompression and lost a significant amount of blood from both femoral arteries. He could potentially regain consciousness, but perhaps the depressurisation had complicated matters.

"Houston, I'm going to get Mike onto the rover."

"Copy that, Sue. Please take some hi-res photos of the drill when possible."

"Copy."

Sue rushed back to the rover, disconnected the powerline for the drill, and then drove it next to Mike. Then she lifted him, possible in lunar gravity, but still not easy, and placed him lying across the rover behind the seats. She found some more straps to secure him in place.

She checked his vitals on her display and noted that his blood pressure had dropped a little again, which was not promising. In reality, she knew there was very little that could be done for Mike.

Sue grabbed one of the cameras, stepped over to the drill, and took photos and video from many angles. She knew that pictures and video were also being captured from her suit cameras, so she wasn't too worried about being overly careful, but she did want to try and get all available angles.

"George, I've taken the photos and video, I'm just gathering up the tools here, and I'll then drive back to the lander."

"Copy that, Sue," replied George, as CAPCOM.

Sue picked up the small number of tools they had been using and placed them in one of the storage lockers on the rover. Then, after quickly checking that Mike was secure, she sat in the rover and strapped herself in.

She drove as quickly as she dared, following the trail they had made on the way there, which made navigation simple.

As they entered the boulder field, an alarm sounded. Looking at her display, Sue sobbed. Mike's heart had stopped.

63

Sue lay in her bunk in the lander, numb.

She had returned with Mike's body to the lander. Mission Control had been working on a checklist for her. They had abandoned all further experiments and sample collection, but she still had to store samples and secure equipment before her lift-off so that the lander wasn't damaged.

Once that was finished, her final task was to carry Mike's body, in his suit, up the lander's ladder and into the airlock. That had been awkward and exhausting.

Once both of them were inside, she could finally close the hatch and repressurise the airlock. And then she had sat there for an hour in her suit while pressures stabilised.

Crying in a space suit is problematic, but at least it wasn't in zero-G, so the tears could run down her face and not just pool around her eyes.

Then, once she got out of her suit, Mission Control informed her of the location of the body bags. Yes, preparations had included having body bags on board. She didn't know why there was more than one. Maybe it was an oversight since future missions would have 4 members on board.

Wearing a mask, Sue had opened Mike's suit hatch and then hauled his body out of the suit.

Mission Control wanted photos. They wanted to see what the damage was to the suit. They wanted to see what Mike's injuries were. She even had to use an inspection camera to view the inside of the suit legs. It was bloody.

As Sue placed Mike's body into the bag, rigor mortis was starting to set in. She cupped his head in her hands and whispered a farewell before zipping the bag closed.

Then, Mission Control had conducted a brief private ceremony with the crew on the Orion patched in and Lisa and Mike's parents present. Sue had left the airlock, and then it was depressurised. Mike's body, exposed to a vacuum, would freeze, and all microbial activity would stop allowing his fragile body to be safely returned to Earth without poisoning the return crew with decomposition gases.

Finally, Sue was able to clean herself and eat some food before performing some crucial system checks.

And now, she could just stop.

What had happened? How had that drill exploded like that? She just couldn't process it, even though she was trained to. Her mind shut down, and she dozed.

The incoming call on her private pad woke her. Sue sat up, startled. She had fallen asleep. Then she remembered the events of the day. She looked at the time on the pad before answering. She had probably only dozed for half an hour, but she did feel a bit refreshed.

The call was from Ron.

She answered the call, "Hi, Ron."

"Sue, I'm so sorry about Mike. How are you?" asked Ron, concerned.

"Ahh, I'm ok physically. I'm pretty stunned. I just dozed for a bit when I lay down."

"That's pretty understandable. Do you want to talk about it?"

"There's not much to say. You've probably seen the footage. The drill just exploded and tore Mike's suit around his upper legs. So, he lost pressure and a lot of blood.

"I just did what I could to save him, taped up his suit and applied tourniquets, but that wasn't really a survival incident."

"You did all you could, Sue."

"I know. Getting him back here, packing up and bringing him inside, and then putting him in his body bag was brutal."

"I bet. Your parents have called and asked me to pass on their love."

"Thanks. How are the kids?"

"Jerome is fine, but Jessica is a bit quiet. She's old enough to realise it could have been you. I've tried to talk to her, but she doesn't want to."

"NASA will have someone who she can talk with. Ask them. Same for you."

"How's Lisa?"

"I don't know. I haven't been able to talk to her. The liaison said she is ok."

"I'll call her after we finish."

"Are you sure?"

"I have to. That is the job of the commander. Mission Control can set it up."

"Ok. Take care of yourself. I guess everything else just happens on schedule."

"I will. Yes, a factor of orbital dynamics. I'll take off in the morning."

"Be careful. I love you."

"Thanks, Ron. I love you too. Hug Jessica and Jerome for me. Bye."

"Bye," replied Ron.

Sue took a deep breath. She contacted Mission Control, asked them to organise a call with Lisa, and washed her face.

Ten minutes later, the call came through on her NASA pad. Sue took a deep breath and answered the video call. "Lisa, I'm so sorry for your loss."

"Thank you, Sue. It's devastating. Are you ok?"

"I'm a bit shaken up, but I'm ok. I'm so sorry that the ceremony happened so quickly."

"That's ok. I was expecting it after going through the scenario exercises."

"That's good, but all the practice in the world doesn't really prepare you for this," said Sue. "Mike was a good guy, a great astronaut, and he loved you and Jasmine."

"Thank you. I know he wasn't perfect, but he was mine."

"I know. He changed so much from when he first came to Houston. I know he was thinking about a lot of stuff recently. He deliberately meant his last radio call for you."

"I know. That was amazing," sobbed Lisa.

"We are here for you if you want to talk. And we'll be home in about a week. If you need anything, just ask your liaison."

"Thanks."

"I'll talk to you later, Lisa. I'd really like to give you a hug, but that's not possible."

"That's ok. Keep safe."

Sue closed the call.

64

—·—

The crew prepared the cabin of the Orion for re-entry. They had carefully placed Mike's body bag in his seat for the landing to help balance the craft.

Sue strapped herself into the commander's seat, with John beside her and Christina in the rear.

Over a week ago, she had successfully launched from the Moon and rendezvoused with the Orion, and she had finally been able to grieve together with John and Christina. Then after transferring their samples and Mike's body to the Orion, they undocked the lander and fired their main engine to leave their orbit and return to Earth.

The remainder of the week had been routine. They had their scheduled maintenance tasks, fitness routines and occasional science experiment. That left a lot of time for thinking and chatting. She, John and Christina had been able to talk through what happened multiple times, and she had also needed to debrief a couple of times with members of the mission team. That kept the incident fresh and helped her process what happened.

There would be more reviews after they landed. The investigation would no doubt be far-reaching.

Sue took a deep breath and focussed on the task at hand, a safe re-entry. Their speed was much, much higher than the re-entry speed of capsules from low earth orbit, such as the Soyuz, Dragon and Starliner capsules.

In low earth orbit the vehicle enters at about 7.8 km/s, whereas from the moon, their entry velocity was around 11 km/s. The protective systems on the Orion had to be better to cope, and the calculations performed to model the re-entry were even more complex. Since the Apollo era, only the early Artemis missions and the Orion test program had reached such entry speeds. Since the Apollo program, this was only the second manned mission to enter at these velocities.

Sue started the next checklist and coordinated with Mission Control. The process would be automated, but she and John would be monitoring at all times and could override it if anything unexpected occurred.

"Ok, guys," said Sue on the internal communications, "we are about to initiate the re-entry burn and then separate from the service module. Do you have any concerns?"

"No," said Christina from the back row.

"No," said John from the pilot's chair.

"I concur," said Sue.

"Houston, Orion, we are ready for re-entry," she said on the radio.

"Orion, we copy that, and you are go for re-entry burn," replied the familiar voice of George as CAPCOM.

"Roger, Wilco," replied Sue. "John, proceed with re-entry burn."

"Copy that, initiating re-entry burn," replied John, selecting the command on his screen.

The Orion and service module had already been orientated so that it was flying the service module first. At the scheduled time, the main engine on the service module fired, slowing down the stack so both vehicles would re-enter the atmosphere somewhere over the Pacific Ocean.

The crew were pushed deep into their seats as the engine fired. This was the first significant acceleration they had experienced since leaving lunar orbit, and they weren't used to it. Sue coped best, having spent a week in lunar gravity.

"Burn complete," reported John, reaching for a sick bag.

"Orion, that burn was nominal. I'll get back to you shortly with any corrections we need to make," reported George.

"Copy that," said Sue.

"Are you ok, John?" asked Christina.

"Yep, I guess I should have taken the anti-nausea meds anyway," replied John.

"There's still time. I'll get them for you," said Christina, unstrapping herself. She pushed over to the locker containing their medications, retrieved the dose for John, and then floated over to his chair before returning to her seat.

After several checklist items and numerous conversations with Houston, they were finally ready to separate from their service module. Once this occurred, they would be committed to the landing sequence and only have limited power and consumables.

"Orion, you are go for separation," said George.

"Copy that. Go for separation," replied Sue.

"Initiating separation", replied John, confirming the command on his screen. They heard several pops as explosive bolts connecting the Orion to its service module fired. The Orion's thrusters fired briefly to distance the vehicle from the service module, and the crew felt a sudden push.

"I'm seeing good separation," reported John.

"The service module is firing thrusters," reported Sue. The service module would move a couple of kilometres away from the Orion module so that the vehicles did not interact during re-entry.

"We have about three minutes before we start interacting with the atmosphere," reported Sue.

"I can't believe we are actually almost home," said Christina.

"I'm looking forward to a nice shower," said John.

"Aren't we all," said Sue.

"And a burger and my family," said John.

"I want a decent coffee, as well as the shower and family," said Sue.

The craft wobbled a bit, and the thrusters started firing intermittently. They sounded a bit like a high-pressure tap being opened and quickly closed with a short water hammer.

"Houston, we are interfacing with the atmosphere," reported Sue. "Here we go, guys."

Gradually a rushing sound grew, together with the thruster firing, as the light out the window started glowing crimson red with a white core. The capsule was falling through the atmosphere at more than Mach 25, and the atmosphere was instantly turning to plasma. The ablative heat shield was slowly eroding and heating up, releasing gases that protected the capsule from the intense heat.

Sue looked out her window briefly. The entire view was now taken up by the reddish glow surrounding the craft. She returned to watching the vehicle displays that showed the orientation of the craft and thruster firings.

The buffeting was getting worse, with the thrusters firing longer in an effort to keep the capsule in the correct orientation, although that would diminish as aerodynamic forces increased.

Suddenly the colour of the plasma changed to yellow, and Sue could see the earth and horizon once again.

The thrusters now occasionally fired to orientate the capsule and steer it towards their landing zone.

The g-force started to increase as the Orion capsule slowed faster as the atmosphere increased.

Now, all Sue could see out of the windows was black which slowly became blue sky.

"Subsonic," reported John.

"Twenty seconds to forward bay cover jettison," reported John.

"Ten seconds," said John. "Five."

There was a loud pop as the forward cover was jettisoned, and small chutes whisked it away, and three small chutes were ejected into the slip-stream. A few seconds later, she felt slight tugs as they started deploying.

The g-forces tugged at Sue and crew as the capsule slowed even further, and after a time, the drogue chutes were jettisoned, and the 3 large chutes deployed.

Sue watched them fly out of the top of the capsule, initially reefed, and she willed them to fill with air correctly. Two of them looked good, but one seemed a bit oddly shaped, but then suddenly, the reefing was released, and the giant parachutes billowed open, bouncing around off each other. At the same time, she felt a violent tug that pushed her deep into her seat and then there was just a gentle falling sensation and a slow swaying as the Orion slowly descended through clouds to its splashdown.

"Well, that was a ride," said John. "We are on target."

"Sure, was," said Christina, "now can you stop the world spinning?"

"Sorry, as you know, we've got a few minutes of this, but it should settle down to a gentle sway."

Sue heard a rustling behind her as Christina grabbed a sick bag. She took a deep breath herself and focussed her view outside, which didn't help. Her vestibula system was telling her all sorts of strange things. And she's spent a week in gravity recently, and the others would be feeling it worse than she was.

Mission Control informed them that they were on target and that there was only a slight swell running, so they should not have long to wait for retrieval, which was good because if they didn't like hanging from para-chutes, they definitely wouldn't like floating on an ocean.

A little while later, John called out, "One thousand feet".

"How are you feeling, Christina?" asked Sue.

"A bit better, thanks," Christina replied.

"We'll be in San Diego in no time," said Sue.

"100 hundred feet," said John. "A pity we don't get time to sightsee there."

"After a month in space, none of us are up to wandering around a zoo or anything like that," said Sue.

Just then, they splashed down into the Pacific, fairly gently on the whole. But then they started to bob around.

"I'm glad the sky is blue, and we aren't in the middle of a squall or something," said John.

"Orion, we read you splashed down. Welcome back to Earth," said George as CAPCOM.

"Thank you, Houston. We are glad to be home."

It took forty minutes for the retrieval team to secure the crew module and tow it to the retrieval ship, where it was towed into the ship's well deck, a water-level landing area. The hatch was then opened, and the crew assisted to exit the vehicle. Sue was able to carefully walk from the vehicle, but both John and Christina were carried out.

Then they started a period of exhausting tests and interviews.

65

— • —

WEDNESDAY, JUNE 12, 2024

Three days later, after their initial tests and a bit of time with families, the remaining crew members reunited in Houston, together with George and some key mission staff. They were meeting with Lisa and Mike's parents, John and Clare.

Sue entered the informal meeting room where Christina and John were already seated in comfortable chairs. She had to walk carefully and deliberately as her body was still recovering from their time in space. She noted the two wheelchairs in the corner of the room that had brought John and Christina, and she was glad that her time on the Moon had helped her avoid the worst muscle wasting the others had experienced.

"Hi, Christina. John," said Sue, walking to each and giving them a hug.

"Sue, fantastic to see you again," said Christina.

"You look like you are doing better than us," said John as Sue took a seat.

"A bit better," said Sue. "How are you doing?"

"Having a shower was wonderful, but I prefer to float while sleeping," said Christina.

"I must say my bed does seem harder than I remember it. And I really enjoyed eating a steak," said John.

"Ahh, everyone is here," said George as he entered the room. "Mike's family will be here shortly, so I hope you guys don't mind getting down to business.

"I know you guys debriefed a lot on the journey home, and Sue has had a few meetings with the team and investigators in the last day, but we are aware that this is the first time you, as a team, will be talking about what happened with Mike, and you'll be doing that with his family present. The mission management team would like us to focus on the facts as we know them and try not to speculate on why or how things happened. If you get ideas, I suggest you note them, and we will debrief this event afterwards, and you can share them then. We don't want to confuse the family."

"OK. What level of detail do we want to share with the family?" asked Sue.

"As much as they ask for," said George. "If something is likely to be distressing, then please warn them and give some minimal detail. If they ask for more, then do so. We don't want to hide anything from them, but we don't want to unnecessarily distress them.

"Your attempts to save MIke will probably be the most distressing for you and them, and we'll have the flight surgeon here to explain things medically and explain his communications to you."

"That's good," said Sue.

"There will also be a member of the board of inquiry present, both to represent the board to the family and to gather data in case something new comes out of discussions," said George.

"So, this is a formal hearing?" asked John.

"No," replied George, "there won't be any recordings, etcetera, but since we are so early in the process, they expect that all of you may have new recollections as you talk about what has happened, and they want to be across that. You don't need to worry about it, and it's the Astronaut Office representative on the board, Gary Mollier, so don't be worried about it."

"Anything else we should know?" asked Christina.

"I think that's it. The main purpose is for you to share what happened and for the family to hear it from you, and for you to show your support for them. I know it won't be easy, and we'll have the support team here for you and them," said George. He checked his phone after it pinged. "The family have arrived, so they will be here soon.

"One final thing. Sue, this is your meeting, as discussed. The rest of us are here to support you and the family."

John and Christina slowly and carefully started to get out of their chairs so they would all be standing to greet Lisa and Mike's family when they entered.

Sue heard the distant ping of a lift bell and a slight murmur as a group exited and walked down the corridor to the room. She took a deep breath. This was going to be hard.

Lisa entered the room first. Sue walked over to her, took her hand, and said, "Lisa, I'm so sorry." They hugged.

As Lisa greeted Christina, Sue moved to John and Clare Trellis, Mike's parents. She took Clare's and then John's hands. "Clare and John, I am so sorry for your loss. Mike was a great man."

"Thank you, Sue," said Clare. "We know how hard it was for you up there. Thank you for doing this."

"Oh, we couldn't not do something like this," said Sue.

During the greetings, the other members of the meeting arrived. Once the crew and family had exchanged greetings, Sue asked them to take their seats.

"Thank you, Lisa, Clare and John, for coming," said Sue. "I know there's a number of people here with us. They are here for support and to answer questions in the main. We, the crew, wanted to meet with you, explain what happened, and answer your questions as well as we can. Almost everyone here was involved in some way during the tragic events when Mike died. And we are all deeply sorry for your loss.

"If it is ok with you, I'll start by going through the events of the EVA from my perspective. I'm not going to go into any great detail. However, if you want me to explain something in more detail, please ask. This will not be easy for any of us, but you need to understand what happened, and we, especially I, need to tell you what happened so that we can all move forward. Is that ok?"

Lisa, John and Clare all exchanged looks, and then Lisa nodded, "Yes, thanks, Sue, go ahead."

Sue then described the lunar walk that morning, the drive to the drill site, the accident, and her attempts to save Mike's life and the return. The family asked very few questions during her account, and the flight surgeon carefully helped Sue explain why Mike's injuries couldn't be treated as well as they might have been on earth.

After a few more medical questions, Lisa asked, "How did this happen?"

"I don't know," answered Sue. "As a crew, we had no expectation that the drill could explode in such a manner. It's not even a particularly high-speed drill, so I personally am at a loss to explain it."

"Sue, if I may," said Gary Mollier. "Lisa, we are investigating that thoroughly through the board of inquiry and several other teams. As Sue stated, there was no expectation that this drill could cause such injuries in such a manner. The team that developed it also have no explanation."

"Then it could have been sabotage?" asked John Trellis, Mike's father.

"Clearly, we can't exclude that," replied Gary. "We are running some tests to see if the evidence supports that conclusion."

"Wasn't there other sabotage found? I seem to remember Mike talking about a disconnected cable in the lander's airlock?" asked Lisa.

"That may or may not have been sabotage. It could have just as easily been an accidental disconnection during testing," said Gary. "Again, we are investigating further."

"Why would anyone want to sabotage the lander?" asked Clare.

"We don't know they did, Clare," said Sue. "At the moment, we just have suspicions, and we are working to prove or disprove them."

"But would anyone want to?" Clare asked again.

George spoke up, "There are a lot of valuable resources on the Moon. There is also a lot of national pride taken in our achievements. So, there are forces who would like us not to succeed."

"Like China," said John Trellis.

"That is one possibility," replied George. "But only one."

"Then Mike might have been murdered?" said John Trellis.

"I think that is a remote possibility, but it is very remote," said Gary.

John slumped back in his chair, shocked. "I thought this was some bizarre accident, not international assassination," he said.

"As I said, it is way too early to assume that and also too early to assign any blame," said Gary.

"Sue, do you think he was murdered?" asked Lisa.

Sue turned to her and said, "Lisa, I really don't know. The way the drill exploded was very unusual and not at all an expected failure mode. Given the international tension around the launch, I can't say it's impossible. It would certainly explain a lot. But as Gary says, we don't have enough information to confirm it or to lay blame."

"I know this is even more of a shock," said George, "and we want to be open with you. However, I think you can understand the possible implications if word of this possibility got out to the press and the world. That could have some serious international consequences, and the government wants to avoid that without cause."

"So, we aren't allowed to talk about this to others?" asked Lisa.

"Your NASA support team have been briefed, so you can talk with them, and if there are others who you want to talk about this with, just let them, or myself, or Sue know, and we will have a talk with them," said George.

"What is being done to investigate this?" asked John Trellis.

Gary responded, "As well as the board of inquiry that I am part of, the mission project team has its own investigation, the drill manufacturer is investigating, and the coroner is also looking into the circumstances of Mike's death. Given our concerns, the FBI has representatives on the board of inquiry, as does the State Department. The FBI is working with NASA's security teams to review security incidents, and they are reviewing videos from the processing of the drill tool.

"There is a lot of work going on to understand what happened. Some of this started very soon after the incident, so are fairly advanced, whereas some other evidence only arrived back with the crew."

"Gary, can you pass my thanks to those people for their work," asked Lisa.

"I certainly will, Lisa."

"If that covers your questions, I suggest the crew and Mike's family proceed to lunch, and we can talk informally there," said Sue.

After checking with Mike's parents, Lisa said, "that would be great, Sue. Thank you, all."

66

— • —

FRIDAY, JUNE 14, 2024

Sue sat at her desk in the NASA Astronaut office, pondering the day ahead. She was dressed in her US Navy Service Dress White uniform, ready to appear before the board of inquiry into Mike's death. It was being held in a meeting room on a nearby floor, and she would leave soon to attend it. It was unusual for anyone to be in the office in a formal uniform, and she felt a bit out of place.

She had been rereading her mission reports from their time on the Moon and her written debrief of the mission. She couldn't think of anything else she could do to prepare.

She looked around the room, noting Ann Williams in her Marine Blue White Dress Unform with Lieutenant Colonel stripes. Ann had been Sue's backup for the Artemis 3 missions, and Sue had asked her to be her support person during the review. Ann was likewise reviewing Sue's reports and debrief.

Ann looked up, saw Sue looking at her, and stood up and walked over to her. "Are you ready?" she asked in her distinctive New York accent.

"I can't think of anything else I can do," said Sue. "I might go and freshen up, and then we probably should go up."

A few minutes later, they meet in the elevator lobby.

"Did your reading give you any new revelations?" asked Ann.

"No, nothing I haven't seen before. What about you?"

"Not really. I wouldn't have been surprised by a suit problem. I can't see that you have anything to worry about personally," said Ann.

"I still think it was design flaw or sabotage, and I lean towards the latter with everything else that had happened."

"I agree. However, I suggest you keep that to yourself unless they really push for your opinion," said Ann. "Let someone else come up with those hypotheses. Let's go up." Ann pushed the elevator call button.

"After you, Ma'am," said Sue as the door opened. It was strange how wearing uniforms changed how they interacted, even though they ignored the rank distinction on a day-to-day basis. Obviously, her basic training had been effective!

They entered the elevator, and Sue took the short time in there to take some deep breaths. The last time she had been to a similar hearing was four years ago after Eric Hipps had died during their descent from the ISS.

The bell chimed, and the doors opened. Ann led the way out of the lift and to the waiting vestibule outside the conference room being used for the board of inquiry.

A clerk greeted them and asked them to sit until they were called. He did not expect they would need to wait long since there were currently no witnesses in the room, and the board was currently undertaking the meeting formalities at the start of their day.

Ann and Sue each took a seat and nervously waited.

After a few minutes, the clerk called them into the meeting. They entered, finding the 8 board members behind several long tables directly ahead of them and a few administrative staff scattered along tables at right angles on the left and right of the board members. There was a table with 2 chairs in the centre of the room to which the clerk directed them. They stood behind their chairs and saluted, which was returned by the one military member on the board.

The board consisted of the Chair James Hargraves, a member of the House Committee on Science, Space and Technology, Gary Mollier, a NASA Astronaut, a member of the judiciary, three academics, a former astronaut, and a retired space systems engineer.

"Lieutenant Colonel Williams and Lieutenant Commander Bright, please take a seat," said the Chairman. "Thank you for attending. This is the board of inquiry into the death of Michael Trellis during the Artemis 3 Mission. Lieutenant Colonel Williams, you are a support person and, as such, cannot answer questions for Lieutenant Commander Bright, nor can you prompt her. However, you can ask the board questions regarding the process and clarify questions. Do you understand?"

"Yes sir," replied Ann.

"Lieutenant Commander Bright, the first part of today's proceedings will be fairly tedious as we review your report and debrief and clarify details to ensure we correctly understand them. After we have completed that, members of the board may have questions that may be more broad-ranging. Are you happy to proceed?"

"Yes sir," said Sue.

The next three hours were spent tediously going through her report and debriefing, explaining details that were unclear to the board members, especially technical details. While laborious, it was not particularly emotional, and Sue began to relax.

The meeting broke for lunch, and Sue and Ann had an opportunity to talk and reflect on the morning. There had not been much that was surprising, and they were more relaxed as they returned for the afternoon session.

"Lieutenant Commander Bright, thank you for your testimony this morning," began the Chairman. "We will now examine areas that the board members consider relevant. First, could you please tell us about the nature of your relationship with Mr Trellis?"

Sue took a deep breath. She had expected something like this. "I knew Mike well. He, Christina, and I were all in the same astronaut class. So, we have spent a lot of time together, studying, training, travelling, and at times socialising. Astronaut classes become very close, and ours was no exception. Mike and I worked well together. We had our differences at times, but we were able to work them out. Obviously, this was very important as we had to work together in confined quarters for several weeks. I would define our relationship as colleagues and friends."

"I understand that both you and Mr Trellis have young families?" asked the member who was a judge.

"Yes, sir," said Sue.

"And your families know each other?"

"Correct. The primary and backup crews for the mission regularly socialised together. Ann, as backup commander, and I encouraged this, as did mission management, to help build team cohesion and support structures for the families," answered Sue.

"I find it interesting, Lieutenant Commander, that your son Jerome and Mr Trellis' daughter Jasmine appear to have a rare hypermobility issue. Would you like to comment on that?" asked the judge.

"The medical history of our children is private, and I'm not prepared to discuss it in this meeting," said Sue. Ann had sat upright and was leaning forward.

"I have to agree," said Gary. "The medical records of astronauts and their families are private and generally should not be relevant, except in this case for the deceased. Mr Chairman, could we please move on from this line of questioning."

"I have to agree," said the Chairman. "unless the reason both children have such as rare condition is that they both have a common parent and that Mr Trellis was the father of both children. Lieutenant Commander, could you comment on that?"

"Sir, I am not going to comment on the medical history of my or my colleague's families," replied Sue.

"Then can you answer this question: Is Michael Trellis the father of your son Jerome?" asked the Chairman.

"No comment," said Sue.

"You are not prepared to answer that question?"

Sue sat in silence.

"Lieutenant Commander, is it true that you and Mike Trellis argued about your children's health and disclosure to your partners during the mission?" asked the judge.

"No comment", said Sue.

"Mr Chairman, is it reasonable to ask such questions where no evidence has been presented to support them? Clearly, the Lieutenant Commander is not prepared to discuss this topic with the board, and I am not aware of any relevance," said Ann.

"There have been submissions that there may have been some level of conflict between Mr Trellis and the Lieutenant Commander during the mission. We are trying to determine if that was of sufficient concern to initiate a violent action against Mr Trellis," said the Chairman.

"Any dispute Mike and I may have had during the mission was resolved, or we agreed to delay resolution until after the mission. I think my efforts to save Mike's life demonstrate that I was not trying to hurt him," said Sue.

"Mr Chairman, I think this line of questioning should cease, or I will advise the Lieutenant Commander not to continue without legal representation," said Ann.

"Lieutenant Colonel, your opinion is of no consequence in these proceedings," said the Chairman.

"Sue, I suggest we leave," said Ann quietly.

"Mr Chairman, as suggested, I will terminate my testimony to the board at this time. If the board wishes to ask me further questions, I will do so with legal counsel present. Thank you for your time," said Sue. She and Ann stood, saluted and left the room while the chairman banged his gavel and demanded they stay.

67

— • —

Sue parked in the car park at Christina's church, Clear Lake Community Church. The church consisted of 2 large red brick buildings, and one appeared to be an administration building, so Sue followed others to the front of the chapel.

In his final letter to Lisa, written in case something went wrong, Mike had asked for his funeral service to be organised together with Christina. Sue knew he had been thinking about faith and that he had spent a lot of time talking with Christina, but she did wonder how Lisa felt about this.

As she approached the church porch, she noted some NASA personnel assisting with the welcoming and US Secret Service agents protecting various dignitaries, including the Vice President. As this was a formal event, she was dressed in her US Navy uniform. After signing the condolence book, Sue picked up a program and entered the church.

Sue walked towards the front of the medium-sized church that she estimated seated 300 to 400. As the crew commander, Sue had a short speech to give, which she carried in a leather binder. It had taken her days to write, and then the NASA communications team had gone over it, so it was now a carefully honed two-page, double-spaced speech.

George and Jean were seated in the fourth row, on the right, and Sue joined them. After leaving her things in her spot, Sue went forward and spoke with Lisa and the minister who would conduct the service. After confirming details of her part in the proceedings, she walked back to her seat just as Ron walked up, together with Christina and Graeme. She kissed Ron.

"Hi, Sue," said Christina, "you didn't have any trouble finding the church? We found Ron outside looking a bit lost."

"No problems," said Sue. "I've even had time to talk with Lisa and the minister. I'm sitting here with George if you want to join us."

"Sure, there should be room for John as well," said Christina.

Just then, John walked up in his Air Force uniform. Sue saluted him, and he returned her salute.

"Good morning all, on this sad day," said John. "Beautiful church, Christina."

"Thank you, John," said Christina. "I gather you haven't been here before. We try and make it as welcoming as possible. We were all about to sit next to George if we fit."

"That sounds good to me. I suspect it will get crowded with all the brass and politicians here," said John.

"I'm still surprised you and Lisa were able to keep the funeral here and not somewhere bigger," said Sue to Christina.

"It was not easy. Lisa isn't used to our church, but she much preferred it to some big event space or a mega church. Mike had visited here a couple of times as we talked about faith, and Lisa even came with him once. So, the invite list was pruned, which made the Secret Service very happy. And we do have the live video stream," Christina replied. "I know there's at least one auditorium here at NASA Houston streaming that."

"And TV," said John, looking around at the discreetly placed cameras. Sue remembered seeing some outside broadcast vans at the back of the church when she was parking.

Just then, an announcement was made, "Ladies and gentlemen, please be aware that the live broadcast and streaming of this event will begin in 5 minutes."

"I gather the VIPs turn up after we go live," said George.

"Hi, team. I'm glad to see that you are all here and ready," said Callum, the Artemis 3 Project Lead, shaking their hands. "The NASA Administrator and I, and some other NASA brass, are going to be sitting just in front of you, and the Vice President and other folk from Congress are in front of us. We've left the front rows on the left for the family.

"Sue, are you all ready for your speech?"

"Yes, thanks, Callum," said Sue.

"Great. The Administrator and the VP will want to talk to you after the service. Since Mike's casket is not being carried out after the service, and there is no welcoming line, that will likely happen in here after they've spoken to Lisa."

"Lisa didn't want to greet everyone, which is fair enough given the number of people expected," said Christina. "So, there will be 5 minutes or so for some greetings, mostly family and VIPs, and then she and her family, and ourselves, and a few VIPs will leave with a few others to the burial."

"It sounds like organising this was a lot of work?" said Sue.

"Funerals are never easy. I've only been involved with a couple," said Christina. "Adding VIPs, TV, Secret Service and so on has just made it harder. A team from NASA have been helping us sort through all the details so that Lisa and I could focus on the service's content."

"Ladies and gentlemen, video broadcasts are now going live," said an announcer.

The next ten minutes became a bit of a blur for Sue as VIP after VIP arrived. Some, such as the NASA Administrator, interacted with them. Others were just a distraction. In some ways, it was odd that so many influential people had seats behind them.

More quickly than Sue expected, the minister stood at the front of the church and addressed them, "Lisa and Mike's family, Madam Vice President, the crew of Artemis 3, dignitaries, NASA family and friends. We gather today to farewell Mike Trellis, child of God, husband of Lisa, father of Jasmine, son of John and Clare, NASA Astronaut, member of the Artemis 3 lunar crew, and geologist.

"This is a sad day as we grieve the loss of Mike. Yet, in the Christian faith, it is also a time of celebration. During his recent lunar mission, Mike accepted Jesus as his Lord and Saviour, as Christina Pak, a member of our church, will testify. As followers of Jesus, we have a sure hope of resurrection and new life with God. Mike knew this and amended his funeral instructions during the mission so that this hope would be celebrated if an event should occur during the mission that would cost his life.

"We are all witnesses of this fact, as we all heard his last words: 'Lisa, Jasmine, Mum, Dad, I love you all. Jesus loves you too. I'm sorry.'"

Sue looked across and saw Lisa weeping, being hugged by her mother. She looked down her row at her crew and suddenly noticed Christina, and George who was originally scheduled to be part of the crew. Rather than sad, they looked something else, a sort of weepy happy.

"Our church," continued the minister, "has a modern music style, which I think Mike enjoyed on the few occasions he visited. There is one old song that sums up this life change that Mike underwent very well. Amazing Grace. Please join us as we sing together the Chris Tomlin version of this well-known song, Amazing Grace, Our chains have gone."

Sue stood with everyone else as a band started playing the well-known tune, and some singers led the congregation. It was something alien to Sue. She rarely entered a church. The only time she and her friends sang was at a karaoke party, and that just about never happened!

The congregation sat as the hymn finished, and the minister continued, "Dr Michael Trellis, PhD, was born in 1989 in Colorado Springs to John and Clare Trellis. As he grew up, he enjoyed camping and canoeing, developed an interest in science, especially the formation of planets, and was fascinated with the NASA Space Shuttle programs. He even managed to attend the launch of the USS Discovery in 2001 with his father. During his high school years, he attended Space Academy.

"Mike attained a Bachelor's in Geological and Environmental Sciences from Stanford University, California. He also completed a Doctorate in Geology from the University of California, Los Angeles.

"He was part of the NASA JPL Mars Curiosity Rover team in Pasadena when he was invited, on his second application, to become an astronaut candidate, and joined the class of 2017. Later, Lieutenant Commander Sue Bright, Commander of Artemis 3, will detail Mike's career at NASA.

"In July 2019, Mike met Lisa Sturbridge, who works at NASA as an educator. Lisa and Mike have one daughter, Jasmine, who is just 11 months.

"I'll now ask another member of the Artemis 3 crew and a member of this church, Christina Pak, to witness to Mike's faith journey."

Christina stood up from the end of the row and walked to the dais.

"Lisa and Mike's family, Madam Vice President, the Artemis 3 crew, dignitaries, NASA family and friends," Christina began. "It saddens me today that we are farewelling Mike. He only just found faith in Jesus, which is a cause of celebration for those of us in the church.

"Mike and I are both scientists. I think the fact that I could be both a Christian and a scientist intrigued him. We also had a conversation once where I shared that I felt that God had called me to be an astronaut. That made no sense to him.

"In the last month or so, as we went into isolation as a crew, Mike started thinking more about death and faith. We had one scenario thrown at us late in training in which we lost the entire crew. We could not survive. That made us all think about death. In this job, we must face death. We even run large-scale scenarios to plan out how to manage the loss of 1 astronaut, what impact that has, and how to manage that situation as an organisation, and Lisa has been a part of them.

"For some reason, this event made Mike think more deeply. Perhaps it was that he was now a father. Maybe it was that our schedule had slowed down a little, so we had a bit more time to think.

"We had a few talks, both here on the ground and during our mission. He read some books, watched some videos and read some of the Bible.

"During the mission, he was vacillating a bit, not deciding whether following Jesus was a good idea. A couple of nights before his last lunar walk, Sue suggested he talk again with me to clarify things. I challenged him that following Jesus meant giving Him control, making him Lord of our lives, and in return, He saves us from our sins and their consequences, eternal death. That challenged him.

"The next day, he called me again after another difficult day. He said that Sue had pointed out to him that none of us have control of our lives. He could see that Jesus was worthy of being followed and wanted to follow him. We prayed together, and I know that he not only died as a fellow crew member but also as my brother in Jesus."

Christina continued, wiping tears away from her eyes. "Lisa, I know this was a surprise for you, but he loved you. He knew he had done wrong to you and others and shared a few things with me. However, I know, and he knew, that Jesus forgave him those things. And as he said in his final letter that he wrote that night, and as he said in his final words, he loved you and wanted you to know that Jesus loves you too."

"Thank you, Christina," said the minister. "At Christina's suggestion, Mike updated several instructions to NASA in case of his death, including letters to Lisa, his parents, and his fellow crew. As Christians, we have confidence that Jesus died to forgive our sins and give us life eternal. Mike shared that faith and wanted us here today to know that, celebrate that, and grieve his loss.

"Let us pray.

"Father, we thank you for bringing Mike into a relationship with yourself. Even in his last days, you were challenging him to know you more. Thank you that he placed his faith in Jesus and made him his Lord. We praise you for your love for us, saving him from his sins and giving him life with You forever. Amen.

"I'll now ask USA Navy Lieutenant Commander Sue Bright, NASA Astronaut and Commander of Artemis 3, to talk about Mike's service with NASA."

Sue stood and walked out to the front of the room. She took a deep breath as she walked behind the dais and placed her notes before her.

"Lisa and Mike's family, Madam Vice President, dignitaries, NASA family and friends," began Sue. "I first met Mike during the Astronaut selection process before our intake in 2017. He then worked for NASA on the Mars Curiosity Lander project as a scientist. Mike was selected as a trainee astronaut in 2017 in the same cohort as me. For the next two years, we trained together. In 2019 Mike graduated as a Mission Specialist. Shortly after graduation, his skill and experience were recognised when Mike was assigned a flight to the International Space Station on the SpaceX Dragon for one month in 2021. He was assigned as the backup mission specialist for Artemis 3 and the primary mission specialist for Artemis 5. Within NASA, such assignment schedules have not been common since Apollo. During Mike's one-month ISS stay, he was involved in several scientific experiments. On his return, during training for Artemis 3, Mike replaced George Scorby of the Canadian Space Agency as Mission Specialist for Artemis 3 as George had to stand down due to medical issues. George was CAPCOM for Artemis 3 and is here today.

"Mike trained hard for the role and performed admirably during the Artemis 3 mission. He saved my life multiple times. As astronauts, we prepare to be ready for any situation, to not panic in circumstances where panic is absolutely natural, and to work the problem. Those of us from pilot backgrounds already have some of that training. I know I saw Mike grow and develop those skills since we started our training, and we had many opportunities to practice them during our mission.

"Personally, I know Mike was not perfect. It took him a little while to settle into life here in Houston. But I do know that he loved Lisa and Jasmine.

"The crew of Artemis 3 was close, and we had lots of time to ponder the loss of our crew mate during our return voyage. We miss him and are grieved by his loss, and our thoughts are with his family."

Sue, glad she had maintained her composure, picked up her notes and returned to her seat, catching Lisa's eye on the way.

Sue sat back, relieved that her official role was now over. As Mike's father stood to talk on behalf of the family, she started to weep. He spoke of Mike's life as a young boy and into high school and his passion for space. This made Sue think about the loss of Mike.

She felt Ron place his arm around her shoulders, and she leaned into him.

To lose someone under her command, though, was devastating. During her training, such an event had been discussed, but the reality in NASA's history was that the whole crew was always lost, except for her mission to the ISS. This was her second mission with the death of a crew member.

The service continued with a sermon, some more hymns and the dedication of Mike's body to God's care, but Sue was focussed on her own grief.

As the service ended, she tried to control her emotions and dry her face.

The crew and partners were led as a group to an area at the front of the church, and the NASA Administrator brought the Vice President to them after she had spoken with Mike's family. She thanked them for their service and inspiring leadership and expressed sorrow for their loss. Finally, she invited them all to visit the White House and meet with the President in the near future.

With the formalities over, Sue walked to Lisa and the family and waited to again express her condolences to them and to give Lisa a hug.

Sue was considering departing the church when Christina came over to her.

"Are you ok, Sue?" asked Christina.

"I'm not too bad. I think it all just hit me again," said Sue.

"Funerals have a way of doing that. It looks like the family is moving out now or trying to."

They walked over to Graeme and started walking to a side door with Lisa and Mike's parents ahead of them.

"Ron, can you drive me to the burial, please," Sue asked.

"Sure, but I'll need to go to work straight after," said Ron.

"Christina, do you mind if I ride with you from the cemetery to the wake."

"Of course," said Christina.

Sue and Ron walked to Ron's car and drove to the cemetery, with the other vehicles, with little conversation.

The smaller group gathered around the grave site, with the casket carefully arranged above the grave.

The service was simple, with a couple of prayers, and then the casket was lowered into the grave. Sue watched it sink into the ground, remembering all that had happened with Mike.

As they dispersed, Sue walked over to Lisa and hugged her again.

Ron had to leave to attend a meeting at work. His project was at a critical stage. He would join Sue at the wake later.

NASA had organised a private wake at a nearby venue for the family, crew, key project people and some close friends.

They got into Christina's car, and Sue sat in the front with her.

"The burial was nice, simple," said Sue.

"Yes, that was Lisa's request. There was the option of a more formal event, but she wanted the smaller, simpler event."

"The service was pretty intense, with VIPs and TV," said Graeme.

"I guess it was, but I'm a bit used to the cameras and VIPs these days," said Sue.

"It's a bit of a crazy world we live in now," said Christina. "At least we only have to worry about NASA bigwigs at the wake, but I don't think there will be too many of them."

"So, we can relax a bit," said Graeme, "That's good."

They drove for a while in silence, each contemplating the day.

"I think your speech was perfect," said Christina.

"You don't think it was too clinical?" asked Sue.

"No, it was fine. And it wasn't too long, and you had that personal touch," said Christina.

"Thanks. I'm not sure I could have kept it together if I did more, anyway."

They drove into the restaurant's parking lot, found a spot and entered, being directed to the function area. They were some of the first arrivals, and they walked out to the balcony, greeting a few people on the way. They found a table and sat down while Graeme went to the bar to get their first round of drinks.

"A lot has happened in the last seven years since we joined NASA," said Sue as she gazed across Clear Lake.

"Yes, it has," said Christina.

"I definitely would not have expected three of us to be on Artemis 3 and two of us to walk on the moon when we got accepted. I was just grateful to be accepted," said Sue.

"I know, and I expected them to give the Moonwalk to more experienced astronauts."

There was a pause. Sue glanced over to see where Graeme was and noticed that someone was talking to him.

"Christina, I was asked about my relationship with Mike at the inquiry. I'm going to have to tell Ron."

"Wow, that's going to be hard," said Christina.

"Yes, it will be, and I'm going to need to talk to Lisa as well."

"Ouch. I gather you, and Mike sorted things out during the mission?"

"Yes, Mike wasn't that worried, and he thought it was a coincidence. We were waiting for the test results before taking any more steps."

"So, it doesn't factor into the accident?"

Sue looked at Christina indignantly. "Of course not!"

"I'm sorry, I had to ask. I know you wouldn't act that way," said Christina.

Sue relaxed back into her chair. "I know, and if you feel you need to know, then others will also think our relationship was involved in his death."

"Yes, I think you will be answering a few questions. Maybe I can be with you when you talk to Lisa if that would help."

"I'd like that, thanks."

68

SATURDAY, JUNE 22,2024

Ron drove their SUV into their garage, and Sue got out to help Jerome out of the back seat.

After the busyness of the funeral, Sue had spent most of Friday at home, apart from a meeting with her lawyer in preparation for her second appearance at the board of inquiry on Monday.

Today they had gone for lunch at a local restaurant and watched the latest Disney release. It was a nice escape from the world, and Jessica and Jerome loved it and were still singing the theme song.

"Can we watch the videos of the songs again?" asked Jessica to her dad.

"Yes, Daddy, please," said Jerome.

"Maybe we can do that later," said Ron.

"How about you both play outside while Daddy and I have a talk," said Sue as they walked into the house. "Why don't you get a juice box out of the fridge."

"But Mum," said Jessica.

"No, come on. You've been inside all day. Go outside and play," said Sue.

She went to the coffee maker, turned it on, and grabbed the milk from the fridge. "Ron, do you want a coffee? I'm making a latte."

"Sure, same for me. What do you want to talk about?"

"Well, this is going to be difficult," said Sue as she started making the coffees.

"Ok, right. What's going on?" said Ron.

"Well, let me finish making these and we can sit down."

They sat down at the kitchen table.

"You know that I love you, don't you, Ron?"

"Yes."

"But we've had our rough patches."

"Oh shit, you slept with him."

"I'm sorry, Ron. It only happened once, and it was years ago, and it didn't mean anything."

"When? How? Why? You said you loved me," said Ron, raising his voice.

"You were away, we had dinner and had too much to drink, and I was stupid."

"You've been working with him all this time and just spent four weeks on a mission with him, and you expect me to believe nothing else ever happened?"

"Yes. Truly. We realised it was a mistake. Not long after that, he meet Lisa."

"So is Jerome his? Is that why he has the same condition as Jasmine?"

"Maybe."

"Why are you telling me now?"

"Somehow, the board of inquiry have found out about our relationship, so they are asking me about it and think I killed Mike."

"So you got caught. Did you kill him?"

"Of course not. Do you really think I could have killed him?" asked Sue.

"Until 5 minutes ago, I didn't think you were an adulterer, so who knows what you are capable of. You've been lying to me for, what, four or five years?!"

Sue didn't know how to answer that.

"Did he know about Jerome?"

"Only recently, when Jasmine started to show some of the same symptoms."

"Why didn't you tell me sooner?"

"I was in space. This is hard enough face to face."

"Mummy, are you ok? You are crying," said Jessica, standing at the door with Jerome.

"Mummy is ok. We are just talking about things. Go back outside and play."

"I hurt my knee," said Jerome.

"Did you? Let me have a look," said Sue. She knelt down and checked his knee, which had a minor abrasion. "Ooh, that doesn't look too bad. Let me wash it, and I'll put a band-aid on it. Is that ok?"

Jerome nodded.

Sue picked him up, got a wipe, cleaned his knee, and took him to the bathroom to stick on the band-aid.

"Are you and Daddy fighting?" asked Jerome.

"All parents do, sometimes, when they don't agree on something. Now, is that better?"

"Thank you, mummy," he said as he ran outside.

Sue returned to the kitchen and saw Ron picking up his car keys and walking to the garage door.

"I'm going out. I need time to think," said Ron.

"Can't we talk about this more?"

"No, I can't talk to you right now," said Ron, shutting the door firmly behind him.

69

MONDAY, JUNE 24, 2024

Sue stood in front of her bathroom mirror, dressed once again in her US Navy Service Dress White uniform. Ron was downstairs with Jessica and Jerome. He had slept in the spare room. They had talked a bit more, but he was still very upset.

Her face looked a bit haggard in the mirror.

This morning she was appearing again at the board of inquiry. This time she would have her lawyer with her as well as Ann.

She took a deep breath, turned and walked downstairs.

"Ohh, I like it when you wear your uniform," said Jessica. "You look very smart."

"Thanks, honey. Have you had your breakfast, and are you ready for school?" said Sue.

"Almost."

"You are taking her to school, aren't you?" asked Ron.

"Yes, then I've got the inquiry."

"I hope it goes well," he said.

"I don't think it will be easy," she said, fetching herself some juice. She had already eaten breakfast.

Jessica finished her breakfast and put her plates in the dishwasher.

"Go get your school things, and I'll take you to school," said Sue. "And are you eating your breakfast too, Jerome?"

"Yes, Mummy."

"Good boy."

"I'm not sure when I'll be finished today. I'm not sure if they want me for the whole day. So don't expect me home until around my normal time," said Sue to Ron.

"Uh-huh," said Ron.

"Ok, Mummy, I'm ready," said Jessica, running down the stairs. She ran to Ron, kissed him, said, "Bye, Daddy," and headed to the door.

"Great, let's go. Bye," said Sue, placing her glass in the disk washer, picking up her bag, and following Jessica to the car.

Sue arrived forty minutes later at the parking lot near the Astronaut Office. She was meeting Ann and her lawyer, Max Heagler, at the café, and she was early. She waited in her car for a few minutes, gathering her thoughts. Ron was clearly unhappy and stewing, but she didn't think he was about to leave her. At least she could now honestly answer questions at the inquiry without needing to worry that he would find out about Mike. She should have told him sooner, at least a few days after she had arrived home.

Sue got out of her car, picked up her bag, and walked to the café, enjoying the sunshine.

Sue ordered a latte, found an isolated table, and sat down to wait for Ann and Max, who were due in about five minutes. Checking her phone, she saw an email from the Astronaut Office requesting her to attend a meeting with the Chief Astronaut later that week.

"Hi Sue, how are you?" said Ann, and she walked up and dropped her bag on a seat.

"I'm good, Ann, Yourself?"

"I'm great. I'll grab a coffee and be with you in a minute. Do you want anything else?"

"No, I'm fine. Thanks."

Ann placed her order and came back to the table to wait. "How was your weekend?" she asked.

"Well, it was okay until I told Ron about Mike."

"That would probably ruin a weekend. How did he take it?"

"He is upset and not really talking to me. But he hasn't walked out, which I thought could happen."

"I suppose that is good. I'm not sure how Jane would cope if I told her I'd cheated on her."

"Yeah. And the timing isn't very good. We got interrupted by the kids. I should have organised someone to look after them, but it was short notice."

"What are you expecting at the inquiry?"

"Well, if I was on the board, I'd be asking about my relationship with Mike, possibly querying about my use of the drill, and they'll probably review the death of my commander on my last mission."

"That is not going to be fun," said Ann.

Max Heagler, Sue's attorney, walked up to the table, deposited his bag, and greeted Sue. He was tall, dark-haired, in his early forties, and wearing a smart dark grey suit, white shirt, and red tie. "Good Morning Sue. I gather this is Lieutenant Colonel Williams?"

"Mr Heagler, good to see you," said Sue, standing and shaking his hand. "You are correct. This is Lieutenant Colonel Ann Williams, my support person and also my backup for the Artemis 3 mission."

"Good to meet you, Mr Heagler," said Ann. "Please call me Ann."

"Likewise," said Max, shaking her hand. "Both of you, please call me Max. Can I get you, ladies, anything? Coffee refill? Donut?"

"No, thank you, I've fine," said Ann.

"Actually, I didn't eat anything for breakfast, so a blackberry Danish would be great. Thanks," said Sue.

"He is younger than I expected," said Ann. "Where did you find him?"

"Christina knows him. He is a defense lawyer with a technical specialty, and he actually initially studied systems engineering and converted to law. He has been involved in some similar inquiries, which is great."

"Right, here you go, Ann. Hope that's what you want. Well, I wanted to meet before attending the board so that we can touch base and clarify anything you may have thought of," said Max.

"Yes, I haven't really come up with anything new since we talked. However, I have talked to Ron about the affair with Mike," said Sue.

"Ok. That's good, so you will feel free to answer questions."

"I guess so. Of course, I haven't spoken to Lisa, Mike's partner."

"Hmm, well, you might want to consider doing that soon," said Max.

"So, Ann," he continued, "we need to clarify your role in the meeting. I've taken over some of your functions, such as looking out for Sue's interests. I think you now will be more of an emotional support person, peer support, and perhaps technical support if questions go that way. So you may get involved in clarifying technical questions, but you probably should not need to talk to the board much."

"Ok, I'm happy to leave the speaking to you," said Ann.

"We can huddle amongst ourselves and pass notes to prompt thoughts," said Max. "I suggest that we ask to make a short statement at the beginning and that you briefly explain you and Mike had a brief affair several years ago. You should explain that it was possible that he is your son's father, that you had been discussing these matters during the mission, and that your relationship had remained amicable. I've written a short statement to that effect. Have a read of it." He handed Sue a page.

Sue read the page. It was straightforward. "This looks ok," she said.

"Good. Do you want to change any phrasing to make it more natural for you?" asked Max.

"No, it is fine."

"Ok. That might short-circuit some questions, but I think there will still be a few relating to this topic. Be truthful, but keep answers short and to the point. That goes for the rest of the questions too."

Just then, Sue noticed Lisa walk into the café and glance in their direction.

"Umm, this might be awkward. Here comes Lisa," said Sue as Lisa walked over.

Lisa glowered at Sue. "Is it true? Did you sleep with Mike?"

"Lisa, do you want to sit down. This is Max, my lawyer, and you know Ann," said Sue.

Lisa hesitated and then took a seat. "Is it true?" she repeated.

"Before you met Mike, he and I did have a one-night stand," said Sue.

"Before I met him?"

"Yes, not long before, but he had not met you. He didn't cheat on you with me."

"But Jerome may still be his son?" said Lisa, calming.

"It is possible, but he only started suspecting that during the mission."

"But you've known longer?"

"Well, the timing wasn't good, as Ron and I were trying for another child at the time."

"But you slept with another man."

"Yes, I know. It isn't good. Things between Ron and I weren't going well at the time, and Mike and I had dinner after training and drank too much. It was stupid. We both realised that, and it never happened again."

"So, does Ron know?"

"Yes."

"And is he happy with it?"

"No, of course not. He is still processing it," said Sue.

"You just told him?!"

"Yes, over the weekend."

"Can I get you a coffee, Lisa?" asked Ann.

"Ahh, yes, thanks, filter and a Danish."

"We have to go to the board of inquiry soon," said Max.

"Yes," said Sue, "and it was in some ways fortunate we saw each other here before I made any statements to them. I was planning to talk to you later today. I'm sorry this happened and that you found out by some other means."

"Thank you. I guess it would have been nice if Mike had told me himself, but I can see that he probably didn't want to tell me during the mission with everything going on," said Lisa.

"Yes, Jasmine's medical issues made us suspect, but we still don't know for sure. When Ron calms down, I'll see if he wants to do DNA tests."

Ann returned with Lisa's coffee and Danish.

"Time for us to go," said Max. "My condolences on your loss, Lisa. " He stood up and gathered his things.

"If you want to talk further," said Sue to Lisa, "I'm available."

"Thanks," said Lisa.

Sue, Ann and Max walked out of the café and towards the building where the inquiry was being held.

70

The board of inquiry was meeting again in the same room. Sue, Ann and Max took seats in the waiting area. They had done a quick review on the walk over from the café.

"Lieutenant Commander Bright, they are ready for you now," announced the clerk.

"Thank you," said Sue. They stood and entered the room, saluting the board and then sitting at the table, with Max on Sue's left and Ann on her right.

The Chairperson, James Hargraves, said, "Lieutenant Commander Bright. Thank you for returning, although we did not give you leave to depart. I gather you have counsel?"

"Max Heagler, Lieutenant Commander Bright's attorney, Mr Chairperson," said Max, standing.

"Thank you, Mr Heagler. Is your client willing to continue testimony?" asked the chairperson.

"Yes, sir. If the board agrees, she wants to start with a short statement."

After conferring with the other board members, the chairperson said, "Lieutenant Commander, please make your statement."

Sue stood and said, "Mr Chairperson and members of the board. I apologise for my sudden departure at our last meeting. It became apparent to myself and Lieutenant Colonel Williams that I should have legal representation, and I also needed to discuss certain facts with family members before confirming them here.

"I can confirm to the board that Mike Trellis and I did have a brief affair. We both recognised that it could not continue. However, we remained friends and colleagues. It is possible, but not confirmed, that Mike is my son's biological father. This possibility became apparent during the mission and was discussed by myself and Mike. We both decided it was best to delay talking to family about this possibility until we returned home after the mission. This in no way affected our relationship as colleagues and the execution of our mission. Thank you."

Sue sat down. Max leaned over to her and quietly said, "Remember to keep your answers short without extra detail."

"Thank you, Lieutenant Commander, for your statement. I think members of the board will have follow-up questions," said the chairperson, looking across the table at other members. Gary Mollier indicated he had a question. "Go ahead, Mr Mollier."

"Lieutenant Commander, I assume that you know that relationships between NASA astronauts are discouraged, and you knew that at the time of this interaction?" asked Gary Mollier, another NASA astronaut.

"Yes, Sir. Mike and I were aware of that policy, which was a driving factor in not continuing the relationship. This occurred fairly early on in our training for this mission, and alcohol consumption and circumstances meant we performed actions we would not have done in other circumstances," said Sue.

"Did you inform any NASA management of this indiscretion?"

"No, Sir."

Amanda Torres, a former astronaut, gained permission from the chairperson and asked, "Lieutenant Commander, I have some sympathy for your situation. I know powerful bonds are formed during training, and it can be difficult not to blur boundaries. However, the policy of non-fraternisation is there for a reason. Why are you sure that this did not cause issues during the mission?"

"It didn't cause issues," said Sue. "We did discuss it on a couple of occasions, but it did not affect our mission duties. Mike's considerations on the meaning of life probably had a much greater impact since he seemed to be spending a lot more thought on that topic, as well as having discussions with Christina. Enough of our days were spent on an open mic during space walks that you should be able to identify any issues if there were any, and I don't think there were."

Brian Herron, a retired space systems engineer, asked the next question. "Lieutenant Commander, do you remember the events of your third moonwalk?"

"Yes, sir. There were quite a few," said Sue.

"Do you recall the geological samples being taken?"

"Yes, I do."

"Do you recall who used the drill to gather those samples on those occasions?"

Sue looked at Max. This was not something they had discussed. But the mission videos would show the answer, so there was no point in not answering. "I used the drill on that walk."

"And why was that the case?"

"That is what the mission plan called for."

"So it wasn't your decision?"

"Not on that day. I don't recall the process of how it was decided that I should use the drill on the third walk."

"Thank you, Lieutenant Commander. Is it also true that you placed the drill into storage after your walk?" said Brian.

"Yes, sir."

"And you also took it out of storage at the beginning of the fourth and fatal walk?"

"Yes, sir."

"Why?"

"It was on my checklist," said Sue.

"And why was it on your checklist?"

"I don't know, sir. The mission controllers developed the lists and assigned tasks."

"Lieutenant Commander, please look at the image on the screen." Brian displayed an image from her suit camera. "This image shows the drill in your hands when you stowed it. Do you see anything unusual?"

Sue looked closely at the image and saw nothing unusual. "No, sir, it looks normal to me."

"So those orange objects seen inside the drill are what you expect?"

"I can't say that they are or aren't. Most of the time I have used the drill or the training items, I have been looking at the other end of it. It is a fairly simple item, and we had no training regarding any maintenance or repair for it."

"Thank you, Lieutenant Commander."

Similar questions continued to be asked for the next fifteen minutes, with Max stating a few times that the question had been asked and answered.

Then a large older balding gentleman, Judge Paul Bents from Appalachia, indicated he had a question. "Lieutenant Commander, first, may I congratulate you on the success of your mission and on being the first woman to walk on the Moon. I know that accomplishment has been overshadowed by other events, but it must make you very proud," he said in his southern drawl.

"Thank you, sir, it does when I have time to reflect on it," said Sue.

"I'm sure you had to work hard to be chosen for that role?"

"Well, sir, I think all of my colleagues worked hard to get into their roles. Becoming a NASA Astronaut is not easy."

"That, may be true. Do you describe yourself as a driven individual?"

Sue looked at Max. He shrugged and nodded. "I think I have been strongly motivated to reach my career goals."

"I'll take that as a 'yes'. Do you think you were ready on November 20, 2020?"

Sue swallowed. "I was as ready as anyone else on that crew was, sir."

Max, realising the reference to the death of Eric Hipps on the Starliner flight, stood. "Mr Chairperson, I don't see the relevance of this line of questioning."

"I'll get to the point quickly, Mr Chairperson," said Judge Bents.

"Please do," said the chairperson.

"Lieutenant Commander Eric Hipps died that day during a flight where you were deputy commander and had to take command, didn't he?"

"Yes, sir."

"So you are in the unfortunate position of being the only NASA astronaut to be present when not one, but two astronauts have died during their mission. Isn't that correct?"

Sue slumped. "Yes, sir," she said, looking at the desk.

"Lieutenant Commander, were you in an intimate relationship with Eric Hipps?"

Max shot to his feet. "Objection," he cried.

"Mr Chairperson, I believe it is relevant to this case. We may have a serial killer here."

"Mr Chairperson, the Lieutenant Commander was not in command of that mission, and there is no hint that she did anything wrong," said Max. "The vehicle was hit by a rare micro meteorite which injured Eric Hipps. The crew, including my client, were commended on their efforts to save him during their descent, putting their own recovery at risk."

"Judge Bents. There is no evidence that the witness caused any injury in that case, so any relationship she may or may not have had with Mr Hipps is irrelevant. Please sit down, and we'll move on to other questions."

"Mr Chairperson, I'd like to ask for a recess for my client, please," said Max.

"Granted, we'll have a 20-minute recess," said the chairperson.

"Wow, that was brutal," said Ann. "Are you ok, Sue?"

"Why would anyone think I killed Eric?" said Sue.

"I think the Judge is playing devil's advocate so they can say they investigated thoroughly," said Max. "I don't think anyone seriously thinks you murdered Eric Hipps. Go and take a break. In fact, let's all go out of the room together. You can get a coffee if you want."

They all stood up from their table and walked out of the room. Sue and Ann took the opportunity to visit the lady's washroom.

While washing their hands and checking their makeup in the mirrors, Ann asked," Are you really ok, Sue?"

"It did shake me up a bit, but I think I'm all right. But you know he is right about being present at the two most recent NASA astronaut deaths."

"That is just unlucky. It has nothing to do with you," said Ann.

"But it does make you think."

"Well, Christina is also in the same boat, having a person die on her two missions. I'm going to recommend that you both get counselling about that."

"I guess she is, isn't she. Let's go join Max. He might be getting worried."

They found Max waiting in the corridor. "Hopefully, there's nothing more like that. Are you ready to return, Sue?"

"I think so. Do you think there will be much more?"

"It's hard to say. I don't think so, but there may be other technical issues they want to discuss."

"I hope you are right. Let's go."

They returned to their seats, and a few minutes later, the chairperson reconvened the board.

"Fellow board members, does anyone else have any questions for this witness?" asked the chairperson. Looking along the board, no one indicated to ask a question. "If there are no further questions, we can excuse the witness. Thank you, Lieutenant Commander, for your time in helping us understand what happened to Mike Trellis. I know this has not been easy for you. As we just heard, you have been unfortunate enough to be involved in two deaths during your missions. I encourage you to take advantage of all available resources to process that. And we, as a board, would like to congratulate you on your recent success in being the first woman to walk on the moon."

"Thank you, sir," said Sue.

"The witness is dismissed," said the chairperson.

"Well, that was quick," said Max. "Let's go."

They gathered their belongings and left the room.

71

Sue drove home. The inquiry meeting had gone pretty much as she had expected, although the suggestion that she had killed Eric Hipps stung. Meeting Lisa that morning had been unexpected, but it did clear the air. She expected Ron to be working at home alone, with Jessica at school and Jerome at daycare.

She drove up the driveway, parked in the garage, and sat for a moment, taking a deep breath to calm herself. She got out of the car and opened the door to the house, dropping her things in the kitchen.

"Ron, I'm home," she called. She walked to the room he used as an office.

Ron turned to her. "You're back from the inquiry?" he said.

"It went fairly well," said Sue.

"Lisa called."

"Ahh, yes, she bumped into us at the café. We briefly talked."

"She says she didn't know about it."

"I believe her. Mike hadn't told her anything. He wanted to be sure first."

"I want Jerome tested," he said.

"We can do that."

"You know, regardless, he is still my son."

"I know that. But he may not be mine."

"Will that make any difference?"

"Maybe."

"Ron, can you forgive me for betraying you?"

"I don't know yet."

"You know we are in a much better place than we were in 4 years ago. We've changed. I've changed," said Sue, sitting opposite him.

"But you've hidden it from me for 4 years too."

"Yes, but it was a one-off thing, and I didn't want to hurt you."

"And you were never tempted again?"

"As I said, we realised our mistake, and he had Lisa. And we were on different teams for a while, so we were just friends and colleagues."

"I need some time."

"That's ok."

Sue's mobile rang, "I'll give you some space. Looks like Christina is ringing me."

Sue walked back into the lounge room and answered the call. "Hi, Christina."

"Sue, how did the board of inquiry go?"

"Not too bad in the main. There were a few brutal things."

"Oh, that doesn't sound good. I've been praying it went well."

"Umm, well, ah... I think the chairperson stomped on the nasty allegation. So I guess that is good."

"What allegation?"

"That I killed both Mike and Eric Hipps."

"Eric?!"

"I'm not sure if you realised, but you and I are the only two astronauts to have been on 2 missions where a crew member died."

"We are? ... I guess we are!" said Christina.

"So, you can understand why some questions were asked."

"But Eric's death was clearly an accident."

"That was pointed out by my attorney and accepted."

"Wow."

"Yeah, and expect some additional counselling due to that revelation."

"Ok. Do you have any more info on what happened with the drill?"

"Apart from the fact that I was the last person to handle it before Mike?" said Sue.

"Oh no."

"They asked questions about some material in the drill. I'd never noticed it, but you can see it in the photos. I didn't know it wasn't supposed to be there. It was Mike's device, and he'd done the in-depth training on it and never noticed an issue."

"Hmm, do you want to investigate that more?" said Christina.

"I guess we could, but I'm sure others are better qualified to do that."

"I just thought it might be helpful to try and understand why it exploded if we can."

"Do you want to meet at the office tomorrow and see what we can learn?"

"Sure, we've got medical tests there tomorrow anyway."

"Right, so we do. How about we meet after them."

"Ok. Is there anything else I can do to help, Sue?"

"No, that's fine, Christina. See you tomorrow."

72

—◆—

TUESDAY, JUNE 25, 2024

Sue attended her medical check in the morning, taking along some samples, and performing various physical and mental challenges for the medical team, along with John and Christina.

The doctors were generally happy with their progress, although Sue's doctor commented that her blood pressure was a bit high. "It's not part of a trend," she said, "and it's probably due to the extra stress you are under. We'll keep an eye on it, and I'll only be concerned if it is high on your next check-up. I recommend that you make good use of the post-mission counselling."

Sue smiled her thanks to the doctor.

Afterwards, they returned to their desks in the NASA Astronaut Office. John joined Sue at Christina's desk. They'd filled him in during their morning of tests.

"So I had a dig around and found some of the reports that the inquiry is using. You can see the pictures of the drill, and they've highlighted the suspicious material," said Christina.

"Can't say I would have noticed that as unusual," said John, " but I didn't train much with that device."

"The training device in the Neutral Buoyancy Lab isn't that high fidelity, and that is probably the only place you would have encountered it," said Sue.

"I had a bit more training than that on it," said Christina, "in case I had to replace Mike for the landing, but still, it's not something I would have noticed."

"So that device was on the Lander, which launched way before us," said Sue.

"Yes," said Christina. "I suspect any change would have had to have been made 6 or more months ago, and the report suggests the same. It would have been in the clean room, in the Lander, after that."

"Well, there should be video coverage during that period," said John.

"Can we see the video?" asked Sue.

"I wouldn't know where to start looking," said Christina.

"Neither would I," said Sue. "I guess it would be security. Are there any other reports about this?"

"Yes," said Christina. "There are some trying to analyse what happened. There's a video that shows the explosion. Some data shows a power draw increase in the drill, but that could be post-explosion. There's a report looking at your use of the drill with photos and video. But it doesn't find anything usual."

"What about security threats or events, especially relating to the Lander or the contractor who supplied the drill?" asked Sue.

"Umm, let's try and search," said Christina.

"I bet you there will be a lot," said John.

"Yes, about three thousand over the last two years. I can probably refine the search a bit, but there will still be a lot," said Christina.

"What about just in the clean room during the last maybe nine months?" said Sue.

"Still about six hundred," said Christina.

"I seem to remember a security briefing just before the launch where some possible suspects were identified. Can we find that report, and maybe we can correlate their activities," said Sue.

"I remember that report," said John. "But I don't know if we'll have access to the data showing a person's movements."

"They do in the movies," said Christina. "I found the briefing you are talking about, but it looks like the report it is based on is classified."

Sue sat back in her chair, considering the inconclusive evidence they had found and the difficulties involved for them to investigate further. She looked at her crew mates, realising that they had her back and she was okay. She didn't know what the future held, but she felt more comfortable with it. Her crew, her friends, believed her and would stand by her. They had developed great trust through their years of training and the mission.

More troubling was her relationship with Ron. That would take some work to restore after his discovery of her betrayal. Yet she was confident that his trust in her would be restored.

"I'm coming to the conclusion that we need to trust the process and see what the inquiry finds," said Sue. "We don't have enough access to the data to draw any reasonable conclusions."

"I think you are right," said John. "I do think sabotage is the most likely, or a critical failure. If it was sabotage, I don't know how it was triggered."

"Well, then, I guess there isn't much we can do here. Anyone want lunch?" said Christina, pushing back from her desk.

"Sure. Let's go off campus. We haven't had much time as a crew together lately," said Sue. "I'm buying."

"Fine with me," said John.

The remaining crew of Artemis 3 headed out of the office together.

EPILOGUE

ARTEMIS 3 INVESTIGATION CONCLUDES SABOTAGE CAUSED MOON WALKER'S DEATH

The NASA Accident Investigation Board has today ruled that Michael Trellis' death on the Moon during Artemis 3 was caused by sabotage of the drill he used during his last moonwalk.

Analysis of particulates on Trellis' space suit showed traces of explosives that were not used on the vehicle. Tests had shown that it was improbable that the drill could fail as it did.

The Board noted that while there had been several suspicious occurrences related to reportedly Chinese covert actions, it was impossible to definitively assign blame to a particular country.

The sabotage likely occurred two years before the lunar walk, when the drill was assembled and tested. Intelligence agencies were reviewing available information regarding access to the tool.

The US State Department stated that no country had been identified as being involved, and therefore little direct action could be taken. However, concern has been expressed to several countries.

The Chinese government has not commented.

AUTHOR'S NOTE

Thankyou for reading Artemis 3: The Journey. I hoped you enjoyed it. I enjoyed writing it and learnt a lot along the way. I progressively got ads for houses in Houston, climbing equipment, baby stuff and planes. Yes, jet planes.

Space has always been an interest for me. We literally got a TV to watch the Apollo moon landings in 1969, and I was in high school when the Shuttle launched. A group of us at school would have loved to be involved in the space program, but opportunities were limited for Aussies. One has had some involvement on the medical side of things. Now that Australia has a Space Agency, things are starting to heat up in the industry.

I would really value your feedback. The best way to do this is to write a review on Amazon. It helps others work out if they want to read the book.

If you would like to keep track of my future work, please sign up for my newsletter at https://davidmiller.online .

ACKNOWLEDGEMENTS

First, thanks to Katrina, my wife, who encouraged me during this project over the years.

Thanks to my alpha readers Tim Young and Katrina Miller.

Thanks to Tim for designing the cover, and for publishing advice.

Thanks to my sister Michelle for publishing and marketing advice. Who thought there'd be two authors in the family!

My family for putting up with listening to shortwave broadcasts of Shuttle launches way back when.

ABOUT AUTHOR

Growing up during the Apollo and Space Shuttle eras, David has a passion for space, science and faith. Artemis 3: The Journey is his first novel.

David has been an avid reader since childhood, and a fan of science fiction, action and mystery novels. As a Christian, he finds it interesting to read stories about characters whose worldview is challenged. Some science fiction contains all the interesting theories, but how do they impact how characters think, feel and relate?

He works in Information Technology and has volunteered as a first responder, and has a Bachelor of Science and a Master of Information Systems.

You can follow David Miller on Facebook, and at davidmiller.online